T0374242

THE Black Sea

Book One of the Dunham Saga

ELM BRYANT

Scripture taken from the King James Version of the Bible.

WestBow Press books may be ordered through booksellers or by contacting:

WestBow Press
A Division of Thomas Nelson & Zondervan
1663 Liberty Drive
Bloomington, IN 47403
www.westbowpress.com
1 (866) 928-1240

ISBN: 978-1-5127-5573-2 (sc)
ISBN: 978-1-5127-5572-5 (hc)
ISBN: 978-1-5127-5574-9 (e)

Library of Congress Control Number: 2016914608

Print information available on the last page.

WestBow Press rev. date: 9/28/2016

For all the women who live in the shadows, trapped, addicted, neglected, and abused.

Acknowledgments

"Thanks be to God for His Indescribable Gift!"
-2 Corinthians 9:15

I wish to express a great deal of thanks to the people surrounding me. You are patient and understanding beyond measure.

I owe boundless gratitude to my husband and my brothers, David, James, Jerry, and Dave. They are the kind of men I want my sons to be.

Mom, you are the source of endless encouragement. Thank you for believing in me.

I owe special thanks to Rachelle Baz Kerr, who is simply the best proofreader ever! Her quick eye and gracious personality vastly improved the quality of this work.

Also, many thanks are owed to the people who read and reread my unfinished text – Billie, Marlene, and especially Judy, who had a major influence on the story.

Finally, I wish to express loving gratitude to my children, who endured their mother's unyielding possession of the family computer for hours on end.

You are so loved!

Prologue

The cold fog hung thick in the Boston night, threatening to settle as icy droplets on the young girl's shoulders. Her breath had already crystallized on the stringy, blonde hair drooping around her face. She pulled her crocheted shawl closer. It was mostly decorative, meant to call attention to her dainty shoulders rather than to keep her warm. Still, the girl could not help but tie it around her, seeking comfort in its futile threads.

Looking each direction down the street, she searched for a fine carriage that might house a gentleman who required her services. She detested most of the men who sought her companionship, but would welcome any excuse to be out of the cold. Even though it was early, the lanes were empty, except for the miserable fog and the eerie light of the gas street lamps.

She crossed her arms and rubbed her shoulders, eying the empty lane as she shivered. Worry creased her pretty brow. Things would not go well for her if she returned to Mr. Drake empty handed.

She heard the rhythmic footsteps of boots on the cobblestone street, then saw her friend round the corner, fog swirling around her long skirts and dark curls. Her friend wore an excited expression on her face, something that was entirely foreign to them lately.

The dark haired girl spied her friend and quickened her step. "Edith!" she cried, catching the girl's hands in her own. "I have found a place for us, for both of us! We can escape this wretched place! Come with me!" Her voice rang with an Irish lilt, and the girl eagerly tugged on Edith's hands toward the direction from which she had just come.

"Wait, Clara!" Edith pulled back from Clara's grasp, not understanding her friend's sudden enthusiasm. "What are you talking about? What place?" Edith's voice betrayed the same melodic accent.

Clara was almost breathless. "A man came up to me. He said he had work for us. Real work! Not this... life." She swept her hand across the empty street to emphasize the hopelessness of their current situation.

"No, Clara," replied Edith, keeping her voice calm to steady Clara's enthusiasm. "You know we cannot trust strangers. You don't know this man!"

Clara stood motionless for a moment, and Edith could see the frost that had accumulated on her eyelashes. Clara spoke, her tone firm and decided. "I have to take the chance, Edith. I cannot do this anymore."

Edith sighed. "At least we know that Mr. Drake will give us a warm place to sleep as soon as we make enough coin for him. We know we will not freeze, or starve. But this man? We know nothing about him."

"I'm with child, Edith." Clara's statement was matter-of-fact, though Edith could see the desperation in her eyes. "If Mr. Drake finds out, then... who knows what will happen to me?" She looked hard into Edith's face. "I have to take this chance."

Edith took her friend's hand sympathetically. She knew that Clara was right, that Mr. Drake had no use for a pregnant girl. Clara's life was over. And then what would Edith do without her only friend? Clara tugged Edith's hand once again, gently. This time Edith willingly followed after her.

They rounded another corner, and Edith saw a black carriage waiting under one of the dim lamps, its horses stamping impatiently in the cold. When the heavily bundled driver saw the girls, he jumped down from his seat and opened the carriage door. Apprehension filled Edith's chest. This was foolishness. No one in Boston was going to help two Irish prostitutes. No one.

A black, gloved hand emerged from the darkness of the carriage interior and offered itself to Clara. She looked up hopefully, then accepted the hand and stepped through the door. Edith strained to see into the shadow, then the same gloved hand was suddenly before her, beckoning her to enter the carriage.

The driver stood patiently as Edith hesitated, holding the door open for as long as was necessary for her to make a decision. She looked behind her, surveying the foggy, empty streets. She returned her gaze to the still waiting hand, then quickly took hold of it before she could change her mind.

As the gloved hand tightened on her own, fear bit through her heart. Still, she allowed herself to be pulled into the foreboding unknown of the carriage.

1

Byron Drake stood on the pier of Boston Harbor, relishing the January breeze that blew off the chilled ocean and whipped locks of blond hair to one side of his handsome face. He pulled his thick, wool coat tightly around him. This harsh winter would drive people from the inhospitable streets and into one of his many establishments. And that meant money.

He smiled as his steel-blue eyes assessed the flow of humanity spilling off of the newly docked *Charlotte Jane*. None of the travelers disembarking from the sailing ship were wealthy—no vacationers returning from holiday in Europe, and no fine businessmen managing their trade. Those with money made the voyage across the Atlantic by steam, not by sail. The vast majority of souls flooding down the filthy gangplank were impoverished Irish, and their stories were all the same.

They were leaving their beloved Ireland to make a new start in America, and many had become indentured just to pay the passage across the sea. Captain Munstead, first in command of the *Charlotte Jane*, had made a small fortune transporting the poor Irish who were fleeing the deadly potato famine, or the influenza, or whatever else plagued people in that wretched country. Drake, in turn, had been able to profit. The two had a fine partnership.

Most of the immigrants hoped to find a better life right here in Boston—a job, a small shack to keep out the elements, and enough food to feed the whining mouths they had hauled along with them. A decent expectation, but not a realistic one. People in Boston were sick of the Irish. They were everywhere, knocking on doors, begging for work, huddling together on the streets. Many shops now began displaying signs in their windows reading NINA—no Irish need apply. Those without prearranged indentured service often found themselves in dire circumstances, especially those who arrived in winter.

But Drake was waiting. He knew the men would need jobs, and he had jobs to offer. He could pay these Irish a fraction of the wages that Americans demanded, provide them with cheap housing, even food and clothing, all to be taken out of their wages, of course. By the time they had worked for him a month, they owed him two months' wages. It was a convenient system that allowed him to expand his financial empire with very little monetary input.

Drake knew that the women would work, too. Many of them were not willing employees, but that mattered little to him. The girls he acquired from Captain Munstead and a few other pragmatic captains made him more money than even he had foreseen. So, he waited on the pier next to the *Charlotte Jane* until most of the passengers had dissipated away from the gangplank. Perhaps the captain would have a few new female employees for him today.

Captain Munstead hailed him from the ship's railing in a grating voice, then led two charges down the gangplank after him. The first was a young girl of no more than sixteen, and the next was a boy who looked to be her younger brother. Just one. Drake had been hoping for three or four girls. He had lost that many just in the previous month. One girl, a petite brunette, had succumbed to the whiskey three weeks earlier. Drake had found her dead in her room, a glass in her hand, and the whiskey spilling on his fine, Victorian rug.

The other two, a blonde and another brunette, had vanished into thin air last week, not returning from their evening ventures. Losses were a part of the business. Sometimes a girl was lost to sickness, other times to a violent client. They never ran away, though. No one in Boston would take in harlots, especially Irish harlots, and just one night in the merciless cold was enough to bring them to their senses and their employer. No, those girls had not run away. He almost pitied them, certain that they had met some horrible end by the hand of an evil drunkard.

If Drake could find the devil who murdered his girls, then he would end him in a most unpleasant fashion. After all, he couldn't afford to lose too much business.

Drake turned his attention to the red-haired lass as she set foot on the wharf. She kept a protective arm around the boy at her side. Only one. Drake sighed. He would take what he could get.

"Captain Munstead. It is a pleasure." Drake greeted the older man with practiced civility and a smile.

"Pleasure's mine." The old captain's voice was dry and flat. He barely nodded to Drake. His grizzled beard reeked of brandy and cigars, and Drake detected small bits of decaying biscuit in its matted, gray tangles.

The young girl looked at Drake expectantly, hoping that his handsome appearance and fine smile indicated a much more pleasant person than the captain. Both she and the boy were clothed in a hopeless array of tatters, no doubt thinking that enough layers of rags would keep out the cold. The girl pulled her little brother closer, trying to guard him from the chilly air.

"And who is this beautiful lady?" Drake inquired of the captain while nodding to the girl. The girl smiled and seemed put at ease by his manners, which was Drake's intended affect. She was of average height and quite thin from the voyage. Long, red ringlets flowed from under the green shawl that was pulled around her face. He was hoping for a blonde from this voyage to replace the one he lost, as blondes were always in high demand. But she was fairly pretty, with blue eyes. Not a striking beauty, but pretty enough for the job.

Captain Munstead spat on the pier, a few drops of spittle sticking to his beard. "This here's Miss Erin Moore," he said, nodding in the direction of the girl, who promptly curtsied, "and this is her brother Murray."

"It is a pleasure to make your acquaintance, Miss Moore," said Drake with a small bow. He turned his attention to the boy and addressed him with a grin. "Hello there, Murray."

"Hello, sir." Murray's reply was tired and cautious, and his accent was thickly Irish. His hair was just as red as his sister's.

"You must be about eight or nine?"

"Yes, sir. Eight, sir."

Captain Munstead interrupted. "Their mum didn't make the voyage. Had to bury her at sea. Shoved her right over the side, we did. These two need work to pay the fare." At this, Murray turned into his sister's skirt to hide his tears. Miss Moore glowered at the captain for his insensitivity.

"So sorry, sir," she said to Drake, "but this past month has been quite difficult for us." Her voice was melodic and rich, and the Irish lilt only made her prettier. "The good captain is right, though." She placed the smallest emphasis on the word *good*, and Drake smiled at her sense of irony. "We do need jobs and we are hard workers, both of us. If you have anything open, sir, we would be grateful to be in your employ."

Drake could see the nervous apprehension in her eyes. This was always too easy, and the fact that Miss Moore had a younger sibling to care for made it especially so. Drake was sure that she would do anything to ensure her brother's survival through the remainder of the Boston winter. They didn't come all this way to freeze.

"I am always in need of help at one of my establishments, Miss Moore. I am certain I could find a position for you. And as for you, Mr. Murray," who raised his head slightly, "I happen to need an errand boy. Are you any good at running errands?"

Murray sensed redemption from his previous showing of tears, and he stood up straight as he wiped the last drop from his face with the back of his hand. "Very good at it, sir."

"Then I think you two shall work out nicely."

Miss Moore hugged her brother happily. "Thank you so much, Mr. Drake. I can't say how relieved I am. You are a godsend."

"Of course, Miss Moore. But this is not charity. I have work that needs done and have to find people to do it." He was certain that Miss Moore would bring him quite a bit of business. As for the boy, he would employ him as an errand boy for now.

"I certainly understand, Mr. Drake," she replied, though he was quite sure she didn't.

"I also have to pay for the fare for you and your brother, and also for your poor mother, God rest her soul." Drake lowered his head slightly. "That will have to come out of your wages until the debt is paid."

"Yes, sir, Mr. Drake. As long as we have enough pay for food and warm shelter, then we will be quite happy with those arrangements."

"I provide housing at a very modest cost for most of my employees and will do so for you as well if you wish," Drake stated warmly.

Miss Moore looked like she wanted to leap for joy, but she restrained herself. She was exactly where Byron Drake wanted her. He turned to Captain Munstead. "Are you agreeable to the usual compensation?"

The captain nodded, then spat on the pier again. Drake retrieved four notes from the inside of his black overcoat and handed them to the captain, who took them unceremoniously, turned around without a word, and trod back up the gangplank. He knew that he would see the good captain again this evening.

Drake smiled down at Miss Moore, who was watching the captain with disdain. He agreed with her sentiment about Munstead. The man was revolting. But he did bring Drake profit, a great deal of profit.

"Well, Miss Moore," Drake said almost merrily, offering her his arm, "shall we away?"

"Of course, sir," Miss Moore replied.

With that, Byron Drake and his newest means of profit walked briskly toward his tavern on Ann Street, the district of Boston that housed the harlots, thieves, drunkards, and derelicts—the most wretched of humanity. Boston locals simply called the area the Black Sea.

2

Josephine Hamilton strolled quietly along one of the many cobblestone paths that traversed her estate. Even though the late-winter air was frigid, the walk warmed her nicely. Still, she pulled the fur lined hood of her cloak over her head, covering the dark chocolate strands that were currently tamed into a sensible bun at the nape of her neck. Pretty, light brown eyes looked out from a rather plain face and surveyed the dormant rose garden she was walking through. In another few weeks, this garden, and the many others on her estate, would be sprouting sprigs of green, readying themselves for a summer's worth of luxuriant blooms. Josephine looked forward to walking these paths in the summer.

Her morning's business had taken her to the private school, Rosewood Hall, that was situated in a secluded corner of her estate. Her father had established the school as a place to educate the servants' children when he first built Hamilton Manor. But Josephine's mother had changed its purpose many years ago, and now Rosewood Hall was filled with young girls who were learning skills that would make them employable in the finer homes throughout New England.

It was a happy and thriving place, due in large part to the compassionate and intelligent headmistress, Mrs. Stoddely, who oversaw the students and their studies. The girls inhabiting the walls of Rosewood Hall also contributed to the air of pleasant productivity. Each of them had been given a second chance, the possibility of a good future when, before, that possibility had not existed. Mrs. Stoddely saw to it that the girls thrived both in their health and in their training. Josephine felt fortunate to have her as an accomplice.

After a few more minutes of pleasant walking, Josephine topped the last hill standing between her and her home. The rust colored, stone walls of Hamilton Manor rested among the frosty, winter lawns that surrounded it. Clusters of stone spires rose from the walls and thrust themselves high into the cloudless morning, and graceful stonework arches adorned the tops of the many doorways and windows. More dormant rose vines climbed the walls and twined over the arches, promising glorious springtime fragrance and color.

Josephine followed the cobbled path that wound to the front of her home as the cold finally made its way through her heavy cloak. As she rounded the last corner, she was surprised to find her father and two other gentlemen lingering on the avenue just outside the main entryway.

Mr. Hamilton's gray hair jolted sporadically from his round head, and the warm coat he wore amplified his frame. His face was smiling, and his bright eyes twinkled in the morning light. He was a graceful man for his age, even though his girth had expanded slightly with the years, making him almost portly, but not quite. He still had a full head of hair, and he wore immense, gray sideburns. Josephine could only guess they were a leftover piece of glory from his younger years. He smiled joyfully when he caught sight of his beloved daughter.

"Hello, my love!" Her father's voice was warm and rough, and always filled with kindness. He strode to her with arms open, embraced her warmly, and planted a kiss on her cheek. The older visitor frowned at the display.

"Hello, Papa." Josephine returned her father's embrace and kiss, and bestowed him with a radiant smile. She then turned her attention to the visiting gentlemen with a friendly nod. Of the two men who were with him, the older one was perhaps sixty, and the younger one was quite handsome. Josephine surmised that the older man was the Duke Dunham, with whom her father had been conducting business of late, and that the younger man was his son.

"My dear," began her father as he held out an arm to the older gentleman, "this is Duke Leopold Dunham and his son, Lord William

Dunham. And this, my dear sirs, is my daughter, Josephine." The introduction was brief and to the point, just as her father liked things, but it was hardly proper for royalty. The complete lack of formality seemed to irritate the duke even further, but he still offered Josephine a tight, formal smile.

She curtsied low and inclined her head gracefully, in part to acknowledge the gentleman's royal position, and in part to compensate for her father's lack of proper social observance. The two gentlemen bowed politely, though the younger man seemed sincere in the gesture. The subtlety was not lost on Josephine.

"Your Grace, it is my great honor to make your acquaintance." Josephine first addressed the duke, then turned to the younger man. "And yours, as well, Lord Dunham."

Duke Dunham's expression changed from that of irritation to one of pleasant approval, as Josephine had hoped.

"Thank you, Miss Hamilton. It is always a pleasure to meet a lady of refinement." The old duke's voice rang out in proper British, and somehow his polished, superficial, tone matched up to his thin facial features and long nose. His hair was just as gray as her father's, but it was carefully combed underneath his hat. His expression and clothing conveyed the look of wealth and prestige.

The younger Dunham also seemed proper, but in an approachable manner. "The honor is mine, Miss Hamilton," he replied, greeting her with a warmth in his accent that contrasted his father's coolness. His smile was pleasant and genuine, and it reflected in his piercing, blue eyes. A few locks of dark hair escaped from under his hat and lay on his neck. Although he resembled his father somewhat in the face, his smile and demeanor were friendly and warm, which lent even more to his handsome features. His frame was sure and solid, tall without being wiry. Josephine detected an honest friendliness about him.

Mr. Hamilton took reign of the conversation and addressed his daughter. "The good duke and I actually concluded our business yesterday afternoon, but I invited them for tea this morning so I could meet his fine son. So good of them to come. I am glad you happened along when you did. They might have ridden off without having had the chance to meet you."

"That would have been my misfortune," Josephine replied.

"Miss Hamilton," began the older Dunham, "will you be attending the Spring Ball next month? I hear it is to be quite the event."

"I rarely have time to attend social events, sir," she answered, "so in all likelihood, I will not be present."

"No time to attend!" exclaimed the duke. "What could occupy a young lady so much that she has no time for a ball?"

"Business, good sir," replied Josephine. She was aware that most young ladies her age only concerned themselves with social matters, and that she was quite the peculiarity. "My father's estate is extensive, as are his business endeavors," she continued. "It is no easy task to manage them well."

"Good heavens, sir!" The duke turned in genuine alarm to Mr. Hamilton. "You let your daughter manage your business affairs?"

"Now Father," the young Dunham tried to calm his elder in a soothing voice, "I am certain Miss Hamilton is a very capable young woman."

"Indeed!" cried Mr. Hamilton, who seemed uncharacteristically offended. "My Josephine has been managing all of my affairs for five years now, and my businesses have seen impressive growth and profit under her hand. I'll have you know that she is the shrewdest business mind in all of Boston!"

"My apologies, sir." It was now the duke's turn to calm his host. "I am not accustomed to a female being acquainted with business matters, much less fluent in them." The duke then turned to Josephine, "Please forgive my assumptions, Miss Hamilton." The grace with which the apology was delivered took Josephine by surprise, as it seemed in direct opposition to his earlier chilled demeanor. The younger Dunham looked on the scene with curiosity, and more than a little humor.

"Well," said Mr. Hamilton, clearly trying to return to more pleasant conversation, "shall we return to our previous subject? I think we were discussing the upcoming ball. I am sure that Josephine is attending this year." He placed a fatherly hand on his daughter's back. Josephine didn't reply, but instead smiled in acquiescence to her father's suggestion. She could tell that he was up to something, but she would wait until their guests were gone before she questioned her father.

"In that case," added William, "I hope you will save a line for me on your dance card."

"I would be most happy to, sir."

"Just one dance?" the duke chimed in. "Why William, I would think that you would spend most of your dances with the lovely Miss Hamilton."

An awkward silence followed as William struggled to find a correct response. Josephine decided to come to the poor man's rescue.

"I am certain, Your Grace, that the gentleman's dance card is already full." She offered a knowing look to William, then continued speaking to the duke. "Your son and his lovely Miss Beech are the most agreeable couple in Boston. It would be a shame if we were not able to observe their wonderful pairing for most of the evening." Even though Josephine barely took part in Boston society, she was hardly ignorant of it. Ignorance was bad business.

For a number of months now, the younger Dunham had been publicly courting a lovely young lady named Elisabeth Beech. Her family had modest means, but that appeared to matter little to William Dunham. It was refreshing to see a match of genuine affection instead of financial arrangement, as often happened in higher society.

William was visibly relieved, and showered Josephine with silent thanks. The duke, however, seemed quite vexed. "Very well," he said, ending the matter abruptly. "We must be off. It was a great pleasure to meet you, Miss Hamilton." Duke Dunham took her hand and bowed slightly, then addressed Mr. Hamilton as he shook his hand. "Good sir, I am in your debt. I hope our endeavors prove fruitful."

"Miss Hamilton," William addressed Josephine as he took her hand and kissed the back of it, "you are a most gracious and perceptive lady. Thank you."

"Of course, sir."

William energetically climbed into the carriage after his father as the driver snapped the reigns, whisking the two royal guests down the cobblestone lane toward Boston. Mr. Hamilton and his daughter watched them for a few moments, then Mr. Hamilton offered a gentleman's arm to Josephine. She looped her own arm through his as they made their way up the stone stairs and into the warm, generous foyer of Hamilton Manor.

Ophelia, the head housekeeper, greeted them and closed the door on the cold outside. Her brown eyes, blonde hair, and delicate features made her very pretty, and a head full of common sense made her unequaled among most other young women. Ophelia and Josephine were about the same age, and had spent much time in each other's company during their childhood years.

Josephine's mother had found the young girl when she was ten, abandoned and starving on the streets of Boston. She had scooped her up and taken her straightway to Mrs. Stoddely. Ophelia was working in the house soon after, and she and Josephine had taken to one another right away. Josephine counted Ophelia as her oldest and closest friend.

Ophelia took each of their coats and directed them to the sitting room where two cups of hot coffee waited. Josephine smiled warmly at her friend. "What would I do without you, Ophelia? I will be up soon." With a nod, Ophelia was away, leaving Josephine and her father alone.

An aged butler, regal in his stance but also slow in his movements, came into the sitting room after them. Under one arm he bore a single, short log, and this he placed on the already thriving fire that warmed them. Jeffrey had been looking after Mr. Hamilton since the latter's early childhood, and it did not seem that age would deter him from his continuing task.

"Thank you, Jeffrey," Mr. Hamilton remarked, obvious affection for the elderly man showing in his eyes, "but you really should allow one of the younger staff to tend to the fires."

"I am still of some use, sir," the old man replied, taking the poker from its hook and repositioning the log in the flames. "Now," he continued, his voice as slow as his movements, "can I bring you anything more? I see that Ophelia has already attended to your beverage."

"No thank you, Jeffrey. You have seen to us quite nicely."

The old man nodded to Josephine, then to Mr. Hamilton. "As you wish, sir." He retreated slowly from the sitting room, poised and gracious despite his advanced age.

Mr. Hamilton was already slurping his coffee, rather loudly. "Ahhh. Is there anything better than a hot cup of coffee on a chilly day?" He eyed his daughter over the rim of his cup as he sipped more of the steaming liquid.

Josephine laughed out loud. "Papa!" she scolded. "What atrocious manners! And your mistreatment of the duke was simply unforgivable."

"Humph," he retorted. "I will not pander to all the pomp and ceremony that royalty expects by giving them a grand introduction. The duke is in America now. He needs to learn the idea that all people are equal. Much more practical than those silly niceties of English society."

"Well," Josephine replied, "don't expect too much from the duke. People don't often change except under extreme circumstances." She took a sip from her own cup, feeling the welcome warmth spread down her throat and through her chest. Then, arching one eyebrow and staring over at her father, she asked, "Speaking of the duke, what brought him here today? Besides tea?" It was time to get to the bottom of whatever her father was scheming.

Mr. Hamilton became suddenly thoughtful. "A good deal of business," he began. "The duke's current business manager has been mishandling his funds, so much so that the Dunham family is on the verge of bankruptcy. To make matters worse, the business manager disappeared without a trace last month."

"That is a great misfortune. And the duke came to you for funds?" Josephine was not at all surprised at the news. Royals were often in dire financial straits. It took a great deal of resources to maintain the royal lifestyle. Some managed this delicate financial tightrope with discretion and practicality, while others tended to squander their riches and titles.

"In a sense." Mr. Hamilton handed a stack of ledgers to Josephine. She opened one and began perusing the pages. "Duke Dunham does indeed need a great deal of funds," Mr. Hamilton continued, "but he also needs to find the holes in his change purse, so to speak. According to the ledgers, all is accounted for. But the numbers in his American accounts are showing alarming losses. It is a complicated task to rectify the situation."

Josephine understood immediately. "So we are to be the eyes that find the holes?" She continued to turn the pages, becoming acquainted with the endless rows of entries.

"Our accountants, yes." Mr. Hamilton replied. "Once we determine how the duke's money was misused, we can correctly restructure his finances, and hopefully, discover the location of his absent business manager and recover his funds."

"Our accountants? Is this not my task?" Josephine was perplexed. This was her area of distinction, the kind of puzzle she excelled at. The accountants that were employed by Mr. Hamilton were the best in their field, but her own skill and business savvy had made a thriving success of her father's finances.

Mr. Hamilton smiled sympathetically as he took the ledger from his daughter, closed it, and placed it on the table. He then took her hand in his own. He knew her better than anyone, and could read the disappointment in her brown eyes. He knew also that her mood would soon turn to a far more unpleasant air. The news he had for his daughter was not good. He had been planning and dreading this conversation for two months.

"My Josephine," he began, his tone much too serious for Josephine's comfort. "Josephine..." he paused, not quite knowing how to start.

Being alarmed at his change in demeanor, Josephine took her father's other hand between hers and turned in her chair to give him her full attention. "Go on, Papa," she urged as a frown deepened her brow.

Mr. Hamilton took a deep breath, then decided that he would only tell her the good news today, though he doubted that his headstrong daughter would see it as such. The bad news could wait for another time.

"I have decided that it is time for you to marry."

Josephine sat straight up in her chair, a look of complete incredulity seizing her face. "What?" she asked, dropping her father's hands.

Mr. Hamilton's voice was soft and soothing as he began his case. "My dear, I don't want you to be alone for the rest of your life. And I won't be here forever. It is time for you to marry a good man and begin a family."

Josephine couldn't believe the words coming out of her father's mouth. They were almost always of the same mind on every subject. How could he think this was acceptable?

"Papa," her voice was calm, even though she felt utterly perplexed, "you know I am perfectly content being alone. We have discussed this before. Why the sudden change of mind?"

Mr. Hamilton reclaimed his daughter's hand before answering. "I was never comfortable with the thought of you living your life in solitude, and now that I am getting on in years, well... I want to protect you."

"Do you think I am not capable of taking care of myself?"

"I think nothing of the sort. But the banking industry in Massachusetts is uncertain, the laws are constantly changing, and you might find yourself robbed of your inheritance because you are an unmarried woman. And, sometimes," he held up his hand defensively to calm her rising objections, "you follow your instincts too quickly. Every person needs another opinion besides their own. Iron sharpens iron, my dear."

"You are my other opinion, Papa," Josephine retorted gently, "and frankly, I do not wish for any other." She knew her father had her best interests at heart, but she also felt that he underestimated her. He seemed set on this matter, and Josephine needed to gently coax him out of this lunacy.

"Papa," she began, "if I were to agree to this, how would we even begin to choose a proper suitor? I have never found a man that I would consider, and any man that agreed to marry me would only do so for our fortune, not for love."

"Nonsense!" countered her father. "You hold so many attractive qualities. Any man would be proud to have you for his wife!"

Although her father meant his words, Josephine was quite familiar with her own reflection in the mirror. She was not ugly, by any account. But neither was she a beauty, or even pretty. Long ago, Josephine had accepted the fact that she was plain.

At first, she was bitter, perhaps even angry at God for making her so. But after she had aged into her early twenties, witnessed several unhappy matches based on nothing more than social standing, and more importantly, realized the enormity of the suffering of people in her own city, Josephine counted her plain appearance as a gift rather than a burden. It allowed her to cast off normal social encumbrances and pursue things of a deeper nature – education, business, and devotion to her Lord.

Then there was her life's passion, her own method of philanthropy. These activities often demanded late hours and strange visitors. Even her father was unaware of her more clandestine and risky efforts. But Josephine had found a way to make a meaningful difference in many lives, and she had no intention of abandoning any of her activities. This was her God given responsibility as well as her joy, and a husband would surely complicate this most important aspect of her life.

"I know you mean well, Papa," she tried to reason, "but I simply have no desire for any kind of marital relationship. Also, I am twenty-six and practically an old maid." Laughter crept into her voice. "Even if you were to find a suitor, my age alone would scare him off, and I would have it no other way!"

Mr. Hamilton did not immediately respond to the comment, and he wore an almost guilty expression.

In that instant, Josephine realized that a suitor had already been found. "Oh no, Papa," she exclaimed softly, "you can't mean the duke!" A merger of their two families would solve the Dunham's financial predicament and secure a position of stability for her, thus fulfilling both of Mr. Hamilton's objectives in one fell swoop.

Laughter rang from Mr. Hamilton. "For such a level headed woman, you are being very melodramatic," he scolded cheerily. "Of course not Duke Dunham. He is four decades your elder." Her father's laughter eased into a circumspect smile. "I have spent the last several weeks with Duke Dunham arranging your marriage to his son, William. The event will stabilize their finances and open many more doors to our businesses. But more important..." Mr. Hamilton paused, carefully brushing a strand of stray, brown hair behind his daughter's ear before continuing in a somber tone, "most important, you will have the shelter of a husband to protect you – from whatever life may bring."

His words were so tender, so serious that Josephine's objections could not voice themselves. She searched his face for a few moments, finding compassion, but also resolve. And something else. Sadness? It caught her off guard.

She spoke softly. "The younger Lord Dunham will not agree. His heart is already taken by Miss Elisabeth Beech, and I am certain that she is just as enraptured with him."

"That is unfortunate," he replied. "Even so, Duke Dunham was determined to secure a profitable marriage for his son. Miss Beech cannot afford William Dunham."

"So he sought you out on this matter?"

"He did," Mr. Hamilton replied, thoughtfully. "And, after a great deal of reflection, I found it to be a wise proposal, considering all the circumstances."

Josephine was silent for a few minutes, trying desperately to think of a way to dissuade her father.

"I am not sure, Papa. I am not ready." Mr. Hamilton sat silently. As she realized that her father would not be swayed, she cast a last, pleading look into his eyes, trying to pierce his very heart. "How do you know that William Dunham is a good man, Papa?" she implored, a touch of sorrow spreading to her own demeanor. "How can you know that with certainty?"

Mr. Hamilton squeezed Josephine's hands reassuringly. "Because I have witnessed him being kind to strangers, and honorable in his dealings." He smiled before adding, "And I have had him followed and thoroughly investigated for the last two months. I know all there is to know about William Dunham, and he is a good man."

Josephine tried very hard not to smile, but a grin escaped to her mouth, and a weak giggle followed. "You are incorrigible, Papa. Shame on you!" She half laughed, then half cried, brushing away a stray teardrop with her fingertip.

Mr. Hamilton rose and put a comforting arm around his daughter, drawing her close. "I ask that you trust me, Josephine. Come what may, promise that you will trust me." He set a gentle kiss in her hair.

"I promise, Papa," she answered, laying her head on his shoulder, "though I cannot be happy about your decision."

Mr. Hamilton held his daughter, relief flooding his soul. He had been certain that this conversation was going to be more of a battle. He was happy to be wrong. His future battles, however, were not going to be as merciful.

3

Shannon Tiernan sat on a large crate that had just been unloaded from the *Charlotte Jane's* hold. She was exceedingly grateful to be off of that wretched boat and feel solid ground beneath her feet. The voyage from Ireland had been brutal and cruel. She had embarked from Dublin in late February, under the care of her ailing father. After two horrific months at sea, she had arrived an orphan.

Upon docking in Boston Harbor, Captain Munstead pointed to the crate and told her to stay in that spot until he could find someone to relieve him of her debt. He then stomped off in the direction of some questionable looking buildings adjacent to the docks. Shannon pulled her father's coat closer around her to ward off the sea air. That coat was the only thing she possessed in all the world besides the dress that she wore.

This section of the harbor was busy as ragged sailors disembarked from vessels and huddles of cold, confused, Irish immigrants dispersed into streets lined with ramshackle warehouses. The warehouse just across from where she was sitting, however, was much nicer than the others. Its structure seemed solid and sure, and its walls were neat and freshly painted, sharply contrasting the peeling and cracked facades of the other buildings. A large, round sign was posted over the warehouse doors. It read, "Warehouse 17. Property of Byron Drake. No Trespassing."

Her attention turned to a small group of immigrants making their way through the crates and sailors that were still flowing off of the *Charlotte Jane*. The bustling people seemed busy, unpleasant, and unhappy. This place was so different than the countryside of Ireland.

No green hills, no broad oaks, no pleasant scent of heather rising from the meadows.

Here, she could only see crowded docks and ramshackle buildings. What had her father been thinking? Their hut may have been tiny, their living poor, but there was a peace there, a quiet beauty that nourished the soul. This place was horrible. She could not find one friendly face, and that frightened her.

Captain Munstead returned, wearing a satisfied expression over his unpleasant features. "Well miss," he said, "I think I've found someone who will buy your indentureship. He'll be along shortly."

Shannon felt a spark of hope light inside her chest. "Then I will have a job? I will be able to pay off my debt?"

"You'll be working alright." His laugh made Shannon uneasy, but a job was a job. As long as she could make enough extra money to feed and shelter herself, she would be fine.

"Where will I find a place to rent? Is there someplace close to my work that you know of?"

"You won't need to worry about that, miss. Your employer will feed and house you, and clothe you, too, as long as you do a good job."

"Really? That is quite fortunate. Thank you, Captain."

Instead of seeming happy with her thanks, the captain frowned and grunted. "Stupid little wench." Shannon felt the sting of his words, and was too shocked to even venture a reply. He was about to march up the gangplank, but turned suddenly to address her again. "Listen, you'll have a better time of it if you don't say much. People don't like the Irish here, and your sweet little accent will just give you trouble. So do yourself a favor and keep your mouth shut! Stay put until your employer comes."

Now Shannon was truly alarmed, not only at the captain's warning, but also at the blatantly abusive remark she had just suffered. Perhaps she could save enough to buy passage back to Ireland. Famine or no, Ireland was far superior to Boston in every way.

"Hello miss." A clear, strong voice addressed Shannon. She looked up and saw a handsome man with an easy smile striding down the dock toward her. He didn't have the disheartened demeanor of so many of the others here, but seemed calm and pleasant. He was clearly a man of means, attested to by his crisp business attire. But Shannon mostly noticed his eyes – large, brown eyes smiling at her and easing her fright.

"Are you my new employer, sir?" Shannon spoke before she remembered the captain's warning. But the gentleman didn't seem to notice her accent.

"I'm afraid not, miss. At least, not yet. I saw you sitting alone and wanted to inquire about your circumstances." He frowned slightly, "This is not a good place for a young woman to be alone."

"Ha! You there!" Captain Munstead bellowed from the top of the gangplank, his voice grating and hostile. "What do you want?"

The gentleman tipped his hat slightly, revealing thick, chocolate brown hair underneath. "Just inquiring about the young lady, sir."

The captain immediately became friendlier and strode down the gangplank. "Captain Munstead at your service, sir." Shannon had never seen the captain so amiable. He actually looked decent when he smiled.

The young man extended a gloved hand and grasped the captain's outstretched paw, shaking it firmly. "Darcy Adams at yours, sir."

"So, you're wondering about Miss Tiernan, here?" the captain asked.

"She seems rather alone and forlorn. Is she your charge?"

"Her father bought passage on my ship with the promise of his service. Unfortunately, he died during the voyage, leaving the debt to the young miss. I would be happy to sell her indentureship to you for a good price." Captain Munstead paused and perused Shannon with his eyes in a most indecent manner. "Those blonde curls are rare. Her beauty would rake in a nice bit of coin for you."

Shannon gasped, realizing the exact meaning of the captain's intentions. She shrank down into her father's coat, suddenly terrified beyond words. She looked from Captain Munstead to Mr. Adams, aware that her future was in a very precarious place.

Darcy Adams reacted as if nothing were amiss. His expression took on a more serious nature, and his tone changed from pleasant ease to all business. "And what might that price be, Captain Munstead?"

"Twenty pounds, sir." The captain spit on the wooden wharf, staining his already filthy beard with more stray spittle.

Adams narrowed his eyes shrewdly, then grinned knowingly at the captain. "Captain Munstead," he began in a chiding tone, "we both know that twenty pounds is robbery - even if I were compensating you for a luxury steamship passage. I would be willing to part with five dollars for this pretty young lady."

Shannon watched in horrific silence as the two men bartered for her as if for a bag of barley. Neither man even looked at her as they spoke. A lump of terror rose in her throat.

"Five dollars!" roared Captain Munstead indignantly. "I had to make room for two passengers. Not my fault that her dad keeled over on the way! And I'll have none of your Boston dollars! I want British pounds. At least fifteen of them!"

Darcy Adams was silent and thoughtful. He looked at the terrified Shannon, then at Captain Munstead. "I'll give you eleven pounds, but even that is outrageous – and you know it."

"Done." Captain Munstead was quick to seal the deal with a handshake. "Give me the money, and I'll fetch her papers."

"I'll have to visit the bank to acquire your British pounds, as I only have Boston currency," replied Adams. "I will be back within the hour." He then gently addressed Shannon, "Come along, miss. All will be well."

As Shannon began to reluctantly take the arm that Adams offered her, Captain Munstead roughly grabbed her wrist and pulled her away from her new employer.

"Not till you pay, sir," he spat hatefully. "Money first."

"Fair enough," Mr. Adams replied. "May I speak with the girl for a moment?"

The captain looked a bit uneasy, but nodded his assent with a grunt.

Mr. Adams leaned in close to Shannon's ear. "I mean you no harm, Miss Tiernan, and offer you an honest job. The other men who frequent this dock are like our good captain here, and will use you for their own profit. Make sure you go with no one else. Tell them you are already employed." He pulled back and looked closely into Shannon's face. "Do you understand what I am saying?"

Shannon stared back at the frowning man, not knowing what to think of the dreadful events of the last ten minutes. She glanced to Captain Munstead, then back to Mr. Adams. If she had to entrust her future to one of these men, the choice seemed crystal clear.

"I understand perfectly, Mr. Adams," she replied, her voice sure. The look of relief on his face was immediate.

"I shall return soon, captain," Mr. Adams cheerfully exclaimed. "Kindly take the young lady back on board to keep her safe for me."

"Of course, sir," replied the captain. "For a fee."

"Will you accept the currency I have on hand then?"

"I suppose that one of your Boston dollars will do as a holding fee."

Reaching into his pocket, Mr. Adams produced a silver coin and handed it to the captain, who held it up and examined it before dropping it in his own pocket.

"A pleasure doing business with you, sir," remarked the captain.

Mr. Adams nodded, then spun on his heel and traveled down the dock with great strides. Shannon's trepidation grew with each step he took away from her. She looked once again to the captain, who stood solidly in his place, then started for the gangplank.

Captain Munstead held out a rough arm to block her path. "Where do you think you're going?" he asked brusquely.

"I am returning to the ship, as Mr. Adams asked."

"And if Mr. Adams doesn't come back, then what will I do?" he growled. "No, you can stay right here." Pointing to the crate that had served as her seat earlier, the captain ordered, "Sit there."

Shannon briefly thought of bolting after Mr. Adams, but could not find the courage in her knees to even stand. She sank woefully onto the crate, pulling her father's coat protectively around her once again as Mr. Adams disappeared into the streets of Boston.

"Ah, Mr. Drake," she heard the captain chime pleasantly. Shannon turned to see a blonde man shaking hands with Captain Munstead. The man wasn't looking at the captain, however. His eyes were riveted on Shannon.

The chill shivering up her spine had nothing to do with the frigid Boston air.

Darcy Adams nervously glanced at the pocket watch in his hand as he hurried back toward the wharf. He had been gone for exactly fifty-eight minutes, exchanging his Boston currency notes for the more stable British Pounds. He could understand the Captain's reticence, but severely mistrusted the man. He winced at the thought of leaving Miss Tiernan in his care.

It was the blonde curls that had caught his eye. He knew that those rare curls would catch another man's attention as well. But other men were looking for a way to line their pockets. His intentions originated from a completely different motivation. For a moment, his throat caught with emotion as his mind traveled back to his boyhood. He shook his head and put the memory underfoot.

As Darcy neared the dock, he scanned for the worn sails of the Charlotte Jane. He could not find them. With each step, it became clearer that the ship had already disembarked from the dock. Darcy hurried to the place where Miss Tiernan had been sitting. Only a few salty, old men wearing bedraggled sailor's garb hurried by, eying the well-to-do stranger suspiciously.

"Sir!" Darcy called to the nearest one, who stopped, though it seemed to pain him to do so.

"What you be wantin', mister," the man replied, showing the few remaining, blackened teeth in his mouth. His companions also stopped, watching the exchange.

Darcy politely tipped his hat to the man. "I am inquiring about a young lady that was in this spot about an hour ago. She had remarkable blonde curls. Have you seen her?"

The old man snickered. "If I would've seen a woman like that, you think I'd still be here?" The other men laughed.

"She's likely already been swallowed up by the Black Sea, mister," another sailor put in, almost sympathetically. "You'd best find someone else to suit your fancy." The men went back to their errand, making raucous comments about their favorite working girls as they left.

Darcy stood alone on the wharf. They were right, of course. The girl was gone, swallowed up into the sin and hell behind him. He turned, slowly facing the line of buildings that marked the beginning of Ann Street. She was there, somewhere.

His sister's flashing, brown eyes jumped back into his mind. Then they changed into the frightened, green eyes of Shannon Tiernan. He had failed her.

Darcy Adams walked briskly toward Ann Street, determined. If Shannon Tiernan had been plunged into the Black Sea, then he would find her and pull her from its merciless waters, and anyone else crying out for rescue.

Byron Drake had kept a firm hold on Shannon's arm during their entire stroll down Ann Street, as if he could sense her trepidation. He had been pleasant enough, even when she informed him that another gentleman had bought her indentureship from Captain Munstead. He simply ignored her comment, instead flashing his handsome smile through charming compliments about her beautiful, blonde locks.

A black dread started growing in the very pit of Shannon's core, making her feel hollow and helpless inside. Whenever Mr. Drake laid a gentle hand on her back to guide her around a corner, fear tingled up her spine and spread through her shoulders. She could sense the evil spilling from this man, and she was certain that Mr. Drake could feel her every pounding, terrified heartbeat.

"And here we are," he smiled, sweeping his arm toward a two-story brick and stone tavern nestled in a line of similar establishments. The Crimson Dagger was carved in elegant letters on an oval sign hanging over a heavy, oak door. He gingerly stepped forward and opened the door, gesturing Shannon through with his other hand. Shannon glanced behind her, looking for any sign of salvation in the faces of the haggard populace of Ann Street. Despite the cloud of aversion that she was sure was apparent to every passerby, not one person paid her any mind.

Mr. Drake continued holding the door, then commented, "There's no one but me, Miss Tiernan. No one." Finality pervaded his voice.

With his free hand he persuaded Shannon through the door, nudging her on the small of her back. Then he pulled the door shut behind them. Shannon had little time to take in the rich, burgundy fabrics obscuring the windows, or the richness of stained, oak tables glowing in the light of the massive fireplace. Byron Drake didn't linger on the first floor, but escorted Shannon to the ample staircase ascending to the second floor.

At the end of the landing stood another beautiful oak door, with black, ornate hinges and shining grain. In any other building, Shannon would have admired its beauty. Mr. Drake opened it to reveal a dimly lit hallway lined with smaller doors, five or six on each side. He guided her to the third door on the left, unlocked it with a key pulled from his pocket, and led her inside. Mr. Drake then relocked the door and gestured for Shannon to sit down on one of the small chairs that accompanied a round table.

Shannon did as she was told, looking around the room as she did so. A bed was centered on the far wall, covered with rich linens. A grand vanity sat across from the bed, with the largest mirror Shannon had ever seen hanging above it. Golden candlesticks shed flickering light in the otherwise darkened room, and thick, velvet curtains covered the far window. Everything was arranged to give an impression of excess and opulence.

"Do you know why you're here, Miss Tiernan?" Mr. Drake began. He pulled the other chair closer to her and sat down, lightly stroking the worn fabric of the dress covering her knee.

Shannon's insides began to tremble, but she gathered her courage. "I'm afraid you've made a mistake, Mr. Drake. As I told you earlier, my papers were already purchased by Mr. Adams." She lifted her head and held the gaze of the man opposite her, though it took all of her nerve to do so.

Mr. Drake sat up and smiled, his blue eyes ice cold. He reached over and picked up a small crystal glass from the vanity and filled it with an amber liquid from an equally beautiful decanter. He brought the glass to his lips and downed the liquor with one pass. Firmly replacing the glass on the vanity, he leveled his piercing eyes on Shannon and smiled.

"I don't care who bought your papers before me, Miss Tiernan," he said. "I am your employer now, and this," he gestured to the room with a sweeping arm, "is your new home. Shall we begin?" He stood and walked to the bed, shedding his jacket and loosening his tie.

Shannon swallowed hard. All the strength had left her legs. She wasn't even sure where she would run to if she could – the door was locked and the window was on the second story. Instead, she mustered all her dignity and her strength, and stood from the table like Queen Victoria herself.

"We shall not, sir!" she replied, authority resounding in her voice. "You will escort me at once back to the place you found me, and then leave me be!"

Byron Drake began to laugh. The sound of it filled Shannon with a terror she did not know existed. He dropped his tie on the floor and returned to the table, taking Shannon's hand in his. She promptly yanked it away.

"You seem a bit tense, my dear," he gestured to the brandy decanter, his tone becoming as cold as his eyes. "Take some." She watched as he refilled the glass and offered it to her.

"No!" she snapped back firmly, her green eyes full of fire. Before she knew what was happening, Byron Drake snared her arm and forcefully yanked her closer, letting the glass of brandy fall and shatter on the floor. He spun her around and held her against him, her back to his chest and her arms pinned to her sides.

She struggled against him, but had no chance of breaking his hold. "Let go of me," she yelled again and again, hoping someone in an adjoining room would hear the altercation and come to her rescue.

Drake put his mouth to her ear. "The one word you are never allowed to say to me, Miss Tiernan, is *no*." He spun her out of his grasp and struck her cheek hard with the back of his hand. She cried out and put her hand to her face, still in shock from the sudden, violent turn of events. Drake pulled her hand from her face and struck her again.

And though the sound of her struggles and screams filled the room, no one came to her rescue.

4

Melodious phrases crafted by the finest musicians in the city drifted through the ballroom, accentuated by laughter and the bright conversation of young socialites. The home of the Cabot family was perhaps the most elegant and magnificent in all of Boston, and the ballroom even more so. Three massive, crystal chandeliers hung gracefully from the impossibly high ceiling, illuminating the swirling guests below. Michelangelo style panels adorned the walls, each framed by gilded, golden trim. Thick, damask fabric in various shades of beige and gold were swept back from the doorways and windows with long silk tassels. A more glorious Spring Ball could not have been imagined, even by the wealthiest residents of Boston.

Josephine herself was dressed resplendently, thanks to Ophelia's insistence. Her silk gown was a striking cobalt blue, the scooping neckline and full skirt trimmed with ornate white and gold. Delicate lace dripped off her shoulders, forming banded sleeves on her otherwise bare arms.

Ophelia had been overjoyed about Josephine's betrothal, and had been showering her with extra attention and excited conversation. Whatever Josephine lacked in enthusiasm for her upcoming marriage, Ophelia more than made up for. This evening, the sentiment translated into ensuring that every detail of Josephine's attire was perfect.

Josephine had put her foot down when it came to the jewelry, however. Ophelia had chosen a lavish diamond pendant supported by a sapphire collar necklace, a piece that Mr. Hamilton had given to his wife long ago. And though the jewels accented Josephine's gown beautifully, she refused to wear such an extravagance. Instead, she wore nothing around her neck, partly to annoy her maid, and partly to contrast herself to every other lady at the ball.

Almost as soon as she entered the ballroom on her father's arm, Josephine had been swept away by one gentleman or another. As always, her dance card was full. Most of the gentlemen had made her acquaintance before, and were eager to vie for a more prominent place in Josephine's affections. She knew, however, that their motivations began not in sincere attraction, but in simple greed.

Josephine's current dance partner was a prime example of why she loathed these types of social gatherings, and usually shunned them altogether. Mr. Charles Holmes was a prominent banker who had extended too many risky loans too quickly. His bank was on the edge of insolvency, though few outside of Boston business circles knew of his plight. He had spent the entire waltz praising Josephine's unequaled beauty and social privilege, hardly taking a rest between his practiced compliments.

Josephine largely ignored him, nodding politely only when a response was required. She was focused instead on the young Lord Dunham and his companion, Miss Elisabeth Beech. The couple had danced almost every dance together, smiling easily at each other and laughing often.

They were clearly in the springtime of a beautiful romance, completely enraptured with one another. From their behavior, Josephine knew that Duke Dunham had not informed his son of their "arrangement". On one hand, she felt regret and sadness that such a beautiful courtship would be brought to an end. On the other, she had to admit to herself a measure of jealousy. She would never know the rapture of a genuine romance like theirs.

"...and so, Miss Hamilton," Mr. Holmes rattled on, "I was hoping you would agree to a more formal courtship between the two of us. Rest assured," he added as Josephine's attention snapped back to his conversation, "your age makes no difference at all in my estimation. A lady owning more years than most is often more graceful and refined than younger companions. And," he added in an assuring tone, "your status overcomes any disadvantage caused by your age."

Josephine took a moment to overcome her incredulity before responding. "Mr. Holmes," she stated emphatically, "I *cannot* tell you the regret I feel at having to decline your offer of courtship." She had wanted to say something entirely different to Mr. Holmes, but good manners prevailed. The waltz mercifully ended, and Josephine put polite, but noticeable, distance between her and Mr. Holmes.

The man seemed mildly alarmed, and took a step to close the distance. "Miss Hamilton. How can I persuade you otherwise?" he asked rather assertively.

"Ah, Miss Hamilton." William Dunham's deep, smooth voice rang out behind her shoulder. "I believe I have the pleasure of this next dance." As she turned, William held out his hand to her just as the next waltz began. She gratefully took it. Mr. Holmes still stood in his place, not wanting to relinquish his invented opportunity for financial salvation. William leveled a stare at the man, a small frown escaping his demeanor.

"Sir," he said, "please find your next partner. You are obstructing the dance floor." A clearly flustered Mr. Holmes left the floor, retreating into the sea of people in the ballroom.

"Lord Dunham," said Josephine as they began to dance, "Thank you for rescuing me from that rather unpleasant gentleman."

"It was my pleasure, Miss Hamilton," he replied. "You clearly were not enjoying his conversation as much as he was."

Josephine laughed. "Was it that obvious, then?"

"Only a bit," the young duke replied. "Besides the last gentleman, are you enjoying your evening?" Josephine hesitated slightly. She didn't know how to reply politely without being dishonest.

"These occasions are always spectacular," she finally responded. "And you, sir? You and Miss Beech are quite lovely together."

William flashed a breathtaking smile at the mention of Elisabeth. "I am particularly happy this evening, Miss Hamilton," he responded as he spun her gracefully across the floor.

"May I inquire as to the reason?"

"Of course, Miss Hamilton. My father informed me that he will announce my engagement tonight. I have been waiting for his permission to marry Miss Beech for some time."

Josephine frowned, certain she had misheard the young man. William frowned as well, not expecting this particular reaction from Miss Hamilton.

"Are you well, Miss Hamilton," he asked when Josephine didn't respond. "Have I said something to alarm you?"

"No," she replied immediately, still trying to unravel the puzzle in her mind. "Excuse me for asking, Lord Dunham," she added, "but did your father inform you of the nature of his business with my father?"

William seemed perplexed by such a question. "No, my lady, he did not." A suspicion began to grow on William's face as he started to grasp the full situation. He looked down at Josephine with an expression somewhere between panic and anger. "My marriage is not to be to Miss Beech, is it?"

Josephine could feel his resentment growing by the second. "I am so sorry, Lord Dunham," she quickly offered. "I was informed just last month, after you and your father left our estate." William looked from Josephine's face to find Elisabeth, who was happily waltzing with another young gentleman on the far end of the ballroom. "I am so sorry," she repeated, trying to somehow ease his distress.

"I assumed my father meant Elisabeth," William said slowly. "We have been celebrating all evening." They continued to dance in time to the waltz, though neither one added anything more to the conversation. These were, without a doubt, the most awkward and unhappy moments Josephine had ever spent at a ball.

As the music came to a close, William bowed politely to Josephine. "Please excuse me, Miss Hamilton. I must find Elisabeth."

Josephine curtsied in reply. "Of course."

As he hurried away, a clear, loud ringing filled the ballroom. Duke Dunham had taken a prominent place at the head of the dance floor, and was summoning the attention of the guests with a wine glass and spoon. All turned their gaze to the duke, wondering what announcement an English royal would make in their presence. William was trying to make his way as quickly as possible to Elisabeth.

Josephine cringed at the duke's social insensibility. Either he didn't understand the effect his public announcement would have on the unsuspecting Miss Beech, or he didn't care. Either way, Josephine was beginning to understand why the elder duke had difficulties finding a trustworthy financial manager.

When the conversation quieted sufficiently, Duke Dunham cleared his throat and began speaking. "Thank you for your kind attention. William," he called, gesturing to his son, "will you please make your way to my side?" All eyes found the younger Dunham, who had not quite made it to Elisabeth. With some reluctance, he changed direction and took a place next to his father. Josephine looked again to Elisabeth, who was radiant with happiness. Her own heart fell. This was beyond disaster.

"I want to thank you for your gracious reception of my son and I into your fair city. Our time here has been well spent." Short applause erupted before the duke continued. "I will be returning to my beloved England soon. I am happy to announce, however, that my son and heir will be taking a bride and making his new home here, in Boston." The ball goers clapped with gusto at the happy news as the duke smiled graciously and waved for silence. A few of the ladies turned to Elisabeth, offering smiles and happy applause. She was beaming. The duke continued, "May I present to you the future Duchess of Bedford, Miss Josephine Hamilton."

This time the applause was delayed, then polite instead of joyous. Most of the guests were clearly surprised at the choice for the bride. Josephine kept her eyes on Elisabeth, whose countenance fell to disbelief as soon as the duke finished speaking. Elisabeth returned Josephine's gaze, anger and hurt washing over her lovely features. She turned to leave the ballroom, and Josephine started to follow after her.

"Please, Miss Hamilton," the duke continued, "join your future husband in a celebratory dance." Duke Dunham gestured to the orchestra, who promptly began a beautiful melody suitable for romantic celebration. Instead of moving to the center of the ballroom to meet her future husband, Josephine replied to the duke's request with slight irritation, exhibited by a raised eyebrow in his direction. Then, with her usual air of authority and command, she calmly followed the path of the distraught Miss Beech out of the ballroom. The orchestral strains stalled awkwardly as she left. The guests stood aloof for a few moments, ladies whispering to their partners behind their hands, no one quite knowing what to do with this situation.

As Josephine retreated from the ballroom completely, she finally heard the music resume and the sounds of shocked conversation die down. The elder Duke Dunham was either one of the most callous, manipulating men she had ever come across or a socially inept imbecile. After a moment's reflection, she decided he was the former. No one of the duke's social standing would be ignorant of the humiliation this situation would throw upon Miss Beech. She was certain that this was a deliberate, calculated attempt by the duke to severe Miss Beech's attachment to his son.

Cad!

Another word crept to Josephine's mind, but she asked forgiveness and put it out of her thoughts just as quickly as it had intruded.

A few more steps brought Josephine around a corner and into a darkened sitting room. Miss Beech was already on the other side the room and was about to exit into the home's foyer.

"Miss Beech!" she called, quickening her stride to catch the fleeing woman. Elisabeth turned immediately, her face flushing with anger when she saw Josephine. Instead of holding her place, the young woman closed the last few steps between them. Before Josephine could react, Elisabeth's hand flew from her side and slapped Josephine smartly across the cheek.

"You already have everything anyone could ever want! Everything!" She furiously hurled the words like stones as Josephine stood shocked and silent, her hand covering the red sting on her face. "Why do you have to have him?" Elisabeth waved her arm toward the doorway where William emerged. He stopped, dismayed at the violent display he had just witnessed.

When Josephine didn't answer, Elisabeth turned and fled from the room. William began to follow, then stopped at Josephine's side, clearly torn between pursuing his distraught love and being a gentleman to the wronged lady.

"Go," Josephine nodded in Elisabeth's direction. "I am uninjured."

William shot off after Elisabeth without another moment's hesitation, leaving Josephine alone and quite unhappy in the darkened room. She sank down in one of the armchairs, suddenly very weary of the evening. Soft footsteps fell behind her, and the weight of Mr. Hamilton's gentle hand lay upon her shoulder.

"I suppose that could have gone better," he said, sighing as he did so.

Josephine raised an eyebrow at the massive understatement. "That was horrible!" she added, looking up at her father. "I am quite unhappy with your choice for my father-in-law."

Mr. Hamilton grunted his agreement. "As you should be, my dear."

She rose and took his outstretched hand. Together, they walked through the foyer, out the door, and down the great stone staircase to their waiting carriage. Both were eager to retire from the night's misfortune.

5

William had not been able to comfort Elisabeth in any way. She had completely ignored his pleas for rational conversation, shutting her carriage door on his voice as the driver sped away. When he had returned to the foyer, he found that Josephine and her father had also left. Unwilling to enter into the public scrutiny of the ballroom, William had made his way to his own carriage to wait for his father.

After a time, Duke Dunham emerged from the Cabot mansion and entered the cab, seemingly unfazed by the drama of the evening.

"Ah, there you are, William!" he exclaimed with surprise as he opened the door and found his son sitting miserably in the dark. "I was wondering what had become of you."

William eyed his father with contempt as the duke ordered the driver back to their residence.

"What, exactly, was that farce that just took place?" he questioned coldly.

The duke sat upright with indignation. "Change your tone at once!" he ordered. "You will show more respect to your father and one of my standing!"

"I will not!" William roared back. "It was not your place to announce a bride that was not of my choosing."

"You cannot be so naive, William!" Duke Dunham retaliated, as if talking with a child. "Did you really think you could happily live out your days with a woman who can barely afford her own wardrobe? Her family has nothing! It is your obligation to..."

"Obligation or no, Father! I will not marry Miss Hamilton, no matter my title, or lineage, or standing! I will happily abdicate it all in order to have Elisabeth."

The duke sat calmly back in the seat and folded his hands in his lap, a somber look overtaking his thin features. "You can't," he stated simply.

"Of course I can," replied William, somewhat puzzled by his father's change in demeanor. "I know a handful of royals who have done that very thing."

"If you do not marry Miss Hamilton," countered the duke, "then our family will lose everything we have, both here and in England."

William was too shocked to respond immediately. His face filled with incredulity, and he sat back slowly, his eyes never leaving his father.

Duke Dunham took advantage of the silence and continued. "We have been losing massive amounts of money from our accounts. I have had to borrow profusely just to keep up with the expenses of our estate at Bedford." He looked squarely at William. "Why do you think we came to America? As a pleasure retreat?" Cynicism punctuated his voice. "The only purpose was to find a suitable heiress for you to marry. It is the only way to rescue our finances and ensure that your mother and sisters in England are not humiliated by being put out of our estate."

Finally finding his voice, William asked, "Why didn't you inform me of your purpose earlier?"

"And bear your noble scorn?" his father answered, derision edging his voice. "Your over inflated sense of honor would have driven me mad, and most likely thwarted my designs."

"There has to be another way, Father," William began, though the duke was already shaking his head.

"I have been trying to solve the problem for months, William. I am exasperated beyond description. At this point, the Hamilton estate is our only salvation."

"Blood and ashes!" William angrily slammed his fist against the carriage wall. "Have you explored every other avenue?" he probed heatedly.

"Of course I have!" his father snapped back. "Do you think I wanted to put you in this position? Do you think I wanted to rely on you to resolve my financial dilemma?" He looked out the window of the carriage, staring at the sleeping buildings of the financial district. "No, William," he finished. "I'm afraid there is no other way."

William stared out the window as well, considering his options. "I can still refuse, Father," he said calmly. "I can let you fall and bear the consequences of your mismanagement."

The duke's laugh was almost silent. "Indeed you could, William," he replied. "I believe that you are fully capable of dooming me to a pauper's life. But," he added, "I don't believe that you are capable of rendering the same judgment on your mother and young sisters. As of yet, they are unaware of our financial peril. It would be quite a shock for them to be reduced to poverty, don't you think?"

The young Dunham sat silently, anger and helplessness seething out of his every pore. Finally, he leaned forward and asked one more question of his father. "Why did you humiliate Miss Beech this evening."

"Yes, well," his father responded, mildly uncomfortable. "I had to make sure the young lady would discontinue her affection for you. I severely misjudged the strength of the attachment you had for one another. For that," Duke Dunham looked his son level in the eye, "I am truly sorry, William."

William sat back heavily, the bitterness of defeat washing over him. How could his father let things get to this point? What had he been doing all this time? William realized that he didn't know most of his father's business, or his family's dealings. He was twenty-eight years old, heir to the Bedford Duchy, and had not taken it upon himself to be acquainted with the family's holdings or business arrangements. Perhaps some of the responsibility for this dilemma lay upon his own shoulders.

William continued to look out the window, wondering how he was going to explain all of this to Elisabeth. How was he going to live without her? There had to be a way to resolve this matter. He could not just walk away from the love of his life.

The carriage slowed to a stop, and William impatiently thrust his head out the window, searching for the cause of the delay.

"Spencer!" he yelled to the driver, "what is the hold up?" William's voice was steeped with irritation, which made him seem harsher than he intended. He immediately regretted his tone with the driver.

Spencer, however, didn't seem put off at all. From his seat, he heard almost everything that transpired between father and son in the carriage, and knew that his master had cause for aggravation this evening.

"Just some drunks crossin' the road, sir," Spencer replied without fuss. "Won't run em' down, though I might be doin' humanity a favor," he added.

Peering around the horses, William could make out four or five well-dressed gentlemen laughing and staggering in the middle of the road, clearly trying to calculate the best route across the street.

"Idiots," he remarked, mostly to himself. As he sat back once again, another carriage caught his eye. It was stopped on the street perpendicular to his, not even a stone's toss away, though it was not waiting for the intoxicated men to clear the street.

A dashing, young man with brown hair was standing beside the open door, courting a poorly dressed girl who was clearly distressed. She was perhaps fourteen or fifteen, and pretty, though she would have been much prettier had she worn a smile and some decent clothing. William sat up and watched carefully. The man spoke a few more words through charmed and reassuring smiles, and beckoned the girl into the cab. To William's dismay, the frightened girl looked from side to side, then hastily entered the carriage.

"Ay there, sir!" William shouted angrily from his window while opening the carriage door. His father looked on with curiosity. The other man spoke to the girl inside the cab, shut the door firmly, then sauntered merrily toward the Dunham's carriage.

William's feet were firmly planted on the street by the time the man made his way over. "Can I help you, sir?" he asked, a smile on his handsome face. Then he added in a quiet tone, "You are alarming the young lady."

"You can help me, sir!" William replied forcefully. "You can let that young lady out of your carriage at once!" He stood his full height as he spoke, letting the anger he felt flood through his voice and bearing.

The young man laughed, his brown eyes almost sparkling. "And put her out in the cold this evening? I think not!"

Without thinking, William wrapped the man's collar in his left fist and pulled back his right. The younger man grabbed William's arm, his black, gloved hands working uselessly to unhinge William's fingers from his collar. Only his father's restraining arm kept William from delivering a devastating blow.

"William!" The duke's harsh tone surprised William, and the man shook free of his grasp, his expression no longer merry.

"I suggest, sir," the man spewed heatedly at William, "that you mind your own business!" With that, he turned on his heel and marched back to his own cab.

William turned angrily to his father. "Why did you interfere? Don't you know what is about to transpire?"

"Don't be an idiot, William!" his father exclaimed. "Get in the carriage!"

William looked about him, noticing that the drunken noise of the street had ceased. The eyes of everyone in the vicinity were fixed on him. Even the inebriated businessmen who had finally succeeded in crossing the street were staring. The other cab hastily pulled away, and the duke ushered his son into their own carriage and shut the door behind them. Spencer casually urged the horses into a trot, and they were again on their way home.

"What were you going to do, William?" Duke Dunham asked calmly. "Rescue the poor girl? Take her home? Feed, clothe, and educate her?"

"Of course not!" he defended. "But I wasn't going to stand by and let that man take advantage of her!"

"Then how would she eat tomorrow?" the duke asked. "Tell me that. How would she pay for her housing or her bread? Hmm?"

William frowned. He honestly had never considered such things, had never seen further into the unfortunate situation.

"That's what I thought," said the duke, less than kindly. "You are always ready to be a chivalrous gentleman, never thinking of the harsh consequences of your noble intentions."

The oddity of his father's statement and the memory of that scared little girl left William in a very sour mood and compounded his feeling of helplessness. As of a few hours ago, everything in his life had been turned upside down.

He wished he had never come to Boston.

Only a few blocks from that intersection, in the warm and richly furnished Crimson Dagger, sat Erin Moore. Her latest client had just left, but she knew Mr. Drake would be severely displeased if she did not get dressed and downstairs in a hurry. At midnight, the evening was young, and there were still plenty of gentlemen callers to be entertained.

She looked into the mirror and watched curiously as tears slid down the face of the stranger looking back at her. Lifting the glass of brandy from the vanity, she downed it with one swallow.

She looked into the mirror again. Everything was going to be fine. But the stranger staring back at her was still crying.

After Josephine and her father returned home from the disastrous social foray, Mr. Hamilton bid his daughter good night with a kiss on the cheek and a gentle reassurance that all would be well. She made her way to her own chambers, looking forward to putting this unfortunate day to an end.

"Josephine?" Ophelia's softened voice beckoned to her from the hallway, and she entered Josephine's room bearing a note in her hand and Josephine's thick cloak over her arm. "It seems that Mr. Darcy has found another," she said, wrapping the cloak around Josephine's shoulders.

Josephine read the note as she and Ophelia quietly made their way downstairs. "Is Mrs. Stoddely prepared for another ward?" she asked.

"I believe so, ma'am," Ophelia responded. "She has come to expect guests at these late hours."

"So she has," replied Josephine. She turned to Ophelia. "Keep a good watch on my father while I am out," she said in a hushed voice.

"Of course, my lady," Ophelia replied. "Josephine," she added, her tone that of a concerned friend rather than of a maid, "perhaps it is time for you to pass the reins on to someone else. After all, you are about to be married. It is hardly proper for you to be attending to these activities."

Josephine smiled, clearly amused at her friend's suggestion, and placed a gentle hand on Ophelia's shoulder. "My dear Ophelia," she answered, "when have these activities ever been proper?"

Then Josephine Hamilton entered the black carriage waiting at the foot of her steps and rode back into the Boston night.

6

Josephine sat on the edge of the wing chair in the library. Two ledgers lay open on the small, round table next to her. In the fireplace a generous flame crackled, more for light than for warmth. Jeffrey always kept up the fire in the library, as this room was a favorite haunt of both her and her father. Bookshelves as tall as the ceiling lined three of the walls. The fourth wall was the exclusive property of the fireplace and the carved mantle above it.

Everything in the room, except for the books, was either deep red or stained wood. Even the two wing chairs were covered in luxurious red velvet. The effect at night, when the only illumination was the fire, was quite enchanting. Even now, with the late morning sun streaming through the arched windows, the color was vibrant and vivacious.

Perhaps that was the reason Josephine loved this room. It surrounded one with warmth on every level. Or perhaps it was the dusty fragrance of the old books filling every sliver of space on the shelves. Her mother has been quite the collector, furnishing their library with everything from The Iliad to Blackstone's Commentaries on English Law. Josephine had acquired her great love of reading from her mother.

The one book that did not find its home on a shelf was their Bible, which lived on the round table between the two wing chairs. This was the only book that Josephine read every day, usually in the morning hour before breakfast. After breakfast, her father would retire to the library and read the same Bible, then place it back on the table for Josephine's use the next morning. Sometimes Josephine would spy him through the ornate archway that served as the library entrance. He would be holding that Book between his palms, his eyes closed, his expression somber. She knew he was praying and thinking of her mother.

Perhaps it was because of her mother that Josephine loved this room.

It did not matter today, though. Josephine sighed and closed both ledgers. After the sour events of the Spring Ball, Josephine had calmed herself by immersing her mind in numbers.

The Dunham ledgers and their mysteries had kept her company when sleep eluded her. She had spent the darkened morning hours detailing transactions, resolving ambiguities, and looking for errors. The Dunham ledgers were a labyrinth of exchanges and conversions, often involving multiple currencies. Even the hand writings were varied, indicating that too many people had their noses in the Dunham accounts. The task at hand would not be easily completed.

Sometimes Josephine wondered if she would be happier living life as her female contemporaries did. Their only worries encompassed social functions, new beaus, and ball gowns. Josephine had her father's financial empire to manage, as well as her own pressing affairs to attend to. She had little time for the silly social games that those of her class seemed to enjoy.

And now she had a marriage to manage. What was her father thinking? Marriage was not supposed to be a business venture, not in this day and age. But the duke and her father had set the mechanism in motion, and there was no going back. All she could do was try to smooth the damage caused by the duke's insensitivity at the Spring Ball. If she were going to be married, she needed an understanding and cooperative relationship with her spouse. She simply did not have the time for an ill-disposed husband.

She sighed again, sat back, and sipped her coffee, eyes closed in weary repose. All was quiet for a few moments, then Ophelia's bubbly voice caught her attention. Opening her eyes, she saw William Dunham being escorted through the archway by her maid, who was happily chatting to the young royal about the history of Hamilton Manor. He nodded politely in response to her comments, then stopped when he saw Josephine. His demeanor was not pleasant, and Josephine could not tell if he exuded anger, sorrow, or both. She felt for the man.

"Here we are then, sir," finished Ophelia. "Would you like me to bring you coffee or tea?"

Josephine rose as William answered the housekeeper, "No, thank you. You are most kind," he responded, his voice deep and steady. Ophelia smiled and blushed as she curtsied to the man. Josephine softly shook her head at her friend.

Ophelia almost giggled as she left the room. Of all the people in the household, she was the most delighted about the engagement."Just call if you need anything, ma'am."

Josephine watched her go, then turned her gaze to William Dunham. He was still one of the most handsome men she had ever seen, even with this stressful scowl marring his brow. For just a moment, she found herself wishing that she were his equal in appearance, so that he might think her beautiful as well. Realizing that she had been staring, Josephine quickly extended her hand to William.

"Lord Dunham, thank you for responding to my invitation. Please sit."

William took her hand and nodded slightly, then sat in the opposite chair. "I think it would be more appropriate if you addressed me as William," he said stiffly.

"Of course," she replied. A few moments of silent, awkward formality followed. Now that William was actually here, Josephine was having a harder time than she had anticipated. She had not counted on this strange nervousness tying knots in her stomach, or the sudden abandonment of her wit.

She cleared her throat. "How is Miss Beech?"

William shifted uncomfortably in his chair. "Frankly, she is inconsolable."

"I am truly sorry, William," Josephine began. "I do not...," she searched for the correct words. "I do not approve of a marriage of financial convenience, especially when such hurt is inflicted."

Softening, he replied, "No, I know that is not your character. You have shown yourself to be nothing but gracious." He suddenly studied her face. "Forgive me. I should be inquiring about your well-being. Have you recovered from the other evening's...drama?"

Josephine unconsciously covered her cheek with her hand. She remembered the sting of Miss Beech's slap well, though the mark was no longer visible. "I am fine," she said. "I feel so badly for Elisabeth, though." She looked up intently at William, summoning all the sincerity she possessed. "This was not what I wanted, William, and I am so sorry for the damage done to you and to Miss Beech."

William slowly sat forward. He seemed drained, and all of the previous anger was gone from his demeanor. Finally, he said, "You owe an apology to no one, Miss Hamilton. As a matter of fact, it is I who should apologize to you. This arrangement was not of your making. As I understand it, you also have no choice in this matter?"

She was relieved. "No. This was a transaction between our fathers. And I have given my father my word that I will trust his judgment."

William sat back thoughtfully. "I, also, am bound by my honor. My father has 'enlightened' me to our financial distress."

Josephine gestured to the two ledgers still resting on the table. "I will get to the bottom of that dilemma, I assure you."

William looked as if he were summing her up, his blue eyes piercing. He replied, "I believe you will, Miss Hamilton. I think my father has underestimated this arrangement."

She smiled. "Perhaps so." She sipped her coffee before continuing. "William, I wanted to meet with you so we could...," she faltered for a moment, "come to an agreement about this marriage."

"Yes?" William sat forward, listening.

"I know that there is no affection between us, and I do not expect such after we are joined. But I would like for us to at least behave in an amiable fashion toward one another."

"I agree," William replied, nodding slowly. "Rest assured, I only wish for things to go as smoothly as possible."

"Thank you, sir," Josephine answered. "One last matter," she continued. "I would like for my residence to remain here at Hamilton Manor. I have many obligations and duties, and it would be most inconvenient to relocate to your residence in the city." William raised a quizzical eyebrow. She continued quickly, "You are welcome here, of course. Well," she faltered, "if you wish."

Nodding again, William said, "I think those terms are quite agreeable. And, frankly, our city home is only ours until my father returns to England. I will be happy to make my residence at Hamilton Manor."

Josephine held out her hand in a business like fashion. "Friends, then?"

William shook her hand as he would that of a business partner. "I would be honored, Miss Hamilton."

"I think," she said, "that you should address me as Josephine."

William donned his hat as he strode down the stairs and to his carriage. Waving to Spencer to keep his seat, he opened the door and stepped firmly into the cab, shutting the door after him. The vehicle lurched to a start, making its way back to Boston.

He was relieved, maybe even in good spirits. He was certain Josephine had summoned him for a severe conversation after the incident with Elisabeth, and he had not been looking forward to it, though he knew it was merited. But he felt a peace as soon as he entered Josephine's presence, and his spirit became more settled. He was sure then that Josephine's intentions were kind.

He knew Josephine did not deserve Elisabeth's wrath, nor was Elisabeth justified in her furious rage of words. But she had been distraught, as had he, and she had acted out of blind hurt. He was grateful that Josephine had reacted with grace and poise. If he had to be thrust into an unwelcome marriage, then at least his wife was going to be pleasant instead of high strung.

His spirits faded a bit with the thought, however. For the last few months, he had planned on Elisabeth being his bride. He loved her. He loved her beauty, her vivaciousness, the light in her eyes when she saw him. He loved their easy conversation and her frequent laughter. So many things about Elisabeth he loved. She was his very breath.

Now his father was taking it all away. William sighed, trying to ease the agonizing pain churning inside his chest. All he wanted was for Elisabeth to be in his arms. For a moment, he saw himself knocking on Elisabeth's door, sweeping her into the carriage, and carrying her far away. They would find a place, someplace where he could work as a commoner, someplace where they could live as other people do. Elisabeth would accept that life if it were the only way they could be together. He was sure of it. They could leave this very evening.

Then another image filled his mind. He saw his mother and sisters being put out of their estate in Bedford. He imagined the derision they would be forced to endure. Worse, the stigma of shame that his family would bear would not be shaken for decades. His own honor would be compromised, and he would be remembered as a man who had willingly contributed to his family's demise.

How could Elisabeth love such a man. Life had entangled him in a loathsome dilemma, with no easy solution. As William stripped away his superfluous rationale, all he was left with was his honor – hanging about his neck like a shackle.

The carriage jolted to a stop. Looking out the window, William saw that he had already arrived in front of the tasteful, but modest, Beech home. He doubted this conversation would go as well as the previous one had. Knowing what he had to do, he slowly exited the coach, his chest heavy with heartache.

Elisabeth herself answered the door. She took his coat and hat, then showed him to the sitting room, where she poured two cups of tea. Her golden hair softly framed her delicate features, making her eyes seem bluer and her lips fuller. Her powder blue gown hugged her figure, and barely rustled as she gracefully seated herself next to him. Her familiar fragrance caused his heart to beat faster.

"I can't even begin to say how sorry I am, William," she began, her voice soft and full of regret. "I acted dreadfully toward Miss Hamilton."

William placed his tea on the table, then took Elisabeth's hand in his own. "Things are often more exaggerated in one's mind, Elisabeth," he replied gently. "I assure you that Miss Hamilton fully understands our distress."

She pulled her hand from his and looked down at the floor. "You have seen her, then?"

"She requested a meeting this morning." William reached out and reclaimed her hand, then turned her chin to meet his gaze. "Her only concern was for our plight."

She looked hopeful. "Then Miss Hamilton is not agreeable to this union?"

"No, she is not."

"William!" she exclaimed excitedly. "We are saved!"

"Elisabeth," he began, dreading his next few words, "I am bound by my father's word, as is Miss Hamilton by her father's wishes."

Elisabeth looked straight into William's eyes, her own filling with tears. "Did you speak with your father?" she asked, her pleading voice ripping his heart in two.

William put his arms around her and drew her close to him. This was an impossible situation. "I'm so sorry, Elisabeth," he whispered in her hair, "there is nothing to be done."

She lay her head on his chest as silent tears streamed down her cheeks. "Please don't say that, William," she whispered back. "We could leave Boston. I don't care where we go or how we live. I don't care about your titles or your wealth. I just want you, just you."

William sighed heavily, feeling the warmth of her against his chest, very aware that this was the last time he would ever hold her.

"If we did that," he answered, his own voice thick, "my family would fall into ruin. I can't, Elisabeth." Her tears were undoing him.

"I know," she answered softly, placing her hand on his chest. "I know the man you are. When... are you to be married?"

"Within the month."

They sat together for many minutes, her face and hand resting on his chest, his arms surrounding her protectively. Finally, William pulled himself away from Elisabeth. He brushed her wet cheeks with his thumbs, then softly, intimately kissed her lips. She cried as he walked out the door.

As the carriage made its way through the streets of Boston proper, William Dunham dropped his weary head into his hands. For the first time since his childhood, he wept.

7

Erin Moore tapped softly on the heavy, wooden door. There was no answer from the other side. She tapped again, a little louder this time, but not loud enough to risk detection from the neighboring rooms.

"Miss?" she whispered into the door crack. "Miss, are you there?" The poor girl behind the door had been shut up for three weeks now, and Erin had not seen even a glimpse of her. Mr. Drake was the only one who entered the room, sometimes merrily bringing up a tray of food for the girl, sometimes staggering up with a bottle in his hand.

He had taken quite a liking to the girl, which meant that he left most of the other women in the establishment alone. While Erin was grateful for the reduced attentions of Mr. Drake, she felt horrible for the most recent target of his abuse. He kept her under lock and key like a prisoner.

Erin paused at the thought. They were prisoners. All of them. She stayed at The Crimson Dagger for the sake of her little brother, Murray. Because she 'worked' for Mr. Drake, Murray had his own room on the first floor, a job running errands during the day, and warm clothes and meals. If not for Mr. Drake, no matter how detestable the employment, Murray would be starving, freezing, and homeless in some back alley. Mr. Drake knew exactly how to keep Erin at his establishment.

But this poor girl, she was kept by wood and iron. Mr. Drake had not even allowed any clients to visit her. The only face that girl saw was his.

"Miss," Erin called again. "I know you are there. You are not alone." Erin stooped down and slid a small paper square under the door. It was the only kindness she could do for the girl.

She quickly stood up and hurried down the hall. It would not do for anyone to see her trying to talk with the girl. She did not want to risk Mr. Drake's anger.

Erin knew Murray would be waiting for her in the kitchen. They would eat breakfast together, like they did every morning. She would listen to her brother's enthusiastic stories about the people he met the day before, or the different places he was able to explore in Boston, or the grandiose buildings he saw. Erin lived for these mornings, for her brother's smile. And when he left for the day to run his errands, she died inside all over again.

Shannon Tiernan slowly made her way to the door. A small scrap of paper was lying on the floor just inside the room. She had heard the girl's call from the other side of the oak, heard her kind words, but did not dare to answer back. She bent over and picked up the paper. Something was inside. Her thin fingers slowly pulled apart the folds to reveal a small square of toffee.

She had seen toffee once before in Ireland, years ago. Her father had come home after a particularly good fishing trip, bearing enough coin to pay expenses for the entire month. He had also brought six pieces of soft, sweet toffee – three for her and three for her mother. Shannon had never tasted anything like it before or since.

Bringing the candy to her mouth, Shannon relished the sweetness of the gift. She thought that all of her tears had been spent days and days ago, but as the toffee dissolved in her mouth, memories of her family and a life gone forever spilled down her cheeks and onto the floor, even as thankfulness for this small kindness filled her.

8

The late spring morning promised nothing but good fortune and fair weather, and Josephine's gown echoed the color of the clear, blue skies overhead. She had chosen a beautiful, but simple dress for her wedding, one that would reflect the attitude of the ceremony and the size of the wedding party.

The duke had wanted a large event to celebrate the marriage of his son, with a guest list including over half of Boston's social elite. Josephine had insisted otherwise, not wanting to put her new husband and his less-than-joyous demeanor on public display. Duke Dunham finally acquiesced, giving the final say to the persistent bride.

Josephine had seen William only a handful of times since their conversation in the library. He was always polite, and even tried to seem pleasant, but something had been quenched in his eyes, and his spirit reflected the emptiness. It almost made Josephine shed tears every time she saw him.

She never thought that she would marry, given her circumstance in life. But when she had allowed for the daydreams that fill a girl's mind, she had never imagined a man who lamented his marriage to her.

The first time she thought on these things, she accused God of being unfair, perhaps even unjust. A second later she had repented, tears in her eyes, thinking of the young girls suffering horrendously just miles from her own luxurious home.

No. William was a good man, full of kindness and nobility. Even if her husband-to-be had no love for her in his heart, her life was still vastly better than most.

She stood calmly in the soft, morning sun, with William on her left. Her father and his were seated behind them, as well as the few distinguished guests whom the duke had insisted upon. The entire party consisted of no more than thirty persons.

The minister stood before them, reciting his sermon on the virtues of love, quoting most often from 1 Corinthians 13. Josephine felt that if his tone were not so monotonous and dry the sermon would be quite lovely. She immediately caught herself, not wanting to be irreverent in any way to the Holy Word.

The minister finished his discourse, then addressed Josephine and William. "Please join right hands," he commanded. Josephine looked up to William as he took her hand. His face was a mask, totally expressionless. Only his eyes betrayed the barest hint of sorrow. He did not meet her gaze.

The minister continued. "No other human ties are more tender; no other vows are more sacred than those you are about to assume. You are entering into the holy estate which is the deepest mystery of experience, and which is the very sacrament of divine love." He turned to William and addressed him.

"William Dunham, in taking the woman whom you hold by the right hand to be your lawful and wedded wife, I require you to promise to love and cherish her, to honor and sustain her, in sickness and in health, in poverty as in wealth, in the bad that may darken your days, in the good that may lighten your ways, and to be true to her in all things until death alone shall part you. Dost thou so promise?"

William finally met Josephine's eyes. He frowned slightly, though she could tell that he was trying not to. His face was still solid, but his eyes were so expressive. Josephine could see the struggle in them, the unwillingness to make this most solemn vow to a woman he didn't love. She saw regret warring with his sense of duty. But mostly, she saw sadness.

The tear that had been threatening to escape during the whole ceremony finally made its way down her cheek as she saw him... grieve. Yes, that was the word. He was grieving.

William's eyes tracked the tear falling down her face. "I do." His voice was strong and sure. Josephine knew that his heart wasn't so.

The minister turned to Josephine. "Josephine Hamilton, taking the man who holds you by the right hand to be your lawful and wedded husband, I require you to promise to love, cherish, and obey him, to honor and sustain him, in sickness and in health, in poverty as in wealth, in the bad that may darken your days, in the good that may lighten your ways, and to be true to him in all things until death alone shall part you. Dost thou so promise?"

She looked deeply in his eyes, thinking hard on the words she had just heard. She could end this now just by saying 'no'. She could free William from this responsibility. She could give him back his joy, give him back Elisabeth. To do so would be to rebel against her father's wishes, to doom the Dunham family to a legacy of disdain. But William would be free.

In that moment, she realized she loved him already.

The word almost fell off of her tongue, but just as she had seen the battle in his eyes a few moments earlier, he saw the conflict in her hesitation. He leaned forward slightly, and with the faintest of whispers mouthed to her, "Say yes."

She breathed in. "I promise." The words were out of her mouth without her realizing that she had said them. William barely nodded, and smiled sadly.

"William," the minister asked, "what token do you give of the vows you have made?" William reached into his pocket and pulled from it a small circlet of gold, wound about with tiny filigree vines and leaves. Small diamonds were studded about the vines, but they did not overwhelm the beauty of the design. The goldsmith had obviously applied all of his skill to craft something so ornate and dainty.

The minister took the ring from William's outstretched hand and held it toward Heaven. "Bless this ring, O Lord, that he who gives it and she who wears it may abide in Thy peace, and continue in Thy favor, unto their life's end, through Jesus Christ our Lord."

William took the ring when the minister handed it back to him, and gently slid it on Josephine's finger.

"Josephine," he continued, "what token do you give of the vows you have made?" Josephine turned to her father, who held out a gold band. She took the ring, and passed it to the minister. He held this ring skyward, as well. After it was blessed, she took it and placed it onto William's finger. He looked at the ring with some surprise. Perhaps he had been expecting a simple gold band. Instead, the ring had the letters D and H engraved in beautiful calligraphy on the circular face, entwining gracefully. She hoped that one day, the ring would be a proper representation of the merging of their two families.

The minister, satisfied with the exchange of rings, uttered the final words of the ceremony. "You now have common interests and occupations. You hold property and possessions in common, and you have essentially one history and one destiny. Inscribed in the Word of God is the counsel you will need for this mutual and blessed relationship." He looked solemnly at both of them. "These vows are to be broken only by death. Mr. Dunham," he concluded, "you may kiss your bride."

William leaned down to Josephine and placed the softest of kisses on her lips. She caught her breath, and returned his kiss, her heart pounding unexpectedly. When she opened her eyes, however, her momentary exultation fled. William's face had resumed its mask, and his eyes retreated back into their sorrow. Ever the gentleman, he offered her his arm as they turned to face the clapping of their guests. Slowly, they retreated from the lawn and made their way through the grand double doors that led to the dining hall.

As she walked, she smiled her thanks to the fine ladies and polished gentlemen offering their congratulations. She could not wait to be away from their presence and their prying eyes. But between the seven course feast and an evening of dancing to the orchestra, there were still hours of celebration ahead.

They both sat quietly through dinner, smiling when a guest came by their long table at the head of the dining room to congratulate them. But they spoke little to each other, and Josephine noticed the furtive glances and occasional whispers of the guests. It did little to improve her mood.

As the servants cleared away the last course of dinner from in front of the guests, lovely strains of music drifted into the dining room from the ballroom. William pushed away from the table, then looked at Josephine.

"May I have this first dance, my lady?" he asked, holding out his hand for her to take. Surprised, she placed her hand in his, and smiled.

"I would be very pleased to dance with you, William," she answered. The couple exited the dining room hand in hand, and various guests also excused themselves from their table to view the first dance of the Lord and Lady Dunham. As they made their way to the center of the ballroom, the quintet took notice and began the traditional waltz. Josephine placed her free hand on William's shoulder as he embraced her around the waist, leaving the proper amount of distance between them. They moved easily and lightly to the tune, turning and swaying as the music wound around the room.

William finally looked Josephine in the eye and smiled, though it seemed to Josephine as if a mask were forcing itself into an unnatural expression. "I have to apologize, Josephine," he began. "My attitude has not been what it should, and I am afraid it has clouded your wedding day."

"Our circumstances," she answered, pondering the best way to phrase her words, "are not as joyous as others. So I understand your demeanor, and I do not expect you to put on any front for my sake."

His mask broke for a moment and allowed a glimmer of shame through. "I am afraid you are revealing me to be a cad. This day above all should be your happiest, and I am stealing that from you with my poor temperament."

They waltzed another few moments in silence as Josephine thought on what to say. "William," she offered, "do not think of me as your wife this day."

"What?" he asked, clearly surprised.

"No, not your wife," she continued. "Think of me as a friend, one who will keep you company in this difficult hour."

He began to protest, but she shushed him gently before he could say anything. "Think of me as your companion who will rescue you with a dance when our gossip laden guests become too trying, or when your father becomes too … obnoxious."

William's eyes widened slightly at her frankness, but he laughed genuinely for the first time that day, perhaps for the first time that month, and the mask that he had been wearing melted away.

"My dear," he replied, lowering his voice and swinging her gently with the music, "what would our guests think if anyone heard you?"

She smiled, feeling an easiness between them that had been absent before. "Should you not be more concerned about what your father would think?"

Without hesitation William responded, "No, I should not. He has removed himself from my good graces by arranging this..." He caught his words before anything more could come out of his mouth, his frown returning.

"William," Josephine responded matter-of-factly, "I am not a sensitive child that will wilt into tears when confronted with the realities of our situation."

"No," he answered, "you are not."

"Then," she said, "do not be afraid to be frank with me. Remember, I am your friend this evening."

"No," William said. "I will not accept your attempted kindness in this matter. You are my wife, Josephine. And even though our circumstances are not what we wanted..." He paused. "Neither am I delicate. I will not pretend at your expense, nor will I require you to rescue me from our marriage. I am a man of honor, and will honor you as my wife."

Josephine looked intently in his eyes, clearly seeing that he meant every word he was saying. Perhaps she had misjudged him. Perhaps William Dunham was stronger than she had first ascertained. She smiled fiercely, suddenly proud, instead of sad, to be Lady Dunham.

"Then, perhaps sir," she said, "*you* can rescue *me*."

He frowned again, confused. "How so?"

"The song is coming to an end, and my new father-in-law is waiting for the next dance." William began laughing, and swept Josephine past the waiting hand of Duke Dunham and into the center of the ballroom.

Once the evening passed and most of the guests left, William escorted Josephine upstairs to her suite. At her door, he kissed her hand gently and bade her goodnight.

She smiled and nodded. "Thank you, William." He knew she was referring to his change in demeanor, his attempt to make the evening a happier one for her.

"Of course, my dear," he replied. He waited until she shut the door behind her, then he walked down the hall to his own suite. It had taken every ounce of inner strength and most of the dinner hour to compose himself enough to be a proper gentleman for his new wife.

It was the tear that had brought him to his senses. Before that one tear fell down Josephine's cheek, William had been completely consumed with thoughts of his Elisabeth and the life he would never have with her. Furthermore, he had been brimming with anger at his father for creating this catastrophe.

He had tried to close off his emotions, to remain stoic and unmoved throughout the day, but then he had seen that one tear. It had shamed him. It was then that he knew he must conjure up some form of joy, even if it was false, for the sake of Josephine. He felt nothing for her beyond the mild affection of friendship, but that – paired with his honor – demanded that he not abuse this poor woman by being aloof on their wedding day. He did not know how his demeanor would fall tomorrow, but tonight, at least, he would allow Josephine some happiness.

"William, my dear boy!" Mr. Hamilton's voice broke into William's reverie. William turned and smiled as Mr. Hamilton strode happily down the hallway. He shook William's hand sturdily and pulled him into a manly embrace, heartily patting his shoulder as he did so. "It does my heart good to see my Josephine married, young man. Welcome to the family." Mr. Hamilton's affectionate pats were a bit more enthusiastic than William was accustomed to, and he winced involuntarily.

William inclined his head with a more formal attitude than his new father-in-law displayed, though not disingenuous. "Thank you, sir. You do me honor with your words," he answered truthfully.

Mr. Hamilton puffed on his pipe, then said, "I was perfectly happy with a daughter, you know. Never once did it enter my mind that I was missing out because I didn't have a son. But," he continued, "I find that it is comforting to have another man in the house."

"I am glad," William replied. He was truly happy to hear the kind words from Mr. Hamilton, though it did little to uplift his spirit.

Mr. Hamilton eyed his new son more thoughtfully, and blew a smoky ring from his lips. "I know it is a bit early to be offering advice," Mr. Hamilton ventured, "but I couldn't help but notice your earlier demeanor."

William's pulse picked up nervously. It seemed that Mr. Hamilton was just as observant as his daughter. He did not want to get off to a bad start with this man.

"I am always open to your counsel," William answered, hoping that he had not offended his new father-in-law on his first day of marriage.

"Good," nodded Mr. Hamilton with an air of seriousness settling uncomfortably around them. "I was not fully aware of your circumstances when your father and I first made our plans."

"Sir," began William defensively, "you do not have to -"

Mr. Hamilton held up a quick hand. "Young man," he continued, "I want only to say that sometimes it is better to put the former things behind you, and this," he pointed his pipe toward Josephine's door, "is one of those times. You will find yourself a happier man when you do."

William stood silent, frozen. He had no idea how to react to this man's frankness. Mr. Hamilton smiled warmly at his unsure son-in-law. "Good evening, William," he finally said. "I hope you rest well." Then Mr. Hamilton was off to his own quarters far down the hall.

William entered his suite and shut the door tightly behind him. He supposed that the conversation could have gone better, but it did not go badly. Mr. Hamilton was proving to be a kind man, but that fact did not erase his dejected state. He only felt worse now that he knew Mr. Hamilton was aware of his turmoil.

Moving as if he had a hundred years added to his shoulders, he sank on the edge of his bed and pulled off one boot, then the other. He let them fall to the floor and wearily dropped his shirt on top them. He fell back onto the pillow and stared up at the ornate ceiling, then forced his eyes to close. When they did, he saw Elisabeth in her sitting room, her eyes wild and blue, her smile sparkling as he walked through her front door.

He opened his eyes again and counted the flourishes outlining the trim on the ceiling above his bed. But even though his eyes were occupied, his thoughts still fled to Elisabeth. He finally gave in to fatigue and closed his eyes again, letting the visions of his lost love consume him. The day of his marriage was meant to be her day. Yet, here he was – married. Married to a woman who was not Elisabeth Beech.

He put away thoughts of the day and delved back into his memories of Elisabeth, her hair and her laughter and her kisses. He finally fell into a broken sleep as Elisabeth's face filled his tortured dreams.

9

Shannon sat on the small chair in front of the vanity mirror, not daring to look at her reflection. In her hand she held a white, linen bedsheet she had found in the large wardrobe next to the bed. Drake had already left that morning, and she did not know when he would return.

She never knew when he would return. Sometimes he brought her food or dresses, sometimes he brought drunken, angry blows. He always brought his lustful expectations, which Shannon found were pointless to fight against. It only left her more wounded and bruised, and Drake seemed to thrive from the conflict. So Shannon learned to acquiesce, though each time the effort plunged another piece of her soul into hell.

But the bedsheet promised one kind of salvation. She only had to tear it into strips, then wind those strips into a makeshift rope. It didn't have to be long. The pole in the wardrobe supporting the dresses Drake had bought her was more than high enough for her small frame. All she had to do was tie the rope tightly, then kick the chair from under her.

She was certain that hanging would be one of the more unpleasant things she would experience, but it was preferable to enduring a lifetime of Byron Drake, or even another day of his wretchedness. With shaking hands, she pulled on the edge of the sheet, tearing a rip along the edge. She knew that if she did not hurry, Drake would return and thwart her escape.

Would her parents be waiting for her? Was she only moments away from their presence? Or would she just fade away into nothingness, never to feel or know anything ever again?

Her stomach turned inside of her, and nausea threatened to send her to the lavatory. She wondered if the fear of death was affecting her composure and causing her queasiness. But she did not feel afraid. She only knew that once her spirit departed her body, she would be free of Drake's brutal grip. Her determined hands ripped the sheet further, gaining at least two more feet of makeshift rope.

Shannon felt the acid come up in her throat. She dropped the sheet and ran to the lavatory, suddenly grateful for the modern convenience supplied by Drake's insistence on luxury. The meager breakfast that she had eaten only half an hour ago came up violently.

A new panic filled her chest, one that had nothing to do with the anticipation of death. Death was her freedom. Death was her salvation. But this new possibility held a different kind of dread. Shannon had not had her menses for almost two months. And this state of sickness could only mean one thing.

Tears of desperation sprang from Shannon's eyes and rolled down her cheeks. Her own life was worthless now, she despised every hour she had to endure. But taking the life of the innocent inside her, that she could not do. Still weeping, Shannon crawled from the lavatory to the floor beside the bed. She did not bother to pull herself onto the bed when she heard the heavy footsteps of Drake outside, though she did slide the torn sheet under the bed.

The latch clicked as Drake turned the key in the lock and pushed open the door. He took two steps into the room, then stopped short as he spied Shannon crumpled and crying on the floor.

"What now?" he asked, exasperation dripping from his voice. He walked over to Shannon and lifted her face up by her chin. He squinted his eyes as he turned her face one way, then the other. "You seem pale, Shannon," he commented. "Are you ill?" Shannon pulled her face halfheartedly from his hand and turned back to the floor, not bothering to answer Drake.

She expected to feel the back of his hand on her cheek for her silence. Instead he lifted her off the floor and placed her in the bed. With uncommon concern, he felt her forehead for telltale signs of fever. She stared back at him through blank eyes.

"What is ailing you, woman?" She still didn't answer, and Drake left her and opened the door to the hall. "Erin!" he called loudly. "Erin!" Shannon heard hurried footfalls, then the voice of a young woman at the doorway.

"Yes, Mr. Drake," the voice answered melodiously.

"She's sick," Drake said, rather tersely. "Take care of her."

"Yes, sir, Mr. Drake."

"I'll be back in a few hours." With that, he turned to leave. "Oh," he added before striding down the hall. "The key." He handed the large, metal key to Erin. "If she happens to leave while I'm away," he waved toward Shannon with his hand, "your brother's future will be quite dire. Do we have an understanding?"

Erin nodded nervously. "I understand perfectly, Mr. Drake," she smiled.

"Good." He tromped off down the hallway, leaving a curious Erin to look after the sick girl. Erin glanced over at Shannon as she shut the door, turning the key firmly in the lock. Then she softly walked over to the bedside and sat on the edge.

"Hello," she offered. "My name is Erin." Shannon looked up at her red curls and pretty smile. She recognized the voice. It belonged to the same girl that slid the taffy under the door a few weeks ago.

"You were kind to me," Shannon said matter-of-factly as she sat up against the headboard. "Thank you."

"What is your name, girl?" returned Erin.

"Shannon."

Erin extended her hand gently. "It is nice to make your acquaintance, Shannon." Shannon took her hand, realizing that it was the first time in a long time that she had felt any touch other than Byron Drake's. She looked into the kind eyes of the red haired girl sitting beside her.

"Mr. Drake said that you are ill?" Erin asked, her frown showing genuine concern. Shannon just nodded, suddenly too ashamed to say anything further. "I see," said Erin sympathetically. "You must not let him find out, do you understand me?" Her tone was deadly serious. "The last two girls that were with child disappeared shortly after Mr. Drake learned of their condition."

Shannon looked up at her with desperate eyes. "What am I to do? There is only one way out of this place, and now that I'm..." She couldn't bring herself to say the word. "I cannot do this anymore."

Grabbing both of Shannon's hand in her own, Erin exclaimed, "You have to. You have to do what you must until you find a way out. An open window, a cracked door... anything."

"And you?" Shannon asked. "You seem to be able to come and go as you please." She remembered something Drake said at the door. "Is it your brother?"

Erin nodded. "Mr. Drake takes proper care of him. He isn't at all unkind to the lad. If I were to leave and take my brother with me..." Erin's brows knit together in worry. "Where could I go where Murray would be warm and full every night?" She looked at Shannon, the desperation on her face almost as great as that on Shannon's.

"There's no way out, is there?" Defeated permeated Shannon's delicate voice. "For either of us."

"God will make a way," Erin returned. "Just keep praying." She rose from the bed and fetched a cloth for Shannon's face, then delicately washed the parts that weren't bruised. "Keep praying, Shannon."

Shannon said nothing. She didn't care to talk to any god that allowed her to suffer in place like this, allowed her to endure this brutality, allowed her mother to die from starvation and her father to die from influenza.

No. Shannon Tiernan would not be praying any time soon.

10

William awaited his father's departure as the morning fell warm across Boston proper. The two had spent the last week preparing for Duke Dunham's return to England. The task required multiple visits with the bank's financiers and the drawing up of an array of legal documents transferring all the duke's American holdings to his son.

William's marriage into the Hamilton empire two months ago had already bolstered the Dunham's financial situation, and the large hole in their accounts had decreased to a small trickle. The person who had been flagrantly embezzling from the Dunham's purse had taken pause about doing the same to the Hamilton estate. But there was still questionable activity needing attention, and William was determined to recover the bulk of his family's stolen assets.

The driver, a man younger than Spencer, loaded the last of the duke's trunks onto the top of the carriage. The duke himself was walking down the steps of his city residence toward his son, who stood waiting.

"Well, my boy," he said as William opened the carriage door, "I wish you well."

"Thank you, sir," William replied. The two men stood awkwardly for a moment. "Please give my love to my sisters and mother," he added.

The duke nodded. "Of course." He held out his hand to William, who shook it heartily. Duke Dunham gingerly patted his son's shoulder, then entered the carriage as William shut the door. "Take care, Son," he said through the window, a touch of concern underlying his usual, stiff demeanor.

"I will." As William answered, the driver urged the horse into a trot, pulling William's father out of his life for a very long time. At this moment, William could not tell if it would be for good or for ill.

He watched until the carriage rounded a corner and headed for the docks. Then he walked back to his own cab, where Spencer was waiting for him.

"You ready, sir?" the old driver asked.

"I suppose," William answered heavily, climbing into his carriage. Spencer pulled away from the affluent dwelling and briskly made his way through the city toward Hamilton Manor. William watched the people and buildings slide by as he reflected on the events of the past two months. He had gone from a pleasant existence to being a captive of sorts. How quickly one's life could change.

As William's eyes stared out the window, a wisp of blonde hair and a rustle of powder blue fabric caught his attention. He sat up and focused on the young woman who walked down the sidewalk only feet from his carriage. It was Elisabeth. He recognized her walk, the sweep of her hair, and even the cut of her favorite dress.

William leaned out the window and called to his driver, "Hold, Spencer!" Elisabeth turned at the sound of William's voice as the carriage pulled to a stop. Here blue eyes were wide with surprise and delight, and she hurried to the carriage as William climbed out onto the sidewalk.

William took her right hand and kissed it, not daring to get too close for fear that he would embrace her. "My Elisabeth," he breathed, "how are you faring?"

Elisabeth did not let go of his hand, but rather held onto it with both of hers. Her lovely blue eyes charted every inch of his face, finally resting on his troubled gaze.

"I am very well, William," she finally answered. "My father was offered a new position with much better pay. He says I am to begin private tutelage." Her voice, which should have been filled with excitement, was weighed down as her delight quickly transformed into sadness. She caressed his hand with hers, and her delicate fingers stumbled upon his wedding ring. She involuntarily looked down at the ring on his hand, then back up to William, her eyes heartrending.

"That is wonderful news, Elisabeth," he replied, trying hard to keep his demeanor light, even though his chest was breaking inside. William stared down into her lovely face, his mind racing with possibilities. With his father gone, his time was suddenly his own. Josephine had placed no constraints or expectations on him whatsoever. Indeed, she attended to much of her own business, and was often absent from his presence when he was at the manor. No one would ever notice if he resumed his relationship with Elisabeth.

William could see his own thoughts echoing behind Elisabeth's beautiful eyes, and sudden shame filled him. How could he ever consider reducing Elisabeth to the life of an adulteress, slinking to his side in the night and walking with her head held down in the sunlight. He felt deplorable for even thinking it. He pulled his hand gently from Elisabeth's hold and took one step back.

"You are a most wonderfully young lady, Elisabeth," he added. "I am certain you will enjoy great success in your studies."

Confusion altered her expression at his sudden change in demeanor, then sorrowful understanding lit her eyes.

"Thank you, sir," she responded, also stepping back slightly. "I wish you only the best, as well." Elisabeth nodded briefly, then turned and walked away from William. She stopped abruptly and turned back to him.

"William. If ever..." Her words trailed off, but the implication in them was not lost on William.

"Goodbye, my lady."

For a split second, her departing expression held so much pain that William almost reached out for her. It took all of his strength to stand rigidly and silently by the carriage as she traveled down the street and out of his view. William was still standing on the sidewalk when Spencer's voice interrupted his stillness.

"Sir," he said gently, "it's about time we get home."

William looked up at the old man in the driver's seat, wondering if he had an old woman at home he loved.

"Yes, of course," William replied, nodding. He entered the carriage again, a renewed sorrow his only companion as he made his way to Hamilton Manor.

Elisabeth continued slowly down the sidewalk, her destination almost within sight. Had she known that she would have seen William, she would have rescheduled her appointment. But one can never know these things.

For a moment, his expression had given her heart wings. She saw in his face that he still loved her. It was as obvious as the morning sun that gently warmed her. She also saw the desire in his eyes, his longing to hold her. She could almost hear his invitation. But he had composed himself at the last moment, and Elisabeth had to make a quick recovery from her profound disappointment. She would still do anything for her William.

Anything at all.

Elisabeth paused before a small office housed in an ordinary brick building. The sign over the white door simply read 'Dr. Stone'. With a heavy sigh, she turned the handle and entered the office. A small bell rang as she opened the door, announcing her arrival. Elisabeth found herself in a sitting room, sparsely furnished with four simple chairs. There were two open doors at the opposite end of the room, one revealing part of an office, and the second displaying the foot end of a wooden examination table.

"Please have a seat, Miss Beech, I will be with you in a moment," a man's pleasant voice called out from beyond the door. Elisabeth did as she was instructed, though her earlier excitement for this appointment had been quenched by the abrupt and brief visit with William. She feared that her demeanor would leave a bad impression on her new tutor, as she was sure that she could not put William out of her thoughts.

She only had to wait for a few more seconds before a nicely dressed man, on the younger side of middle-aged, strode through the door. He had a busy air about him, as if some task was always waiting in the wings to be accomplished. His hair was short and crisp, a nice color of light brown, and his demeanor was sure. It was the sureness that made him handsome, and not his features, as they were average.

Elisabeth forced a smile and rose from her chair as the man took her extended hand. "Dr. Stone at your service. You are Miss Beech, I presume?" he asked, gesturing for her to return to her seat.

"I am," she answered softly.

Dr. Stone turned his head slightly, as if assessing his pupil. "You are aware that the medical profession is a difficult one, that you will see many unpleasant things as a nurse?"

Elisabeth nodded. "I am," she responded, then, remembering her manners, "I am grateful for the opportunity, Dr. Stone. Thank you for agreeing to instruct me."

Dr. Stone nodded. "Well, right to it then. Please come this way." He held his arm toward the office door, indicating that Elisabeth was to enter. She did so, and was immediately taken aback by the sheer number of thick books resting on the massive bookshelves surrounding half of the small room. Against the other two walls were more shelves, these housing a myriad of bottles, solutions, medicines and medical instruments, different sizes of mortars and pestles, and a variety of herbs hanging upside down from the top three shelves. A massive, oak desk sat in the middle of it all, piled with more books, half of which were open, even though they were stacked on top of one another.

Dr. Stone surveyed the desk, then said, "Excuse me, Miss Beech." He stepped quickly into the waiting room from which they just came and grabbed one of its chairs. This he put at the end of his desk and commented, "Here you are, Miss Beech, this is for you." As Elisabeth sat down, Dr. Stone went to one of the bookshelves and retrieved a thick volume, which he placed in front of her.

"This text contains basic anatomy. You are to be familiar with the contents of the first three pages by morning." He paused, raising one eyebrow as Elisabeth looked at the tome with disbelief. "You can read, Miss Beech?" he asked cautiously, as if wondering if he were to instruct her in letters as well.

"Of course, Dr. Stone," she responded, almost offended. "Quite well."

The doctor seemed relieved. "Excellent. Busy yourself with the anatomy text unless someone enters the front seeking care. If they do, escort them to the examination room, obtain a succinct medical history, and retrieve me from my office." His words were sure and quick, as if a matter had been settled and all was back to normal.

"Medical history?" Elisabeth queried. She had imagined private tutoring to be completely different from the experience she was being thrust into. This felt more like a job than tutelage.

"Yes," Dr. Stone answered. "Their reason for seeking medical attention, their recent symptoms, whether they are afflicted with a fever-" He held his finger up at this last point. "The fever is of particularly importance. Do you understand?"

Elisabeth felt as if her head were whirling, but she was still composed enough to respond, "Quite well, Dr. Stone."

"Very good, Miss Beech." Elisabeth opened the pages of the thick text as Dr. Stone resumed his own seat behind the desk. Her eyes widened in disbelief as she looked over the first page.

"Dr. Stone?" she asked, quite sure that the doctor had made a mistake. "This text is in German. You cannot expect me to complete this task with a German text."

"Ah, yes. So it is, Miss Beech," Dr. Stone answered, rising again from his chair and running his finger across a particularly dusty row of books. "Most anatomy texts are either in German or French. Some are even in Latin."

He found the volume he was looking for, pulled it with some difficulty from the shelf, and set it rather heavily on the desk beside the first. He then pulled some blank paper from the desk drawer and lay it on top of the text, along with a pen and ink well.

"You will have an easier time remembering the nomenclature if you translate the text as you go," he added casually.

Elisabeth eyed the other book suspiciously, then blew the dust from its cover. Its title read, "A Comprehensive Dictionary of German Words and Phrases for the English Speaker". She looked at the doctor incredulously. "Surely you are jesting, good sir."

Dr. Stone shook his head, though not with any sympathy. "I can think of no better way to educate you than to throw you directly into the fray, Miss Beech. Now," he said, seemingly satisfied with the situation, "I have a great deal of work to attend to." With that, he sat again and began writing in a hasty manner in the journal in front of him, often referring to yet another text that was at his right.

"Oh," Dr. Stone added, raising his finger once again, "don't forget to reproduce the illustrations onto your own translation." Elisabeth didn't answer, though she did eye him through an irritated expression. The doctor didn't seem to require a response, as he went directly back to his work.

She considered shutting the thick text and stomping out of the office right then. How could anyone complete this kind of task? Dr. Stone was clearly exploiting the agreement her father had made with him. Still, she had given her word to her father that she would apply herself to this venture.

With no small amount of trepidation, Elisabeth searched through the dictionary and found the first word of the anatomy text. She carefully wrote it on the top of the blank page. After five minutes, she had translated the title of the first section, "Musculature of the Face".

Elisabeth continued on with the text, her thoughts intent on the task before her, and, incidentally, quite far away from the young duke who had commanded them only minutes earlier.

11

Josephine stood silently under the elegant archway that served as the entrance to the library. Her fingers traced along the intricate trim outlining the gentle curve of the opening. Within sat William, reclined in the plush arm chair, his handsome face troubled by some sorrowful, inner musing as he watched the flames dance in the fireplace. He didn't seem to notice his wife hesitating under the arch.

He had been despondent ever since their marriage, and Josephine had tried to give him the time and space he needed to recover from the circumstances. But seeing his sadness this evening touched Josephine's heart. She could no longer watch this man grieve. After taking a deep breath, Josephine set her resolve and stepped through the archway. William looked up from the fire, then stood as she made her way to the chair next to his.

"Hello, my dear," he greeted, placing a gentle kiss on the back of her hand. William continued to hold her hand until she seated herself, then he returned to his own chair. He was always a gentleman, the epitome of chivalry.

"I hope your day has been pleasant?" he asked, giving her his attention. Josephine smiled sadly. It was this very trait, his chivalry, that had ensured his unhappy participation in this situation. "Josephine, you seem so troubled. What is the matter?" he asked, genuine concern etched in his brow.

Josephine placed her hand on top of his and sighed softly. "You are a good and noble man, William."

William seemed perplexed. "Thank you, my dear."

She watched the flames cast their light throughout the library. How complicated life could be! "May I speak frankly, William?"

"Of course," he replied, "as always."

This was Josephine's point of no return. She would spill her heart to this man who was her husband. Perhaps, by the end of this conversation, one of them could pursue love. She looked into his deep, blue eyes and began.

"William, ever since I was old enough to consider such things, I have known that I would never marry for love." He was about to protest, but she quieted him with a graceful raise of her hand. "Please, sir, let me finish."

"As you say," he answered, his look becoming more quizzical and attentive.

"I am not a beauty – I know and accept this. And my family's financial standing makes a marriage of passion an impossibility. I have accepted this, also." She smiled gently at him. "And you, William, are already more than I could have asked for in a husband. You are always a gentleman, and very kind. You have never been cross or cruel with me."

"I would never be so."

"I know," she replied. "Next to my father, you are the most noble of men." She breathed in deeply. "But I see your sadness, William."

He seemed surprised, but held his silence. So she continued. "Ours is a compact of convenience. You were thrust into this marriage because of your family's financial misfortune. And I," she paused, trying to steady her voice. "I know that the object of your affection lives outside these walls."

"Josephine..." he began.

"Please, William, I'm almost finished." He nodded, listening intently. "In short, I will never take notice of the hour upon which you come home, the length of your travels, or the nature of your company. You are as free as you were before our union." She searched his face for some hint of emotion, some reaction. He was silent, his expression settling somewhere between surprise and alarm.

"My dear," she finished, "one of us, at least, should know the joys of love. I will not withhold that from you." She turned to make a graceful exit from the library, but her hand was still caught in William's grasp. He had risen from his chair when she did, and was looking at her as if he had never seen her before this moment.

"Josephine," he said, searching her face for words, "I do not know what to say."

She replied gently, "There is nothing else that needs to be said." She tried to leave again, but William didn't relinquish her hand. Instead, he gently brushed her cheek with his other. The emotion sweeping through Josephine caught her off guard and left her breathless.

"You are a most extraordinary woman, Josephine," he offered, kissing the back of her hand, then finally releasing it. "Good evening, my lady." William exited the library with a determined air, while a bewildered Josephine sank back into the wing chair, quite undone. She was certain he did not know the effect he had on her, especially at this moment. She preferred it that way.

But William seemed happier, as if something was settled, and Josephine felt as if her purpose had been accomplished. The way he strode from the library left no doubt in Josephine's mind that he was off to renew his ties with Elisabeth. It had been a long time since Josephine had felt sorrow grip so strongly on her heart. She touched her hand to the place where he had caressed her cheek, certain that she would never feel his hand on her face again.

William seated himself at the polished oak desk in his quarters. Plume and paper were already before him, and he felt he could lose no time in penning his sentiments. For the second time today, shame poured into him as he reflected on the conversation with Josephine just moments earlier.

William thought he had been holding tight to his nobility of character by keeping aloof where his marriage was concerned. He felt justified in clinging to his love for Elisabeth, in grieving for the life he would never have with her. But one plain woman offering him permission for infidelity had proven nobler than all of his misplaced sentiment.

He had been selfish, not even seeing what his preoccupation had been costing others around him. Although she had tried to hide it, William had heard the sadness in Josephine's voice this evening, and it was because of him.

She was correct, he did not love her. He had never even allowed himself to develop an affection for her. After seeing Elisabeth, William knew that if he did not move forward in his life, he would become a bitter, bad-humored, old man.

Perhaps the noblest path he could pursue was fulfilling his duty toward his father and nurturing a relationship with his new wife. He had always been amenable and kind to Josephine, but he had never considered that this circumstance was unfair to her as well as to him. Never once did he assume that he might not be her choice, as she had not been his. Was she also grieving a lost love? Did their wedding day break her heart in two as it had his? He had never bothered to inquire.

He was sure that his love for Elisabeth would remain with him until his dying day, but perhaps it was time to move on and embrace the life that had been handed to him. Perhaps he was ready.

"Selfish cad!" he exclaimed, scolding himself aloud.

"Ah, is that you, William?" Mr. Hamilton's voice grated from the hallway, causing William considerable surprise. "A cad, you say," Mr. Hamilton continued. "I certainly hope you are not referring to me!" His eyes twinkled with humor as he stuck his head through the open doorway. William noticed that the older man was not as portly as he had been upon their first meeting, though his gray hair was still thick and untamed.

"Of course not, sir," William quickly answered. "I was reflecting on my behavior of late."

Leaning against the door frame, Mr. Hamilton thoughtfully puffed on his pipe before remarking, "A little introspection by a man is never a wasted effort. And how," he continued, "do you plan to amend this so-called behavior? Hmm?" Mr. Hamilton pointed his pipe at William and raised a hoary eyebrow, coughing slightly. It did not escape William's notice that Mr. Hamilton did not ask the specifics of the behavior. He was certain that the older man already knew.

"I think, sir," replied the younger man, "that I shall take your advice and put the former things behind me."

Mr. Hamilton returned the pipe to his mouth and puffed a small billow of sweet smoke out the end. "Well said, my boy. And it's about time." He was about to continue down the hall, but leaned back into the doorway for a final comment. "I get my advice from the Good Book, young man. I suggest you do the same." The pleasant odor of his pipe lingered behind him as he retired from the hallway.

The Good Book? William had not picked up a Bible since childhood. He doubted it had anything relevant to offer him, though he was sure Mr. Hamilton meant well.

Putting pen to paper, William lost no time in scripting a letter. He made several starts, and threw several crumpled sheets to the fire before accepting his writing as appropriate. He carefully folded the note, though he did not address it for travel through the general post. Rather, he wrote one name in his most beautiful script across the back of the envelope.

On the front, he dripped the crimson wax of the candle on his desk and imprinted the seal with his wedding ring. An outdated practice, he knew, but he was certain its significance would not be lost on the recipient.

He sat back in his chair, finally satisfied with his efforts. It was time William Dunham regained his nobility.

12

Gentle, morning sun filtered through Josephine's balcony doors. The golden light spilled through the trees, onto the glistening lawn, and filled her room with cheery possibility. Josephine eased up in bed, immediately struck by the beauty of the new day.

She thanked God. Every morning, she thanked Him.

As was her custom since childhood, she slipped from her covers and knelt next to her bed, beginning the day in quiet praise to her Father. Usually her prayers were steadfast and focused, but this morning they were intruded upon by her conversation with William the previous evening, and by the memory of his caress. This, also, she finally took to God, not knowing if she had said and done the right thing concerning William and Elisabeth.

Part of her business success came from her ability to make hard decisions quickly, though sometimes this required her to wade into gray areas her father was not completely comfortable with. Was this one of those gray areas? Had Josephine made a mistake by giving William leave to betray their marriage vows?

As she prayed, Ophelia came in, quietly setting a serving platter on the small table by the French doors. Most mornings Ophelia left just as silently as she entered, but this morning Josephine did not hear any departing footsteps. Instead, she heard Ophelia softly preoccupying herself in Josephine's wardrobe, rustling through the hanging dresses while trying to remain as silent as possible.

Josephine sighed softly to herself. If there was one morning when she needed to focus on listening during her prayer, it was this one. She felt irritation rise in her spirit, but resolved to keep a kind demeanor. She would not hurt Ophelia's feelings for anything.

Finishing her prayer, Josephine rose and pulled a bed coat over her shoulders, tying it at the waist. She cast a glance toward Ophelia, who was still musing through the wardrobe, considering each dress she came across before thrusting it back into its place. How odd for this early morning hour! The amused puzzlement at Ophelia's behavior chased away any previous irritation that Josephine felt toward her friend.

"Good morning, Ophelia," she said, making her way to the table and her waiting coffee. "Am I not dressing myself today?" she asked with humor.

Ophelia turned her head just long enough to engage Josephine. "Good morning, ma'am. And no, not today," she responded, a smile and a mischievous twinkle lighting up her face before she went back to the wardrobe. Josephine sat down at the table, baffled at her maid's response.

As she reached for her cup, she noticed a single white rose lying on top of a folded piece of paper. So this is why Ophelia had lingered. She picked up the rose instead of her coffee, and held it under her nose. Its scent was mild and clean, with the softest of perfumes coming from its petals. She replaced the rose and gently lifted the note. Her name was beautifully crafted across the back in a strong, elegant script. She knew this handwriting. It was William's.

She hesitated over the note, a nervous lightness fluttering in her chest. Turning it over, she saw a crimson wax seal holding the page closed. The letters DH were impressed into the wax. Josephine recognized the impression as that of William's wedding ring.

"Well," Ophelia asked excitedly, breaking Josephine's breathless reverie, "are you going to open it?"

Josephine frowned as she held the note between her thumb and finger. What if this was William's goodbye note to her? Perhaps he had already left to find Elisabeth, and was explaining his purpose in this note.

Josephine raised her large, uncertain eyes to Ophelia, not able to hide the apprehension from her friend. Ophelia's demeanor changed immediately as she seated herself next to Josephine, placing a comforting arm around her shoulders. "Why are you so troubled by this, Josephine?" she asked gently. "What is the matter?"

Sighing, Josephine set the note back on the tray. "I spoke with William last night, Ophelia. I gave him leave to pursue his intentions with Miss Beech." She sat back wearily in her chair, her emotions clearly a heavy weight. "I am sure this is a gracious farewell note. And frankly," she met Ophelia's eyes, "I have no desire to read it."

Ophelia smiled and took the note from the tray. "Mr. Dunham himself placed this note – and this rose – on the tray as I came out of the kitchen, with instructions to prepare you for a morning of riding." Handing the paper to her mistress, she said firmly but kindly, "Open the note, Josephine."

With some reluctance, Josephine took the note from Ophelia's outstretched hand, then gently broke the seal and opened the folded page to reveal more of William's beautiful script.

"My Dearest Josephine,

Please allow me the pleasure of your company as I tour the grounds of Hamilton Estate this morning.

Your husband,

William"

Josephine lowered the note slowly, pondering William's words. "What do you think this could mean, Ophelia?" she asked, puzzled. She could feel her heart thud against the inside of her breastbone, and her heartbeat itself seemed a foreign thing.

Ophelia laughed as she resumed her search through the wardrobe. "The fearless and brilliant Lady Josephine, reduced to uncertainty by a man!"

"Ophelia!" Josephine scolded halfheartedly.

"It means, my lady," Ophelia answered simply, not a bit vexed by her scolding, "that your husband would like to spend the morning with you." Finally satisfied with her search, Ophelia lay a suitable riding ensemble on the bed. "I will be back with your breakfast," she added happily.

As Ophelia left, Josephine sat back in her chair, sipped her coffee, and wondered how the morning would unfold. Father, she prayed, resuming her interrupted prayer. Please calm this feeling in my heart. It is only a simple ride. Why am I so nervous? Please calm my heart, Father.

An hour later Josephine found herself strolling toward the stables, the gentle kiss of sunshine gracing her face. The weather was as pleasant as one could want, and Josephine hoped the rest of the day would follow suit.

The clipping of horses' hooves became evident in her ears, and Josephine turned her attention to the stone path in front of her. A hundred yards ahead walked William, leading two saddled horses up the path. The early sun sprayed golden light on his dark hair, and his walk seemed to be less taxing than of late. He waved a hand in greeting when he saw her. Josephine's smile widened, and she waved back.

"Good morning, Josephine." William greeted her pleasantly when the two finally met, and he kissed the back of her hand, as was his custom. Even though she knew it was a gesture of courtesy, she could not help but feel a small flutter in her stomach each time he took her hand to his lips.

"I believe it is, William," she answered pleasantly. "How are you this morning?"

"I am well, thank you. And you?" William's voice seemed calm and sure, and Josephine sensed some kind of peacefulness beneath his demeanor. Something had changed, she was certain of it.

"I was pleasantly surprised at your invitation this morning," she responded.

William smiled softly and nodded. "With my father off for England, my days are suddenly my own. I was hoping that today you could acquaint me with my new home."

"It would be my pleasure," she answered, smiling genuinely.

William held out his hand to Josephine and positioned himself next to her horse. "Shall we, then?"

"Yes, we shall." Instead taking his hand and allowing him to place her sidesaddle upon the horse, Josephine grasped the saddle horn herself and nimbly mounted her horse the way a gentleman would. She looked down unapologetically at William. "I am far too practical to ride sidesaddle, as a proper lady. I hope you don't object."

William laughed as he mounted his own horse. "Would it matter if I did?" he queried.

Josephine shook her head. "Not in the least."

From his third story window Mr. Hamilton watched the pair trot down the stone path toward the kitchen gardens. The sight gave him a peace that settled deep in his soul.

"Breathe in once more, Rutherford," instructed Dr. Stone.

Mr. Hamilton was sitting on his desk, looking through the window while the doctor examined him. He took a long, slow draught of air as Dr. Stone pressed a funnel shaped instrument against his back and listened deeply. In mid-breath Mr. Hamilton felt the air catch deep in his chest, and he coughed so violently that the physician could not keep the instrument against his back.

Dr. Stone stood upright and placed a firm hand on Mr. Hamilton's back until the coughing ceased. "Rutherford," he began, "I wish I had better news for you."

The old man nodded slowly. "I've known for quite some time that this was coming," he replied.

Following the gaze of his patient, Dr. Stone looked out the window at the couple that was riding from their view. "Have you told your daughter yet?" he asked.

"I will have to find the proper time." Mr. Hamilton chuckled softly to himself. "Honestly, Dr. Stone," he added, "I will have to find the courage to have this conversation with Josephine."

The doctor nodded in understanding. "You need to have that conversation soon, Rutherford." He looked thoughtful, then asked, "If you like, I can arrange to stay on the premises for a month or so. I will be here for you when the time comes, so you won't be alone."

Mr. Hamilton smiled. "I am never alone, Dr. Stone," he said, his old voice raspy and peaceful. "You have your patients in the city to attend to, and when my time comes," he paused for a moment, "then I will have better attendants than any earthly company could provide."

Dr. Stone smiled. He held out his hand to Mr. Hamilton, who shook it warmly. "Send for me if you need me. I will come immediately."

"I will. Thank you."

As Dr. Stone left the room, Mr. Hamilton returned his gaze to the stone path where he had last seen his beloved daughter. He was happy to see William finally take an interest in his marriage. He knew that William was a good man, and now he knew that Josephine would be well taken care of after he was gone. As he pulled on his shirt and fumbled clumsily with the buttons, a small drop of moisture made its way down his cheek.

He missed his daughter already, but he knew who was waiting for him. His tear was not all sorrow.

William and Josephine spent the better part of the morning touring Hamilton estate. The many gardens were extensive, and were quite lovely as they bloomed profusely for summer. Even the kitchen garden, though it's purpose was not for beauty, was pleasantly overtaking its borders and flooding its space with a variety of edibles.

As they explored the stone paths, they often encountered the staff who cared for the estate. William counted at least eight young men who were busy spading, weeding, planting, or otherwise tending to the grounds. The Hamilton estate was proving to be larger and grander than he had first imagined.

They rounded another gentle curve in the path and made their way toward the carriage house, riding comfortably in each other's presence. Their easy conversation continued as they meandered toward the building.

"And the estate?" asked William. "How old is it?"

Josephine smiled happily at the question. "It is quite young, actually," she answered, "especially compared to your estate in England."

"Did your father build it?"

"He did," she nodded, "for my mother. After he became prosperous in business, he bought this acreage and had the manor constructed. He wanted to build her the grandest home she had ever seen." William smiled at Josephine's expression. She was obviously caught up in some pleasant memory.

"The gardens, however," Josephine continued, sweeping her arm toward the flowerbeds behind them, "were my mother's doing. She knew exactly what she wanted for each section of the manor."

"I am sorry that she is gone," said William. "What happened, if I may inquire?"

"Influenza took her ten years ago." There was only a trace of sadness in Josephine's voice.

"I am truly sorry," said William. "She must have been quite wonderful."

Josephine smiled happily, then nodded. "She was wonderful. My father never ceased to be enthralled with her."

"Your father is remarkably resilient for bearing such tragedy and still having the chipper demeanor that he does," William said. He could only imagine the pain if something similar were to happen to Elisabeth.

Josephine was thoughtful before she responded, her brown eyes searching past the forested hills in front of them. "My father is a man of deep and genuine faith. He knows that he will be reunited with my mother one day." She looked over at William as she said this, examining his face. "I think when that day comes, it will be a happy one for him."

"Really?" William remarked. "It seems quite odd to look forward to one's death."

Josephine smiled. "He sees it only as a physical death. His spirit lives forever." They rode on for a few more moments in silence. William was clearly pondering her words.

"And you?" she finally asked. "What do you believe about such things, William. What do you truly believe in your heart of hearts?"

William considered the question for a moment. It was such a strange and unique inquiry. No one had ever ventured it to him before.

He tilted his head in thought. "To be quite honest, I have never given it much deliberation. I suppose that God is there, somewhere. If He has business with me, then I suppose He will let me know."

Josephine's reply was rather cryptic. "Indeed He will, William."

William was silent for a moment, then his thoughts went back to Mr. Hamilton. "Still," he added, "I would be devastated if..." William caught himself before he finished. He almost said, "if Elisabeth were to pass away."

His awkward silence spurred Josephine to speak.

"We have agreed to be friends, have we not, William?" she asked.

"We have," he answered, still uncomfortable with his blunder.

"Then let us be candid with one another, shall we? I know full well your affections. You will find no judgment on my part."

Once again, William was thankful for her gracious kindness and gentle strength. He knew that many men did not fare so well in an arranged marriage.

"I saw Elisabeth yesterday." William stated the subject plainly, hoping to find some solace in open conversation.

"I thought as much when I saw you last evening," she replied. "May I ask," she continued, "why you are with me today instead of seeking out Elisabeth? Did I not make myself plain last night?"

Shame returned to William's face. The next words were obviously hard for him. "You did. And I thought about just such a scenario when I spoke to Elisabeth. But," he looked over to Josephine's face, "I could never live with myself knowing that I had cheapened her to the position of a mistress." He frowned heavily, then continued, "I could not dishonor myself – and you – by breaking my vows to you."

Josephine nodded, a thoughtful frown on her face as well. "You are honorable, William. I honestly wish the circumstances were favored toward your happiness."

William smiled softly. She was shaming him with her words again, though he was sure it was unintentional. "I am looking forward, Josephine," he replied, trying to lighten the tone of the suddenly somber conversation, "just as your father advised. There is nothing behind me and everything before me."

Josephine's smile was wide and happy. She could be quite pretty when she smiled. "I am glad, William," she said.

A large two story house loomed in front of them, with an ivy covered wall encasing the generous yard. Several girls were sitting on the grass, laughing and enjoying a picnic lunch. One of them, a pretty brunette girl, was obviously with child. She turned excitedly to the blonde girl next to her.

"Edith, the baby is moving!" With joy she pulled her friend's hand to her belly, while the blonde girl smiled as the young life made its presence known. The two were obviously close friends.

Even though the scene was happy, Josephine was dismayed. They had ridden past the carriage house and down the path to Rosewood Hall. She had been so caught up in William's companionship that she did not even notice their course.

William was surprised. "What is this place?" he asked, observing the pleasant scene through the open, wrought-iron gate. "I have not seen it before."

Josephine silently chided herself. She had not meant to allow William to see the school. It would surely open up too many questions that she was not prepared to answer.

"This is a school for the impoverished girls of Boston." It was the closest explanation she could think of with without being dishonest.

"I had no idea a school such as this even existed," he remarked, "especially on your grounds. For impoverished children, you say?"

"Yes," she answered. "My father and I consider education as one of the most important necessities for children. It began as a place to educate the servant's children, but grew into a more charitable institution."

"But that girl is obviously expecting," remarked William. "Where is her husband?"

Josephine didn't answer, but casually turned her horse back toward her home. She didn't want to seem eager to leave, but she also didn't want to linger for too long at the school.

William turned his horse as well, then pulled up short, looking intently at another one of the girls dining on the lawn. A flicker of recognition sparked in his eyes as he stared through the gate.

"I know that child," he said, gesturing to the young girl sitting with the group. "The night of the ball, as my father and I were returning to the townhouse, I saw her get into a cab with an unscrupulous young man." William eyed the girl with confusion, then looked questioningly at Josephine.

"Then it is very fortunate that she found her way here, don't you agree?" Josephine responded. William waited for her to elaborate, but she did not. "Shall we return home and find our own lunch?" she asked, filling in the silence.

William knew that something more was going on than Josephine's explanation offered. He decided to afford her the same grace that she had shown him earlier and not press the issue. And seeing that the girl had somehow made her way to a safe haven also helped to lighten his mood.

"I am more than ready for lunch," he responded graciously, as the two began a mild trot down the path that would lead them home. They conversed pleasantly about less serious matters as they rode, but Josephine's reluctance to further explain the school stuck in William's thoughts.

It seemed that the candor Josephine offered earlier was only going in one direction.

13

The soft clanking of the key turning in the lock alerted Shannon that Byron Drake was returning from his evening's ventures. She hoped that he would be too drunk to stay awake longer than it took to pull of his boots, but those evenings were few and far between. She pretended to be asleep, hoping for the best.

Drake sank onto the edge of the bed, and Shannon heard his boots land heavily on the floor. He pulled off his shirt and rolled into bed next to her. "Wake up, Shannon, I'm back," he said, rubbing her shoulder. His breath had the aroma of whiskey, but he was clearly not drunk.

Shannon turned and looked at him, realizing that she would not escape his attention this evening. She sat up and decided to be bold. After all, what more could he do to her? "This is a brothel, is it not?" Shannon asked directly, catching Drake by surprise.

His eyes narrowed cautiously, wary of her change in demeanor. "Of course it is," he answered, sitting up, also. "Why do you ask?"

"Because I want to know why you have imprisoned me in this room for months instead of using me to fatten your wallet."

Drake sat up and studied Shannon closely, not sure what to make of her boldness. "Fair enough," he answered. "It is because I like beautiful things. When I saw you sitting next to the *Charlotte Jane...*" he caressed her blonde curls with his fingers. "You are quite simply the most beautiful woman I have ever seen. And that makes you mine," he stated. "I will not share you with those filthy imbeciles crowding the bar downstairs." He sneered the words, clearly disdainful of most of his clientele.

Then, to Shannon's horror, he placed a gentle hand across her stomach. "Not now, especially."

She pulled his hand from her middle while shrinking away from him as far as the headboard would allow. "I will never leave this room, will I?" Shannon's voice was bleak, as if her futile desperation had slain even the remotest hope of escape from this man.

Drake contemplated for a moment. "I won't risk you running away, not with my child in your womb," he said casually, wrapping his fingers around her neck and pulling her mouth to his. She pulled away from him, though he did not release her until he wanted.

"You are a demon!" she hissed, wiping her mouth with the back of her hand.

His smile was wicked and sincere. "So I am," he answered.

14

Josephine and William sat quietly at the small table on the veranda just outside the dining room. The last few days of summer were proving to be splendid, and Ophelia set lunch for them outside to take advantage of the weather.

They were waiting for Mr. Hamilton, as was their midday custom. The three usually found entertaining conversation to amuse themselves with, and often Josephine would discuss the most recent developments about the Dunham financial mystery with her husband and her father. Not only did the books have to be examined with a fine tooth comb, but the people with whom every transaction had occurred were being identified and spoken with. The process was lengthy and tedious, but Josephine was determined to get to the bottom of the matter.

"I wonder where your father is?" William said casually. "I have never known him to be late for lunch."

"Hmm," she answered, concerned now that she noticed his absence. "Perhaps he is taking his afternoon nap earlier than usual." He had seemed tired lately, like the kick had gone out of his step. Josephine attributed it to the nagging cold that seemed to be hanging onto him, causing him to cough frequently. But perhaps his age was finally catching up with him. Maybe her father was finally old. Odd that she had never seen him as such, even though he was decades her senior.

A strange expression made its way onto William's face. "Ophelia," he called, concern in his voice, "would you be so kind as to check on Mr. Hamilton?"

Ophelia popped around the corner of the French door, carrying a tray with three teacups and a steaming teapot. She set them down gracefully on the table and turned without missing a step. "It would be my pleasure, Mr. Dunham," she answered, sporting a lovely smile and a curtsy. Josephine turned her head and hid the secretive grin her friend evoked.

Every time Ophelia was in the room with Mr. and Mrs. Dunham, she smiled largely at Mr. Dunham, and often winked to Josephine behind his back. She was shameless in her good-natured teasing of Josephine, often noting how she had landed the most handsome husband England had to offer.

"What has caused the happy air, my dear?" Josephine's smile had not gone unnoticed by William, and he was watching her with some amusement, though she could still see a shadow of concern behind his eyes.

"My Ophelia," she replied with a small laugh. "She thinks that the ground you walk on sprouts miraculous blossoms that can heal the masses."

William laughed. "She is quite the charmer, isn't she?" he answered. "She dotes on you like a mother hen looking after her only chick."

"Yes, she is attentive," Josephine said. "Actually," she added thoughtfully, "aside from my father, she is my best friend." Perhaps it was time to confide more in William.

He caught the serious note creeping into her tone and sat forward, sensing a story forthcoming.

"May I tell you about the day I met Ophelia?" she asked.

William opened his mouth to answer, but Ophelia's frantic voice echoed from inside the house. "Jeffrey!" she shouted. "JEFFREY! Send Albert for Dr. Stone at once!" The running steps of the old man as well as the other household servants could be heard from the veranda, and William and Josephine sprang from the table immediately, sending their chairs flying backward behind them.

William was the first to reach the stairs, but he waited for Josephine to run ahead of him. She ran through Mr. Hamilton's open door and into his bedroom. Her father was lying on top of his covers, still dressed in his morning clothes, his breathing ragged and shallow. He held his hand out to Josephine as she flew into the room, William close behind her.

"Papa!" she cried, clutching onto his hand. "Papa, what's wrong?"

Mr. Hamilton chuckled slightly, then coughed hard as he did so. "There is nothing wrong, my love," he answered when the coughing died down. "It is simply my time to go home to see your mother – and meet my Lord." His words were slow and pained, his voice gravelly, but determined.

Josephine sat in the chair that William placed behind her, and scooting it closer to her father's bedside. She grabbed his hand with both of hers and leaned close to his face. "What are you talking about, Papa? Why are you saying such things?"

He squeezed her hands and looked lovingly in her eyes. "I have been sick for a long time, Josephine," he explained. "Since before you even met William."

"Dr. Stone is on his way, Papa, everything is going to be fine," she answered, tears creeping into her voice.

"I know it will, Josephine," he smiled softly. "My Josephine." He closed his eyes and coughed again, his body shaking violently. Josephine squeezed his hand tighter as the coughing spell continued. When it was over, he opened his eyes and looked past Josephine to William. "It is your turn, now," he said in a strained voice. "Perhaps it was selfish, but I wanted my daughter to be protected when I was gone. To have a good man to look after her."

William placed his hand on Josephine's shoulder. He could feel its almost imperceptible trembling. "I will take care of her, sir," he said, understanding that the old man needed this last assurance before he could let go of this world. "You have my word."

Mr. Hamilton nodded weakly, then turned his attention back to Josephine. "I'm sorry for not telling you earlier, my love," he said, "but I could not bear to sadden you before it was time."

Josephine was openly crying, tears running down her cheeks. "There is no sorry, Papa," she replied. "You know that I love you."

He smiled. "And I you, dear daughter. I will miss you."

"I love you, Papa," she answered, laying her head on his chest. "I love you."

Mr. Hamilton lay his hand on Josephine's head and closed his eyes. His breathing was still strained, but it eased slightly as he slept. She kept her head there, wetting his shirt with her tears, feeling his chest rise and fall with each shallow breath.

"Tell her I love her, Papa," Josephine whispered with difficulty. "Tell Mama." But Mr. Hamilton didn't respond, and his sleep seemed to deepen into a more restful state.

Josephine sat up and looked at her father, then placed her hand on his cheek. Her tears were still falling, but her demeanor was peaceful. "Go home, Papa," she said quietly, her voice catching with sorrow. She sat back and held onto her father's hand, determined to be there for him until the end.

William pulled up another chair and sat next to her in silence. He was quite fond of Mr. Hamilton, and this event saddened him deeply. He thought of his own father, suddenly realizing that most likely he would not be present when he passed away. He might never see his father again. The thought saddened him even more.

He placed a gentle arm around Josephine's shoulders. She was no longer crying, and her head was bowed slightly. She still held her father's hand, but her eyes were closed and her lips were moving silently. She was praying. William was not sure what to do, so he waited quietly, watching Mr. Hamilton's breathing become more and more scarce.

William started in surprise when Dr. Stone came through the door, bringing Josephine out of her extended prayer. She looked up at the doctor, but there was acceptance already in her face. She didn't say anything.

Sitting on the bed next to Mr. Hamilton, Dr. Stone opened his bag and retrieved the long, funnel shaped stethoscope. He opened Mr. Hamilton's wet shirt and placed the larger end on the dying man's chest while listening intently through the narrow end. A look of sad resignation came over his face, and he replaced the stethoscope in his bag.

In a muted tone he addressed Josephine. "I'm afraid it won't be long, Mrs. Dunham." He sat down in the chair opposite Josephine and waited. Jeffrey had come in behind the doctor, and now the elderly man made his way forward, placing his hand on Mr. Hamilton's chest.

"Go in peace, lad," the old man rasped, "I won't be long to follow." Dr. Stone rose from the chair and stood at the foot of the bed so that Jeffrey could sit by his master.

Mr. Hamilton breathed out a last time, and a gentle smile lit on his face. Josephine knew it was in that instant her father had indeed gone home. A few farewell tears made their way down her cheeks as she turned to William. He embraced her compassionately as she rested on his shoulder. She stayed for a few moments more, then pulled away slowly, her hands on his shoulders. She looked in William's face, and he could see the gratitude in her own.

Without saying anything, Josephine made her way around the bed to Jeffrey, whose forehead was resting next to the deceased Mr. Hamilton. She stood behind him and lay a gentle hand on his back as the old man wept. William watched her, more surprised and curious than sad, wondering what strength allowed her to put aside her own grief and comfort the old man.

Jeffrey raised his head and patted Josephine's hand kindly. "We should let Dr. Stone attend to your father," he said, his old eyes red and wet.

"Of course," she answered, nodding to Dr. Stone. The doctor went to the linen closet and pulled a sheet from the cupboard. He was unfolding it to drape over Mr. Hamilton as Josephine and William made their way back downstairs, hand in hand. William led her downstairs to the sitting room where she sank onto the settee. He settled beside her, reclaiming her shoulders with his arm and drawing her close to his side. Ophelia came through the opposite door to attend to them both, but her own eyes also bore the signs of grief, so William dismissed her in gentle tones.

"I am so sorry, my dear," he said kindly, smoothing the back of her hand with his.

"Thank you, William," she answered, her voice still precarious. Another lone tear traced down her cheek, and William brushed it away with his thumb. "I will miss him dearly," she added.

"Yes," William replied thoughtfully. "You two were very close. I will also miss that dear, old man."

Josephine wiped the tears from her eyes and sat forward. "At least he is home now," she said. "I should contact the minister and start making arrangements."

William sat forward, a quizzical look in his eye. "Josephine," he began, not quite knowing how to delicately probe the issue, "please forgive me for seeming insensitive at this difficult time, but..." Josephine frowned as she waited for him to continue, giving him her full attention.

"What is it, William?" she asked.

"Well," he continued, clearly uncomfortable, "I don't understand why aren't you more grief stricken over your father's passing. You are already abandoning your tears and thinking about making his funeral arrangements." William ventured a look with his question, making sure that he had not injured Josephine with his words.

She smiled sadly, then sat forward to meet him. "I am grieved," she answered, "but not like others who have no hope."

"No hope?" he asked, confused. Perhaps her father's death was affecting her more deeply than it seemed. Clearly, she wasn't fully understanding the situation. William frowned, not sure how to proceed gently. "Josephine," he took her hand in an understanding manner, "my dear, your father has died. There is no hope for him now. I am so sorry."

"William," she began calmly, not addressing his comment, "how would you react if your father went on holiday to the finest retreat in Europe? Would you be sad for him?"

"Well, no, of course not," he answered. "I would be quite pleased for him, actually."

"And if he were to retire there, never to travel again. If you were to never see him again?"

"I would be sad at the prospect of not seeing him, of course, but I would still be pleased at his pleasant state... Ah," he said, "I understand the point you are trying to make."

She sat back, still holding onto his fingers with hers. She could see the skepticism rising behind his striking, blue eyes. Instead of pressing the matter, she was silent. Waiting. Waiting for God to open an opportunity. Even through her grief and sadness, God could work.

He sat back easily, and she could see his thoughts churning. But instead of saying anything more on the matter, he smiled kindly at his wife, apparently deciding that this was neither the time nor the place for a discussion on theology.

"After things settle a bit," he said, "I will send someone to town to notify the minister. If you don't mind, I would like to make the arrangements." William paused, looking down at the floor. "He was a good father-in-law to me, and I don't want you to be burdened with this."

She nodded slowly, truly grateful for his consideration. It was a thoughtful kindness, which Josephine was unused to receiving outside of her father and Ophelia. She was touched by it. "Thank you so much, William. I..." She caught herself quickly. The words "I love you" almost slipped casually from her lips. She frowned again, wishing she could lean on him the way lovers lean on one another in times of sorrow.

"What is it?" William asked.

"I … am grateful to have you to lean on." It was the truth, even if it wasn't the truth she wanted. Suddenly, the weight of losing her father seemed heavier than before. He had always been the pillar supporting her. Now, without her father to confide in, she was truly alone.

'No child,' came the whisper in her heart, the still, quiet voice that spoke when her soul was deeply troubled, 'you are never alone.'

"I am going to miss him a great deal," she said. Another tear formed, and she wiped it away with her hand. "I know he is so much happier now, but I don't know what I will do without him."

"My dear," replied William, "give your father the honor of a few more tears. Do him justice. And perhaps, you can learn to lean on me the way you leaned on him."

She smiled. He meant well, she knew, but she also knew that her relationship with William would never be as close as the one she had with her father. Still, the comment touched her heart.

"I will try."

Two days later, Josephine buried her father in the plot next to her mother. It was situated in one of the more secluded gardens on Hamilton Manor. Her sorrow had settled in deeper, but the thought of her mother and father finally together again made the moment bittersweet. William was by her side, and the household staff, their numerous employees, and business acquaintances were filling up the small corner of the manor. It seemed that Mr. Hamilton would be missed by many.

As the minister spoke in soothing tones, William stood quietly with the other mourners, his eyes casually moving from person to person in the assembly. Then, his gaze fixed curiously on one man. It was the same man that William had confronted the night of the Spring Ball. He clearly recognized the cut of the man's brown hair and the youthful features of his face. What business did a man like that have at Mr. Hamilton's funeral?

William studied the man more carefully. His eyes were fixed on the grass and his expression was pained, though he was trying to hide it. Was he some business acquaintance of the Hamilton family? If so, why did Mr. Hamilton's death seem to affect him with so much weight?

Josephine and the others bowed their heads as the minister prayed, and William followed suit, making a note to speak with Josephine about the man's affiliation with the Hamilton family at a more appropriate time.

Afterward, the guests slowly filed by the casket before making their way toward the home, offering their quiet condolences to Josephine and William as they did so. William noticed that the man stood solemnly by the casket for a few moments, his head down, then walked directly toward the house without offering condolences to Josephine. Josephine seemed too busy with the other guests to even notice the oddity.

As the man reached the curve in the path that would take him beyond their sight, he paused, then cast a direct, but casual glance to Josephine. To William's silent shock, she turned subtly and nodded almost imperceptibly to the man. The movement would be lost on anyone else who was not watching. Apparently, the man was satisfied, and he retreated down the path. William looked over at his wife, hiding most of the anxious perplexity he felt at this strange turn of events. Her expression was merely sad, however, and if anything were amiss in her mind, she did not show it.

There had to be some logical explanation. Josephine's character would not allow for anything unscrupulous, so perhaps she did not realize the type of man this acquaintance was. William resolved to speak with her after the activity and grief of the last few days had subsided.

He stood quietly and suffered the few remaining guests to voice their sympathies. When the last person has retreated from their presence, Josephine stepped forward to the casket and placed her hand lovingly on the top. Bowing her head, she whispered softly into the breeze. William knew she was praying. He waited quietly, but Josephine finished quickly. She turned to William, a few tears remaining in her eyes, and took the hand he held out to her.

"Are you ready, my dear?"

She took his hand, and he gently wrapped his fingers around hers. "I am," she replied, as they followed the path of the last guest to the house. The ladies and gentlemen quietly milling in the dining room were all dressed in their finery, black, as was appropriate for the occasion. William casually let his eyes wander around the room, even as he kept his hand protectively on the small of Josephine's back, but the young man was no longer among the company of mourners. It seemed that he had left the house entirely.

The other persons stayed long enough to exchange memories of Mr. Hamilton over coffee or tea, conversing softly as they circulated about the dining room. Quiet laughter was often heard, and more than one business acquaintance sought out Josephine and shared a narrative about her father's great generosity or humorous social conduct. It struck William that this funeral gathering harbored just as many peaceful smiles and pleasant stories as it did tears. Even his wife was able to laugh gently at one of her father's more outrageous social blunders as retold by an elderly businessman.

Indeed, it seemed as if Mr. Hamilton had taken a holiday instead of perishing from life. Seeing the demeanor of Josephine and the other men and women who had known Mr. Hamilton reinforced this sentiment. Frankly, it was the oddest, but most pleasant, funeral he had ever attended.

15

Darcy Adams sat alone in the corner of the darkened tavern with a brandy in his hand. Attending Mr. Hamilton's funeral had been difficult for him. The old man had practically been his father, but circumstances dictated that he not even grieve as he wanted to. No one could know of his connection to the Hamilton family. The discovery could lead to the ruin of both Josephine's financial standing and her clandestine philanthropy, of which he played a pivotal role. The best way to deal with his loss was to fill his mind with the most pressing task on hand – his continuing search for Shannon Tiernan.

He had spent the first few weeks after her disappearance roaming the frozen streets, then more weeks combing the bars and brothels situated directly on the wharf. But he had seen no trace of the scared, blonde, Irish girl. Darcy knew that he had not imagined her, that she was still somewhere in the dark, Boston underworld. He had not searched in the right places yet.

The Crimson Dagger was a nicer establishment than most, set back from the docks, and one he had not been in before this evening. The walls glowed golden with the light of the main fireplace and dozens of candles mounted at regular intervals. Cigar smoke hung thickly in the air, its sweet aroma wafting around the occupants in the room. Long, red folds of scarlet hung at the windows, adding an air of richness to the inside and keeping out any curious eyes from the street.

The long bar was all polished mahogany and crystal snifters, and over a dozen finely dressed men lined the stools. A lively debate was circulating among them about possible business opportunities in the

Oregon Territory. A few more men were seated at another table, carrying on a poker game that showed no signs of slowing. Darcy recognized several of the businessmen as prominent figures in Boston society. Even Judge Charles Patterson, who was known for ruling his courtroom with an iron fist, was seated at a table, cards in one hand, a brandy in the other, and a beautiful brunette sitting in his lap.

Women dressed in lovely silk gowns of all colors wove their way through chairs and men, refreshing drinks and engaging in conversation when appropriate. There were only beautiful girls here, with perfect teeth, flawless skin, and delicately piled curls spilling down over their bare shoulders and into their cleavage. And they were young. Of the twelve or so girls in the room, the oldest might have been nineteen, the youngest looked to be fifteen. The owner of this establishment was making very good money.

But the one woman he was looking for was not anywhere to be seen. For months Darcy had scoured the taverns on and around Ann Street looking for Shannon Tiernan, but she was simply nowhere. So he decided to expand his search into the nicer establishments bordering the harbor.

This change in tactic was more dangerous for him. He knew that the women here were not facing death on the streets, but they needed rescuing, nonetheless. However, if one of them should suspect foul play on his part and breathe a word to the bartender, Darcy would find himself inside a burlap sack, sinking to the bottom of the harbor.

A pretty girl with red, curly locks eased over to Darcy's table with a brandy bottle and refilled his snifter. She smiled, then asked, "How are you this evening, sir?" Darcy found her Irish accent charming, and she carried an air of intelligence. He knew all too well the circumstances that had driven this young woman to occupy a brothel. The opportunities for immigrants were very limited, and most women had to take what was offered them or perish in the harsh, Boston backstreets.

"I'm faring very well, miss. And you?" Darcy rose and pulled out a chair for the young lady.

"I'm having a lovely evening, sir," she replied. He heard the barest hint of sarcasm in her voice, and knew in that instant this young lady held promise. She seated herself gracefully, giving her full attention to her next client.

"May I inquire your name, miss?"

"Of course. My name is Erin." She cast her eyes up at him flirtatiously, playing the role she was supposed to. "And may I ask yours?"

"James," he replied. "James Smith." In a place like this, Darcy felt that giving his true name would be quite foolish.

"Most gentlemen don't give their last names," she commented.

"I imagine that most gentlemen don't give their real names."

Erin laughed softly, but genuinely. "I imagine you are correct, Mr. *Smith*."

Darcy took a sip of brandy before continuing. "What do you do here, Erin? What is your job?"

Erin looked him directly in the eye. "Whatever you tell me to do, Mr. Smith. That is my job."

Darcy leaned forward to close the distance between the two. Erin leaned in as well, preparing to hear whatever proposition 'Mr. Smith' had to offer. "Erin," he began, whispering softly in her ear, "you are wasted in this place. If you could do something else, would you?"

She pulled back sharply and looked at him, clearly not expecting this question. The barkeep cast a glance at their table, the sudden movement catching his attention. The last thing Darcy Adams wanted was attention.

"Would you like to continue our conversation upstairs?" Darcy asked, gently taking her hand in his own.

Her confusion lasted only a moment, then curiosity crept into her eyes. "I think I would," she replied, rising from the table and nodding at the barkeep. Darcy followed Erin toward the staircase, discreetly handing the barkeep a generous amount of currency before ascending the stairs.

Erin opened an oak door that was framed in more red velvet curtains. It turned soundlessly on its hinges, revealing a darkened corridor with five closed doors along each side. Darcy could tell that the gentlemen clients who frequented this establishment expected privacy and secrecy.

Opening the last door on the left, Erin gestured Darcy through. The room was small, but plush, with the ornate bed dominating most of the space. Lush quilts and satin sheets were draped lavishly across the mattress. Erin pulled a small chair from the corner of the room and placed it next to the bed. She seated herself on the foot of the bed and invited Darcy to sit down in the chair.

"We have a small measure of privacy, Mr. Smith," she began, "but I suggest you keep your voice low." She leaned forward and asked, "Now, what exactly did you mean by your previous comment?"

"I meant that I can bring you to a place where you will be housed and educated, then gainfully employed. You can leave this life." He gestured to the bed she was sitting on.

Erin narrowed her eyes suspiciously. "Why, Mr. Smith? Why would a stranger help me? What is your profit in this arrangement?"

Darcy wasn't accustomed to these questions. Most of the women he rescued were freezing in the night mists of Ann Street, and gladly exchanged their current situation for the promise of better things. "Do you want to be here?" he asked quizzically.

"Of course not!" she frowned, keeping her voice to a low whisper. "But at least I am warm and fed. I am protected, unlike many other women in my situation, and my younger brother is cared for and employed. You understand that I cannot just trade my situation for a worse one should you prove to be deceitful."

"No, of course not," Darcy replied thoughtfully. He did not know how to explain to this woman that he was trying to help her without revealing his employer and putting their efforts at risk. But there was something different about Erin. She had not yet been beaten down by this profession. She still had a spark of life and intelligence behind her eyes and in her speech. And she was thinking. A rare quality these days in anyone. Darcy decided to extend a small, but risky piece of trust.

"I do not profit, Erin. My employer does."

Erin sat back on the bed with her hands supporting her, an "I thought so" look settling on her features. "And what exactly do I have to do?"

"Well," answered Darcy, "you have to leave this place, go to a school where you will be taken care of and educated, then be released to an employer as a housekeeper or a governess, perhaps even a tutor. My employer receives a five percent fee for providing a family with a valuable, trained employee. And you gain your life back."

Erin was listening intently now, but skepticism was still clouding her face. "Again, Mr. Smith, why?"

"Because this is wrong. Because you are being abused. Because you will be thrown out on the street once you are worn down. Because you and girls like you will not live past twenty-two or twenty-three." The anger rose in Darcy's expression as he spoke, but he managed to keep his volume down.

Understanding dawned on Erin's features, and she looked at Darcy with her piercing eyes. "Who was it, Mr. Smith?" She leaned forward, suddenly captivated by this man. "Who was it that you could not save?"

Darcy sat upright, completely caught off guard. This girl was sharp. No one else had even suspected his motives, or, at least, no one else had ever asked.

He breathed in deeply before answering. "It was my sister, my older sister," he said. Erin sat back and nodded. "She was only ten, you must understand," Darcy continued, "and I was seven. But I still felt it was my duty as her brother to keep her safe." Darcy looked straight into Erin's eyes. "And I failed."

She frowned. "You certainly have passion, Mr. Smith, and if you are being honest, a good plan. But what of my younger brother? I cannot leave him to fend for himself."

"No, of course not," he replied. "Bring him with you. There is a place for him."

Erin sat thoughtfully for a while, the fingers of her left hand tapping on the coverlet as she mused over her choices. Darcy understood her reluctance. For all she knew, Darcy was just another man seeking someone to profit from. Here at least, she and her brother were fed and warm, even if she had to do terrible things to ensure that security. He was asking her to leave that security for the unknown, which was possibly far worse than their current situation.

"And if I do decide to take advantage of this offer, Mr. Smith?"

"A black coach will slowly drive in front of The Crimson Dagger at the one o'clock morning hour. If you wish to leave this place with your brother, then simply get in the coach."

Distress showed in Erin's eyes. "I will not see my brother until breakfast. Is there any other way you can retrieve him?"

"What is his name?" Darcy asked.

"Murray Moore. He is eight, with a mop of red hair. Mr. Drake has him running errands in the banking district."

Darcy smiled. "I know of the lad. I have seen him several times over the past few months. I will retrieve him for you."

"Thank you, Mr. Smith," Erin said, relief easing her expression. She seemed to have come to a decision. "If at all possible, I will be on the coach. If I cannot, then I do not wish to be separated from my brother. Please leave him in Mr. Drake's employ." She paused, then looked down at the floor. "He is, at least, good to my brother."

Darcy placed a comforting hand over Erin's. "All will be well, Erin. I promise." She looked up to his face, uncertainty and worry clouding her thoughts.

"Did you ever see your sister again, Mr. Smith?"

Darcy smiled largely. "I enjoy breakfast with her every Saturday morning."

Erin smiled as well, daring to hope for something better.

"When I see you tomorrow," he added, "I can tell you my real name."

"On the morrow, then." She rose and opened the door for Darcy to exit, shutting it firmly behind him once he was out.

As Darcy traveled down the hall, another door opened right upon him, almost striking him in the ribs. He sidestepped quickly to avoid being hit. The blonde man emerging was quite startled, as well, but apologetic.

"So sorry, Mr...," he began.

Darcy nodded his head in greeting. "Mr. Smith. And no harm done."

The young man smiled warmly and held out a hand. "Byron Drake. I hope you are enjoying yourself, sir."

Darcy shook his hand and put an equally warm smile on his face, killing the revulsion creeping into his stomach. This was the owner of The Crimson Dagger and many other brothels in this area. This man had practically enslaved dozens of young girls, profiting from their misery. This was his enemy.

"I am enjoying myself immensely," Darcy answered. "Your young ladies are as beautiful as they are... talented."

Mr. Drake laughed, leaning against the still open door. "Indeed they are. I hope you will visit my establishment again soon."

As Darcy glanced past the open door into the room, his heart fell inside his chest. A young woman with blonde curls sat on a small chair by the vanity, her head down, her locks covering her face. But Darcy could see her reflection in the vanity mirror. Her left eye was blackened and part of her lip was swollen and bloodied, but she was still recognizable. Shannon Tiernan.

Darcy looked Byron Drake in the eye, maintaining his pleasant expression. His gut told him to do away with this man here and now, strangling him slowly until the last bit of life left his worthless body. But the struggle would surely alert the barkeep and any other hired men working here, and Darcy would not see the morning light.

Instead, he replied in his merriest voice, "I plan to return very soon, Mr. Drake."

Drake clapped him firmly on the arm. "Until next time, then." He shut the bedroom door, locked it from the outside, and escorted Darcy to the end of the hallway, opening the door to the tavern below. Darcy descended the stairs and made his way to the main exit, while Mr. Drake quietly conversed with the barkeep.

Darcy Adams was going to return, all right.

16

Byron Drake watched with cautious eyes as Mr. Smith left The Crimson Dagger. There was something about him that left Drake uneasy. He was too friendly, too conversational. Most of Drake's clients did not chat happily in the corridor of a brothel.

Not so Mr. Smith. Something was amiss here.

Drake put away another shot of brandy, then focused on his barkeep. "That man," he gestured to the door, "the one who just left. Who did he see tonight?"

"I believe he went upstairs with Miss Moore," the man answered, refilling his boss's brandy glass.

"Did he say what his profession was, or where he was from?"

"No. He just came in and sat down, watchin' the girls."

"Thank you, Sam." Drake set his glass on the counter and made for the staircase. He needed to pay a visit to Miss Moore.

"Hey boss," Sam called after him. "When are you going to let that sweet little blonde out and about? I'd like to get to know her better." Sam winked cheerfully at his boss, clearly looking forward to time spent with Miss Tiernan.

Drake paused on the first step, then turned and walked slowly back to the bar. He casually reached across the bar and grasped the front of Sam's collar with his fist, pulling his face to within an inch of his own. Sam's eyes widened in surprised fear.

"The next time you mention Miss Tiernan," he said, his voice steady, controlled, and cold, "I will kick your dead corpse off the wharf and into the sea for the crabs to feed on. Do you understand what I'm telling you, Sam?"

Sam's white face indicated that he understood perfectly. "Yes, sir," he replied, his voice not as merry as a few moments earlier.

Drake let go of Sam's shirt, and without another word, climbed the staircase. He wanted to know more about his newest client, Mr. Smith.

Erin nervously moved around the crowded room, filling empty snifters and shot glasses that sat adjacent to sloppy stacks of cash and coin on the poker tables. She tried to keep her demeanor pleasant, but the earlier visit from Mr. Drake had rattled her badly.

He had asked a great deal about Mr. Smith. Did he mention a wife? Did he live in Boston? What business was he in? Did he tell her his real name? She answered as honestly as she cared to, saying that she believed he lived somewhere on the outskirts of Boston and was employed by a wealthy business owner. Beyond that, she was ignorant of the man.

Mr. Drake had pressed on. Was she sure there was nothing else? The intensity of his eyes had almost convinced Erin that he already knew everything that had transpired between her and Mr. Smith, and that she should tell him everything before she had to endure his wrath.

Instead, Erin had replied that the man had not been interested in idle conversation. Mr. Drake had left then, with an order to get downstairs and find another gentleman caller.

As she made her way to a table occupied by five men playing poker, one of the men beckoned to her. She gracefully refilled his shot glass from the flask that she carried. The man looked at her chest, focusing his eyes on her cleavage.

"You'll do," he said, not even looking at her face as he drank his whiskey. Erin nervously glanced at the clock sitting on the mantle above the fireplace. It was ten to one – almost time for the black carriage. The man pushed back his chair from the table while collecting his cash from the other protesting players. "Didn't you hear me?" he said irately, his voice slurred from too much alcohol. "Up you go!"

"Wait a minute!" cried one of the men. "You can't just leave in the middle of a game! We have a lot of money on the table!"

The man rose unsteadily from his seat and grabbed Erin by the wrist. "Since you just lost," slurred the man, "it's my money now." He clumsily scooped up the notes from the table and shoved them in his pants pocket, dropping several of them heedlessly to the floor. He put his arm over Erin's shoulder, using her to support his drunken frame. "And I'd rather go upstairs than play any more with your ugly mugs."

Erin had no choice but to hold up the man, or they would both topple to the floor. As she put her arm around his waist, her hand felt something small and square in his jacket pocket, about the size of a deck of cards. She deftly slipped her hand into his pocket. Sure enough, there was a small stack of cards resting there.

If Erin had to put money on it, she would bet that every card was an ace or a face card. She gripped the deck with her fingers, then gently lifted them out of his pocket. As the man turned toward the stairs, still hanging onto Erin for support, she let them fall out of her fingers and spill on the floor.

"Sir," she commented, "you seem to have dropped something." The man looked down at the floor. Aces and kings of all four suits lay scattered everywhere. The other men stood from the table, their eyes scouring the floor, murderous anger forming on their faces.

"You worthless cheat!" shouted one. "Do you know what we do to thieves?" The men left the table and started toward the charlatan, who then looked down at Erin, his face twisting into a vile scowl. He pushed her from him and slapped her hard across the face, sending her backward into a table.

"That'll be enough of that!" exclaimed one of the cheated players. He decked the scoundrel squarely in the jaw, and Erin heard the crack of bone as she clambered off the floor and away from the brawl. A burly man, who had apparently lost quite a bit of money, bent over and hauled the thief off the floor. Elevating him into the air, he threw the flailing man over the bar, barreling him into Sam the barkeep.

Several more men jumped over the bar to retrieve the man, knocking over bottles of liqueur and smashing brandy glasses into oblivion. Everyone in the room was either trying to kill the man who had been caught cheating or separate the would be killers from their victim.

Erin fled to a table close to the door and looked at the clock. Five to one. The door was within her reach. She fought the panic rising in her throat even as her hand crept toward the door.

"What is going on down here?!" The voice of Byron Drake thundered across the room as he hurried down the staircase opposite Erin, his face aghast at the scene in front of him. Erin yanked her hand from the door and shrank against the wall, the brawl still roiling around the bar. Surely Drake had seen her reaching for the door. She expected his painful fury to descend on her any second.

Drake glanced at Erin for a moment, his eyes narrow. Then he dismissed her and waded into the mass of legs and fists, cursing and pulling men off of each other. Perhaps he assumed her terrified expression was caused by the very real threat of physical harm. No matter. It afforded Erin the split second she needed to swallow her fear, pull open the heavy oak door, and slip out into the night.

The street outside was lit by the full moon and a single gas lamp hanging on a post a few feet from The Crimson Dagger. Its light was bright enough to illuminate Erin's form as she pressed herself against the wall. She could not remember the last time she had been outside. A few drunk stragglers stood across the street from her, not seeming to notice the pretty redhead shrinking back from the light.

Slow, steady clipping from the end of the lane caught her ear. She looked to her right and saw a black carriage, about twenty yards away, slowly driving in her direction. She started for the cab, then stopped. What if it wasn't the right carriage? What if Mr. Smith was false? What if she was dooming herself and her brother to a life of poverty and cruelty? With each step of the horse, each foot closer that the carriage came, her doubts grew. Was she really making the best decision?

The carriage was upon her, the horse walking at a leisurely pace in front of the tavern. Sitting in the driver's seat was an old man with mostly gray hair, wrapped in a heavy black coat to keep out the chill of early morning. As he passed, he looked directly at Erin, then jerked his head to the cab behind him, still keeping the pace of the horse steady.

It was now or never. Erin took a deep breath and stepped up to the moving cab. It did not stop and thus call attention to itself, but it was going slow enough so that Erin could open the door and climb in with ease. She shut the door tightly behind her and sat on the seat, trying to calm the wild beating of her heart. She ventured a quick look out of the window toward the door of The Crimson Dagger. It was still shut tight. No one from the street would even suspect the tumult that was going on inside. She sat back and breathed in deeply.

Had she really just escaped from Byron Drake?

The driver maintained silence until they reached the end of the lane. "You alright, Miss?" His aged voice crackled through the silence from the front of the cab, catching Erin by surprise.

She jumped at his voice, but answered quickly, "I am fine, sir. Thank you." She felt, rather than saw, the old man nod his acknowledgment. "Where are we off to," she ventured, her uneasiness fading into curiosity.

"To safety, lass," he answered. "To safety."

As she heard the old man's words, the reality of the situation finally sank in. She was free. Never again would she look at that stranger in the mirror and turn away in shame. Never again.

Byron Drake took the stairs from the cellar two at a time, the gun in his holster still smelling of burnt powder. When the fight in the bar had finally been sorted through, a cheat had been revealed. And a cheat in Byron Drake's games would not be tolerated. The man now lay dead in a corner of the cellar, one hole directly between his eyes. It had been awhile since Drake had killed a man. He missed it.

With his spirits lifted, he sauntered through the kitchen to the bar room, his boots crunching on the broken glass covering the floor. Sam looked at him nervously.

"Sam!" Drake barked, but not unhappily.

"Yes, sir?" Sam answered quickly, doing his best to sound normal.

"You and Jones dump that pile of filth in a burlap sack and throw it off Woodman's Wharf by my warehouse before morning."

"Yes sir, Mr. Drake!" Sam knew exactly what pile of filth Drake was talking about, and he was incredibly happy that it wasn't him lying in the cellar right now.

Drake slapped Sam's shoulder heartily. "Guess those crabs will get a meal after all." He looked around the room, surveying the damage, not even disheartened by the amount of broken furniture. All of the girls were on the lower level, collecting bits of chairs and glasses and helping Drake's men set tables straight again. All except Shannon, of course. He scanned the room again, this time looking for curly locks of red hair. Erin Moore was not there. His eyes narrowed as a realization stole over him.

"Sam," he said again, though his tone was completely opposite from that of a moment age.

The barkeep noticed the change and answered him warily, concern clearly shaping his expression. "Sir?"

"Did Miss Moore go upstairs?"

Sam looked around the room as well. "No," he answered slowly. "The last time I saw her was right before the brawl."

Drake bolted for the staircase. "Get my horse ready! Now!" He stormed through the oak door at the top of the stairs, then yanked open the last door on the left of the hallway. It was empty, except for the luxurious bed and chair that furnished the room. One by one, he opened every door except for Shannon's. Each time, he found that Erin Moore was not there.

Wretched woman! She was one of his best money makers. How dare she abandon him like this! He fumed down the stairs for the second time that night, his fury rising like a storm blowing in from the Atlantic. Sam already had his stallion saddled and waiting in front of The Crimson Dagger. Drake mounted hastily and clopped across the street where a group of four or five drunks were milling restlessly.

"You there!" he called, catching their attention. The men looked up at Drake, curiosity awakening their senses slightly. "Did you see a redhead pass by? Perhaps ten or fifteen minutes ago?"

Drake's horse pranced back and forth, not content to be standing in one place.

"What's the matter, mister?" one of the inebriated men called back. "Lose your lady for the night?" Drunken laughter erupted among the group. A loud click sounded above the laughter, and all of the men fell dead silent, looking down the barrel of Drake's pistol.

"One more time, gentlemen," Drake said calmly. "Where is the redhead that came out that door?" He gestured to the door of The Crimson Dagger with his gun, then returned his aim to the man closest to him.

"I didn't see no redhead, mister," the man answered nervously. "But I did see a coach come along this way, about the time you said."

"A coach?" questioned Drake, his gun still drawn.

"Yes, sir," replied the man. "A regular, old, black coach, just drivin' slow down the road."

"Which way?"

The man pointed to his right. "That way."

Drake holstered his pistol. "Thank you, sirs," he offered. "You have been very helpful." Turning his horse, Drake urged him into a gallop and tore down the street. Ten minutes, at the earliest. That was the head start that Miss Moore had on him. Now he knew without a doubt that she had help, probably from Mr. Smith. He would have to put a bullet in his head, as well. No one took anything from Byron Drake. No one.

17

Darcy Adams impatiently pulled out his pocket watch. "It's half past one," he spoke through the coach's window to Josephine, who was waiting inside to receive the newest addition to her school.

Darcy sat on horseback beside the coach, both of them waiting on the opposite side of the bridge that crossed the Charles River. The full moon illuminated the landscape in gentle shades of black and gray, and glinted brilliantly off the river as its deep waters rolled peacefully under the bridge.

Josephine was anxious to talk to Miss Moore. From what Darcy had told her, Miss Moore had worked directly for Byron Drake, a man who perpetuated this horrible industry in Boston. Perhaps Josephine could learn enough from her to find a legal way into Mr. Drake's dealings, a way that would eventually bring him to justice.

She knew that this would be no easy task. The crime of prostitution was always laid at the feet of the woman involved, never at the man behind it. She would have to find some other illegal activity on the part of Byron Drake that would be inflammatory enough to put him in prison. With men like him, there was always something.

A woman of her means had other ways to deal with Byron Drake, if she so desired, but Josephine would never seriously contemplate ending someone's life. The threat to her family would have to be dire for her to even consider such a thing.

"Should I go forward and locate them?" Darcy asked, pulling Josephine from her thoughts. Before she could respond, the distant sounds of galloping hooves and carriage wheels came from across the bridge. They both strained to hear. The noise grew louder with each passing second, and the unmistakable pop of gunshots echoed through the tumult. Darcy pulled his revolver from his side and rode toward the bridge.

At that instant, the black coach carrying Miss Moore tore around the corner of the road into view, dangerously tilting onto two wheels as it did so. The driver was furiously churning the reins, inciting the horse to ever greater speeds. A horseman came into view twenty yards behind them, riding at top speed with his gun drawn, aiming for the careening carriage in front of him. Another shot cracked through the night.

Josephine bolted forward in horror as the horse pulling Miss Moore screamed in pain, its terrified cry echoing across the bridge. She was vaguely aware of Darcy advancing to the bridge and firing shots at the horseman. But her eyes were riveted on the horse and carriage.

She saw the scene as if time had slowed. The horse reared up on the bridge, still screaming in agony from the bullet in its flank. The driver of the carriage was desperately trying to pull the creature away from the edge of the bridge. She could just make out the horrified expression of a young woman in the cab, her red curls obscuring part of her face.

The horse came down from its rearing, its front hooves just missing the firm stone of the bridge and toppling over the side. As the horse's body plummeted toward the river, it pulled the carriage, driver, and passenger with it, plunging them all into the cold, deep waters of the Charles River. Josephine's heart froze with terror as she heard the woman's horrified screams mingling with those of the horse on the way toward the water. Then, for just a moment, she heard the most dreadful silence imaginable.

Another shot rang into the night, and Josephine's driver slumped over in his seat. Darcy was on the bridge, firing his gun toward the retreating horseman. He emptied his gun, then pulled another from his back before Josephine fully realized what was happening. When his second gun was empty and the horseman was fleeing at full gallop in the opposite direction, he dismounted at the water's edge and shouted to Josephine, who was already climbing out of the cab.

"Get to safety! You and the driver! He's been hit!" He hurriedly stripped off his boots and plunged into the waters, diving headlong into the dark current.

Josephine wrapped her arms around her groaning driver and pushed the semi-conscious man into the cab. After firmly closing and latching the door, she climbed into the driver's seat and turned the spooked horse toward home. One look back found Darcy's head breaking through the waters and gasping for air before he went under again. Josephine snapped the reins urgently and incited the horse into a full gallop toward Hamilton Manor.

"Oh God," she prayed frantically, repeatedly. "Oh please, God. Please save them, God. Please, God."

William made his way into the foyer, hoping that Josephine was still awake at this late hour. It had been two weeks since her father's passing, and he felt it was time to tell her about the strange man at the funeral and what he had seen the night of the Spring Ball. If a Hamilton business was in some kind of partnership with this man, then she needed to be warned.

Truth be told, William also felt a bit lonely this evening. He was wanting to have tea and conversation with Josephine to ease this disconcerted feeling. However, he had never sought her out at this late hour before. Come to think of it, he rarely even saw her in the evenings. He caught Jeffrey making his way down the hall toward the wing that housed the old servant's quarters.

"Ay there," William called in a friendly manner to the man, who turned at the summons. "Do you know if Mrs. Dunham has retired yet.

"Ah, good evening Mr. Dunham," greeted the elder man, bending slightly at the waist as he faced William. "Mrs. Dunham has not yet retired," he replied, his manner slow and calm, as always.

"Very good," said William. "Would you ask her to join me in the library, then?"

Jeffrey cocked his head to one side, as if the request were something odd he had never heard before. William smiled slightly and raised an eyebrow. Perhaps the old man was still affected by his master's death.

"Jeffrey?" William prodded the elderly man after a few moments of inaction. "Will you please find Mrs. Dunham and ask her to join me in the library?"

Jeffrey looked pleasantly at William and nodded his head. "I'm afraid I cannot, sir. Have an excellent evening." As William watched, a bit irritated and more than a bit baffled, the elderly man turned on his heel and made his way down the hall without even a backward glance to his superior. When the old servant was finally out of sight, William realized that he was still standing in the same place, staring after Jeffrey like a dolt.

"Ophelia!" William called for the maid as he turned and headed for the kitchen. "Ophe...!"

"Here Mr. Dunham!" Ophelia rounded the corner hurriedly just as William called her name. She curtsied slightly. "What can I help you with, sir?"

"I am trying to find my wife," he said, his voice betraying his slightly flustered state. "But Jeffrey is acting quite odd this evening. Would you please bring your mistress to the library, then fetch some evening tea for us?"

Ophelia smiled pleasantly, but William detected a nervousness about her. "Please excuse old Jeffrey, sir," she explained. "Ever since he turned seventy he's been slightly off. But he has been with the family since Mr. Hamilton was a child, and they would never consider letting him go." Ophelia paused sadly. "I think Mr. Hamilton's passing has broken old Jeffrey's heart."

"I did not know," William responded, "Though I know Mr. Hamilton's death was difficult for him." The poor man must have grieved for Mr. Hamilton like a son. He recalled Josephine comforting Jeffrey as the old man wept at her father's bedside. The thought eased his irritation.

"Well, sir," Ophelia answered, "I will retire for the evening, then." She turned quickly and almost sprinted down the hall.

"No... Ophelia... wait!" The young maid ignored him and made her way toward the kitchen and down the hall to her quarters. Such insubordinate servants! What happened to this household in the evening? Apparently, William was going to have to do his own bidding.

Perhaps Josephine was already in the library. It was her favorite destination in the house. With any luck, she was already there, reviewing some business document or legal brief. William tromped up the stairs, still debating with himself if he should reprimand the servants on the morrow.

The library arch came into view, the orange glow of a fire emanating from inside the room. He boldly entered the library, expecting Josephine to be reclined peacefully in her wing chair with a book in her hands. It was vacant.

A disappointment that he did not expect filled his chest. He was truly hoping for Josephine's company this evening. Where was his wife?

He marched back down the stairs and made his way to Ophelia's quarters. He was about to pound on the door, but stopped abruptly. This was a most improper situation. He could not call on his wife's maid at this hour.

He looked up and down the deserted hall. There was no one else here to help him. William loudly hammered the door with his fist, intent upon receiving some kind of assistance this evening.

"Ophelia!" he called through the door, "what is going on here this evening? Where is Josephine?"

The door opened abruptly to reveal a very alarmed Ophelia, her bed coat pulled tightly around her. "Mr. Dunham!" she scolded. "You are going to upset the entire household with that thundering!"

"Blood and ashes, woman!" he retorted sharply. "Just tell me where my wife is!"

Ophelia stepped out of her room and into the hall, shutting the door behind her. "She is out on business, Mr. Dunham," she said firmly. "Frankly," she added, "she will not be home until much later. Now please, Mr. Dunham, just go to bed!"

William staggered back. Out on business? Not home until later? These were the terms used by worthless husbands to camouflage their philandering to their pitiable wives. How could his Josephine possibly be engaged in such behavior? Then the image of Josephine nodding almost imperceptibly to the man at the funeral filled his vision. She had clearly been aware of the man, but had not wanted to call attention to him, or even speak to him in public.

Suspicion began to nag at his heart. This contravened everything William knew to be true about Josephine, but would also explain the puzzling behavior of her household staff this evening. They were trying to protect their mistress.

He looked again at Ophelia, disbelief engulfing his entire demeanor. She immediately realized the impact her words had on him.

"Oh no, sir," she began hastily. "Josephine is nothing if not honorable and kind. She really does have business at these late hours..." She faltered, not wanting to disclose anything more.

"What legitimate business could Mrs. Dunham possibly have at this hour?"

"Legitimate business...?" she answered, her brows knit together in a frown. "Really, sir!" Ophelia retorted, suddenly nervy, "you have never once taken notice of her other late evening outings. I don't understand why you are so upset this evening."

William could hardly contain himself. "Of all the insolent, insubordinate, disrespectful...!" His anger and frustration were so hot he could not even continue speaking.

Ophelia stood at the doorway a moment more, then opened the door behind her while speaking. "If that's all then, sir," she said, as if their exchange had been a pleasant chit chat, "I will return to my room." She disappeared quickly back through the door and closed it securely, leaving William, once again, standing alone in a hallway.

He turned and stomped back up the stairs and into the library. Sinking unhappily into the chair, he decided not to rest his head until he had spoken with Josephine and resolved this madness.

Insolence! Ophelia would have to go first thing in the morning! He would not have this insolence! After a few minutes in the silence of the library, William's mind quieted. There were no stirrings either in the house or outside the open window. All he could hear was the song of crickets and the occasional crackle of the fire.

Things simply could not be as they appeared. Josephine had not even wanted to marry. He could not imagine her wanting to deal with the burden of a secret affair.

But perhaps that was the reason she didn't want to marry. Perhaps her first choice was unacceptable to her father, and so she kept the relationship shrouded. Mr. Hamilton would never accept a man of such questionable character.

What if their marriage had no impact whatsoever on that relationship, and so Josephine had kept her habit of being away from home late at night? Maybe that was the very reason that she encouraged William to pursue an adulterous relationship with Elisabeth, because she was doing that very thing herself!

It could not be! His affections were just beginning to edge past the bounds of friendship. If Josephine were being unfaithful, then William would not tolerate this marriage another day – not after all he had given up. Even as he made the determination, his heart sank uncomfortably in his chest. William realized that he was hoping for another explanation, any other explanation, than the most obvious one.

The boredom and silence started to wear on William, and more than once he caught himself nodding off in the firelight. After what seemed only a few seconds, the thunder of hooves galloping up the front lane jolted William out of his uneasy sleep. He sat up straight, disconcerted for a moment, then rose and went to the window. A black carriage raced toward the house at a frantic pace, then stopped right at the front steps. What insanity now? William leaned closer to the window.

Josephine was climbing down from the driver's seat! "Ophelia!" she yelled, heedless of her volume as she jerked the carriage door open. "Albert! Hans! NOW!" The whole house seemed to awake in an instant and rush out the front door to their mistress. William watched in alarm as Josephine reached inside the carriage and pulled a man from the cab. Albert and Hans rushed to her side to assist her, pulling him out completely as Hans hoisted him into his strong arms.

"The guest room, Hans," she ordered. "Quickly!' Hans turned and raced into the house with the unconscious man, passing Ophelia who was still dressed in her bed coat and making her way to Josephine.

"Albert! Go fetch all the hands on the grounds and ride to the bridge! Search the river by the bridge – and downstream."

"Ma'am?" Albert questioned, the request seeming too absurd to be legitimate.

"A woman, Albert! A red haired girl. She fell in the river with her carriage!" As soon as Albert heard the words, he wasted no more time, but ran at breakneck speed down the lane toward the carriage house.

William turned from the window as he heard Josephine order Ophelia into town to retrieve Dr. Stone. On his way down the hall, he spied Jeffrey following Hans into the guest room, carrying a pitcher of water, a towel, and bandages.

By the time he reached the foyer, Josephine was already in the house and shutting the door. Something in her demeanor was so foreign that it stopped William in his tracks. Her head rested heavily against the door frame, and her shoulders were slumped. Everything about her posture exuded weariness and defeat.

She did not turn from the door after she shut it, but stood there, eyes shut, taking one ragged breath after another. "I can't do this, God," she whispered dejectedly, sinking to the floor beneath her. "I can't do this anymore." Her dress was smeared with crimson, and her hands were shaking and bloody as she covered her face and began to weep bitterly.

William covered the distance between them in an instant and knelt down next to her, his arm resting protectively across her back as she wept into the floor. Even after her father's passing, she never mourned like this.

"Good heavens, Josephine," he asked gently, carefully raising her to a sitting position so he could see her face. "What has happened?" She covered her face with her hands once again and turned away, the sobs disabling any capacity for speech.

William rested himself on the floor against the wall and pulled his wife into his lap, surrounding her with his arms and whispering comfort into her ear. She did not try to resist, but continued to weep, hiding her face in his neck and soaking his jacket with her tears. Whatever it was causing Josephine to be so distraught, William was sure to learn of it later. His immediate concern was for her overwrought state. He had never seen her like this.

After a few more minutes the wracking sobs lessened, though she still did not bring her face to the light. William decided that the floor was not the best place to be when Ophelia returned with the doctor. He slid one of his arms under Josephine's legs and lifted her up, walked to the sitting room, and eased himself and Josephine onto the sofa. It was darker here, only the light from the foyer reflecting through the arched entry.

"Josephine," William whispered, pulling her damp hair away from her cheek while trying to see her face. "Please confide in me. What happened this evening?" He waited patiently, stroking her arm as Josephine lay her head on his shoulder and rested her hand against his chest. He felt her take a deep, solid breath and relax against him.

"Do you remember," she began, her voice little more than a whisper, "the morning we toured the estate?"

"Yes," William replied, his hand resting on her shoulder. "I remember it quite well."

"When we arrived at the school, you recognized one of the girls there."

William nodded.

"She had been a prostitute, William."

William frowned. "I knew the nature of her transaction the evening I saw her, but she was so young. Too young for that type of profession."

Josephine nodded. "Most people don't understand what is actually happening to these poor girls." She pushed away slightly so she could see him face to face. "They are no more than fourteen or fifteen, some even younger, and have been indentured for the voyage to America. When they arrive, their papers are sold to someone else. Some, for honest labor. Others," she paused, "others force these girls into the business of unscrupulous profit. The girls have no choice, William. They must either work or starve. Most of them die in an alley in their early twenties." She shook her head. "You would be horrified to hear what some of these girls have endured. Little girls, William!" She closed her eyes as if to put the images out of sight.

William took Josephine's hand in his own and looked squarely in her eyes. "How did she find the school?" He was finally piecing together these little mysteries surrounding Josephine.

"She didn't, William," she answered. "I found her. That is what I do. I find the ones that can be saved and I save them. The school is a safe place where they can be educated for a respectable profession."

William nodded his understanding. "And the girl this evening?" William thought back to Josephine's frantic ride up the lane.

"Most of the girls come to me through my employee – a gentleman who finds them and brings them to my carriage. I, in turn, deliver them to the school."

"Why?" asked William. "Why doesn't your gentleman bring them himself?"

"If he were tied to Hamilton Manor or the school in any way, it could put this household and those girls at risk."

"I see." The more William heard, the more uncomfortable he became.

Josephine continued. "I was waiting for the girl across the river, but she was followed by a man on horseback. I believe that he was her employer, angry that she had tried to escape. He fired shots at her carriage just as she was crossing the bridge..." Josephine's voice broke as she recounted the horrible ordeal.

"And the horse was hit and went into the river," William finished.

"I am afraid that the poor girl is lost, William, as well as my man that was driving her carriage. And the poor horse!" She shuddered, remembering the nightmarish, mingling screams of the horse and the girl as the carriage plunged into the black waters of the Charles River.

"My own driver is grievously wounded, William. He was struck by the gunshots. I can only pray that he makes it through the night." A horrible sorrow haunted her face as she searched his eyes. "Those lives are on my shoulders, William. I have failed them miserably. Miserably."

"I am so sorry, Josephine," he said, pulling her against him again, hoping to offer some measure of comfort. "I am so sorry. But you were engaging in acts of salvation. The blame for this is not on your shoulders." A cold dread presented itself in William's gut. If Josephine's driver had been hit, then the horseman had been targeting Josephine's carriage directly, not the one carrying the girl. Josephine had escaped death this evening by a hair's breadth. He breathed deeply and held her tighter, not knowing if she had come to this realization yet.

William heard the door knob turn in the foyer, then heard the hurried steps of Ophelia and Dr. Stone jogging toward the guest room. The two hurried past without noticing William and Josephine in the sitting room. Ophelia's distressed voice carried back through the hall as she conversed with the doctor.

Josephine slowly pulled herself from William's embrace and stood. He stood with her. "I need to check on my driver," she said, concern heavy on her face.

"He is in good hands, Josephine," William replied. "You need to be tended to yourself."

Josephine considered for a moment without replying.

"Josephine," he said gently but gravely, "I am not asking, but insisting."

Her eyes shot up to meet his. He continued. "You cannot keep things from me anymore. Not anything," he stressed, taking her hand. "I cannot protect you, or even help you, if you keep me in the dark." His frown was intense and sober, showing the degree of his concern. "I am not asking, Josephine."

He saw her expression turn thoughtful as she searched over his face, her eyes narrowed slightly, looking for something beyond his physical features. Clearly, this woman was not accustomed to accommodating the demands of a man.

"All right," she answered after a lingering silence. "I will take you into my confidence."

"Thank you," he answered, as they began walking, hand in hand. "Is there anything you still need to tell me?"

"There is," she replied. "When we take the girls from the men who bought their papers..."

Understanding struck William. "You, of course, must leave the papers behind."

"Yes," she replied. They were almost to the top of the stairs.

"You would be held criminally responsible if you were caught."

Josephine stopped at the top of the staircase, paused, then looked at William. "Yes."

William nodded, then led Josephine to his own quarters. He bade her sit in the chair by the fire while he put a pitcher of water on the hearth to warm. His own clothes had become bloody from Josephine's hands and dress, so he stripped off his jacket and tossed it in the corner by the door, mildly hoping that the action would irritate Ophelia in the morning when she came to keep house.

Taking the pitcher, William poured the warm water into a basin and soaked the towel that lay next to it. He squeezed out the excess, then knelt by Josephine, who was quietly watching him. He began with her hands, gently rubbing away the dried blood encrusting them. He plunged the towel into the basin again, then cleaned her face using careful strokes, his eyes examining every inch to make sure that not a drop of blood remained.

She sat motionless, almost not breathing, her eyes on his every move.

After she was clean, William inspected her stained dress. Reaching his arms around her, with his face next to hers, he undid the back of Josephine's dress and loosened the ties that kept it taught about her frame. He sat back and looked into her tired eyes, his hand resting on her cheek.

"I am going to find you something more proper to wear. I will be right back." She nodded in response, and William rose and went down the hall to Josephine's suite. Looking around, he found her gown and bed coat waiting neatly across her bed, no doubt laid out by Ophelia earlier that evening. He hurriedly snatched them and returned to Josephine, who was still seated by the fire.

"Here," he said simply, draping the clothes across the arm of the chair. As Josephine rose, he turned his back so that she could exchange her soiled garments for the clean ones. When the sound of rustling clothes had ceased, William turned around again.

Josephine sat there, small and delicate, looking into the fireplace with uncertain eyes. She had never seemed so unsure. Usually, she was larger than life, with a commanding presence filling every space of the room she occupied.

She did not fare well with blood on her shoulders. He frowned at the thought, even as the compassion welled up inside him.

William took her bloody dress from the floor and tossed it into the corner with his own coat. Then he took her hand and looked down into her eyes. "It will be all right, Josephine," he promised. "You are not alone anymore."

At his words Josephine closed her eyes, and tears slid down her face again. "No, no," said William, brushing them from her cheek. "That was supposed to comfort you, not make you cry."

She smiled for the first time that evening, though it was a tired, defeated smile. "It does comfort me, William," she replied softly. "That is why I'm crying."

William smiled sadly and shook his head. "Come here," he said as he pulled the cover down on his bed. "Stay with me this evening."

Uncertainty clouded Josephine's expression for only a moment as she searched William's face, then she nodded wearily. She eased herself under the blanket, and William climbed in next to her, shirt, pants, and all. He placed a protective arm over her as she settled into the pillow and nestled close to his chest. Within moments, she was sleeping, the weariness and sorrow of the evening overtaking her. He felt her breathing take on a steady rhythm.

His mind raced through the events of the evening and the nature of Josephine's undertaking as he felt the warmth of this extraordinary woman sleeping next to him. He concluded that perhaps his father had made a wise choice, after all. He kissed her hair, then rested his own head on the pillow. Sleep didn't come as easily to him, though. His mind kept returning to the bullet that found Josephine's driver, and to the horseman that tried to kill his wife.

18

The long, weary night finally gave way to the gleaming fingers of dawn stretching across the fragile sky. Dr. Stone had been able to retrieve a single bullet from the driver's side. He was still in the guest room with his patient, watching the man for any signs of ill or good, when William slipped quietly through the door. He had left the still sleeping Josephine early, hoping to speak to the doctor without his wife present.

Dr. Stone was sitting in an armchair, his chin tucked to his chest, sleeping lightly as his patient rested. William's entrance woke him from his tentative slumber.

"Ah, Mr. Dunham," he said quietly, "you have come to check on the driver?"

"Aye," William answered, looking at the older man in the bed. He seemed to be resting well, and his pallor was much improved from last night. "Will he pull through?"

The doctor rose and motioned William into the hall. He shut the door behind them and led William to the sitting room, where he and Josephine had sat the night before.

"We will be able to talk here without disturbing the driver," Dr. Stone commented while taking a seat in one of the chairs. William sat on the couch adjacent to the doctor. "To answer your question, Mr. Dunham, I believe that he will be fine after a few weeks. It seems that the bullet missed his internal organs, though it ricocheted off of one of his ribs, breaking it. But he will live. He is very lucky."

"Indeed," answered William thoughtfully.

"And Mrs. Dunham?" the doctor asked. "Is she all right? I should have made my way upstairs earlier."

"She is sleeping soundly," William answered. "Dr. Stone," he continued, "I also have questions of another nature that you might be able to answer."

Dr. Stone sat back and folded his hands, knowing that Mr. Dunham was seeking more than just patient information. "Of course, Mr. Dunham, I will answer what I can."

"Do you know the nature of the events that led to this man's injury?" William asked.

"I do," replied Dr. Stone, thoughtfully, "as you must also, by now."

William sat thoughtfully for a few moments before speaking again. "Do you know how long Mrs. Dunham has been doing this...rescuing?"

Dr. Stone tilted his head to one side. "Are you looking for the story, Mr. Dunham? The history of this venture?"

"I suppose I am, Dr. Stone," replied William. "I would like to be able to protect my wife, and I need to know the entirety of the situation in order to do that."

Dr. Stone sat back, getting comfortable in his seat. "As you wish, Mr. Dunham," he answered. "Though I might be risking your wife's wrath in the telling." William smiled at Dr. Stone's comment, but nodded for him to continue. "Rosewood Hall, the school on Hamilton Manor, was meant as a place of tutelage for the servants' children when Mr. Hamilton first built this estate, and was used as such. It was Mrs. Hamilton who first thought of using it as a school for rescued girls."

"Mrs. Hamilton? Josephine's mother?" questioned William. "How did that come about?"

"From what I understand, Mrs. Hamilton and her daughter were enjoying a day in Boston together. Your wife must have been ten or eleven at the time. As they were returning home, late in the day, Mrs. Hamilton saw a little girl lying in one of the alleys. The child was barely clothed, using tattered rags as a blanket. And Mrs. Hamilton," Dr. Stone smiled at the memory of the woman, "well, if you would have known Mrs. Hamilton, then you would know she could not pass up that little child. She scooped her up, brought her back to Hamilton Manor, and then sent for a doctor straightway."

William raised his eyebrow in surprise. "You?" he asked.

"Yes," the doctor replied. "I was only twenty at the time, having just received my medical license. The doctor I was working under refused to treat the child when he learned she was a homeless orphan found in an alley. He said it was useless, that those children were hopeless." Dr. Stone frowned, then looked at William with a penetrating gaze. "I didn't believe him then, and I still don't."

William nodded. He appreciated the compassion practiced by Dr. Stone. "And when you saw the girl?" William asked.

"She had suffered horrible abuse," Dr. Stone answered. "She had been starved and beaten, used in the most horrific manner. She was waiting to die. Ten years old, and waiting to die." Dr. Stone's jaw clenched as he remembered. "But," he continued, "under Mrs. Hamilton's care, the girl flourished. We learned that she had a brother, also homeless on the streets of Boston. Mr. Hamilton was able to retrieve the boy.

When the girl was able, Mrs. Stoddely, the head housekeeper at the time, began training her for service in housekeeping. I think it was then that Mrs. Hamilton conceived of the idea of a girls' school. But your wife, the girl, and her brother grew up together, fast friends since the day Mrs. Hamilton brought the girl home. And I have been caring for the others that have come to the school since then – setting their broken bones, delivering their babies, finding suitable parents for the ones given up for adoption, and sometimes," Dr. Stone sighed heavily, "burying the girls who don't survive."

William shook his head and lowered his face at the thought of the trials these children suffered. He had never imagined such evils existed before last night. William's head shot up as something clicked in his mind. "Ophelia!" he exclaimed. "That little girl was Ophelia!"

"Indeed, Mr. Dunham," Dr. Stone said. "She was the first. When her brother was old enough, Mrs. Hamilton sent him out into the slums of Boston, and he told the other girls he found about the school. Some would meet him in the carriage sent by Mrs. Hamilton, some he never saw again. But those who chose to trust him have better lives by far.

Mrs. Stoddely trains many of them to be housekeepers. Others exhibit a talent for letters and numbers, and are trained to be tutors. They are sent to wealthy families for reputable employment."

"This boy," said William, "is obviously a man by now. Yet you speak as if he still engages in this venture."

"He does," Dr. Stone nodded. "After Mrs. Hamilton passed away, your wife took her place, and things kept going as they always had. There are only a few that know of this... organization. Myself, the young man, Ophelia, and certain members of the household staff."

William understood immediately. "If it was known that Josephine engaged in such activity, she would be a social outcast."

Dr. Stone laughed. "As if Mrs. Dunham cared about such things. No, the social aspect does not concern her. The business aspect, however, is another matter. Mr. Hamilton built profitable relationships with many businessmen in Boston, and if they were to withdraw their patronage from his businesses..."

"I see," replied William. And he did. Something with the potential to become this scandalous could destroy a business, even an empire. William's thoughts returned to the young man that Dr. Stone had spoken of. "The man that brings these girls," he continued, "does he happen to have brown hair and a cheery face?"

"I see you have already met Mr. Adams, then," stated the doctor.

"Adams? I did not know his name, but that is no matter. He was at the funeral for Mr. Hamilton, was he not?"

"Of course. I don't think that anything could have kept him away."

William sat back and folded his hands in front of him. All of the pieces were falling into place now. It was Mr. Adams that William had seen on the street the night of the ball. This man was Josephine's accomplice, as well as her childhood friend. Adams had been snatching that girl from the evils of the cold Boston streets, and he had almost undone the rescue that evening.

Undoubtedly, Josephine had retrieved the young woman from Mr. Adams after she had left the ball. That is why William saw the girl at Rosewood Hall, and why Josephine had been evasive of his questions.

William made a note to find Mr. Adams later and introduce himself properly.

Dr. Stone carefully studied William from his chair. "Mr. Dunham," he began, his tone cautious, "I must know what you plan to do now you know the scope of this situation."

"You mean," answered William, "you want to know if I will allow my wife to continue in this venture?"

Dr. Stone smiled again. "Actually, I cannot see Mrs. Dunham allowing you to hinder her. The question is, will you try?"

William ran a worried hand through his hair. "I do not believe the bullet that found the driver was meant for him. It was meant for the passenger, for the one waiting to take that girl last night."

"I considered that as well."

William looked squarely at the man across from him. "What would you do, Dr. Stone?"

Dr. Stone was unhelpfully silent as he returned William's gaze.

"Is there any other philanthropic venture of this kind in Boston?" William continued.

"Mr. Dunham," responded Dr. Stone, "Mrs. Dunham is a very unique lady, with a compassionate heart and a mind of her own. I don't think there is another venture of this kind in the country." He raised both eyebrows and nodded his head to William. "You are a very fortunate man to be married to her, but I do not envy your current dilemma. Now," he stood from the chair, "I need to return to my patient."

"Of course, sir," William responded, rising as well. "Oh," he added before the doctor left the room, "is there any news of the girl or the other driver?"

"The driver was found on the banks of the Charles about an hour after Mrs. Dunham sent the search party. He was cold, but otherwise uninjured. But the girl..." Dr. Stone sighed heavily. "I am afraid that the girl is lost."

"Thank you, Dr. Stone." William sank back in the chair as Dr. Stone retreated down the hall to his patient. He knew that trying to convince Josephine to give up this venture would be fruitless. Perhaps he could keep her safe, though, if he accompanied her on these late night travels. Somehow he knew that persuading her of that would be easier said than done.

19

Elisabeth arrived at Dr. Stone's office precisely at eight in the morning, as always. Though she had been inhospitable to her tasks at first, she discovered that she enjoyed her learning, and rose eagerly in the mornings to make her way to his office, usually with questions about the text she had been immersed in the night before.

Dr. Stone, she found, was fond of questions. It gave him the opportunity to impart his knowledge to another.

Elisabeth found herself being educated not only in German, Latin, and medicine, but also in compassion. She enjoyed the doctor's company lately, and almost felt guilty for not mourning William's company as much as she had at first.

As Elisabeth turned the knob on the white door, she was surprised to find it locked. Dr. Stone was always here earlier than she was. However, he had given her a key at the end of her first day of tutelage should this event ever arise, which she now retrieved from her reticule. She entered the office and began her morning routine of translating and copying a massive procedural text.

After a few moments, the bell on the white door jingled, and Elisabeth heard a child's cough and a mother's worried exclamations. She rose from the desk and gathered two bottles from the shelf beside her. She recognized the cough already, and knew how to treat it. Then she paused.

Would Dr. Stone want her to treat the child without him there? About a month ago, she had dispensed a remedy without consulting him first. He had gently chided her for being too quick to act and too slow to think. The words had stung sharply, even though she knew they were merited. A few skilled questions from the doctor had shown that the patient had needed a different treatment. No harm had been done, but Elisabeth had been left feeling foolish and uncertain. She did not want to repeat the situation.

Elisabeth set the bottles on the desk and entered the waiting room. The well-dressed mother sat on a chair holding a boy of about five or six in her lap. The child was pale and sweaty, and he winced every time he coughed.

"Good morning, ma'am," she said, looking down at the concerned woman. "Dr. Stone has not yet arrived, but I can look at your son, if you like."

"Are you the nurse, then?" the mother asked, looking nervously beyond Elisabeth into the back office, as if Dr. Stone were hiding in its depths.

Elisabeth smiled. "I suppose I am. Will you bring him to the examination table? I can look at his throat and feel for a temperature."

"Oh, he has a temperature," the mother offered as she stood up and led her son to the examination room. "He has been warm since last night."

Elisabeth helped the boy up onto the table, then checked his throat, ears, nose, and eyes. After determining that her original suspicion was correct, she retrieved the bottles from Dr. Stone's desk and instructed the mother on the proper dispensation of the medication.

"You should start seeing an improvement by the morning. If not, please bring your son back. I am certain that Dr. Stone will be in by then."

The woman smiled thankfully at Elisabeth. "I am glad you were here, Miss..."

"Beech," Elisabeth answered. "Elisabeth Beech."

"Thank you, Miss Beech."

As they exited the office, Elisabeth felt a satisfaction that she had never experienced before. Was this what it felt like to help someone, to truly do something important? She liked this feeling.

For a split second, Elisabeth was almost grateful for the cruel turn of events that had taken William away and thrust her onto this path.

20

Byron Drake sat at the kitchen table in The Crimson Dagger, still seething in rage from the events of last night. His only consolation was that Erin Moore was surely dead and gone. He had taken great satisfaction in hearing her terrified screams as her carriage plunged into the Charles River.

But he had learned something else last night. The person who was taking his girls from him had been waiting in the carriage across the bridge. Drake had tried to land a few lucky shots into the cab, but doubted that he had hit his mark. Whoever was behind this, though, would have to be done away with. Byron Drake was determined to destroy, in a most horrible manner, anyone who came between him and his profit.

"Mornin', Mr. Drake." Murray Moore's cheery face poked around the corner of the kitchen where Drake was sitting. He grabbed a biscuit from the stove and looked around the kitchen for his sister. Drake narrowed his eyes at the lad.

"Have you seen Erin, sir?" Murray asked, oblivious to the malevolence that was oozing out the man sitting at the table.

"You ignorant little dolt!" Drake spat, catching Murray's immediate and worried attention. Drake struck the boy across the face, causing Murray to fly backwards into the wall. Murray started to cry. "Your harlot of a sister is dead! At the bottom of the Charles River!"

Murray's eyes widened in shock and disbelief, but more tears started to stream down his cheeks. "You're lying!" he shouted. "My sister's upstairs!"

Drake rose from the table and bent over the boy. "She's not, boy," he answered hatefully. "She was running away from here. She was leaving you behind! And her carriage fell into the river. She's dead."

"No she's not!" Murray defiantly picked himself up from the floor and shouted in Drake's face. Drake hit the boy again, then grabbed him by the scruff of his collar.

"You," he said, dragging Murray to the front door and opening it onto Ann Street, "are not welcome here!" To emphasize the last word, Drake threw the boy onto the sidewalk, then shut and bolted the door behind him.

The little boy rolled a few feet before jumping up and throwing himself against the door. He beat on it with useless fists and shouted over and over, "She's not dead! She's not dead!"

When there was no response, Murray stopped assaulting the door and marched toward the financial district, where he carried out most of his errands. Maybe his sister was there, somewhere. He would just keep looking until he found her, no matter how long it took.

21

The cold, early morning fog rolling off of the Atlantic and into the streets of Boston was still dense, even though it was ten in the morning. It had been that way the past few mornings – cold, damp, and miserable, even though the autumn afternoons had been warm.

For the past four days, Darcy had been subsisting in an alley across from The Crimson Dagger. It was offset just enough from the front door to not be readily noticed by those entering or exiting the tavern, and Darcy placed himself as far back in the alley as he could while still keeping the entrance in his field of vision. He had wrapped himself in old, tattered garments the color of coal and kept as still as possible during his vigil. Any passersby who happened to notice him saw only the darkened form of a homeless vagrant.

The damp, cold hour before daylight posed the greatest challenge. This was when the ocean sent its gray billows creeping onto land, bringing a fog that penetrated into the very bones of those unfortunate enough to be outdoors. During these hours, Darcy pulled his tatters closer about him, huddled his limbs together as tight as he could, and peered closely through the mist toward those oak doors.

He had left his post just once last night, long enough to send a message to his driver about a rendezvous time and location, then he returned to the same spot in the alley and huddled down for the last watch. After scrutinizing Byron Drake's comings and goings for four days, Darcy had a good idea of the best time to retrieve Shannon Tiernan, though he had seen no sign of Erin's brother, Murray.

It was no surprise that Drake was a late sleeper, not leaving his tavern until ten thirty or eleven in the morning. He was gone for six or seven hours, then returned to The Crimson Dagger at five or six in the afternoon, right when the gentlemen callers left their employment for the day and headed to his tavern. After that, the man's schedule was erratic. Sometimes he stayed at the tavern for the duration of the evening, sometimes he left for a few hours before returning. These few daylight hours were the only ones when Drake was certain to be gone.

Darcy would have preferred a more reliable window of opportunity in the night time, but he would take what he could get. Even though the fog these last few days had caused him considerable misery, he still counted it as a blessing. The dense mist was his ally, and he hoped it would persist for at least another hour. Two would be better.

As the door to The Crimson Dagger swung open, Darcy's attention focused intensely on the man exiting the tavern. It was Drake. He waved to his driver just a few yards away, then stepped into the carriage as it pulled up. "To the warehouse," he said, almost melodiously, "then on to the bank." Darcy didn't make a move as the carriage pulled out of sight. He waited for two more minutes, listening. When nothing but the normal sounds of the slums came to his ears, he rose slowly from his spot.

Not wanting to risk being seen on the open street so close to The Crimson Dagger, Darcy stepped to the back of the building against whose wall he had been leaning for four days. He turned right and followed the back alley for three buildings before coming again to Ann Street. The fog was still thick, but not as dense as it had been half an hour ago.

Darcy listened for any hoof beats or footfalls, but heard nothing. Ten was still early for this area of town. He hobbled across the street anyway, hoping that any stray eyes that saw him would mistake him for an old man shuffling along. Once across, Darcy took another alley leading to the back of the buildings on this side of the street, then turned left. He traveled this back alley until he came to the rear of The Crimson Dagger.

The building was tall and long, but not very wide. On each side of the roof were five dormers where the windows of the upper rooms let in the promise of light. If Drake had not moved Shannon, then she was still in the third room on the left. The window was his only way in and out, but he had to consider how to get the girl off of the roof safely. Darcy scanned the alley for anything useful. Except for some discarded crates here and there, there was nothing. Crates it was, then.

Being careful not to make more noise than absolutely necessary, Darcy heaved one of the discarded crates to the corner of the building. He grabbed another and stacked it on top of the first. Two more crates were readily available, which he used to stabilize the stack and add on more height. He gently shook his hasty construction to test for sturdiness. It would do.

Darcy pulled off the tattered cloak he had been covered in for the last four days and dropped it to the earth. Over his other shoulder was looped thirty feet of tough, thin rope. He scrambled up the crates, which took him to about ten feet off the ground. When he stood on the pile, the eave of the second floor roof was beyond his reach, but the kitchen chimney was looming just off to his left.

He took his rope in his hands and secured a wide loop, making sure that his knot was one of the best he had ever tied. Eying the distance from him to the top of the kitchen chimney, Darcy swung the rope over his head twice, then let it fly. It sailed toward the chimney, landed on the corner, but didn't encircle the stout bricks. Darcy grimaced as he gathered the rope back into his hands. Once again swinging the coil over his head, he threw the loop with greater force. This time, the rope gracefully circled the chimney.

Darcy pulled the slack tight, placed a foot against the wall, and started to climb. Each step was carefully and silently placed, even though his arms strained with the effort of keeping his pace slow and his body stable. He could not afford to be discovered. He had failed Shannon Tiernan once. Twice was unthinkable.

By the time Darcy slipped over the edge of the roof next to the chimney, his limbs were burning from the exertion. He sat against the blackened bricks and caught his breath, then pulled the rope up behind him, letting it lie in a coil on the slate tiles of the roof. Carefully, and as silently as possible, Darcy crept over the first dormer, nimbly spanned the distance to the second dormer, then crawled to the third. The fog was still present, but not thick, and someone who was looking would be able to see him from the front of the building. He needed to move faster.

Hopefully, this was still where Shannon resided. Darcy slowly moved to the window and put his ear close to the glass, listening intently. At first, there was nothing, only the occasional sound of a passerby on the street below and the clopping of hooves. Then, Darcy caught the faintest sound, so quiet he almost didn't hear it. Sobbing. The heartbreaking sound of a woman trying to hide her sorrow.

Compassion moved Darcy, and he softly rapped on the window. The crying immediately ceased, and there was complete silence from inside. Darcy rapped again. The thick curtain hanging over the window from the inside inched open slightly, and a perfect, green eye peered from behind it.

When it saw Darcy's face, the eye widened in disbelief and shock, but the curtain was thrown aside to reveal the pale, frightened face of Shannon Tiernan. She still had the remains of the bruises from a few nights ago, but they had faded to an unattractive yellow.

Darcy motioned for her to open the window. With shaking fingers, Shannon unlocked the latch and pulled up the window as far as it would go.

"Hello, Miss Tiernan," Darcy began, as if they were conversing over afternoon tea, "I have come to make good on my offer, if you wish."

Shannon stared at Darcy a moment longer as if he were a ghost, then she laughed slightly as she processed the comment. "Yes, Mr. Adams," she replied shakily, "I do wish it." Then silent tears started to stream down her face.

"All will be well, Miss Tiernan," Darcy comforted, "but we cannot tarry. You must come with me now." Darcy held out his hand to the girl and she grabbed his wrist firmly. It was in that moment they both heard the tromping of heavy boots outside her door and the turning of the key in the lock.

As his cab pulled away from The Crimson Dagger, Byron Drake was lost in thought. Shannon's pallor seemed unhealthy the last few days, and he did not know if it was due to the loss of her friend, Erin, or the pregnancy.

He had suspected early on that she was carrying a child – his child. Her tiny frame had no way to hide the slight swelling in her abdomen, and when he had seen her sick and crying on the floor, he had known for sure. Perhaps he had fathered other children before. Honestly, he did not know or care. A harlot in one of his establishments could be carrying a child from any number of men. Frankly, they were liabilities after becoming pregnant, and had to be disposed of.

But Shannon, no one had touch her before him. And she was so beautiful. A child from her was sure to be handsome. A son, Drake was certain he would have a son. The boy would be blonde, like himself, and intelligent, and full of spirit, like his mother.

Ah, that woman had too much spirit. Drake had been trying to curb his temper with her lately because of the child inside her, but sometimes his temper rose with his intoxication and his hand flew of its own accord. Even while drunk, however, he had been careful to never strike her anywhere but the face. He did not want to damage his child growing in her belly.

His child. The thought did something strange to Drake's insides that he could not quite comprehend. All he could think about was the child's wellbeing.

If Shannon were sick, would his son become sick inside her? What if she lost her appetite? Or didn't get enough air or sunlight? How could the child be healthy? Drake sat forward thoughtfully, a worried look crossing his brow. When was the last time Shannon had been out in the air? Had it really been the day he bought her from Captain Munstead? That must have been over five months ago.

"Wells!" Drake leaned out the window and called sharply to the driver. "Wells, turn around and go back to The Crimson Dagger."

"Sir?" The young man had not been with Drake long enough to know any better than to voice his confusion.

"Just do it, you idiot!" Drake returned hotly. Wells turned the next corner, then the next, until he had reversed their previous direction and pointed the carriage back toward the inn. Drake sat back, satisfied with himself for thinking of his child. It was a risk, he knew, taking Shannon out and about on the streets of Boston. But where could she run to? She probably wasn't even capable of such exertion in her current state, and she needed the fresh air and the sunshine, of that he was quite sure.

Perhaps she would even appreciate being outdoors for a while. Would it make her heart kinder towards him? Drake frowned again. Did he need Shannon to have affection for him? How would it affect his child to have the mother dislike the father? After all, she would be the one caring for the child, nursing and nurturing it. Her words would be in the child's ear almost every moment.

Truth be told, Drake only needed her until the child was born. After that, he could hire a nurse to care for the child should Shannon prove to be difficult. There, it was settled. But the satisfaction that had reigned in him moments earlier now turned to unease. The thought of doing away with Shannon made him uncharacteristically sad. Did he actually love the girl?

Drake laughed out loud at the thought, and Wells cast a nervous glance over his shoulder. Perhaps he did love her. Perhaps it was time to start a proper life, as much as his business would allow. He could buy a house in the country for his son and Shannon, come home in the evenings, go back to the inn when the boy went to bed and attend to business.

And Shannon would finally escape the confines of The Crimson Dagger. He would give her a normal life – no, better than normal. She would be wealthy, with a fine house, a son to love, and a man to keep her. That should make her happy enough to hold some affection for him. Drake wondered if he would have to marry her. No matter. Marriage was just paper. He would do what was best for the child. His child.

The carriage pulled up to the door of its destination, and Drake hopped merrily out of the cab. He usually didn't feel merry, only after his pistol had just stolen the life from someone. But that was a different kind of ecstasy. This was quite different, more wholesome. He would have to get used to it.

Taking the stairs two at a time, Drake quickly made his way to Shannon's room. He turned the key. He was actually looking forward to Shannon's reaction when he told her of his plans. As he opened the door, he felt the breeze from the window blow across his face.

"Shannon?" The girl was sitting on the floor in front of the open window, a terrified look across her face. Drake understood immediately. She needed the fresh air more than he had anticipated. Drake walked over to her and pulled her from the floor. She started to cry. He didn't know what to do with these female emotions. They left him mystified.

"Shannon, my dear," he began cheerfully, "I am taking you out today for some fresh air. Find something appropriate to wear for the carriage ride." He puzzled over her mournful face, then added, "It will do you good."

Shannon made no move to comply, but just stood there with that hopeless expression on her features. "Didn't you hear me, woman? I said to get dressed." Drake could not understand her lack of enthusiasm. Perhaps she was more ill than he thought.

Exasperated, Drake tromped to the wardrobe and pulled it open. Five or six dresses hung there, along with her father's tattered coat that she was wearing when Drake found her. He grabbed the first dress his hand touched and tossed it on the bed. "You can't go out like that, Shannon. Put this on so I can take you into the city." She looked up at him, clearly surprised.

Her reaction encouraged Drake, so he continued. "I have been thinking, Shannon. We are going to be a family, you and I, and the child."

She cringed. "I don't want a family with you, not ever!"

Drake nodded in understanding. "I know. It is because I have not been as good to you as I ought. But I am changing that. Today I will take you into Boston and show you the city. Tomorrow, perhaps we will take a ride in the country and find a house for you. You and the child will need a fine home."

Shannon eyed him as if he were insane, then her expression softened as she looked at the dress on the bed. "You will really take me out of this place?" she asked incredulously.

Drake smiled. He was hoping that with offers of freedom and finery she would come around. He did not expect it this quickly, though. "This very morning. As soon as you get dressed." He stood there, waiting for her to commence dressing.

Shannon remained unmoving. "I would rather dress by myself," she ventured.

Drake frowned. "Are you still so modest after so many months together?" He stepped closer to her and placed his hands on her hips. "What if I help you out of your bed clothes?"

She took one step back before replying. "A lady dresses by herself, Byron."

Brief disappointment filled his frame, then he remembered his true purpose for the day. "As you wish, my dear," he replied. "I will leave the door unlocked. Meet me downstairs when you have made yourself ready." Drake stepped closer to her once again, then kissed her before stepping out the door. True to his word, he left it unlocked.

As he opened the large oak door at the top of the stairs, he paused. There had been something different about that particular kiss. It had been softer, more compliant than Shannon's usual response. It was very much out of character for her, even in light of his new found kindness. He knew her better than to assume that she was so easily won by a few promises. The memory of the breeze easing through the open window caused him to turn on his heel and march back to her door. He knocked heavily.

"Shannon!" A soft, muffled thumping sounded from somewhere above him, and he crashed through the door into an empty room.

"Shannon!" His voice was full of thunder and venom as he thrust his head through the window just in time to see Shannon being lowered down a rope tied to the kitchen chimney by – Mr. Smith! A wordless roar of rage erupted from Drake as he drew his gun and fired at the man from his perch on the window. The shot blew past Mr. Smith's right ear, and the offending man drew his own pistol and returned fire at Drake.

Drake ducked into the window, gathered his fortitude, then made a bold leap straight through the window and onto the roof. He held the edge of the window with one hand so that he wouldn't topple down the steep slope, and with the other he shot more deadly projectiles toward Mr. Smith. The man returned fire again instead of slithering down the rope, keeping Drake at bay.

As the man popped over the edge of the roof for another quick shot, Drake fired again, and the bullet ripped through Smith's shirt and straight through his right arm. Mr. Smith cried out in pain, but managed to keep hold of the rope. Drake darted as quickly as he dared across the steep roof as Mr. Smith pulled a knife from his belt with his injured arm.

Drake immediately realized the danger. If Mr. Smith cut the rope before Drake could get to him, then Shannon's escape would be certain.

"No!" shouted Drake. He was almost to the chimney. The rope was barely attached, and its threads were almost cut through as Drake reached out to grab Smith's collar. The weight of Smith was too great, however, and the last threads of the rope broke, letting Smith literally fall right through Drake's fingers.

Lunging over the side, Drake saw Smith land on a few stacked crates then roll onto his feet, pulling the crates to the ground with him so that Drake could not easily follow. The man grabbed the terrified Shannon's hand and darted out of sight into the foggy alley behind The Crimson Dagger. Drake pointed his pistol in the direction of the fleeing pair, but the gun only clicked uselessly as Drake pulled the trigger. Disgusted, he shoved the empty pistol back into his belt.

"You can't take my child, Shannon!" Drake roared from the rooftop into the mist. "I will find you! I will have my child!"

Drake didn't wait for an answer, but quickly skirted to the window and nimbly jumped back inside the building. "Sam! Wells!" he bellowed at the top of his voice as he sprinted down the hall, taking the stairs two at a time to the first floor.

Smith may have taken Shannon, but not without a price – and that price was the hole in Smith's shoulder that was leaving a trail of blood for him to follow. With any luck, Drake would be able to track them down, kill Smith in the most horrible way he could think of, then deal with Shannon. He would make sure that she never tried to leave him again.

With four of his own men following hot on his heels, Drake tore out the door and to the back of his building, hunting for the scarlet trail that would lead him to his child.

22

Darcy knew that time was not his friend right now. Drake was close behind them, and Shannon's bare feet did not aid their haste of escape. But she still ran as quickly as he did, her hand glued tightly to his.

"Hold a moment, Mr. Adams!" she said breathlessly, pulling up to a stop without letting go of Darcy's hand.

"We don't have a moment, Miss Tiernan. We must continue or we will be overtaken!"

Shannon ripped part of the hem from her night gown and quickly wrapped the rag around his injured arm as she answered him. "He will be sure to find us if you leave him a trail." Tying the two ends of the fabric as tightly as she could at the site of the wound, she staunched the slow weep of blood running down his arm and dripping off of his fingers and onto the street.

Darcy granted her the moment, then nodded to her gratefully as he took her hand once again and resumed a hurried run down back alleys toward the outskirts of Boston. "You are a clever girl, Miss Tiernan," he remarked through heavy breaths. She could only nod, the exertion of the flight was taking its toll on her. "We are almost there," he added, hoping that some encouragement would help the poor girl to persevere.

In the fog behind them, Darcy could hear men shouting. It was far too close for comfort. He quickened his pace, almost dragging the already spent girl. His arm was starting to throb hatefully, and each step was costing him in endurance and pain. Almost there. The carriage should be just ahead.

More shouts from behind filtered through the fog, and Darcy recognized the distinctly angry curses of Byron Drake. He could only surmise that their pursuers had been following the trail of blood he had inadvertently left for them, and had now come to the spot where Shannon had tied off the bleeding.

A soft glow diffused through the mist about twenty feet in front of them, and another five feet revealed that it belonged to a lamp hanging gracefully from the front of a black carriage. Before Darcy and Shannon even reached the cab, the door was thrown open to receive them. Darcy hurriedly lifted Shannon toward the arms that pulled her into the protective darkness before scrambling into the cab himself, shutting the door securely behind him.

"What kind of business are we about today, then?" William cast a curious glance towards his wife, who sat across from him in the carriage. When Josephine had invited him to accompany her on trip to the city this morning, he had assumed they would be going to one of their businesses in Boston. Instead, the driver had taken them to an obscure corner on the outskirts of town, closer to the slums than to the financial district.

Crossing her legs and folding her hands around her knee, Josephine smiled, not happily, but rather with purpose. "The kind you said I could not attend to without you," she responded.

"Ah," William replied. "I should have known when we didn't go directly into Boston. Isn't it early for this kind of venture?"

"My gentleman accomplice informed me this was the only time to retrieve this young woman," she answered thoughtfully.

"Mr. Adams?" William queried.

Josephine raised a surprised eyebrow in his direction. "I see you have been talking to Dr. Stone," she responded, her slight smile growing a bit.

"After the incident with your other driver, I thought it prudent to be knowledgeable of the entire story." Josephine blushed slightly with the mention of the other evening. It had been horrible in one respect, true, but she had also spent the evening in William's sheltering arms.

In all her twenty-six years, she had never felt anything so blissful as just sleeping next to the man she loved.

Giddiness bubbled up in her stomach and threatened to betray her composure. She cast a look to her husband, wondering if he could see her thoughts. William was studying her carefully, with an almost amused expression on his face. She regained enough of herself to realize that an answer would be prudent to avoid any more awkwardness.

"I am rather relieved you know the story," she admitted truthfully. "I was at a loss as how to explain things fully. Dr. Stone did me a service by telling you." William didn't respond immediately, and Josephine wondered if his hesitation was an indication of his disapproval. She frowned, the giddiness changing to something less pleasant. Her friend, Ophelia, was right. William certainly did reduce Josephine to uncertainty, though she was sure it was not deliberate on his part.

"Perhaps you do not approve of these activities, William?" she ventured quietly, making certain her voice was more sure than her emotions.

Reaching across to his wife, William took her hand in his and fixed his intense, blue eyes on her. "I may worry," he offered, "but that does not mean I do not approve." His voice was rich and low, and the way he said his words made Josephine's heart almost stop. Could he really be developing a true affection for her? She dared not hope, but his recent actions suggested just that.

William did not let go of her hand, but leaned forward to close the distance between them. With profound, rapturous surprise, Josephine realized he meant to kiss her.

At that very moment, the sounds of running footfalls and the distant shouts of angry men pushed through the fog to disturb the pair in the carriage. Josephine turned her head from William and peered out the carriage window. It was Darcy, his right hand red with blood. Behind him he pulled a pale, distressed, blonde girl wearing only her bedclothes and a ragged coat.

Throwing the carriage door open, Josephine and William hurriedly pulled in the young woman as the cries of their pursuers rang closer. She quickly pulled the barefoot girl closer to her as Darcy sprang into the carriage next to William. Darcy's surprise at the extra passenger was only surpassed by William's at the sight of the bleeding bandage tied around Darcy's arm.

"Good heavens, man!" William exclaimed as the driver urged the horse into a gentle trot. "You've been shot!"

Darcy smiled through a grimace. "Very astute, sir." He then focused on the young woman whom Josephine was now cradling. He leaned forward and lay his left hand on her shoulder. "You are safe now, Miss Tiernan."

"Indeed you are, Miss Tiernan," added Josephine.

As a group of men rounded the corner, barely visible through the fog, Josephine lowered the fabric shutter of the window, denying any outside eyes from seeing into the carriage. Just before the screen closed fully, she caught sight of a striking, blonde man who was leading the others through the street. His expression was full of murder and hate, and his cold, clever gaze met hers for the slightest of moments.

It was enough. In that instant, Josephine saw the face of her enemy, and she began to pray.

Drake returned to the misty Boston corner where he had lost the blood trail that had been leading him to Shannon. He clenched his fist angrily and cursed. They were simply gone. Smith had waltzed into his inn, taken his woman and child, and disappeared, leaving behind nothing but a few drops of wretched blood. Drake would spill more than that when he saw Mr. Smith next. He would make Smith's blood run down the gutters with the rest of the refuse!

The plain woman in the carriage had struck him as odd. He had only caught a glimpse of her before she shut the blind, but there was something in her demeanor that made him uncomfortable. He couldn't put his finger on it, but it was there.

Drake shook his head. That woman was of no consequence. He needed to concentrate on finding Shannon, and to do that, he needed to find out all he could about Smith.

23

The carriage was still well within Boston when Josephine addressed Darcy. "Punctual as always, Darcy," she said as William began unwrapping the rags from his right arm. Shannon was residing in Josephine's embrace, and seemed to be in a state of uneasy sleep against her shoulder.

Darcy nodded through a pained smile. "And I have never been more glad for your own timing, Josephine." He turned his attention to William. "I believe that we have met before, sir, though not under such fine circumstances."

William tore the man's shirt sleeve open and inspected the bullet hole carefully, then he looked at Darcy and began to chuckle. "Indeed, Mr. Adams," he replied. "It seems you can go nowhere without someone wanting to cause you bodily harm."

"You two have already met, then?" Josephine asked quietly.

Darcy nodded. "Your husband attempted to remove my head from my shoulders with one blow. I am very fortunate his father was there to restrain him."

Josephine smiled as William offered an uncomfortable explanation. "It was the night of the Spring Ball, and I thought he was behaving in an unscrupulous fashion toward the young woman."

"The one you saw at Rosewood Hall while we were riding," offered Josephine. She looked at Darcy. "I simply must pay you more."

Darcy laughed, then winced as the motion caused him pain. "We will take you to the carriage house and call for Dr. Stone," Josephine added, concern clouding her face as she observed his wounded arm.

Darcy began to shake his head and speak, but Josephine broke in. "This injury is too serious, Darcy. You must have proper care."

"The bullet went right through. I don't even think it touched the bone. I can patch it up myself."

She shook her head. "No, Darcy. Not this time."

"Has this happened before?" William asked incredulously, still trying to fully take in the entirety of the situation.

"Minor wounds," answered Darcy. "A few cuts and bruises, perhaps a broken nose. It comes with the territory."

Darcy leveled his eyes right at Josephine's and clenched his jaw. "He saw me, Josephine. He saw me as close as you do now. And he is dangerous. There can be no contact at all between you and I. I should not even be here now. If he ties me to you in any way..."

"It is too late." Josephine's matter of fact statement made both of the men in the carriage stare at her through worried expressions.

"What do you mean?" William asked, a dangerous edge in his voice.

"He saw me, as well," she answered, "just before I shut the blind. It is only a matter of time before he reasons out how you escaped and who I am."

"The one waiting on the bridge," offered Darcy, understanding lighting his expression. Josephine nodded. "He will realize you were the one waiting there that night."

Comprehension fell on William, as well, and anger began to grow on his face. "This is the same man who shot your driver? Who sent that poor girl over the bridge? Who tried to kill you?"

Not answering, Josephine looked steadily at William. Darcy answered in her stead. "I believe the men are one and the same. His name is Byron Drake, and his easy violence acts as his signature," Darcy gazed at the exhausted Shannon, "and these girls bear the brunt of his brutality."

William leaned forward to his wife, anger making his frown seem harsh. "How could you knowingly put yourself in danger again?" He shook his head as he sat back. "Why didn't you tell me, Josephine? I cannot allow you to continue in this. I will not!"

Darcy looked uncomfortably from William to Josephine, who was eying her husband with an expression he had not seen before. It had the attributes of sadness, but also of a fierce determination that made Darcy shift uneasily in his seat.

"I do not need your permission, William. I am not beholden to any man."

"I am not any man, Josephine! I am your husband!"

She did not acknowledge William's demand with a response. Instead, she fixed her gaze on Darcy. "I cannot force you to acquiesce to my wishes about Dr. Stone, but I am asking you as one who is very concerned. And if Mr. Drake indeed knows your face as intimately as you believe, then you must not venture into Boston again until he is dealt with."

"There is one more I must find," Darcy countered.

"Who?" William asked incredulously. "Who could merit such risk? This is all insanity!" He raised his arm to Darcy's shoulder to emphasize his point.

"A little boy," replied Darcy. Josephine and William both turned their heads to him. Darcy continued. "Miss Moore, the girl in the carriage, had a brother. I promised her I would find him. I have not seen him since the incident with his sister, but I have not been able to properly search for him these last few days, either."

Nodding reluctantly, Josephine added, "Then you must find him. But let Dr. Stone attend to you first."

"Dr. Stone must attend to Miss Tiernan first," he said. "She is with child."

Looking down at the girl, Josephine could make out the swelling of her abdomen, which showed her to be four, perhaps five months along. She moved her eyes to the poor girl's face, which still bore the signs of recent abuse. Byron Drake was proving to be more monstrous than Josephine had first imagined.

As her eyes consumed the bruised face of the girl in her arms, a dark thought returned to Josephine, one which she had banished weeks ago. Drake had to be dealt with, but what means was Josephine willing to employ? The man had almost killed Darcy, and had abused this poor girl in the vilest of ways. He deserved to die. She closed her eyes and put the thought from her again, though not with the same disdain as before.

"As you wish, Darcy," she replied. She moved her gaze from the girl to William, who sat with a resolute, stern expression over his features. As her unflinching eyes met his, William's eyes also looked at the girl's face, and his expression softened slightly. Josephine's stare remained determined, however, and Darcy, who had known Josephine for most of his life, was grateful to not be William Dunham at this particular moment.

24

Painful, wracking coughs tore through the little boy's body as he huddled closer to the wall he was sleeping against. For days, Murray had searched all of the Boston that he was familiar with, wandering up and down the streets, peering into the faces of every lady with long, red hair. When he had not found her, he extended his search to the unfamiliar streets, where the fine ladies turned away from him in disgust, and the gentlemen kicked at him to discourage him away from the civilized portion of the city.

The abuse had not deterred him. His sister was somewhere, - she had to be. Mr. Drake was lying. At first, he thought that the man was nice. After all, he had given them a house to sleep in and jobs to do. But after a while, Murray had heard Mr. Drake yell angrily at the other girls that lived in his house. He had even seen Mr. Drake hit them sometimes.

He had never seen Mr. Drake be mean to his sister, though, and that counted for something. But then Mr. Drake had hit him, and yelled at him, and told him lies about his sister. And even if Mr. Drake had not thrown him out, Murray would still have left to look for Erin. But where was she?

Even though Murray's determination never faltered, his little body was not as stout. For a week, his only subsistence had been a few bits of moldy bread he had found in the gutter. When added to the cold nights with no shelter, the result was a nasty cough that began in Murray's throat, and quickly descended into his chest.

As the new morning dawned, Murray knew that he must get up and resume the search for his sister, but he could not will his limbs to raise his body from the alley. Every time he coughed, a miserable burning ripped through his chest and throat, and his head throbbed painfully. Perhaps he would rest a little while longer before going onto the streets. He was so tired. Erin would want him to rest.

Another fitful cough caused him to curl up into a tighter ball on the ground, then whimper in misery when it was over.

"Little boy?" A far off voice made its way into his head, and he braced for the inevitable kick that was sure to follow. Instead, a gentle hand shook his shoulder.

"Little boy, can you hear me?" It was a woman's voice. Could it be Erin? Murray opened his eyes to see a pretty, blonde lady with big, blue eyes stooping over him.

"Do you know where my sister is, lady?" he asked her. Surely someone this pretty would be able to help him find his sister.

The lady put an arm under Murray and helped him sit up. "Where do you live, child? You are burning up! I need to get you home!"

Murray turned his head as another cough tore through him. "I don't live anywhere, lady," he finally answered, "not since Mr. Drake kicked me out." He looked up at her with pleading eyes. "I just need to find my sister. I haven't seen her for a week. Can you help me?"

The lady lifted Murray to his feet and pulled him close to her side. "I am going to help you," she answered, "but we have to get you well before we can find your sister." The little boy was too sick to do anything but go along with the woman.

They didn't have to go far before the woman turned from the sidewalk to a brick building. She took a key from her reticule and unlocked the simple, white door in front of them. After ushering the boy through, she led him to a room in the back and let him crawl onto the examination table. She had to wake him gently when she returned with a bitter, sticky syrup for him to swallow, which he did without complaint. Then, after drinking an entire glass of clean, cool water, Murray fell into a grateful, if somewhat fitful, sleep.

25

Josephine had kept her distance from William for the past few days, though as far as he could tell, she hadn't ventured out in the evening, either, and so didn't violate his wishes. There was a price, however, and William found he sorely missed her company throughout the day.

He settled himself in the library chair in front of the fire, considering how to make amends with his wife while still keeping her safe. He admired what she did, her indelible spirit, and her compassion. But she was placing herself in danger, and it was his duty to keep her safe. He had promised her father.

As he stared miserably into the dancing flames of the fireplace, William pondered his other reasons for asserting his authority over Josephine, and his mind raced back to the night he had sheltered her protectively inside his arms.

He had only meant to make her feel safe, to reassure her all would be well, that he was there for her. But the smell of her hair and the warmth of her skin had not left him, not even after days and days. The light in her eyes and the way she smiled at him after that night left him... what?

This was not the same emotion he had felt for Elisabeth. That feeling had been all encompassing and devouring, not leaving room for thoughts of anything else. This was more like a seedling, small and slight in its springtime infancy, but tall and green and beautiful in the summer sun.

Without him even knowing it, the roots of that seedling had spread deep into him, and the thought of losing Josephine filled him with a dread he had not known before. And strangely enough, he had not even thought of Elisabeth in the past few weeks.

How could he make Josephine understand what he felt, his reasons for keeping her from her philanthropy? At this point, he was at a loss as how to answer those questions.

"May I join you, sir?" Ophelia's cheery voice beside him jolted him out of his reverie. He had been so lost in thought he had not even heard her enter the library. She placed a tray with a teapot and two cups on the table, then seated herself without awaiting his permission.

William frowned under a raised eyebrow. "I suppose," he responded, hoping his tone would convey his disapproval at her lack of propriety. He understood that Ophelia was a close friend to his wife, but she was still a servant, nonetheless.

If Ophelia caught his tone, then she did not acknowledge it. Instead, she poured two cups of tea, handed one to William, then took one herself and reclined in the wing chair, sipping the hot liquid as she did so. William could no longer let her behavior go without comment.

"Ophelia," he began in a rather stern voice, "I know you have been with this family since childhood, but you are behaving as an equal instead of a servant. This behavior on your part simply cannot continue."

"Of course, sir," she responded, but her tone was rather dismissive. "However," she continued without changing her position or demeanor, "I came to speak to you about your wife."

William sat up quickly. "Really Ophelia, that is none of your concern! This very insolence is the type of behavior I am addressing."

"She loves you, sir," Ophelia replied, ignoring his previous comment and commanding his silence with her words. "I have watched these past few months as her emotion for you has grown into something that makes me quite happy. So it pains me to see things strained between you, especially after she has taken you into her confidence."

"What am I supposed to do?" William sat back in exasperation as he answered, defeated in his efforts to reign in Ophelia's attitude to its proper social station. "I cannot allow her to go gallivanting about Boston rescuing these poor girls! I realize they need help, that they need someone to intervene for them, but it can no longer be my wife. I cannot allow any harm to come to her!"

Ophelia nodded in understanding. "I agree with you, sir," she offered, "I truly do. But you do not understand the position you are putting her in."

"What on Earth do you mean?"

"Mrs. Dunham will not abandon her work, nor any of those girls. And should you continue to work against her, well..." Ophelia sipped her tea, though a frown crossed her brow, "she will contrive a way to deal with you, despite her affection for you. I would not be surprised if you found yourself waking up on the finest steamer bound for England for an extended visit to your family."

"Of all the...!"

Ophelia held up her hands defensively. "I would never approve of such a thing, sir," she hastened. "I am just making you aware of your wife's determination. If such a thing were to happen, it would undoubtedly damage your attachment for one another, and Josephine would not be the better for it. But she will do something to continue her work without interference from you. I have seen her deal with her obstacles, and she is quick, creative, and thorough."

Seeing his alarmed expression, Ophelia added quickly, "Though she would never harm anyone, especially you. Please, Mr. Dunham, do not be at odds with her on this."

She gave him a final, earnest look. Satisfied that she had been understood, Ophelia stood and returned her teacup to the tray. Taking William's cup from him, she refilled it, set it back on the round table between the chairs, curtsied quite properly, then left the room.

Insolent, that is what she is, William thought. But was she also correct? Truth be told, he was quite shocked at the idea that Josephine would 'deal' with him. But Ophelia seemed very concerned, more over the effect it would have on his wife than himself.

Then he smiled. The more William thought about it, the more certain he was that his wife would find some creative way to continue her philanthropy without his approval. Strangely, the thought of Josephine's adeptness stirred a sense of pride in his chest. She was the most capable person he had ever met, and she was his wife.

Ophelia was quite correct. He did not want to miss out. Rising from his chair, he poked his head out of the library.

"Ophelia," he called, hoping the maid was still upstairs.

She quickly returned to the hall from her mistress's chambers. "Yes, sir?" she responded.

"Would you kindly ask Mrs. Dunham if she would share lunch with her husband today, then bring our meal to us on the veranda?"

Ophelia smiled largely. "I would love to, sir. But," she continued, "Mrs. Dunham departed for Boston over an hour ago. I doubt she will be back until the afternoon."

William frowned, thinking about Byron Drake happening upon the same place as his wife. "Did she say what her business was?"

"Yes, Mr. Dunham. She said that she needed to visit your father's bank. She left with one of the ledgers your father provided for her." As if Ophelia could read his thoughts, she added, "Mrs. Dunham asked Albert to accompany her, sir."

William nodded. "Thank you, Ophelia. Oh -" he added before she could exit the hall, "please tell Hans to ready my horse. Just the reins – no saddle."

Ophelia wore a confused expression, but she curtsied nevertheless and set off to find Hans. William started downstairs to retrieve his coat. He needed to repair his bond with his wife.

26

Sitting quietly at a small table in the corner of the busy bank, well away from the opening and closing of the main door, was Josephine Dunham. To any bystander who happened to notice, the woman seemed busy reading a ledger by the light of the window behind her. But given her plain face and her modest sense of dress, she was not noticed by many at all in the bustling establishment. Mrs. Josephine Dunham was counting on that very fact.

The bank manager, Doyle Blythe, and her father had done quite a bit of prosperous business in the past, and the relationship had naturally carried over after Josephine began managing most of her father's business affairs. The death of her father had only served to endear her more to many of the long time business acquaintances of the Hamilton family, and Mr. Blythe was no exception. So when Mrs. Dunham had asked Mr. Blythe to personally and discreetly keep track of who was making certain withdrawals, he had been more than willing to assist.

The tangle of accounts weaving from Duke Dunham's former holdings to this particular account was a complex labyrinth, to be sure, but this account was the final pool to which all the other flows of money eventually settled. It had taken her and her accountants months to unwind the path, but they had done it, carefully and quietly.

Mr. Blythe had sent her a letter a week ago, after a gentleman of interest had made three withdrawals in a row on the same day of the week, almost at the same hour each time, from this account. The name on the account was simply Mr. Brown, which was certainly not his real name. Nothing could be learned about this man without actually seeing his face.

So Josephine sat unobtrusively in the corner, waiting for a single man to make a small withdrawal from his account, and thus identify himself as the man responsible for Duke Dunham's near financial destruction.

Albert was waiting, as well. The competent, older man was standing at the opposite side of the bank, leaning casually against the wall. He had worked for the Hamilton's for many years, and his quick wit and decades of experience made him one of Josephine's most valuable allies.

As soon as Albert knew who the culprit was, he would discreetly follow the man, learning where he resided, how he made his living, and who he really was. Hopefully, by the end of the month, the matter of the Dunham's financial distress could be legally addressed, though the money that had been lost would probably never be recovered. The thief could be arrested however, and that would count for something.

The minutes ticked by, and customers came and went through the doors of the bank. Still, Josephine did not see the almost imperceptible nod from Mr. Blythe that would indicate the presence of the culprit. Then, to Josephine's surprise and alarm, a well-dressed young man strode confidently through the doors and up to a teller. His blonde hair and handsome features were those of the man she had seen through the fog from the carriage the day they had retrieved Miss Tiernan. His expression today was pleasant, sharply contrasted to the murderous rage that was displayed on his features when she first saw him.

The man did not seem to see her at all, and Josephine willed herself to shrink into the gloom of the corner and become invisible. She was hoping that he had not yet pieced together her role in the foray of the other morning, and she did not want to remind him of her existence just yet. As she watched the man, who she was certain was Byron Drake, Mr. Blythe casually glanced at her, then barely nodded his head.

So, Mr. Drake was quite industrious! Not only was he making money from the girls he took from the wharfs, he was also embezzling funds from wealthy foreigners. Somehow, he had managed to persuade Duke Dunham's financial manager to do business with him, and thereby gain access to the duke's finances. Josephine wondered how many other businessmen he had exploited financially, and how vast his resources were. Byron Drake might prove to be a very difficult man to deal with.

Drake concluded his business at the teller's window, placed several notes in his inside jacket pocket, then turned and looked directly at Josephine. She caught her breath, but resigned herself to a calm demeanor as the man walked to her table and sat down. Albert started toward her from his position across the bank, but Josephine shook her head slightly.

"Good morning, miss," he began, smiling pleasantly. "I hope I am not too presumptuous in introducing myself, but I recognize your face from the other morning. Byron Drake, at your service, my lady." Drake rose and bowed graciously.

Josephine inclined her head to him and responded, "I am Mrs. William Dunham, sir." She did not extend her hand, but Drake reached across the table, took it, and raised it to his lips. His eyes narrowed slightly as he kissed the back of her hand. Revulsion rose up in Josephine's throat, but she kept it from her face.

Releasing her hand and resuming his seat, Drake continued the conversation. "So you are, or were, Josephine Hamilton. Am I correct?"

Josephine nodded, keeping a pleasant look on her face. "You are correct," she replied, wondering what his purpose could be in singling her out for conversation. She was certain his intent was malicious. She could feel it emanating from the man through his handsome smile.

"Your reputation for business proceeds you. When I learned you were to marry Duke Dunham's son, I had to drastically reduce my activity in his accounts." He smiled slyly at Josephine's obvious shock. Why was he flagrantly admitting his theft of Duke Dunham's funds?

She frowned. This man was arrogant beyond belief, and dangerously confident. Silent prayers were underscoring her conversation, and she felt her Father's peace ease her spirit as she spoke. "What business do you have with me, Mr. Drake? Say it so we can conclude this discussion."

Byron Drake smiled and sat back, crossing his legs and bringing his fingertips together. "First, Mrs. Dunham, your presence here indicates to me that you have uncovered the nature of my business with your father-in-law."

"I would hardly call it business, Mr. Drake. Piracy is more the proper term."

"It matters not what you call it, Mrs. Dunham. The duke gave financial jurisdiction to his business manager, and that manager signed a contract with me. It is all perfectly legal, I assure you."

Josephine's mouth cocked in a wry, half smile. "Then why, sir, have you taken such pains to hide your business? I take no confidence in your assurances, and I highly doubt the legality of your methods."

Drake sat forward, staring Josephine directly in the eye. "Challenge me in court, then, Mrs. Dunham. Try to persuade a judge that the convoluted trail your accountants followed really does lead to me. It will take months to sort it all out legally, and in the meantime, I will be free to ravage your husband's finances." He smiled as he looked her up and down lasciviously. "And yours, as well, now that you are married to the man."

Refusing to be intimidated, Josephine kept his gaze, though she was certain the aversion she felt had finally made its way to her expression.

When she didn't reply, Drake continued. "Second, I know you are interfering with my business ventures on Ann Street. One girl, in particular, is quite dear to me, and I lost her just as I saw you setting off in your carriage a week ago. I wish her returned to me at once."

Josephine raised an eyebrow, her spirit mounting in offense at the arrogant insistence of the man. "Since we are speaking frankly with one another," she replied, "you can be quite certain you will never lay a hand on Miss Tiernan again."

The smile that had been pleasantly sitting on Drake's face fell at the mention of Shannon's name. Josephine turned her head with interest as she observed his reaction. "Furthermore, I will not rest until I see you and your "ventures" undone, Mr. Drake. You are an abomination to humanity, and a scourge to this city."

Drake resumed his previous, cordial demeanor, and his eyes twinkled as if she had just given him the finest of compliments. "Indeed, I am, Mrs. Dunham, and you would do well to remember that fact." He rose and bowed. At the lowest point of his bow, Drake leaned close to Josephine, his mouth almost to her ear, and whispered, "Until next time." She felt the hairs on the back of her neck rise as the evil air of the man brushed against her.

Albert had been watching the encounter closely, and when Drake moved so close to Mrs. Dunham, he started toward them. Drake stood up and looked directly at him. Albert stopped in his tracks, realizing Drake's intention had been to flush out any accomplice Mrs. Dunham might have in the room, and that he had been successful.

Drake tipped his hat at Albert, nodded amiably to Mrs. Dunham, then exited the bank with the same confident air with which he entered it.

Albert made his way to Josephine as she rose from the table. "Are you all right, Mrs. Dunham?" he asked with concern.

"I am fine, Albert," she replied, though her insides felt as if they might revolt at any moment. She took the arm he offered, nodded silent thanks to Mr. Blythe, then made her way to the waiting carriage.

Albert scanned the street in both directions. "Should I follow him as we originally planned?" he inquired, opening the door for her.

As she ascended into the cab, Josephine shook her head. "It would serve no purpose. We already know all too much about Mr. Drake, and you would be put in unnecessary danger." Josephine smiled warmly at Albert. "Instead, would you care to accompany me home?"

Albert returned her smile and climbed into the cab opposite her. "It would be my pleasure, ma'am," he answered.

Urging the horse into a trot, the driver carefully navigated through the pedestrians until the cab was closer to the less populated outskirts of Boston. Neither Josephine nor Albert, who were discussing the events of the last thirty minutes, noticed that the driver of the cab was not the same man who had driven them to town.

27

William enjoyed a pleasant ride toward Boston. His favorite steed, Hero, trotted effortlessly down the smooth, dirt lane, enjoying the unusually light load of his rider minus the saddle. The autumn day was mild, with the warm sun bathing everything in its rich brightness. The lane was mostly uninhabited, as William had seen only one other traveler on his journey so far. These conditions would make for an equally pleasant trip home, and William was looking forward to surprising Josephine with an afternoon ride.

Spying the carriage rounding a far corner in the road ahead, William urged Hero into an easy canter to close the distance between them. As he neared the carriage, he saw Albert's graying head and the lovely brown tresses of his wife through the window of the cab.

"Aye, there," he called cheerfully to the driver, who pulled the carriage to a stop. William didn't recognize the man, but Josephine had several drivers. She recognized his voice and curiously looked out the window.

"William!' she exclaimed, though not unpleasantly. "What brings you to Boston?"

William nodded his hat to Albert politely, then offered a stunning smile to his wife. "My destination is not Boston, my lady," he answered, "it is you."

Josephine blushed mildly and searched her vocabulary for an appropriate response, though her voice fled from her rebelliously. Albert only smiled at her befuddlement, enjoying the unusual sight of Mrs. Dunham at a loss for words.

William let her remain uncomfortable for only a moment longer before addressing her again. "Might I escort you home, Mrs. Dunham? It is truly a fine day, and I thought we should enjoy it together."

She smiled, then finally found her voice. "I would be honored, sir."

Albert opened the door for her and held her hand firmly as she took her leave of the carriage. Standing next to Hero, she eyed the saddleless horse suspiciously. Before she could make any queries as to how to mount the steed, William reached down with both arms and easily lifted her to a sidesaddle bearing in front of him. Placing his arms on either side of her waist, he grasped the reins firmly and urged Hero toward home, deliberately making their pace a little brisker than that of the carriage to ensure some privacy. The carriage also resumed its course, but it quickly fell behind the riding couple.

After the brisk trot had put sufficient distance between them and the carriage, William slowed Hero's pace to an enjoyable walk. Josephine still leaned close against him, and he felt that the expanse that had been between them the past week was melting away. They carried their easy silence for another few minutes, enjoying the nourishing sunlight and fresh breeze gently blowing past. William was not eager to break the spell of serenity, but he did come here for a purpose, and he needed to address that purpose.

"Josephine," he began, rather uncertain as to how to proceed, "I feel I may have been too harsh the other morning, and I wish to mend things between us. Frankly, I have missed you this past week."

Josephine breathed in deeply and turned her head slightly toward William's face. "No, William," she answered softly, "you were not too harsh. You were correct. And," she paused, as if the next few words were difficult, "I am the one that has been too harsh with you. I was entirely wrong to take my leave of your company." She turned to see his face more fully. "For that, I ask your forgiveness, William."

His smile was gentle as he continued to gaze forward. "Always, my dear." William felt as if the stifling cloud that had been weighing upon his brow had suddenly cleared. He was immediately happier. "Your business this morning was rewarding, I trust?" William asked, engaging in what should have been easy conversation with his wife.

Instead of offering an immediate reply, Josephine sighed heavily, and a frown troubled her face. "I did accomplish my objective," she finally offered, "but what I discovered is somewhat distressing."

William unconsciously tightened his arms around Josephine, sensing that something significant and sobering had happened at the bank. "What transpired this morning, Josephine?"

"I discovered who has been embezzling from your father's account."

"That is a good thing, is it not?" He was a bit perplexed.

"The man is Byron Drake, William." Her voice was soft and steady, but William could hear undertones of concern. William's own chest tightened with anger at the mention of Drake's name.

"How did you discover this?"

"The bank manager alerted me that a certain man had been making withdrawals on a fairly regular basis from an account that had been traced back to your father. I waited at the bank to see the identity of the man."

"Good heavens, Josephine! Drake was there, at the bank, with you?" His voice was filled with alarm and apprehension. "Are you all right?"

She quickly laid her hand on his shoulder. "I am fine, William. Though the conversation was quite unsettling."

"You spoke to him?"

"He sought me out directly. He has already pieced together everything." Her eyes were large as she looked into his. "He is wholly evil, William. I could feel the vileness of the man pierce right through me."

"Oh, Josephine," William sighed. "How is it that you keep getting into these situations? It frightens me to think about what might happen."

She nodded in understanding, but spoke confidently. "God keeps me in His hand, William. I draw great confidence from that."

William was silent. He was not going to trust his wife's safety to a deity he was not sure even existed, but he would never hurt Josephine by telling her so.

"Even so," he finally replied, "in light of the events of the morning, and at the risk of playing the hypocrite, I am asking that you do not venture out without your husband by your side. I know you are capable," he added hastily, "but I would never be right again if something should happen to you." In his heart he was preparing himself for Josephine to bristle and resume her silent anger toward him.

Instead, she nodded in acquiescence and said, "You are quite right, William. I should have trusted your judgment to begin with."

Pleasant surprise lit his face, and Josephine smiled up at him in response, then settled back comfortably against his chest as Hero's peaceful gait carried them along. Once again, William was aware of the smell of her hair, the warmth of her closeness. He would have to thank Ophelia when they returned home. Perhaps she was wiser than he gave her credit for.

A sudden thought caused him to draw Hero to a halt. "Josephine," he asked, concern trapped in his tone, "when did you get a new driver?"

Josephine sat up abruptly and looked at him. "I do not have a new driver."

"Blood and ashes!" William turned Hero suddenly and broke him into a gallop back toward the carriage, holding Josephine tightly around the waist with one arm and guiding Hero with the other. The span that had taken fifteen minutes before now only took three, and the stalled carriage soon came into sight, though the driver was nowhere to be seen.

William lithely dismounted Hero then lifted Josephine off the horse's back. He covered the distance to the carriage in three strides and yanked the already ajar door fully open. Josephine hurried to his side, then stood as motionless as her husband at the scene inside the cab. Albert's lifeless body lay across the seat of the carriage, the knife wound across his neck leaving no doubt about what had just happened.

Josephine cried out with an agonizing sound of shock and sorrow, and William immediately turned to shield her from the sight. "Oh God! Why?" she wept. "Why?" William moved her away from the carriage and toward Hero as he continued to embrace her tightly, keeping her face turned from the horrific sight. Once to his horse, William lifted Josephine onto his back, then sprang up behind her.

"We can't leave him!" Josephine exclaimed, her voice almost strangled by her sorrow.

"We must find the constable, Josephine. Immediately!"

"Then I will stay with him, William. I can't leave him!'

William turned Hero back toward Boston. "Absolutely not! The wretch could return at any moment!" He broke into a gallop toward Boston with the weeping Josephine tightly pulled against him, knowing if he had not come to find her today, then she would be laying alongside Albert, broken and lifeless in that carriage.

"That is unacceptable!" William pounded his fist on the constable's desk to emphasize his extreme unhappiness. The busy office on Leverett Street was bustling with uniformed constables and a variety of vagrants and drunkards being hustled to the cells in the back of the building. The large room fell silent for a moment at the thunder of William's fist.

"I want that man arrested and dealt with immediately! He killed my wife's driver and would have dispatched her as well!" His volume was climbing by the second, and by the time he finished his sentence, William Dunham's voice was roaring with anger.

Constable Fairbanks, an unattractive, but fit man, with a touch of gray frosting his sideburns, found it necessary to stand and address Mr. Dunham face to face. "If you had proof Mr. Drake threatened your wife, then I could investigate. But as it is, Mr. Dunham, you have brought me nothing I can address in an investigation." His voice was firm and tinged with irritation.

"You mean the dead man in my carriage is nothing?" William was livid, and his frustration with the constable was more than transparent.

Josephine had regained her composure soon after William started for Boston, and she now sat at the constable's fine desk, watching her husband verbally wrestle with the lawman. She had known where this conversation would end after hearing the first few words out of Constable Fairbank's mouth, and knew also that her husband's efforts, zealous though they were, were in vain. So she sat quietly, waiting for the proper moment to extract herself and her husband from the crowded office.

"Of course I will investigate that poor man's death, sir," replied the exasperated constable. "But I will not jump to the conclusion that Mr. Drake is responsible. He is a well-known, successful businessman in Boston, and I will not ruin his reputation needlessly!"

"But he threatened my wife!"

"Mrs. Dunham," the constable turned to Josephine, hoping some form of reasonableness could be found with her. "What exactly did Mr. Drake say to you in the bank?"

"His parting words were 'until next time'," she replied. Relief quickly crossed the constable's face, and he turned back to William.

"See there, Mr. Dunham," he said, his voice filled with as much advocacy as he could muster. "Mr. Drake was being a gentleman, as usual. How can you expect me to accuse anyone of murder based on good manners?"

William placed both hands on the desk, vexation dripping from him. "Are you a dolt, man?" he asked with exasperation. "It was the manner in which he said it!"

"Were you there, sir?" the constable countered, his manner indicating that he took offense to William's suggestion.

"I already told you I was not."

"Are there any witnesses to this alleged threat?"

William looked as if he were about to strike the man. "The only witness, besides my wife, is lying dead in my carriage on the outskirts of Boston!" William slammed both hands on the desk, causing a considerable noise to again thunder within the room.

Josephine, seeing that the situation was progressing badly, quickly stood and placed her hand on her husband's arm. "William," she said softly, "please take me home. I am afraid I cannot bear any more of this."

William immediately softened, and even looked slightly alarmed. "I am sorry, Josephine," he replied, taking her by the hand. "We will be off at once." He returned his attention to the constable and sent him a withering look. "I expect you to ensure that justice is done, sir!"

Constable Fairbanks looked immensely relieved when Mrs. Dunham intervened, and he answered William with less agitation than a few seconds earlier. "That is exactly my job, sir. And I assure you I will see it through." He took Josephine's hand delicately between his own and said, "I know what a horrible trauma this has been for you,

Mrs. Dunham. Rest assured that I will find the murderous villain who did this."

Josephine nodded, but did not reply. She had already seen the nervous brow of the man as he argued with William, heard the defensiveness in his tone when he spoke about Byron Drake. Josephine already knew from his actions that this man had been bought and paid for, and that justice was not to be found here. She had nothing to say to him.

"Come, my dear," offered William, guiding his wife out of the office with a gentle arm behind her waist. After the constable shut the door behind them they made their way to Hero, and William took both of Josephine's hands in his own. "I truly am sorry, Josephine. I should have considered that bringing you here would be too taxing for you."

"No, William, I am fine. You need not worry. I could see, however, that the constable will be of no use in bringing Byron Drake to justice, and I wanted to be rid of him." William once again lifted Josephine onto Hero's back, then vaulted himself up behind her.

"Then we must consider our options," replied William. "There must be a way to make sure Drake is dealt with." For the second time that day, he urged Hero toward home, with Josephine sitting sidesaddle in front of him.

"I have been considering that very thing, William." A strange calmness accompanied her words, and there was a resolve in her eyes that made William uneasy. His thoughts went back to his earlier conversation with Ophelia, and her insistence that he not place himself at odds with his wife. William's discomfort grew as the silence between them lengthened, and he felt an emotion emanating from Josephine he could not identify. But it felt nothing of the wisdom and kindness that usually marked her bearing.

Watching through the curtained window of his lawyer's office, just across the street from the constable, was Byron Drake. He smiled with contempt as Mr. Dunham lifted his wife onto the horse. He had been hoping, of course, that his man would have been able to do away with Josephine Dunham. His life would have been made less complicated.

But the lady simply endured. Perhaps luck was with her today. No matter – there would be other days.

However, her continued existence most certainly assured an upcoming legal confrontation with the Dunham family, and Drake would not be unprepared. As soon as his man had returned and recounted the unintentional rescue of Mrs. Dunham by her husband, Drake had made his way to his lawyer's office. He was unexpectedly delighted to see the Dunham's exit the constable's office as he looked out the window.

"But sir," the lawyer interrupted Drake's thoughts, and Drake let the curtain fall back in place as he turned his attention to his lawyer. "You say you want to part with all of your holdings and possessions?" The lawyer's voice indicated he thought Drake was somehow jesting or mistaken.

"Did I not make myself clear, Mr. Thompson?" Drake responded curtly. "I said everything, and I meant everything."

"We will need a signature from the young woman, sir, indicating her agreement to this transaction."

"Transaction?" Drake questioned, a wounded air to his voice. "Dear sir, this is not a transaction, but a gift. I adore my lady with all my heart, and all I have is hers."

"I see," replied Mr. Thompson, rather skeptically. "No signature then?"

"As the young lady is not here, Mr. Thompson, I don't see how she can sign a completely unnecessary document."

"Mr. Drake," the lawyer said, sitting back in his chair and folding his hands in front of him, "in order for this gift to be legally binding, the records office will need proof you are actually gifting your properties to a real person, not some fictional character that serves as your legal shield."

Drake's tone lowered dangerously. "What are you suggesting, sir?"

"Nothing at all, Mr. Drake." The lawyer's words were nonchalant, as if he had conducted this conversation a hundred times before. "As your lawyer, I am just informing you that in order to be successful in your venture, you need a legal document stating this young lady is a real person."

"Fair enough, Mr. Thompson," replied Drake, pulling papers from the breast pocket inside his coat. "Will the indentured servitude papers that came with the young lady suffice?"

The lawyer sat forward and took the offered papers from Drake. As he scanned through them he said, "These seem to be authentic, Mr. Drake. I can see no reason to deny your request."

Drake sat back with a satisfied air. "Thank you, Mr. Thompson."

Mr. Thompson sat forward and looked Drake directly in the eye. "I assume you will be managing all of the holdings, even though the young lady will be the legal owner."

"Of course."

Mr. Thompson handed the papers back to Drake. "Very well, Mr. Drake," he said as he pulled a set of blank documents from one of the drawers in his desk. "You will soon have nothing in the world that can be legally taken from you. It will all belong to this lady of yours." He dipped his pen into an ink well on his desk and began to write.

"Once again, Mr. Drake, what is the young lady's name?"

Drake's triumphant smile could not be hidden as he answered, "Erin. Her name is Erin Moore."

28

When the Dunham's arrived at Hamilton Manor, Josephine took her leave of William as he recounted the events of the morning to the distraught household staff. Without a word, she ascended the stairs to her own suite, shut the door behind her, and fell to her knees in the center of the room.

"Oh God," she prayed, too distressed to keep her voice inside herself, "this was not supposed to happen! Albert is dead! How could you let this happen?"

Images from the blood soaked carriage invaded her mind, forcing wave after wave of chest splitting sorrow into her prayer. With them they carried another thought, the seed of which came to fruition in Josephine's heart at the constable's office, when she realized that the law would not hold Byron Drake accountable for his actions.

It was well within her abilities to deal with Byron Drake herself, quickly, silently, and with absolute finality. And frankly, it was what she wanted at this very moment, to do away with this murderous man who had caused so much suffering and bloodshed. If she did not, then Drake would find a way to end her, do away with William, and worse, keep enslaving and abusing those poor innocents who could not hope to fight against him. She knew it as sure as night follows day.

It would be quite easy to find a man who would do the job quickly and dispose of Drake's body efficiently. Her business dealings had exposed her to many unscrupulous characters, and she was sure a few well-placed inquiries would provide her with the name of a man skilled in that particular area.

The image of Albert's broken body rose again in her mind, and the nervous certainty that her driver was also dead caused her sorrow to edge into anger, then into a righteous fury demanding justice. It gave her strength and resolve, and she sat upright from the floor, sure of her path.

"Forgive me, God," she begged, her prayer barely above a whisper. The enormity of her resolve filled her with a horrible dread that crept up her spine, but she was more sure of herself than ever before. "Forgive me, Father, for what I must do."

She almost didn't recognize the voice as it brushed against her thoughts, but its shocking words drove her back to her face on the floor.

Love your enemies, bless them that curse you, do good to them that hate you, and pray for them which spitefully use you, and persecute you.

"You cannot mean it, God," she answered. "This man murdered Albert, my driver, and that poor girl, Erin! He abuses the helpless and profits from misery. He would see me and my family dead! I cannot pray for him!"

Pray for them which spitefully use you. The voice was gentle, full of love and understanding. But its demands were too much this time. Too much.

"I cannot let him continue to live, Father. He will destroy us, destroy William. I cannot! What of William? What of my husband? What of all those poor girls? Byron Drake deserves to die!"

Lean not on thine own understanding. Pray for them which spitefully use you.

"Oh God," she cried, "I cannot do this! I cannot!"

The whisper faded into silence, a burning silence that was almost more painful than the thought of interceding on behalf of Byron Drake. Josephine felt in her soul that this was a moment of utmost importance, and her God was waiting for her to decide. Did she trust Him? Did she truly trust Him?

And what of William? If she dispatched Byron Drake as she desired, what would become of William's soul? With one foul act she would declare her faith worthless and her God useless and untrustworthy.

Could any man ever place his faith in such a god? She knew William never would.

Josephine clenched her fists and brought them beside her forehead, which was still resting on her rug. Then she uttered the most difficult words that had ever left her mouth. "Oh Father," she began, "please have mercy on Byron Drake, and bring him to You." The words were so painful they threatened to choked in her throat. "I do not ask that he evade justice, but rather that You bring him to a place where he can be blessed by knowing You."

At that moment, Josephine felt herself break upon the Stone that the builders rejected, and her body crumpled completely as if all of her bones had dissolved. "Oh God," she pleaded, "please forgive me. I will trust You, Father. Please forgive me. Use me to bring that man to You, if You will."

She had not heard when her husband had pushed the door open slightly a few minutes earlier to check on her state. But he stood there now, watching and listening as the weeping and the words poured from her prostrate form. He did not disturb her, but stood silently transfixed as his wife earnestly prayed for the man that had tried, that very day, to kill her.

After a few more moments, he pulled the door closed, just as quietly as when he opened it, and turned toward his own chambers. As he passed the library, the thick, old tome lying on the round table caught his eye. What could be in that Book that held such sway over a force as unmovable as his wife? He paused at the arch, his memory vivid with the image of Mr. Hamilton sitting in the far chair, bent over that Bible in complete preoccupation.

Instead of continuing on to his room, William entered the library and sat in the same chair that Mr. Hamilton used to occupy. He pulled the old Book off the table and into his hands, then opened the pages and flipped through them unhurriedly. His fingers halted when a certain passage caught his eye, and he gave his full attention to the words in the book of Matthew.

"Ye have heard that it hath been said, thou shalt love thy neighbor, and hate thine enemy. But I say unto you, love your enemies, bless them that curse you, do good to them that hate you, and pray for them which spitefully use you, and persecute you."

Suddenly, William understood Josephine's prayer in full, and instead of closing the Book and replacing it on the table, he read far into the night.

29

The mid October day brought an unusual warmth and a cheerful Darcy Adams swinging a picnic basket over his arm. Shannon waited under the familiar oak tree, and smiled happily as he sat next to her on the blanket and unpacked lunch. This had become their daily routine while Darcy lodged at the carriage house, waiting for his arm to heal.

A bond between the two had sprung up overnight, though, from Darcy's perspective, it had been forming for much longer than that. He had given most of his waking hours the past few months to the purpose of finding Shannon Tiernan, and the beautiful culmination of his efforts now sat smiling in front of him.

"Darcy!" she cried as she saw the overabundance of food he placed on the blanket. "If you continue to feed me in this manner, I shall balloon out like a whale!"

"And a very lovely whale you would make, if I do say so," he replied with a mischievous smile.

"You are a cad, Mr. Adams!" she reprimanded happily, reaching for a bowl of baked apples.

His smile deepened as his eyes continued on her face, but there was a sadness underneath the smile. It did not escape Shannon's notice. She placed the bowl on the ground and studied him.

"What is amiss, Darcy?" she asked, their previous joviality gone.

"Did you know a girl named Erin Moore?" Darcy began.

Shannon nodded, sadness filling her own expression. "I did," she answered. "Erin was very kind to me. Byron told me that she had been…" Shannon looked into Darcy's face, the pain of the memories returning to her.

"Drake was responsible for her death," Darcy said, shaking his head. "I was there, and I tried to save her. I truly did."

Shannon reached out for Darcy's hand and held it in her own. "I am sure you did all you could," she responded.

Darcy shook his head again. "Not all," he replied. "She has a little brother."

"Yes," said Shannon. "His name is Murray, I believe."

"I was to retrieve him for her and bring him here. But after that night, after seeing what Drake did..." Darcy squeezed Shannon's hand and looked her directly in the eye. "I knew you were at The Crimson Dagger, so I gave all of my attention to find a way to free you. I was going to get the boy as soon as you were safe, but then I was injured and unable to look for him." He gestured to his healing right arm. "Now that I am healing properly, I must go and find the lad before any more time passes."

"But how can you find him? There are thousands of little boys in Boston."

"I know he is not living at The Crimson Dagger any longer, so I will comb the slums until I come across him."

Shannon frowned and shook her head. "Mr. Drake will see you, Darcy. He is not a man of mercy. You cannot go out there."

Darcy reached over and touched her cheek, his smile gentle. "I promised her, Shannon. That little boy needs me."

Shannon looked down at the ground, her frown deepening. "I know you are right, Darcy. I just... I fear for you."

Darcy moved his hand from her face to her blonde tresses. "Then pray for me, Shannon. Pray for me every day I am gone."

She returned her gaze to his face, unable to hide the anger and incredulity she felt at his request. "Pray?" she asked. "Darcy, if there were truly a God, He would not allow these horrible things to happen! I suffered, Darcy, and I was one of the fortunate ones. Other girls, like Erin, lost their lives because of that man! How could God allow such suffering? Do not ask me to pray, Darcy, because if there is a God, then I do not wish to know Him!"

Darcy sat back, a thoughtful expression on his face. It was clear he had not expected this reaction from Shannon. A sudden fear rose up in Shannon's throat as she watched Darcy's eyes. Would he reject her now because of her lack of faith? Silently, she chided herself for foolishly unleashing her tongue. The thought of not spending her days with him filled her with a terrible dread, and she found herself wishing that she had just agreed to Darcy's request instead of being so vocal.

After a few more moments of reflection, Darcy found Shannon's eyes and spoke. "I think you know, have somehow always known, that I love you." Shannon's eyes widened in surprise at his forthrightness, and she was about to answer him, but he continued before she could. "From the very first moment I saw you, I loved you with all my heart. A love like that is precious, it cannot be compelled or forced. No one can make me love you. If they did, it would not be love. And while I desperately hope you do love me as well, I would never want you to love me because you had to, because someone forced you to. That would mean nothing to me."

As he paused, her frown deepened. In the end, Drake had tried to make her love him, and it had only caused her to hate him more. The words coming from Darcy's mouth rang true, but Shannon sensed that he wasn't finished speaking, so she held her speech, even though the words "I do love you" were burning on her tongue.

"God gives us the choice, Shannon. It is the second greatest gift He has ever given us, the ability to choose to love Him. And some people do choose Him. Others, well, they choose to love themselves, and their choices lead to evil and suffering for others. God may allow it, but how could He not and still allow us to choose? I am so sorry for what happened to you, but it was not God's doing. And He will be with you, Shannon, no matter what you may go through."

Shannon tilted her head, the frown still present. "The second greatest gift?" she asked. "What, then, is the first?"

Darcy smiled. "It was Jesus, His Son, our key to Heaven."

"Most men do not speak of these things, Darcy." Shannon was uncomfortable now, and did not know how else to answer.

Darcy responded without hesitation, "They should. Promise me you will at least consider what I said."

Shannon studied Darcy's face carefully, saw his unhidden sincerity and affection. How could she not promise anything to this man? "I promise," she answered softly. His smile was one of relief. Summoning her courage, Shannon opened her mouth to share her own feelings for Darcy, but a sharp jolt in her abdomen made her jump.

"What is it? Are you all right?" Darcy's face was filled with immediate concern as he knelt closer to her.

Shannon smiled in surprise and placed her hands on her stomach as the baby kicked again. Her large, happy eyes looked up to Darcy, and she reached for his hand and held it against her. He smiled with wonder as the child made its presence known with another firm kick. Darcy put both of his hands on her rounding belly, feeling each movement of the small life inside her.

"Strong, like its mother," he said, almost laughing. Shannon could not speak for a moment, and happy tears spilled down her cheeks.

"Shannon?" Darcy said, noticing the tears. "Why are you crying? What is the matter?"

"I thought..." she began, trying to collect her thoughts enough to explain her sentiment. "I never thought I would be happy again, Darcy. I thought I would be scorned and condemned, and..." She wiped a tear with her hand. "I am happy for this child."

"As I said," replied Darcy, a hand on her cheek, "strong." He bent and kissed her lightly on her lips, barely letting his mouth linger. "I will not stay away from you for long, Shannon Tiernan." He rose quickly and started toward the carriage house, his stride full of certainty and determination. She knew Darcy would not rest until he found Murray Moore. With a small start of panic, Shannon realized she still had something to say to him.

"Darcy!" she called, rising from the ground. He turned, his infectious smile lighting up the sunshine. "Darcy, I..." Her words stuck in her throat. Why was she having so much trouble saying the words?

She had easily been able to voice her rejection of his God; why could she not now find words to tell him of her affection? His eyes only twinkled more as he realized her intent.

"I know," he said, then he turned and resumed his pace away from Shannon and into the uncertainty that waited for him.

30

Murray Moore had been awake since the first light of day peeped through the window of Dr. Stone's small living room. After the nice lady, Miss Beech, had brought him to Dr. Stone's office, he had taken his medicine every morning, then fallen into a healing sleep. In the daytime, he had slept on a small pallet that the doctor made in the corner of his office. In the evening, Murray went home with Dr. Stone and curled up on his couch.

When he woke up this morning, none of the pain that had plagued his head and chest remained, and the burning cough that had made him more than miserable was gone. Murray felt he was back to his old self, and he also felt it was time to get back to searching for his sister. Now that he was better, he had to go and find her.

He heard Dr. Stone rustling in the other room, so Murray pushed aside his blanket and crept into the kitchen. He quietly rummaged around, located the teapot and two cups, then put the water on to boil.

"Feeling better, I see?" Dr. Stone's deep, kind voice startled Murray momentarily, and he spun around still holding the teacups. "Easy, lad," the doctor chuckled. "It would not do to drop our teacups."

"No, sir. Sorry, sir," Murray stammered, a bit flummoxed at being surprised. He placed the cups on the table as Dr. Stone fetched the tea leaves for the pot from a cupboard. Murray continued, "I thought I would make you something this morning, seeing how you've been looking after me, and all."

"That is quite thoughtful, young sir," Dr. Stone replied. He gestured for Murray to sit down at the table, then pulled out a chair for himself. "You are looking well, lad."

"Thank you. I don't know where I would be now if it weren't for your nice lady finding me and you fixing me up with that medicine."

Dr. Stone smiled. "You mean, Miss Beech? Yes, she is a very nice lady. Not my lady, though."

Murray seemed surprised. "Beg your pardon, sir, but you look at her the way my da used to look at my ma. That's why I thought she was your lady."

Dr. Stone raised an eyebrow, as if he were processing a new thought. "Well, Murray," he said, his tone unmistakably changing the subject, "now you are better, we should try to find your parents. I am certain they are dreadfully worried for you."

"No, sir," replied Murray. The doctor wore a puzzled expression, so Murray continued, "My da died three years back in Ireland, and my ma died on the boat ride over. I imagine they don't have any worries now." His tone was not sad, though it was not devoid of emotion, either. It seemed as if Murray knew this world was one of hardship, and was grateful his parents were someplace better.

Dr. Stone sighed, his own thoughts briefly settling on the cruel difficulties of life that left a little boy an orphan. The teapot announced that the water was hot enough for tea, and Dr. Stone rose and poured some into each cup. The steam from the two cups rose lazily from the liquid and intertwined above the table. "Do you have any family, lad? Anyone who will be looking for you?"

"Yes, sir." Murray's expression lit up. "I have an older sister. I was looking for her when your nice lady... I mean, Miss Beech... found me."

"Why were you looking for her? How did you lose each other?"

"My sister used to work for Mr. Drake, and so did I. Then, one day he up and threw me out. Told me my sister was dead and that I had to get out. I knew he was lying, so I started looking for her." Murray took a grateful sip of the hot tea, then looked out the window. "Now that I am better, I need to go looking for her again." He cast a worried look to Dr. Stone, "Though I don't know how I'll ever repay you for making me better, sir."

Dr. Stone had not sipped his tea yet. He was sitting almost as still as his name, a dreadful realization sinking into his expression. He put the cup on the table and leaned forward. "Murray, is your last name Moore?"

"How did you know that, sir?" Murray's surprise was pleasant, as if the doctor had made the grandest discovery.

"And your sister's name was Erin?"

Murray frowned at the word 'was'. "Yes, sir. But how do you know all of that?"

Dr. Stone sat back, his frown full of concern and sadness. "Son," he began, "I am afraid Mr. Drake was telling you the truth about your sister. I was at the bridge where her carriage went over that night. I am so sorry, Murray."

Murray looked at the doctor with certainty. "Beg your pardon, sir, but you're wrong. I would know it if she were dead." It was quite evident from the young man's tone and expression that he would not be swayed. "Since she isn't, I have to go and find her. I am all that she has left in this whole world." Murray wrapped both his hands around the cup and took a sip of the hot tea, as if nothing about this conversation was disturbing or tragic.

Dr. Stone studied the boy in wonder, marveling at his tenacity of spirit. "Well then, since you are absolutely determined to go about your course, I have a proposition for you."

Murray raised his eyebrows and gave the doctor his full attention. "Yes, sir?"

"You are in need of a job, a place to stay, and schooling." Dr. Stone finally sipped his own tea. "Perhaps you can spend part of your time each day searching for your sister, maybe even running errands for me here and there while you are in Boston. The other portion of your day can be spent learning how to read and work your way around numbers. I will provide you with this instruction and lodging if you agree to look after my home and help me with whatever tasks I need assistance with. Well, son, what do you say?"

Without hesitation, the boy nodded in enthusiastic agreement. "I know a good deal when I hear one, sir," he answered. Finishing the rest of his tea, he plopped the cup down on the table and rose to retrieve his coat. "I will start looking for Erin right now, then be back this afternoon for your chores." Dr. Stone couldn't help but smile at Murray's infectious enthusiasm. The boy addressed the doctor one last time before hurrying out the door. "Are there any errands you want me to run while I am out this morning?"

"Ah, yes," Dr. Stone answered. He rose and found paper and plume, scribbled a quick note, then handed it to Murray. "Take this to the tailor's shop on Temple Street. It is two blocks east and a few more north from here."

"I know the one, sir," answered Murray, happy to have an errand to attend to. "Count it as done."

"Very good, lad. And be at my office by two this afternoon, or I shall have to dispatch Miss Beech from her duties to search you out."

Murray was already at the door. "Two sharp, sir. Yes, sir!" As he exited the door, Dr. Stone felt as if a whirlwind had just left his house. All was suddenly silent, and... lonely.

He sat back and enjoyed the rest of his tea, contemplating the little boy that had just shared the morning with him. He had immediately seen it was useless to try and convince the lad his sister was dead. Useless, and perhaps even cruel.

Instead, Dr. Stone found himself covertly committing to feed, educate, and raise this young man on a moment's whim. He was certain Murray did not understand the gravity of the agreement they had just entered into, or the life changing consequences it would have for the boy. No matter. From now on, Murray would be raised as a doctor's ward, not as a homeless street orphan. At least the child would look the part after a visit to the tailor today.

He chuckled as he placed his empty cup on the table next to Murray's and retrieved his coat. He had been alone for many years. He was tired of being alone. Maybe that was why he had taken Murray under his wing so quickly. Maybe that was also the reason he hurried happily to his office every morning to be greeted by his Miss Beech.

Pulling on his coat, Dr. Stone firmly shut the door to his empty house and made his way to his office, and to the young lady whom he was sure was already waiting for him.

Young Murray Moore received quite the shock when he arrived at the tailor's shop. It had been his plan to deliver the note as expeditiously as politely possible, then flee the uncomfortably refined haberdashery in favor of searching for his sister in the lesser parts of Boston. Instead, the tailor, a sharply dressed fellow with an aristocratic air, read the note through his spectacles, raised a quizzical eyebrow toward the poor boy, then began measuring Murray with his tailor's tape in a most uncomfortable manner. When Murray protested, the tailor told him none too gently to be still and silence his tongue.

To make matters worse, the tailor instructed him to return the hour after lunch for a 'more proper fitting'. The very words induced a new kind of dread in Murray's brain. He realized that the kind doctor was not going to have him running errands in his current tatters. While Murray was grateful for the gesture, he cringed at the thought of a properly starched shirt scratching his neck, well fitted trousers that he had to be careful not to rip, and fine shoes that could not endure an occasional mud puddle.

From a pragmatic angle, Murray was concerned that these clothes would result in more than a few pummelings for him should he venture into the areas around Ann Street. The other boys would not take kindly to a finely dressed prig running about their neighborhood.

As he finally escaped the tailor's clutches and fled out the door of the shop, Murray hatched a plan to keep his old clothes for the morning hours when he was searching for Erin, then change before he met with Dr. Stone in the afternoons. Satisfied with his scheming, he set off in haste toward the poorest section of Boston, where he was certain that today would be the day he would finally find his sister. Grimly, he wondered if monthly baths were also in his future.

He had only traveled three blocks when a loud voice caught his ear. "Aye there, lad!" Certain the man could not be addressing him, Murray ignored the voice and continued on his way. "Moore! Murray

Moore!" the man called again. This time, Murray turned to find the person calling out to him. A man waved to him from across the busy lane, then motioned for him to stay in place. Perhaps this person was someone who knew something about Erin. After all, how else could anyone know his name unless Erin had told them.

The man quickly made his way across the street to where Murray waited. He was youthful and friendly looking, cheery and mischievous at the same time, with short brown hair and brown eyes to match. His relieved smile earned him a moment of Murray's time, though Murray's trust would have to be earned with something more substantial.

"Who are you, mister?" Murray answered as the man approached him. "Do you know something about my sister?"

"I believe so, young man," the gentleman answered him. "You are Murray Moore, then?"

"Yes, sir."

"My name is Darcy Adams," he said, shaking Murray's hand in introduction. "I am here to talk to you about your sister, and to take you to a safe place."

Murray lit up with anticipation. "Do you know where she is? Can you take me to her?"

The man's expression changed from friendliness to one of pained sadness, and he laid a sober hand on Murray's shoulder. "I am so sorry, Murray, but your sister died. She asked me to look after you. I am here to take you to a place where you will be well cared for."

Murray angrily yanked his shoulder from under the man's hand and backed away. "I don't understand why all you people are saying that my sister is dead!" Mr. Adams tilted his head in perplexity, then stepped toward Murray, attempting to calm him.

"Please, Murray," he said, "please come with me, and we can talk things over. I will tell you how I knew your sister, and you can tell me who else you have been talking with."

Murray balked at Darcy's suggestion and turned on his heel, apparently finished with the present conversation. "Murray!" Darcy called after him. "Please!"

As Darcy started after the boy, he suddenly found two dubious looking men on either side of him. With his attention centered on Murray, he had failed to notice the men inching closer. They each took Darcy by an arm and hastily shoved him into an open carriage door. The whole action happened so quickly that Darcy barely had time to call out for help. He brought his knee up into one man's stomach, causing the man to release his arm. He then landed a quick blow to the other man's jaw and prepared to leap from the cab onto the sidewalk.

Another man stepped up to block the open door and Darcy's escape. He recognized the face – it was Byron Drake. Before he could react, Drake struck Darcy square in the jaw with devastating force, sending him crashing into the seat behind him.

Drake eyed the man who was still doubled over from Darcy's blow to his stomach. He was leaning halfway in the cab, using the step rail as a support. Grabbing him behind the collar, Drake pulled him from the cab and tossed him onto the sidewalk. "You're in my way, idiot," he remarked, stepping over the man and into the cab. The last thing Darcy remembered was Drake pulling the door shut, his evil grin penetrating through Darcy's fading consciousness.

31

Josephine had been withdrawn for the last two days, and William did not know if it was due to the loss of Albert or the battle that had taken place on her knees that same night. More than likely, both factors were weighing heavily on her. In any case, he had not left her alone for an extended period of time since that horrible day, except for the hours when she retreated to her quarters to sleep.

In those late hours after dinner, William had not done the same. After Josephine closed her bedroom door for the evening, William found his way to the library and opened the window to the cold, evening breeze. From this vantage point, he could hear any foreign sounds that might be made by someone attempting to scale Josephine's balcony and cause her harm. The open archway of the library also allowed him to hear any sounds of intruders from the hallway, and possibly any sounds of struggle from inside Josephine's room.

He had met the day before with three of the strong, young groundskeepers employed at the manor. Their new task, which came with a significant increase in salary, was to keep an eye on the grounds during the hours when the rest of the household was deep in slumber. After losing one of their own, the men were more than happy to assume their new duties.

William Dunham was not taking any more chances with the safety of his wife or his household.

Josephine had retired early, as she had for the last two nights, and William found himself again seated comfortably in the library. He usually read in Mr. Hamilton's old Bible before drifting off to sleep in the armchair, when the fatigue could not be fought off any longer. This evening, however, he picked up one of the business ledgers Josephine had been writing in earlier. It was the only other book on the round table, so he flipped rather haphazardly through the pages, not really looking for anything in particular, other than a better understanding of his wife's businesses.

It was then that his eye caught a familiar name – Jefferson Beech. Immediately, he recognized it as the name of Elisabeth's father, and he studiously read the entry that followed.

May 18, 1850

Jefferson Beech

> The sum of fifty dollars a month shall be deposited in an account for the sole use of the tutoring and education of any and all children of Jefferson Beech, which is provided as a benefit of his position at The Boston Accounting Firm.

The Boston Accounting Firm was one of Mr. Hamilton's first businesses. William's thoughts flew back to the very last conversation he had with Elisabeth. His heart cringed as he recalled the pain of the experience, but it was only momentary. She had told him her father had secured a new position, and that she was to attend lessons as a result.

At the time, William's pain had kept him from paying much attention to those details of their conversation, and he had never thought on them afterward. In hindsight, it was obvious that Mr. Beech's new position, and Elisabeth's generous tutoring fund, was a result of Josephine's intervention.

Leave it to Josephine to look after Elisabeth. He wondered why she didn't tell him about Mr. Beech, or about arranging the tutor for Elisabeth. Then he realized that Josephine didn't do kind deeds to be noticed by others – she did kind deeds to help people. Nothing more. She did not care what other people thought of her, or how she was viewed by proper society, or if anyone in the world knew of her philanthropy. She often did not even expect simple thanks. Josephine Dunham simply helped people any way she could. How extraordinary!

He frowned suddenly. Why wasn't he more like that? Why hadn't he thought of it before?

"Is anything amiss, William?" Josephine's placid voice snapped him out of his reverie as she walked through the library arch. William stood as she entered the room.

"Hello, my dear," he answered, taking her hand and kissing the back of it.

She thought his lips lingered just a few moments longer than usual, and her heart skipped a beat. Even after all these months, he still affected her like a love-struck schoolgirl.

"Are you well?" he asked suddenly, aware that she was usually sleeping at this hour. "Is there anything wrong?"

"No," she replied quickly, sitting in the other chair. "I just finished drafting a note to our legal counsel. I think it would be prudent to meet with them tomorrow to discuss how to... proceed with this situation. I saw you in the library, and thought you might need company. Your frown indicated that something was amiss?"

"Amiss?" William echoed as they both sat down. He toyed with the idea of telling her what he had found in the ledger, then decided against it. He did not want to bring up the subject of Elisabeth, and Josephine might feel embarrassed discussing her generosity toward Miss Beech.

William let his eyes fall onto the gentle face of his wife. She smiled quizzically at him, as if wondering what strangeness had overtaken him. He didn't quite know himself. All he knew was that Josephine Dunham was beautiful when she smiled.

"Nothing at all amiss, love," he answered, still sweeping his eyes over Josephine, the way her dress curved around her waist, and the way one rebellious, dark curl fell on her neck.

She blushed, but held his gaze, even as she felt a lightness spread from her stomach to her shoulders. "You've never called me that before," she commented quietly, her heart thudding so hard she wondered if William could hear it.

"No?" he answered. "I suppose you are right." William stood from his seat and knelt in front of Josephine's chair, leaning his hands on either side of her. He held his face in front of hers, mapping her features with his blue, blue eyes. She barely breathed. "Josephine, do you remember our first ride together? When we first toured the grounds of Hamilton Manor."

"Yes," she answered quietly, almost in a whisper. "It is one of my fondest memories."

William brought his hand to her cheek, caressing it carefully, as if touching a wild thing that might fly away at any moment. "We agreed to be candid with one another," he said.

Josephine didn't answer, she wasn't sure if she could even speak.

William continued. "Life with you is..." He faltered momentarily. "No one could have ever guessed how extraordinary you are – you hide it so well. But every day I spend with you, every time I discover something else about your life or your kindness, I am more enamored with you."

William leaned very close to her, his cheek brushing hers, his mouth by her ear. "If you but say the word, then I will restrain myself from kissing you." He leaned back slightly, intently watching Josephine's face. When she did not say anything at all, he placed the softest of kisses on her lips. She kissed him back, almost not believing that this moment was even happening.

He moved his hand behind her neck and kissed her again. After a few more moments, he pulled away, gently resting his forehead on hers.

She ran her fingers through his dark hair and smiled. "You haven't kissed me since our wedding day," she whispered, smiling shyly. "I quite like it."

"No, that is not true," he whispered back.

She looked up at him, surprised. "I'm sure I would have remembered," she teased, delicately tracing the line of his jawbone with her finger.

He placed another kiss on her cheek. "I assure you, my lady, I have kissed you since our wedding day."

"When?" she asked, perplexed.

"That horrible night when you drove your carriage up the lane like a mad woman."

She giggled softly. "I didn't know you had witnessed that."

"Aye," he replied after gently kissing her neck. "I saw you from the window. I was waiting for you in this very room, and had fallen asleep in this very chair." Another kiss. "I awoke to the preposterous sound of my wife thundering up the road like a hell hound chasing down Ares."

Josephine laughed out loud. "Yes, well, not my finest moment, I'm sure."

William sat back from her, his face very serious. "Actually, Josephine, it is one of your finer moments. It was the first time I realized ... there is not another woman like you anywhere."

She turned away, slightly self-conscious, unsure of what to do with his comment.

"I held you that night, just wanting to keep you safe."

She met his eyes again.

"And after you fell asleep, I kissed your hair – just small kisses. But I am certain they count."

Josephine took his face in her hands. "They count," she said, bending down to meet his lips.

He leaned forward and pulled her close to him. "I have wanted to have you next to me since that night," he said in her ear. "I have missed lying next to you."

"And I you," she answered breathlessly.

He slowly stood and pulled her up next to him, kissing her again. "Come with me tonight?" he asked softly, offering his other hand to her.

"Yes," she whispered, taking his hand, "I'll go with you anywhere."

William looked at her longingly, then walked out of the library toward his own quarters, holding her hand as she walked behind him. Opening the door to his room, he held it open for his wife as she walked through. He shut the door softly, then locked it behind him.

Balancing Josephine's breakfast tray in one hand, Ophelia silently pushed open her mistress's door. Golden, morning light spilled onto her from the balcony doors as she stepped into the room. It was odd that

Josephine's curtains were already open. After two steps, she stopped in her tracks. Josephine's bed was empty, and still arranged beautifully from yesterday. Josephine had not even slept there last night.

Ophelia knit her brows in concern. Josephine had not gone out last night, at least not without her knowing. Something was wrong. Wherever Josephine had gone, she had not returned. Alarm filled Ophelia's stomach, and she quickly set the tray on the dresser and ran across the hall to Mr. Dunham's suite.

Knocking quickly and loudly, she called in a half panicked voice, "Mr. Dunham, sir. Wake up. Wake up, sir."

She heard the bolt unlatch and Mr. Dunham opened the door a sliver, just enough to address the maid. He was shirtless, but had hurriedly pulled on his pants before opening the door. Ophelia didn't even notice his state of dress. "Good heavens, woman!" he exclaimed softly. "Your knocking could wake the dead!"

Ophelia ignored the remark. "It's Josephine, sir!" Ophelia began, her words quick with panic. "She left last night and never came home." The worry on her face was evident. "I'm afraid for her, Mr. Dunham. You have to go find her at once!"

William put his finger to his lips to shush the frantic woman. He allowed the door to fall open just a bit more, revealing the sleeping Josephine curled under his blankets.

Ophelia's alarm changed into a delighted smile. "You are a lovely man!" she whispered, reaching up to pinch Mr. Dunham's face, much like a grandmother would dote on her favorite toddler.

William frowned as the maid squeezed his cheek. "You are still insolent."

"Yes, I know," she replied happily. "When would you like breakfast for you and Miss Josephine?"

"In an hour, I think." He cast a look back at his wife. "She needs to sleep."

Ophelia curtsied, turned to leave, then paused. She turned back to William and said, "Mr. Hamilton could not have done a better thing for his daughter than when he chose you, sir."

Ophelia left him there and hurried down the stairs, joy bubbling over for her friend. Josephine had been alone for so long, and Ophelia had worried for her. She had seen the lonely sighs, and the look in Josephine's eyes the few times she studied her image in the mirror. Ophelia knew Josephine was not meant to be alone, no matter how much her mistress protested otherwise. Now, it seemed that Mr. Dunham had finally come to his senses, instead of moping about the house like the pouting boy he had been at first.

Ophelia burst into the kitchen, smiling from ear to ear, and started preparations for breakfast. A small, quiet rapping sounded from the far doorway, and Ophelia stretched her neck to see who the owner of the knocking was.

"Hello?" A beautiful girl, with blonde ringlets and a round belly, looked shyly through the doorway and found Ophelia's smile.

"Hello, dear," Ophelia called to her, beckoning her to enter the kitchen and sit down at the sturdy wooden table. "You must be Miss Tiernan?"

The girl smiled and sat gently on a chair, pulling it away from the table slightly to accommodate her tummy. "I am," she answered, rather surprised that a stranger knew her name. "It is nice to make your acquaintance, ma'am."

Ophelia smiled and held her hand out to the girl. "My name is Ophelia, not ma'am," she answered. "And I am very pleased to finally meet you."

"Finally?" Shannon responded, her brows quizzical.

"Ah, I see my brother has mentioned nothing about his life or his family to you. The cad!" Ophelia's tone was not serious, and she winked at Shannon as she spoke. "Would you care for some breakfast?" she added. "You came at just the right time for the morning meal. Perhaps you will eat with me?"

Shannon smiled, but shook her head. "I wish I had come for something as simple as a meal, but I am concerned for Darcy." Ophelia quieted her busy hands, sat down at the table opposite Shannon, and gave the girl her full attention.

"I am listening," she answered.

"You are his sister?" Shannon asked, her tone betraying a lingering apprehension.

"I am, Miss Tiernan," Ophelia answered, reaching across the table and placing her hand over Shannon's. "And if you have reason to be concerned for my brother, I need to know."

Shannon nodded. "Darcy left three days ago to find the young boy, Erin Moore's brother."

"Yes," Ophelia said. "I remember his departure."

"It seems that he should have returned by now. I feel..." Shannon searched Ophelia's face, looking for an ally. "I feel as if something is dreadfully wrong."

Ophelia took a deep breath and squeezed Shannon's hand gently. "At first, I felt terribly ill at ease every time he went out. Sometimes he would be gone for days and days, and my fear for him would almost drive me mad. Now..." she paused, casting a worried glance to the ceiling. "Well, I still worry for him, but I also pray. And God has brought him home every time, often with another poor girl that he has saved from a horrible fate."

"So you think there is no cause for worry?"

Ophelia frowned. "I would not say that," she answered slowly, "but I think Darcy needs more time to find the lad. If he has not returned three days from now, then Mrs. Dunham will send someone to look for him."

"Three days?" Shannon's displeasure was evident. "But if something has happened, then three days' time is surely too long."

Leaning forward on the table, Ophelia held Shannon's eyes with a sober gaze. "You feel very strongly, then? This is not just nervous apprehension because of your affection for Darcy?"

Shannon blushed slightly and looked down at the tabletop, but she answered quickly. "I suppose that is possible, but I do not think so. It is as if my spirit is being blackened by something horrible, something that will only depart when I know Darcy is safe."

Ophelia considered for only a moment before answering, "Then I will send someone myself this very moment. Hans knows most of Darcy's haunts in Boston, and I believe that he is in the carriage house this morning." She rose from the table and pushed in her chair, then looked down with compassion at the young woman with whom her brother was so taken. "Would you care to walk with me, Miss Tiernan? I would enjoy the chance to get acquainted with you more."

Shannon's expression was one of relief and genuine gratitude as she also rose from the table. "Thank you for listening to me, Ophelia," she said, taking the arm that Ophelia offered as the two escaped out the back door of the kitchen and started down the cobblestone path to the carriage house.

"Women have a sense about these things that should not be ignored. Perhaps God is talking to you," Ophelia replied.

Shannon shook her head. "No, God does not talk to me. I only feel as if something is terribly amiss."

Ophelia didn't belabor the point. "When Hans returns this evening, I will send one of the servants down to Rosewood Hall to inform you."

"You are very kind, Ophelia, just like your brother."

Laughing, Ophelia replied, "You do not know him quite as well as I do. But I am sure that will change."

While Shannon enjoyed the fine company and the pleasant morning as they walked to the carriage house, the feeling of dread did not relent. It only grew stronger as each minute passed, eternity after eternity of the terrible certainty that Darcy Adams was in grave distress.

32

The gravelly voices of old sailors cursing one another, the neighing of horses pulling wagons, and the shouts of impatient ship captains all traveled faintly to the ears of Darcy Adams. Light, however, was another matter. The only window in the old warehouse was far up on the eastern wall, large enough to allow the sounds of the harbor, but not so large as to let in the light of day, except for the early morning sun in the eastern sky.

Light would not have done Darcy any good, anyway. Both of his eyes were swollen shut from blow after blow to his face, and his hands were tied firmly to one of the posts supporting the wooden structure. Even if he could somehow twist his hands free of the rough, binding ropes, he would not be able to navigate his way through the stacked crates to the door. He did not even remember where the door was.

The sound of a flaring match caught Darcy's attention, and the sweet smoke of a cigar drifted into his nostrils. He heard a man inhale deeply, then felt the hot breath of exhaled smoke swirling around his face.

"You are proving to be most difficult, Mr. Smith." The voice of Byron Drake was relaxed and pleasant, as if he were spending the afternoon catching up with an old friend. "That's right, it's not Smith at all, is it, Mr. Adams?" Drake grabbed Darcy by the hair and pulled his head back violently, bringing his face so close to Darcy's that the stench of his breath threatened to make him wretch. Darcy said nothing in reply.

"You should have paid more attention to your surroundings when you were trying to persuade that little whelp to come with you." Drake released Darcy's hair and delivered a brutal kick to his gut, causing Darcy to finally release the putrid vomit that had been lingering just beneath his throat.

Drake stepped back casually to avoid the puddle of filth on the floor. "Once I knew your name, I was able to find out all kinds of interesting things about you, Mr. Adams. For instance, I know the name of your dear sister, Ophelia. And I also know you are affiliated with Josephine Dunham and her imbecile of a husband. What is most important, however, is not what I know, but what you know."

Darcy's head still hung limply form his neck, the severe kick and the act of vomiting still taking its toll on his body. He did not even attempt a response.

"All you have to do is simply give me back what is mine. Just tell me where Shannon is. It is that simple, Mr. Adams." Drake bent down and attempted to engage Darcy's face with a severe stare, though the gesture was useless.

"Still not talking, Mr. Adams?" Drake nodded to one of the two men who looked on with nervous interest, then pulled another long breath through the cigar. The man ripped the already torn and bloody shirt off of Darcy's torso. Drake stepped closer, eying the cigar he held tightly in his fingers.

"I think I might have a way to persuade you.

That evening, Ophelia herself walked down the path to Rosewood Hall. Once Shannon had seen her worried eyes and furrowed brow, she knew before Ophelia even spoke that there had been no sign of Darcy. The maid had tried to keep her voice upbeat, perhaps even cheery, noting how Darcy had often been gone for much longer periods than this. Ophelia had assured her all would be well, and that one of the household men was making his way through the streets of Boston, checking the brothels and taverns for her brother. But Shannon saw straight into Ophelia's concerned eyes, saw the distress and uncertainty lingering there. And she knew. She knew Ophelia was just as afraid as she was.

So, early in the morning, when no light had yet touched the sky, Shannon quietly crept out of her room to the stables, being careful not to arouse anyone from their slumber.

A few horses nickered softly as Shannon slipped through the stable door and headed down the center aisle toward the back of the building. A massive, black horse stood patiently in the last stall, his ears twitching lightly as Shannon stroked his nose and neck.

The name "Hero" was engraved on a brass plaque that was tacked to his door. Shannon immediately liked this great creature, and she stepped closer to smooth his mane with her dainty hand. The stallion lowered his great head and snuffed onto her shoulder while she spoke to him in soft, melodic, Irish verse. Yes, this one would do nicely.

Shannon reached for the bridle and reins hanging on the wall next to Hero's door and lifted them off their hook. Her fingers nimbly fitted the bridle over his head and ears and buckled it snugly, and she softly rubbed Hero's nose, praising him with more Irish lilt. Hero tossed his head, apparently happy at the prospect of an unscheduled outing.

She hoped that the Dunham's, who undoubtedly owned the horse, would not be too cross with her for taking him out without permission. She was sure, however, that had she asked permission to go on this venture, she would have been met with swift and sound objections.

Shannon opened the stall door and led Hero toward a stack of hay near the front of the stable. Lifting a heavy saddle and throwing it over the great beast would be difficult for Shannon under ordinary circumstances, but now, at almost six months pregnant, the task was quite impossible. Instead, she climbed onto the stack of hay bales, drew Hero parallel to her, then quickly transferred over to his back. She shifted back and forth until her balance was situated, then urged Hero into a trot.

The morning sun had not risen, though its faint glow in the east threatened the blackness that still lingered. Hero trotted easily along the darkened lane, his hooves very well acquainted with the route leading toward town. She had left an hour before dawn, with no lantern to light the path. Today, darkness would be her friend.

When she reached the outskirts of Boston, she turned Hero south and followed the lane that led to the docks and to the warehouse owned by Byron Drake. She was hoping that most of the men who frequented this area would be asleep, having spent the hours up to dawn engaged in their drinking and revelry. As she traveled down the street, she saw no signs of life whatsoever, confirming her theory.

A line of warehouses came into view, most of them looking as if they had been constructed hastily. Shannon slowed Hero to a walk, quieting the clip of his hooves. She knew exactly which warehouse she was looking for.

Shannon closed her eyes and retrieved the memory of disembarking from the Charlotte Jane. She had sat on the crate that Captain Munstead told her to, waiting. A moment of deep regret stabbed her through the heart as she remembered watching Darcy walk away from her. Shaking her head, she pushed that vision far down into inner blackness. It was of no use to her right now.

Instead, she focused on the memory of looking around her new surroundings, seeing the unhappy people bustle by, taking in the view of the wooden warehouses sitting across from the docks. One name caught her attention, perhaps because the warehouse was more kept and decent looking than the others, perhaps because it was larger than the others, or perhaps because it was directly across from Captain Munstead's ship.

Over the door of the warehouse hung a wooden sign, with proud, scripted letters, "Warehouse 17. Property of Byron Drake. No Trespassing."

Yes, that was it. Shannon had revisited that memory many times, but not for the warehouse number. Most times the memory had served to remind her that one man had offered her a chance of decency, but that chance had been snatched away from her. Now, the roles were reversed. It was Shannon's turn to rescue Darcy, and she would do so, even if the doing of it took her last breath.

In her mind, she again saw that warehouse and the sign marking it as Drake's. If Byron Drake had indeed taken Darcy, then Shannon was hoping she would find him there. A few more minutes of gentle trotting brought Shannon to the docks.

She turned Hero into an alley and carefully slid off of his back. Walking him to the back of a building, she tied his reins to a stack of discarded lumber. Shannon patted the stallion's neck as she collected her nerve. With a final rub, she breathed in deeply to calm the fear knotting her stomach, then turned toward Byron Drake's warehouse.

Her steps were quiet and sure, and she pulled the cowl of her cloak over her head as she walked. Shannon stopped at the wooden side door of the warehouse and listened. She stood motionless for several minutes, straining to hear the slightest sound from within. There was nothing.

She put her hand on the door handle and turned, all the while trying not to shake uncontrollably. The handle rotated a quarter of a turn before it stopped dead.

It was locked.

Of course it was locked, she scolded herself. Byron Drake was not going to leave his activities open to the world. Shannon silently admonished herself for her lack of foresight. She looked up at the brightening sky. Soon it would be too late to do anything.

Suddenly inspired, Shannon stooped down to the filthy ground and rubbed both hands in the black dirt of the alley. She gingerly smoothed it onto both arms, down the front of her dress, and across her face. Hopefully, she looked as if she had just escaped with her life.

Then, remembering the last conversation she had with Darcy, she prayed.

It was the first, genuine prayer her lips had ever uttered.

"Help me, God."

Drawing in a deep breath, Shannon raised both of her arms and pounded on the wooden door as loudly as she could.

"Open up!" she yelled, still pounding. "The Crimson Dagger is burning! We need every man! Open! She's burning down!"

After a few seconds Shannon heard frantic movement from inside, and the door flew open to reveal two burly men in a very excited state.

"It's burning!" Shannon yelled hysterically, grabbing the first man's arm. "We need every man!" The man barely looked at Shannon as he shook her off of his arm and bolted out the door, followed closely by the second brawny character. They sprinted down the alley and turned in the direction of The Crimson Dagger. Shannon hastily ran through the door, knowing that she had only moments before her ruse was found out.

She looked around the large, open space, impatiently waiting for her eyes to adjust to the darkness of the warehouse. There! She saw him! Thirty feet away a man was lying on the floor, his hands tied to one of the thick, wooden poles holding up the massive structure. Shannon lost no time in running over to him and falling on her knees.

"Darcy!" She shook him, then turned his face toward her. His lips were busted and bleeding, and his face was almost unrecognizable from the swelling and bruising that covered every inch of his features. He was stripped of his shirt and littered with bruises, cuts, and nasty, round burns across his torso. Shannon began to hurriedly fumble with the ropes binding his wrist.

"We have to go, Darcy!" she cried. "Please, Darcy, wake up!" She knew if Drake's two men returned, then neither of them would ever see the light of day again.

Darcy turned his head slightly, though Shannon could not tell through the swelling if his eyes were open or not. "Shannon?" His voice was a raspy tangle, barely intelligible.

Hastily pulling the final knots from the ropes around his wrist, Shannon slid her arm under Darcy and pulled. "They will be back any second," she urged. "We must go!"

Darcy sat up suddenly as the gravity of the situation impacted him. For the slightest moment, he stared into Shannon's face through swollen eyes, then he stood up quickly, letting Shannon support him enough to get to the door.

"You should not be in this place," he said with a grated voice as they pushed out into the alley. With each step he moved a little easier, though it was obvious to Shannon that walking pained him. She didn't respond to his comment.

"This way," she directed, grabbing his hand and hurrying toward the place where Hero was tied. Frantic cries and the sounds of running men came from the street in front of the warehouse. Obviously, Drake's two henchmen had sounded the alarm as they ran, enlisting the help of anyone who could be awakened at this hour. Within a minute, a whole group of would-be firefighters was running toward The Crimson Dagger.

Shannon and Darcy quickly reached the stallion, who stamped nervously at the sounds of the chaos just yards away. Darcy grabbed Shannon's waist at her sides, being careful not to injure her rounded stomach, and lifted her up to Hero's back. He awkwardly vaulted himself up behind Shannon and shook the reins gently in one hand, urging Hero into a fast trot. She felt his other arm wrap around her middle and pull her close to him, ensuring she would not fall off of the horse or out of his hold.

He led Hero down the alley and onto the street, hoping that the chaos would mask their strange appearance. Few people even gave them a second look, as most of the street's occupants were already heading away from the dock and clustering toward The Crimson Dagger.

Darcy kept the brisk pace until they were well outside of Boston. He then eased Hero off of the lane and into the wooded hills surrounding the city. As the morning light burst over the trees and lit up the day, Darcy and Shannon were safely sheltered in the forest, slowly picking along a path roughly parallel to the lane they had just left.

"Are you all right, Shannon?" Darcy asked softly, his mouth close to her ear. He put his hand gently on her stomach as he spoke.

She turned slightly to see his face. "Am I all right?" she responded disbelievingly, her lilting voice on the verge of tears. "Did you not notice your own state?" She barely touched his cheek with her fingers, not wanting to cause any pain to his beaten face.

"What you did was far too dangerous," he said, his tone gentle but chiding. "What if you had been caught? What would I have done?"

She was silent for a few moments, resting easily inside the shelter of his bare, bloodied arms. "You came for me, didn't you?" she answered softly. "You came for me when there was no hope." Tears started to stream down her cheek and mar her voice. "I could not leave you to that fate."

"Shhh." Darcy drew Hero to a stop and pulled Shannon closer with both arms, placing small kisses in her blonde hair to ease her distress.

"You are the bravest woman I have ever met, Shannon Tiernan. Braver than most men I've met, even." He brushed away her tears and kissed her cheek, holding her until the tears were done.

"So tell me," he asked when she was able converse again, "what exactly did you do to cause that tumult at the warehouse?"

Shannon giggled slightly. "I told them The Crimson Dagger was burning down."

Darcy smiled as well, wincing as he did so. "If only it were true," he said. "Very clever," he added, nudging Hero back into a walk toward Hamilton Manor. He looked closer at her face. "That would explain why I have never before seen you so filthy."

Shannon remembered the dirt she smeared over her face and hands to mimic the soot from a fire. "You're not exactly looking your best, either!" she exclaimed, leaning contentedly back into his chest.

Darcy laughed again, then groaned from the pain it caused. They continued in comfortable silence for a few more minutes. "Don't you think," Darcy asked finally, "that this is a most inappropriate way to conduct a courtship?"

Shannon laughed out loud, her relief finally finding its way into the open air. "Most inappropriate," she agreed happily.

33

Byron Drake slept fitfully in his room at The Crimson Dagger, his arm draped over the waist of his latest companion, a blonde named Helen. Lately, he could not enjoy a full sleep. In that place between slumber and consciousness, Shannon's face kept tormenting him. He would wake with a start, only to find that the woman next to him was not Shannon. Deep in the blackness of the morning's early hours, in the midst of his torment, he finally determined to do away with the wretch who was fouling the air in his warehouse.

Darcy Adams was not going to reveal where he had taken Shannon. For three days, Drake had attempted to beat it out of him, and had gotten nowhere. After making the decision to put an end to the man and find Shannon by other means, Drake finally fell into a troubled slumber.

"Fire!"

Drake bolted upright immediately, the sound of shouting and heavy boots filling the downstairs parlor.

"Everyone out! Fire!"

Drake leapt out of bed, grabbing the barely clad girl next to him by the wrist and pulling her out the door. As he descended the stairs, he saw a horde of men teeming around the lower story, wielding buckets and axes, throwing water on his furniture, and shouting for the inhabitants of the building to evacuate. Drake grabbed a tablecloth and tossed it to his companion, who was grateful to cover herself. He smelled the air, then looked carefully around the room. There was not even a hint of smoke or flame. Aside from the idiots invading his tavern, everything was in order.

"Stop!" he roared forcefully from the stairway. "Stop! What is going on here?"

"We're here to put out the fire!" answered one of the men, holding his ax above is head enthusiastically.

"You imbecile!" Drake shouted angrily. "Look around you! There is no fire!"

The men paused in unison and took note of the building. After a few moments of chaotic bewilderment, they began to grumble, shooting angry looks and curses in his direction.

"You shouldn't call for help if there's no fire!" one man called out crossly.

"Got us out of bed for nothin'!"

"And he calls us imbeciles," another yelled over the clamor. A few of the men laughed.

"Get out!" Drake ordered loudly. "All of you! Now!" As the party stomped angrily out the door, Drake caught sight of one of his own, bearing a bucket and a look of utter confusion. "You! Jones!" he ordered. "Over here." The man's confusion quickly turned to alarm as he realized he would bear the responsibility for this foray.

"What is happening here?" Drake demanded angrily. "Why aren't you at the warehouse?" As he asked the question, a slow realization dawned on Drake.

"A girl came bangin' on the door sayin' that the tavern was burnin' down, sir. So we ran right over to help." Jones' voice was nervous, and his eyes were scanning the room for his partner from the warehouse. He was nowhere to be seen.

Drake's eyes narrowed, and his face transforming dangerously. Jones shifted tensely. "Did she have blonde hair, Jones?"

Jones did not know the importance of the question, only that he was in more trouble than he desired. "I'm not sure, sir. Maybe."

"Who's with Adams?" Drake snapped. The alarmed look from his henchman was all the answer Drake needed. He looked at the young girl who was retreating up the stairs. "Helen, bring my boots and shirt, now!" he growled. The girl ran to retrieve the items. Drake looked coldly at Jones. "Jones, if Adams is gone, you are a dead man."

Jones stood motionless at the bottom of the stairs, not responding. The girl returned after a few seconds with Drake's shirt and boots, which he hurriedly pulled on. "Come on!" he called as he ran out the door. Jones reluctantly followed after him.

Drake sprinted hard down the street, his untucked shirt flowing behind him. At this pace, it only took a couple of minutes to arrive at the warehouse. Drake immediately saw the side door halfway open. He turned to sharply reprimand Jones, but the man was not there. Drake scanned the street behind him. No one. Perhaps Jones wasn't a complete moron.

Throwing open the door, Drake marched into the warehouse. A small pile of rope lay next to the post where Smith had last been, and a cold, hateful fury began churning in his gut, though his breath was calm and steady. He caught a familiar scent, and breathed in deeply, this time paying attention to the smell. It was her scent. She had been here.

A murderous rage grew inside Drake as he tromped back through the streets to The Crimson Dagger, though no one would know it from looking at him. He calmly climbed the stairway and retreated into the third door on the left, his own room. Shannon's room. Only after the door was shut behind him did his rage emerge, roaring from his throat and throwing the night stands from their place beside the bed. As each piece of furniture hit the wall, it fractured into splinters, spilling its contents onto the luxurious rug.

Drake stood in the middle of it all, breathing heavy from the exertion of his anger. If he ever saw Jones again, he would not give him the luxury of a warning before killing him. But Adams, on the other hand, Adams would feel every ounce of pain that Drake could devise. He would kill him slowly and happily, and he would make sure that Shannon Tiernan was there to watch every moment.

As he scanned the chaotic jumble of papers and kindling that littered the floor, his eyes fell on one folded document in particular. He picked it up and unfolded the papers, reading over the scripted legal text. These were Shannon's indentured servitude papers, ownership of which had been legally transferred to himself. He lifted another similarly folded document off of the floor. These papers were for Erin Moore. Another set documented his ownership of Edith Evan's indentured servitude.

On the floor lay his ownership papers for the indentured servitude of over two dozen girls that had gone missing the past few months.

Byron Drake began to laugh. The sound of it was far more disturbing than the rage that had filled the room moments earlier.

34

Elisabeth heard the office door open softly, though Dr. Stone seemed too enraptured by his text and writings to even notice the entry of a new patient. She smiled softly at the doctor, then left her own chair at the desk to tend to the latest patient. A young man, tall and muscular, and quite healthy, stood in the waiting room.

"Would you like to take a seat in the examination room?" Elisabeth offered kindly, gesturing to the room behind her. "Dr. Stone will be with you in a moment."

"No thank you, ma'am," he countered. "I need to talk to Dr. Stone now."

"Of course," Elisabeth answered as she turned to retrieve the doctor. But Dr. Stone heard the young man and was already exiting his office.

"Hans," he said, concern in his voice, "what brings you out and about today?"

"You're needed at the Hamilton estate, sir," Hans replied, casting a questioning glance at Elisabeth.

Dr. Stone followed his unsure gaze. "It is alright, Hans. You may speak freely in front of Miss Beech." Elisabeth stood quietly, not knowing what to make of the strangeness of the man's hesitation or the reference to William's new home.

"Mr. Adams has been found, sir," Hans continued at once. "But he's been beat up pretty bad. Burned, too, looks like with a cigar, all over him, sir."

Elisabeth gasped in shock, but Dr. Stone was already retrieving his bag even as Hans spoke. He took it with him to his office and grabbed two or three bottles from his supply shelf, as well as suturing needles and thread.

Content that he was well supplied for the job at hand, he started to follow Hans, but stopped in front of Elisabeth. “Miss Beech,” he said, “the office is yours for the afternoon.” He raised an eyebrow, then added, “Remember, be quick to think and slow to act.”

He was referring to her earlier failing, and the words stung slightly, but the smile he gave her was sure and genuine, and he let his eyes linger on hers for a few moments.

“Of course, Dr. Stone.” Elisabeth watched as Hans and the doctor hurried out the door, her cheeks just now starting to flush from his extended gaze. She was certain her heartbeat had increased slightly, and she took a deep breath to slow it to its normal pace.

Had she read the situation correctly? Did Dr. Stone’s eyes hold something more than friendly affection? Did her own affections go beyond friendship and respect? She truly did not know, so Elisabeth reseated herself at the desk in the back office and chased those thoughts out of her head by outlining the treatment of the pox in her ever growing stack of medical notes. Before she could get too far, however, the sound of another person entering the front office demanded her attention.

Once again, Elisabeth returned to the front room, this time to greet a balding man wearing a farmer’s overalls and great, muddy boots. His worried frown betrayed the concern hiding behind his polite nod and pleasant face.

“How can I help you, sir?” Elisabeth began. The man looked over her shoulder into the office.

“I’m looking for Dr. Stone, ma’am,” he responded with a voice sounding older than he looked. “Is he in?”

Elisabeth shook her head. “I am afraid Dr. Stone will be out for the rest of the afternoon. Perhaps I can help you?”

Looking over Elisabeth worriedly, the man continued. “Do you know how to doctor? I have a sick girl that needs tending to.” He looked around the office again, as if Dr. Stone might pop out of the examination room and save the day. “Dr. Stone is the one who usually takes care of us.”

Elisabeth smiled gently at the man. "Dr. Stone has been teaching me for the last few months, and he left me to care for his patients this afternoon," she offered, trying to put the worried man at ease. "What are your daughter's symptoms? I might have something that will help her."

"She's not my daughter, ma'am," the farmer responded, "just a poor girl we found on the river bank some time ago. She was bone cold and almost drowned, so my wife and I took her home and tried to warm her up." The man's frown deepened. "Now she's come down with a fever and this horrible cough. Coughs all the time. And she hasn't eaten a thing this last week. I don't think she can make it much longer."

Elisabeth responded to the man while retreating to the back office. "It might be pneumonia," she said, "especially since she was pulled from the river." She pulled two bottles from the medicine shelf, then located a stethoscope from the supply shelf. She found one of the doctor's older, black bags and placed the medicines and stethoscope inside.

Then, as an afterthought, she took two more bottles from the shelf and one bunch of dried herbs from the rack. It might be pneumonia, but it might also be influenza or tuberculosis. Elisabeth wanted to be prepared for whatever she would face, so she placed these in her bag as well.

"Shall we be off, then?" Elisabeth asked expectantly.

The farmer was hesitant for a moment. "You sure you know what to do?" he queried carefully.

"Sir," she answered, "I won't be certain of anything until I see the young lady and evaluate her symptoms for myself. I will treat her as best as I can this evening, then send Dr. Stone out first thing tomorrow morning."

The older man nodded in satisfaction. "You don't mind riding on a wagon, do you?" he asked as they started out the door.

Elisabeth smiled again. "Not in the least." She saw a ramshackle configuration of planks and wheels, harnessed to an even more questionable looking mule, waiting for them in the street outside of Dr. Stone's office. The day was shaping up to be an adventurous one.

Dr. Stone happily returned to his home later that evening, having tended to the very fortunate Mr. Adams and the heroic young lady who had rescued him. Mr. Adams had received a thorough beating and a great many injuries. The latter had been designed to be extremely painful instead of life threatening. Dr. Stone expected the young man to be the picture of health after a few weeks of restful healing.

The young lady, Shannon Tiernan, had been remarkably courageous, especially for her delicate state. But as soon as Dr. Stone had seen the pair lock eyes as they recounted the story of the rescue, he understood her motivations. The two were very clearly enamored with one another.

When Dr. Stone learned of the reason for Darcy's misadventure, he quickly related his own tale about the finding of Murray Moore, and how the lad was now under his care. Needless to say, Darcy was exceedingly glad for Murray's safety.

Murray was already home by the time Dr. Stone returned, and had started dinner in anticipation of his guardian's presence. The wholesome aroma of biscuits and gravy wafted from the kitchen, as it did every time Dr. Stone allowed Murray to cook. It was the lad's favorite meal.

The two had just sat down to their biscuits and a discussion about the recent passing of President Taylor when a quiet knock sounded from the front door. Dr. Stone looked up at Murray. "Who do you think that could be?" he asked, as if the lad somehow knew.

Not one to miss any excitement, Murray pushed his chair back and wiped his mouth on the sleeve of his fine, new shirt. "I'll find out, sir," he replied, making straight for the door. He opened it to reveal Miss Beech standing on the doorstep.

"Miss Elisabeth!" he exclaimed adoringly. "Are you here to have dinner with us?"

Still on the doorstep, Elisabeth smiled warmly at her favorite redhead. "I shall not impose upon you gentlemen for dinner, I just wanted to discuss a new patient with Dr. Stone."

Dr. Stone also pushed back his chair and made his way to the door. "Never leave a young lady standing at the door, Murray," he chided gently while opening the door wider and gesturing for Elisabeth to enter. "Especially when there are biscuits and gravy to share."

"I made them myself," Murray bubbled as Elisabeth entered the small foyer.

Dr. Stone smiled mischievously and raised an eyebrow. "How can anyone refuse that? Please stay for dinner, Miss Beech," he said, "and we can discuss your new patient."

Elisabeth allowed herself to be seated at the table next to Dr. Stone while Murray fetched another plate and set of silverware. Soon, Miss Beech was seated between the two gentlemen, happily sampling Murray's cooking while the three enjoyed relaxed conversation. Any resentment Elisabeth had felt about Dr. Stone's earlier comment melted away with the friendly atmosphere.

Murray reached for another biscuit and began a description of the "ugliest, little dog" he had ever seen. He had been on an errand for in the finest part of Boston when he had spied the little creature riding in his owner's lap.

"And I swear," he continued, "that dog looked just like the lady holding it!" Dr. Stone exchanged an amused glance with Elisabeth, who was holding her napkin in front of her mouth, trying not to laugh out loud.

"Young man!" she scolded, though lightheartedly, and still trying to contain her amusement. "You should never swear, no matter how unattractive the subject of your story might be." Dr. Stone hid his chuckle behind his own napkin as Murray offered a sheepish "yes, ma'am" in response.

"Well then, Miss Beech," Dr. Stone interjected, pushing his plate to the middle of the table, "tell us about this new patient of yours."

"Yes", said Elisabeth, placing her napkin on the table. "A farmer came to the office soon after you left. He came to find you, but had to settle for me, instead."

"A balding man? Large boots?" asked the doctor.

Elisabeth smiled. "Exactly!"

"Ira Jacobs and his wife. I have known the couple for a number of years," he replied, his smile changing to concern. "Who is ill?"

"Neither of them," she explained. "It seems he and his wife rescued a young girl from the Charles River, and though she survived the near drowning, I am afraid pneumonia has set up in her lungs. The poor girl's fever is high, and she has an unproductive cough that is wreaking havoc on her airways."

Dr. Stone sat up in his chair, his full attention riveted on Miss Beech's words. "How long ago?" he asked.

Elisabeth frowned slightly, thinking back to her conversation with the farmer. "Four or five weeks ago, I believe."

Dr. Stone leaned forward. "And you saw the girl yourself?"

At the doctor's suddenly serious tone, Murray began paying rapt attention to Miss Beech, as well. "I did," she answered, not sure of the reason for Dr. Stone's sudden change in demeanor. "I examined her myself."

"What color was her hair?" Murray asked, suddenly understanding Dr. Stone's concern.

"Her hair?" Elisabeth asked, confusion etched on her face.

"Yes," replied Dr. Stone, nodding for her to continue.

Elisabeth looked at both of them as if they were mad, but continued, nonetheless. "Well, it was fiery red," she said. "A beautiful mass of red ringlets."

"Do you know her name, Elisabeth?" Dr. Stone's expression and voice were intense.

"Erin," she responded. "Her name is Erin."

Dr. Stone addressed Murray as both of them rose from the table in haste. "Don your coat, lad, and go find a coach immediately!" The boy didn't hesitate for a second, and was out the door before Elisabeth could even ask for an explanation.

She also rose from the table and found her coat, following Dr. Stone's hurried example. "What on earth is going on, Dr. Stone?" she asked.

"I will explain on the way," he answered, holding the door open for Elisabeth. He grabbed her hand and they both raced for the coach that was coming to a stop in front of Dr. Stone's home. A very excited Murray already sat in the cab.

35

The morning light found Josephine's face and nudged her from her dreams. Before she even opened her eyes, she heard William's soft breathing beside her. She smiled softly. Thank you, Lord.

Josephine had not slept in her own quarters for over two months – not since that wonderful night she had spent with her husband. Thinking about it, so many things in the past two months had turned out for the better, not just her relationship with William.

The girl whom she feared lost, Erin Moore, had been found at the home of a farmer who lived down river. Murray Moore, the little boy Darcy had been searching for, finally had his sister back. It was reported to Josephine that the lad spent his days running errands for Dr. Stone, and his evenings at the farmer's home, helping to care for his sister. Though Miss Moore was alive, her physical state had been affected by her prolonged struggle with pneumonia. Dr. Stone's efforts were slowly bringing about healing for the girl, but her health would always be delicate.

Darcy Adams had abandoned his residence in the city in favor of the carriage house on Hamilton Manor. While part of his reason was to avoid more unwanted attention from Byron Drake, Josephine was certain his main motive had to do with Shannon Tiernan. They spent the lunch hour together every day, though picnicking under the massive oak had been abandoned during the winter months in favor of lunching in the kitchen.

Dr. Stone checked on Miss Tiernan and her unborn child often, always declaring both of them healthy and sound. As for Byron Drake,

Josephine had neither seen nor heard any news about him since Darcy's encounter with the man.

That thought was the only thing marring her perfect morning. She could hope that Byron Drake had admitted defeat and gone away forever, but she knew men like him simply did not go away. He was plotting, planning, spinning something sinister. Josephine could feel it, like a fly feels the subtle shaking of a spider's thread. And so she waited, looking every day for the bit of news that would signal her next battle with the man.

Josephine's patient respite had not been idle, however. Her lawyers had been preparing a suit against Mr. Drake regarding the flagrant embezzlement of Duke Dunham's finances. The only task remaining was to locate the missing financial manager and secure his testimony for court. Of course, this was the most difficult errand of the whole affair, but Josephine was certain the man would be found soon, as all of her resources were focused on that end.

It was her plan to strike at Mr. Drake before he could initiate any legal grievance against her. However, as the days ticked by without the Dunham's financial manager being found, this plan became less likely to succeed.

Josephine heard William yawn and felt him stretch beside her. Opening her eyes, she put all of her waking worries aside and gazed at the unshaven, half-awake man next to her. Thank you, Lord.

William finally opened his eyes as well and caught her staring. He smiled. "Good morning, love. How are you?" His hand softly stroked her loose, brown hair as he addressed her.

"I have never been better," she smiled back, catching his hand with hers and intertwining her fingers through his. "I am sure today will be extraordinary."

"Hmm," he replied, sleep still clinging to his voice. "Why is that?"

"Because I plan on spending every moment of it with you."

William wrapped his arm about her waist and pulled her closer, both of them enjoying the warmth and comfortable silence. After a few moments, however, a soft rapping at William's door interrupted their morning tranquility.

William growled softly under his breath, "Ophelia!" Josephine laughed quietly as he raised his head from his pillow. "Go away, woman!" he called to the door. "Leave us in peace for a few more moments!"

Contrary to her usual habit, Ophelia actually pushed the door open and took half a step through, trying to maintain the privacy of her mistress while still carrying out her task.

"So sorry, sir," she quickly offered, "but Constable Fairbanks is here for Mrs. Dunham."

William sat upright, clearly irate, and Josephine pushed herself onto one elbow. "What on Earth for?" William demanded, his tone much too brisk for this early in the morning.

Concern drew Ophelia's brow together as she answered. "He said he would only speak to Mrs. Dunham, sir. Something is amiss about his manner, though. I am not sure what to make of it."

"It is not your place to make anything of it!' William's vexation poured out onto Ophelia, but Josephine put a hand on her husband's shoulder and addressed her maid.

"Please make the constable comfortable, and see to it that he has breakfast. I will be down as soon as I am able."

"Already done, ma'am," Ophelia answered, backing out of the door and shutting it behind her.

William looked down at Josephine, his own concern mirrored in her face. "What do you think he wants?" William asked. "Perhaps he has finally found a link between Drake and Albert's murder."

Josephine shook her head. Tension was building inside her chest, but she chose to keep a calm demeanor. "He is here at Mr. Drake's bidding, William," she answered, rising from the bed and tying her bed coat around her waist.

William also rose and pulled on his pants. "How can you know that?" he asked, grabbing a shirt from his wardrobe and donning it hastily.

"Because it is the next logical move," she answered. "We already know the constable is in Mr. Drake's confidence, and that Mr. Drake knows I am behind the rescue of those girls."

Alarm bit at William's expression. "The papers!" he breathed. "The indentured servitude papers! Drake still has them for every girl he lost."

"Quite right," answered Josephine calmly. "Constable Fairbanks is here to arrest me."

"You must leave at once, Josephine!" William insisted. "I will distract the constable while Hans drives you to the docks. I will meet you there and we can be aboard a ship to London before nightfall!"

Josephine was shaking her head before William even finished speaking. "Then what?" she asked. "Fleeing would leave Hamilton Manor vulnerable to Drake. He could legally retrieve every one of the girls at Rosewood Hall who had once belonged to him. Everything I have accomplished would be for naught."

Frustration and anger clouded William's handsome features. "You cannot stay here, Josephine," he pleaded. "You have helped those girls to the best of your ability. There is nothing more to be done. You must think of yourself this time – and of me."

Josephine visibly winced as his words cut through her. She did want to run. She wanted to run away with this wonderful man and spend the rest of her days with him in England, where they would be safe and happy. They would never be bothered by Byron Drake there. She could take Ophelia and Jeffrey with her, and leave Darcy in charge of the estate.

But then Darcy would have to deal with Drake, and find a way to protect the girls at Rosewood Hall, not to mention himself. If Drake ever found the opportunity to end Darcy, he would take it without hesitation. Josephine was certain Drake would make that opportunity a reality if he were allowed to continue in his ventures.

Closing her eyes, she took a deep breath before answering her husband. "This is the only way to proceed, William."

"No, Josephine," he insisted, pounding his fist in his hand. "You will listen to me in this matter. You promised to trust my judgment, and I am holding you to that promise!"

She looked at William through an expression of sadness, and her next words almost broke her heart in two. "No, William. I cannot."

He stood motionless, visibly stunned at her refusal. Josephine walked past him and out the door to her own chambers, determined to meet Constable Fairbanks in something other than her bed coat. William watched her go without another word, anger seething out of his every pore. Finally, he pulled on his boots and tromped downstairs to dispense his wrath on the waiting constable.

When Josephine finally descended the stairs and made her way to the sitting room, she found the constable sitting on the edge of the settee wearing a very uncomfortable expression, and her husband sitting across from him, glaring at the man with undisguised vehemence. The constable rose nervously as soon as he caught sight of Mrs. Dunham.

"Good morning, ma'am," he began, his voice lacking the boldness that had been his mainstay the last time they had met. Whatever his task was this morning, Josephine could see he was not favorable to it.

She smiled graciously. "I suppose that remains to be seen," she answered, seating herself beside William. Ophelia brought her mistress a tray with three cups of hot coffee and placed it on the table between Josephine and the constable. Josephine reached for hers and sipped it casually. Neither William nor the constable reached for theirs.

After a satisfying sip of her coffee, Josephine asked the constable, "What can I do for you today?" She placed her free hand over William's, trying to discreetly calm his mood. It had no visible effect, as William continued to drill into the constable with a dreadful stare.

"Well, Mrs. Dunham," he answered, his nervousness heightening now that the main reason for his visit was being addressed, "to be blunt, it has been alleged that you have committed theft of a grand scale against Byron Drake by stealing many of his employees – indentureships for whom he paid a great deal of money."

William's indigence poured out through his voice as he answered the constable, his frame rising with his voice. "You think you can come into my home and accuse my wife..."

"William." Josephine's soft voice and gentle hand on his shoulder quieted William's tirade, much to the relief of the constable, who continued his address after William returned to his seat.

"I am sure this is a baseless accusation," he continued, eying William warily, "but, as constable, it is my duty to investigate such accusations."

"Just like you investigated the death of my wife's driver?" William added, his voice abundant with angry irony.

"Sir," answered the constable, "I had no evidence to support your accusations against Mr. Drake. Furthermore, I..."

Josephine briskly held her hand in front of her, silencing the constable and demanding the attention of both of the men.

"Sir," she began, addressing the constable, "the allegations made by Mr. Drake are entirely true." Both men started in shock at her frankness, though William found his voice before the constable.

"Josephine, are you mad?!" he exclaimed.

"What would you have me do, William?" she responded. "Lie to the man? I will not."

"Blood and ashes, woman!" he cursed. "That is exactly what I would have you do!"

The constable shook his head, as if he were not sure of what he had just heard. "I'm sorry, Mrs. Dunham," he said incredulously, "but did you just admit your guilt in this matter?"

"Yes," she responded calmly. "I have taken many of the girls indentured to Mr. Drake without purchasing their indentureship from him."

The constable was visibly confused. "Why would you do such a thing, Mrs. Dunham? Didn't you know the act was illegal."

"Of course," she answered. "I knew the legality of the matter." William crossed his arms in frustration as he sat next to her, clearly disapproving of his wife's tactic.

"Then why did you take those girls?" the constable continued.

Josephine took another sip of her coffee and looked the constable directly in the eye. "What occupation do you think Mr. Drake uses those girls for, Constable?" she asked, her voice razor sharp.

The constable readjusted his position on the settee, clearly uncomfortable with the direction this conversation was taking. "Well," he mused, "I suppose Mr. Drake needs maids for his inns and serving girls for his taverns. I am sure he does not act dishonorably towards those girls."

Josephine smiled slyly. "Sir," she continued, "I own the bank where you hold you accounts. Did you think Mr. Drake's regular payments to you would escape my notice?" An ashen pallor settled over the constable's face, and William turned to his wife in surprise, then back to the constable.

"Your livelihood depends on believing every word Byron Drake utters," she continued. "I would ask you to question your own motives in this matter and believe what is right before your eyes. You know what happens to those girls."

"Is this true, man?!" William demanded, his voice flirting dangerously with violence. "I should have you publicly flogged for such despicable behavior!"

"We are not here to discuss my affairs!" the constable fired back, "but your wife's actions!"

"Very true," Josephine answered, before William could retort to the constable. "So we are. I have admitted my guilt, Constable. Is there anything else?"

Constable Fairbanks was still shocked by the whole conversation that had just taken place. He blinked a few times and raised his eyebrows, unsure of how to proceed under these circumstances. "I suppose that I have to insist you return those girls to Mr. Drake's charge at once."

An expression of humorous scorn lit Josephine's face. "And back into a life of abuse and prostitution? I certainly will not!" It was the most emotion she had shown during the entire conversation, and her unconquerable tone and fierce reply caused pride to well up in William's chest, despite his current unhappiness with her.

The constable frowned. "Mrs. Dunham, I must insist," he pressed.

"Sir," Josephine replied, "I will guard those young ladies with my freedom and my life, if necessary. Byron Drake will never lay a finger on any of them ever again."

"You will have to come with me if you do not cooperate, Mrs. Dunham," he answered. "And I will have the grounds searched to locate those girls."

"I will happily go with you," she replied, her detached manner returning. "But," she added, "do you really want to be a party to the return of those girls to a life of abuse and death?"

Shame covered the constable's features momentarily, and he refused to meet Josephine's piercing eyes. "I will not search the grounds," he conceded, "but you must accompany me to the jailhouse."

"What!" William roared, anger propelling him up from the settee. "You mean to take my wife to jail?"

The constable rose quickly in defense. "She has left me no choice in the matter, sir!" he retorted.

Josephine stood and put herself between her husband and the lawman. "I am willing to accompany you, sir," she offered, "if you will keep your word regarding the search." Turning to William, she tried to placate his distress. "It is all right, William. I am able to endure this."

His expression was almost a snarl as he glared at Constable Fairbanks. "This is outrageous!" he answered. "A lady such as yourself should never be treated in this manner!"

The constable's nervous disposition only increased as he reached for Josephine. "Please, ma'am," he said. "The longer we prolong this, the worse the situation will become." He cast another apprehensive glance at William, perhaps fearing a show of physical violence from him at any moment.

"May I have a few words with my husband before we depart?" Josephine asked, her voice still controlled and certain.

"Of course, Mrs. Dunham," he replied, taking a few steps back to afford some privacy to the couple. Taking a refined lady into custody was clearly putting the man out of his element, and his discomfort showed even in the way he stood.

Josephine turned away from the constable and leaned close to William. In hushed and hurried tones, she began speaking. "You must instruct Ophelia to vacate the girls to Lexington. We have a small home there that will accommodate them. They will be crowded, but safe. The constable is gracious now, but his resolve cannot be trusted. He will come back after I am in his custody."

"Josephine!" he responded, his voice also hushed to avoid being heard. "You cannot go through with this! You must follow my plan and flee to London!"

She ignored him. "After I leave with the constable," she continued, "gather Darcy, my lawyer, Mr. Graves, and our banker, Mr. Blythe. Bring them to the jail, but no one else."

"This is utter insanity! You cannot mean to allow this!"

Josephine placed her small hand on William's still unshaven face, her brown eyes steady, and she kissed him tenderly on his lips. "Will you do as I have asked?" she said, when her lips left his and her mouth was close to his ear.

William looked down at her, his own expression twisted with chagrin and defeat. Stroking her soft, brown hair, he answered, "Of course I will."

Josephine nodded and smiled softly. Then, turning to the constable, she announced, "I am ready to go, sir." She strode to the door the same way she did most other things, with command and confidence. The constable had to hurry in order to catch up with her and open the door for her as they exited the foyer.

William watched, feeling helpless as his wife entered the coach with Constable Fairbanks. He knew she could weather the cramped and uncomfortable quarters of the jail without any difficulty. She was not one of those women who would wither without her luxury.

William's main worry was for her safety. What would happen when the constable left, especially since he was on Byron Drake's payroll? Drake could waltz in and do whatever he wished to his wife.

"Ophelia!' The maid was at his side half a second after he called. She had been outside the door the whole time, and was well aware of the entire situation.

"What are you going to do, sir?" she began, not waiting for him to issue orders. "You cannot allow this to continue!"

"Fetch Darcy," he said, hastily finding his coat in the foyer's closet. "Tell him to meet me at the constable's office immediately with Mr. Graves and Mr. Blythe! You will also instruct Mrs. Stoddely to move all of the girls to the house in Lexington this very day."

"Sir!" Ophelia's voice was sharp. "What about Josephine?"

"Ophelia!" William thundered back as he started for the door, "You will do as I say without question!"

Ophelia nodded and curtsied quickly, but her face was contorted into a stressful and worried scowl. William paused as he opened the door.

"Ophelia!" he called, his voice softened slightly. Ophelia turned to face him. "I know we are often at odds," William offered, "but on this matter, we are of the same mind."

Ophelia smiled as best as she could. "Thank you, sir. I will trust you in that." She quickly turned and almost ran to carry out her master's instructions. William shook his head with the irony of the situation as he exited the front door. His wife, the one woman who should trust his judgment and advice without question, completely rebuffed both at a moment of critical decision. Ophelia, on the other hand, seemed to go out of her way to vex him. Yet, she was now trusting her mistress to his action.

Hans was already trotting up the lane with Hero, no doubt instructed by Mrs. Dunham on her way out. "Good man!" exclaimed William as he mounted the impatient stallion and galloped toward Boston.

Ophelia practically jogged to the carriage house, where Darcy immediately saddled up and rode for town. Ophelia lost no time in coming down the path to the ivy encrusted gates of Rosewood Hall. Mrs. Stoddely was sitting on a stone bench with Shannon Tiernan, each woman holding chalk and a slate. Shannon rose with a glad smile as she saw Ophelia approach, her rounded belly very pronounced. The girl's smile faded when she saw Ophelia's expression, however, and Mrs. Stoddely also rose in alarm.

"Goodness, Ophelia!" the headmistress exclaimed. "What is the matter?"

"Mrs. Stoddely." Ophelia nodded a greeting while trying to catch her breath. Shannon put her arm around her friend and guided her to the bench. After a few more moments and deep breaths, Ophelia stated,

"Mrs. Dunham has ordered all of the girls to be moved to the house in Lexington. Today. Now."

Shock registered on Mrs. Stoddely's face, and a few more of the girls gathered around the trio. "What has happened, Ophelia?" The headmistress' tone was gravely serious.

"The constable has arrested Mrs. Dunham at the bidding of Mr. Drake, and she fears he will try to take the girls from here and return them to..." Ophelia could not bring herself to finish the sentence, nor did she have to. Every woman present understood the peril at hand, and panic could be seen growing in their faces.

Mrs. Stoddely, however, stood upright and steady in their midst, her voice rising over the alarmed murmur that was starting to circulate. "Ladies," she announced, "we will leave straightway. Gather what things you can in ten minutes, help any others who may need it, and meet here at the gate. We will go to the carriage house together and depart at once." She looked down at Ophelia. "How many carriages are at our disposal?"

"All three, ma'am," she answered, "and the drivers are making them ready now."

Mrs. Stoddely frowned in thought. "That means only twelve girls can go by carriage. We have nine more that will need to go by horseback. I am not sure all of the girls can ride."

"You can put six to a carriage, Mrs. Stoddely," offered Shannon, "It may be cramped, but it will be effective. The other two young ladies can ride with the drivers."

"Two?" Ophelia questioned, suspicion rising in her voice. "You most certainly mean three. You cannot stay behind."

"Hurry up, girl," Mrs. Stoddely urged Shannon, "you must not tarry here."

Shannon remained seated beside Ophelia. "I am not willing to leave, Mrs. Stoddely. I will remain here with Ophelia and Mr. Adams."

The headmistress stared at Shannon for only a moment, her piercing gaze ascertaining the situation of the girl's bulging middle, and perhaps her attachment to Mr. Adams. After a few seconds of thought, Mrs. Stoddely consented, "As you wish, child." She turned and quickly made for the hall to gather her own things, and to gently urge on the girls in her charge.

Ophelia turned to her friend as Mrs. Stoddely disappeared into Rosewood Hall, "I know your reason for staying, Shannon, but Darcy will object."

Shannon nodded. "I know, but I will not be parted from him again. And," she placed her hand on the top of her pregnant stomach, "I fear a trip would be unwise for me now." She smiled reassuringly at Ophelia and returned her hand to that of her friend. "Besides, I will be just fine here at the school. I will quite enjoy the solitude."

"Absolutely not!" Ophelia exclaimed. "If you are insistent on staying, then you will stay with me in my quarters at the main house." She stood. "Now, I will help you get your things."

Shannon threw her arms around Ophelia and embraced her tightly, then the two made their way into Rosewood Hall to gather Shannon's meager belongings, bidding more than a few goodbyes to the exiting girls who were going on to Lexington.

36

Had it not been for the fact that Josephine Dunham was traveling in the custody of the constable, her trip to town would have been quite pleasant. The constable himself was trying to be polite and conversational, but Josephine could see that this whole situation had rattled the man. His uneasy glances in her direction and momentary frowns of shame betrayed that this task he was carrying out was not agreeable to him. At least his conscience is somewhat intact, Josephine mused.

As the carriage stopped at their final destination, two uniformed constables came to the carriage and escorted Josephine through the ominous looking doors of the building. The constable followed two steps behind as the uniformed men led her to the end cell along a poorly lit row containing many cells on either side.

Each cell seemed as if it were holding too many occupants for its small size. They were mostly men, but some women were among the occupants, sheltered in two cells meant only for females. From what Josephine could see, most of these women resembled the girls she found on the street – disheveled, thin, and hopeless. The noise and calls from the rowdy inhabitants died down as the proper lady dressed in finery was led down the aisle to the end cell, which was empty, obviously waiting for Mrs. Dunham to occupy it.

"I really am sorry for all of this, Mrs. Dunham," the constable offered, breaking through the gloom of humanity with his voice. "If these charges were not so many, or so serious, or even if you had denied them, then all of this would be unnecessary."

Josephine merely nodded. "Thank you for your kindness, Constable. Your efforts are appreciated." Again, a look of shame crossed the man's face as he shut and locked the door to her cell.

"I will be back to check on you, Mrs. Dunham," he announced.

"Of course, Constable." Josephine seated herself on the bench that would serve as both her chair and her bed for the next several days, perhaps even the next several weeks, until a hearing could be conducted. The December chill lingered in the brick wall behind her, and diffused into her back as she wearily leaned against it.

The constable had not even been out of the row of cells a full five minutes before she heard the thumping of heavy boots on the floor. The raucous noise of the prisoners, which had resumed after the constable exited, again fell silent. The hair on the back of Josephine's neck raised, and before she even looked up, she knew who was paying her a visit.

Byron Drake walked confidently up to the bars and flashed his most charming smile to the woman behind them. "Mrs. Dunham," he began, his voice dripping with pleasure, "I cannot tell you how much joy it gives me to see you again – especially here."

Josephine did not stand up to greet her visitor. Instead she folded her hands in front of her in a businesslike manner and looked Byron Drake directly in the eye. She said nothing in reply, and held her expression steady. Only a slight raise of her left eyebrow indicated that she had any interest in what this man had to say.

"You must have determined my plan by now, have you not, Mrs. Dunham?" He walked slowly along the front of the cell as he spoke, letting his hand slide from bar to bar. "And you must also know the penalty you face for your foolish undertakings. Each act of theft carries with it a minimum of five years in prison." He stopped at the center of her cell and looked her over with an offensive smile, visible even in the dim light. "Exactly how many girls did you take from me? Eighteen? Twenty?"

Reaching into his jacket, he pulled from his pocket a dense packet of folded papers and held them up for her to see. "Twenty-three," he said, almost laughing. "You traded 115 years of your life for twenty-three Irish harlots!"

He carefully replaced the papers in his jacket, then bent down and rested himself on one knee, bringing his face to her level. She still did not respond to the man in any way.

He continued, "My reason for visiting you was to work out a solution to this dilemma you seem to have gotten yourself into. You see, I have already replaced all of the girls you stole from me. They come in from the docks every day, and I am waiting for them. Well," he sneered, "for the pretty ones, anyway. Please forgive me," he added, "I digress from the subject. What I am trying to say is all of your efforts have been for nothing. For every girl you have taken, I have replaced her with two more. I am almost making more money than God Himself, and you have not even put a dent in my undertakings!"

Drake smoothed the top of his pant leg before continuing. "As a matter of fact, Mrs. Dunham, the only person in this city with more money than me is, why, you." He smiled slyly and leaned forward. "Which brings me to my gracious offer."

Josephine raised her eyebrow fully, her sense of irony peaked, but she remained silent. He pushed himself from his knee and stood straight, looking down at her. "I wish to have everything you do, Mrs. Dunham. I want your bank accounts, your businesses, your homes, your servants, everything that has your name or your idiot husband's name on it. I want everything. In exchange, I will drop all of the charges against you, agree to not retrieve any of the girls you took from me, even Miss Tiernan, and promise not to murder your husband and his entire family."

Drake's voice held the air of merriment, as if the very thought of murder was, for him, like a day at the park. She knew he was lying, especially about allowing Miss Tiernan to live free of his interference. But if she did not agree, she was certain Drake would carry out everything he had just threatened.

"You, of course," he continued, "will go free. I doubt your husband's father, the most excellent Duke Dunham," his voice held scorn as he said the name, "will allow you to continue to be his daughter-in-law. He will have to find a more... well, a more financially endowed woman to take your place and redeem his family's finances."

Drake laughed out loud. “But not to worry, Josephine. I will always have a place for you, should you ever need it. You will never have to grovel on the streets for your meals, not as long as you lend me your company, if you will, on a regular basis.”

Josephine could not hide the disgust that welled up inside her and twisted her face; and though no words came from her mouth, her expression was enough to give Byron Drake his answer. He merely laughed again, then turned to leave.

“Oh,” he added, addressing her a last time, “I hear you have been seeking Duke Dunham’s financial manager. Did you really think I would leave a loose end walking about Boston?” Drake smiled again and tipped his hat to Josephine as he left her cell door. “I will expect an answer before the hearing.” Just as quickly as he had entered the jail, he was gone, leaving behind a disturbed silence.

Josephine’s heart plunged inside her chest as she realized that the Dunham’s financial manager would never be found. Drake had likely done away with him months ago. She felt profound sadness that another person had lost their life to Drake’s schemes.

She also knew, without any doubt, that all of her legal preparations against Byron Drake would not stand up in court without the testimony of that financial manager. She had underestimated his ruthlessness, and in doing so, had given him the upper hand, perhaps even the victory. Drake was correct. All of her efforts had been for nothing.

Josephine closed her eyes and leaned back against the wall. Father, she prayed, what am I supposed to do? I have been compassionate and obedient, yet this man has won. I spared his life at Your bidding when I had the resources to finish him, yet he has trapped me. What of my husband now? What of my servants? And Miss Tiernan and her child? If I do not do as this man asks, he will destroy us all. He may do so anyway. Show me, Father, she pleaded. Show me what to do.

Quieting her mind and her fears, Josephine listened. Sometimes her Lord spoke to her through memories of Mr. Hamilton’s gentle wisdom, or through verses that were brought to her remembrance, or sometimes, on very rare occasions, through a unique, gentle voice overriding all her other thoughts. She listened for several minutes, but nothing made itself prominent through the resumed comments and curses of the other inmates.

Please, Lord. Please show me.

A few more seconds ticked by, and Josephine heard the barred door at the end of the aisle turn on its hinges. Her eyes opened to the worried expressions of her husband, Darcy, Mr. Graves and Mr. Blythe as they stood on the other side of her cell. Just behind them was Constable Fairbanks, holding the keys to her cell in his hand.

William shot a hostile glance to the constable as the man unlocked Josephine's cell door, allowing the four men to crowd into the small space.

"Sir," she said to the constable, who was still standing outside the cell, "I require privacy for this conversation. Would you be gracious enough to grant it?" Even though Constable Fairbanks had shown considerable dismay at this whole turn of events, Josephine knew he was still on Drake's payroll, and could not be trusted for a moment.

The constable's expression of mild discomfort increased at Josephine's request. The rich, elderly voice of Mr. Graves, Josephine's lawyer, intervened as the constable hesitated. "You are required to allow me a private conference with my client, Constable. If you do not, I will file charges of my own."

Clearly unhappy, the constable turned on his heel and made for the door. "I will return in a quarter of an hour," he announced, exiting the hall.

Losing no time, Mr. Graves turned to Josephine. "Now, my dear," he began in a hushed voice, "your husband has advised me of the details of this matter." Taking her hand in his and patting it in a fatherly manner he continued, "I do admire your bravery and compassion, Josephine, but it has landed you in a very compromising position. We must produce a valid argument for your defense that will keep you out of prison. We must also minimize any damage this news will do to your business affairs. I already have several ideas I would like to put forward."

Darcy shook his head. "It will do no good," he whispered.

"Why ever not, Mr. Adams?" countered Mr. Graves, sounding justly offended.

"Because Judge Patterson is a frequent guest of Byron Drake, and you can be sure Drake will have no qualms about blackmailing the judge to produce his desired outcome," replied Darcy.

Mr. Graves expression was one of shock. "You are certain of this, young man?"

"I saw him myself inside The Crimson Dagger some time ago, and have seen him enter the place many more times since then. Any legal defense you put forward will fail, no matter how sound."

Josephine looked over to her husband, who was following the conversation with concern. Drake's words came back to her, "In exchange...I promise not to murder your husband and his entire family." She was not certain if Drake would keep his promise, but she was certain he would carry out his threat if she refused his offer. Was this really the only way to save her husband? William caught her look, saw the defeat in her eyes. The concern in his own grew.

"Then we must quickly and aggressively pursue a lawsuit against Mr. Drake regarding the embezzlement of the Dunham's finances," replied Mr. Graves. "Perhaps if we find a way to cripple him financially, he will be unable to affect Judge Patterson's decision regarding Mrs. Dunham."

"Even if the financial manager were located today," Mr. Blythe interjected, "I am not sure it would matter. Mr. Drake does not seem to actually own anything."

"What are you talking about, sir?" William asked in a hushed tone. "That man owns half of the slums of Boston. It seems there is no end to his financial resources."

"I thought so, as well," Mr. Blythe answered. "But, while preparing for the suit against him, I discovered that Mr. Drake transferred all of his property to another person some time back, presumable to guard against this type of action. We have not been able to locate this young lady yet, but everything is in her name. Nothing can be taken from Drake if he doesn't own anything."

Josephine sat upright, and a verse fell from her mouth. "Better is a poor man who is blameless... Oh, Mr. Drake is a clever man, indeed!" she uttered, as if the thought were still a long way off. All four men paused and looked at Mrs. Dunham as if this whole experience was proving too trying for the distraught woman.

William glanced toward the other men, then took his wife's hand. "This may be too much for you, my dear. We should carry on this business somewhere else and let you rest as best as you can in this place."

"No," she responded quickly, and a fire lit in her expression. Darcy recognized it at once, and he smiled.

"Ah, I know that look," he offered. "I already pity your contender."

"He was here, actually," Josephine began. "Mr. Drake paid me a visit just before you arrived."

Confusion changed to alarm in William's face. "Are you all right? Did he hurt you?"

Josephine took her husband's hand with reassurance. "He did not touch me," she replied. "But he did wish to 'settle' things."

"You made no agreements with him!" Mr. Graves demanded more than inquired, alarm raising his voice above that of a whisper.

"I said nothing at all," she answered, "but I did ascertain that our missing financial manager will never be found. He has likely been deceased for some time now. Mr. Blythe is quite right. There will be no ground gained in a lawsuit against Mr. Drake."

"What else did he say?" asked William. "And where was the constable when this transpired?" His ire rose with each word he uttered.

Ignoring his last question, Josephine continued, "He said he would drop all of the charges against me, not pursue the girls I rescued, and not murder my husband and family if I signed over everything William and I own to him."

"How vile!" exclaimed Mr. Graves.

"Everything?" Mr. Blythe was aghast.

"Every, single, penny," she replied, her expression finally releasing a sly smile.

"What are you planning?" asked the elderly lawyer, eying her grin with confusion etched on his brow.

Josephine found William's face again and brushed a few brown locks away from his worried eyes. "I plan on losing, Mr. Graves," she answered confidently. "Losing everything."

Two hours after leaving Josephine in the confines of Leverett Street Jail, William, Darcy, Mr. Graves, and Mr. Blythe entered the foyer of Hamilton Manor. Ophelia had already seen to the hasty evacuation of the tenants of Rosewood Hall, and had also made certain that Shannon Tiernan was comfortably moved into her own quarters. Now she was busily taking each man's coat and making ready to bring them afternoon tea.

"Ophelia," William said, as she took his coat and directed him to the sitting room, "I need to speak with you."

"Of course, sir," she responded. "I will make sure to come in after you have conducted your business with the gentlemen."

"No, Ophelia," William answered. Ophelia stopped in her tracks as she realized all four men were staring at her. "Actually, their business is with you."

Ophelia twisted her brow in confusion. "Sir?" she said. "What business could they have with me?"

"You must save Josephine, Ophelia," William answered simply. "You must save all of us." He held his arm toward the sitting room, gesturing for Ophelia to enter. She looked to the face of each man. All of them wore solemn expressions, except for her brother, who was smiling. Both Mr. Graves and Mr. Blythe were holding thick stacks of documents in their arms.

She silently obeyed her master's wish and took a seat in the sitting room, the confusion on her face growing. The four men filed into the room behind her, and Darcy shut the door.

37

The late December weather and stone construction combined to make the environment in Leverett Street Jail exceptionally frigid. Josephine had one blanket at her disposal, given to her by the jailer. She wrapped it around her shoulders as she sat on the long, wooden bench, her head bowed. These hours were limping by slowly, but she filled them with prayer.

In this place, her prayers were focused and direct, more so than at any other time. After pondering this for some hours, and discussing it with her Father, she attributed this focus to the lack of distractions caused by everyday comforts. Her thoughts went to the Apostle John and the amount of time spent in captivity on Patmos. It was there the Lord appeared to him with a great revelation. It was there that he was privileged enough to see his King again as he had never seen him before.

Josephine reckoned that John would not have traded one moment of imprisonment if it meant not experiencing his Lord in such a way. She would give countless hours of her own life in here if she could see Jesus like John did.

Her prayers turned to more current matters, and concern for Ophelia flooded her heart. Father, she pleaded, please keep her safe. My actions will place her in harm's way, and I could not live knowing she perished because of me. Please, Mighty God, please protect her from Byron Drake. Please keep her safe in Your hand. Images of Albert flooded her head, and reinforced the fear she felt for Ophelia.

"Hey! Hey, lady!" A young, deep voice calling from the neighboring cell caught Josephine's attention. She rose from her bench and moved to the far end of the cell, which only took two steps. Then she sat on the floor with her face next to the bars.

"Hello, sir," she responded to the voice, as if the two were passing pleasantries in the park on a fine afternoon.

"I heard what Mr. Drake said to you earlier. You should not be making enemies of that man!" the voice continued, his thick accent very Latin. "Don't you know who he is?"

"I did what I had to," she answered. "But my Father will see me through this."

"Your father? I doubt any man can get you out of this mess with Drake?"

"Sir," she said. "God is my Father."

There was a pause, then the voice continued. "You're a strange one, lady," he finally responded,

Josephine laughed softly. "What is your name, good sir?" she asked.

"I'm not a 'good sir', lady," he snorted. "And it's Victor." A large, dark golden hand came from the other side of the wall and offered itself in front of the bars of Josephine's cell. Josephine reached through her own bars and shook Victor's hand firmly, like the handshake that transpires after a solid business deal.

"Mrs. Josephine Dunham. It is my pleasure to make your acquaintance." The man was silent.

She smiled again, then added. "Victor – like Queen Victoria in England," she offered.

"I don't imagine it's anything like the Queen," Victor scoffed, "but it was nice of you to say. There's nothing nice about Drake, though. If you've gotten on his bad side, then God help you, lady."

Josephine was thoughtful. "He has, Victor," she answered.

"Then what are you doing here? Instead of in your warm mansion?" he pressed.

"Perhaps I'm here to meet you," she answered without hesitation. "I think it's going quite well so far, don't you?"

"You shouldn't take this lightly," Victor responded. "I heard Drake, and what you did to him. You cost him money, hurt his pride, and now he has it in for you. You should be worried, Mrs. Dunham."

"What do you know about Mr. Drake, Victor?" she responded.

"I know he doesn't like to pay full price for his rum. That's why I'm here. I brought him the finest rum from Cuba, and he didn't pay me what he agreed to. When I protested, he took my shipment anyway and had me thrown in here like a dog. Had the port levy false fees against me. Now I can't get out until I pay up, and I can't pay up until I get out."

"Ah, you are a ship's captain, then?" Josephine's voice held pleasant surprise, and she immediately began plotting while offering silent thanks to God for answering her prayer for Ophelia so quickly.

"I was three days ago," Victor answered. "Now I'm just another piece of rubbish rotting in this place."

"No one is rubbish, Victor," Josephine responded, her voice serious. "No one."

There was silence for many moments, and Josephine began working out the best way to approach this man for help. Then Victor's deep voice sounded again.

"You play poker?"

"Poker?" It was quite the unexpected request.

"Yes, cards," Victor answered, sliding a few cards around the brick wall dividing their cells. She took the cards, which had clearly seen better days, and turned them in her hand. She could barely see them. The dim flicker of the gas torch on the far wall gave almost enough light.

"I've played some poker before, but I've never been very good at it," she answered.

"I'll teach you," Victor answered. "Just promise you'll hide the cards when you hear a constable coming our way."

Josephine smiled and squinted, examining the cards in her hand by the inadequate light. They were mostly low cards, with only one face card in her hand. "I promise," she answered.

"We'll try five card draw," Victor said, explaining the nuances of game bit by bit until Josephine had a good grasp of the details. They played many hands, most of which she lost, while Victor's deep voice told her about Cuba, and the rum business, and the other ports he had traded in aboard his ship, the *Reina Dona Isabel*.

After many hours, and many games, and many instances of hastily hiding cards, they heard the hinges of the far door swing and the heavy boots of a constable. Josephine's heart skipped a beat as she heard William's agitated voice complaining bitterly to the uniformed man. William finally stopped in front of her cell as she stood from the floor to meet him.

"You have ten minutes, sir," the guard offered as William reached through the bars to take Josephine's hand. He didn't even notice the large, golden man sitting just two feet from him next to the bars.

William shot the constable a venomous look. "Do you mind, sir?" he retorted. "I would like to have a semi-private conversation with my wife."

"Sorry, sir," the constable replied in a nondescript manner. "Constable Fairbanks says I have to stay with you until you're done."

"Blood and ashes," William responded, the frustration mounting in his voice.

Josephine squeezed his hand. "I am all right, William," she said, offering him a small smile of comfort.

"How can you be all right in this place?" he fumed, taking her other hand and squeezing it tightly. "This is contemptible at best!"

Instead of answering, Josephine brought her face to the bars, and William responded by leaning his ear closer. "Is it done?" she asked, her voice barely audible.

William nodded, then answered by whispering in her ear in the same fashion, "All of the details have already been attended to, and all the documents have been signed. It is done." Then he shook his head and closed his eyes before continuing, "I can hardly believe this has happened."

She rested her forehead against the bars. "All will be well in due time, William. Trust me."

The constable's voice chimed in harshly. "Five minutes, sir," he alerted. William's face contorted in anger.

"We are trying to post bail for you," he continued, "but the judge is being difficult. I was also thinking that we need to send Ophelia to the house in Lexington with the other girls to ensure her safety. Drake will do whatever he must to win this battle."

"Do what you are able in regard to the bail," Josephine answered, "but do not expect that it will be much. If Judge Patterson is indebted to Mr. Drake in any manner, then your efforts may be in vain. However, I think there is a better way to ensure Ophelia's safety."

Josephine again whispered hurried words in William's ear, while her husband's expression changed from worry, to confusion, then to amusement. When she was done, he responded, "You really do like to stir things up, Josephine. But if this will vex that mongrel, Drake, while securing Ophelia's security, then I am all for it." He gently kissed her cheek through the bars, then accompanied the waiting constable down the corridor and out of the jailhouse.

Josephine sat back against the wall, her heart heavy with the sight of William leaving. Still, she smiled slightly to herself. All would be well. She trusted in that. She trusted in God.

"Seems like you have a good man." Victor's accent broke through her reverie.

"Yes," she responded, "and I will miss him very much in the next few days."

"You don't think you'll make bail?"

"No. I am certain Mr. Drake means to keep me here as long as possible."

Victor snorted. "That man's a pig," he added, "but at least I will keep you company." Josephine heard the sound of cards being shuffled, and she returned to her seat on the floor to play another round of poker with Victor.

"Not many fine ladies would sit on the floor to play cards with a Cuban captain," Victor remarked, dealing the cards from around the brick wall.

"I suppose," she answered, picking up the cards, "that not many fine ladies have ever had the opportunity." Victor laughed, his rich voice full of humor for the first time that day.

The pale morning light brought another constable down the cold corridor. His footsteps echoed against the ceiling as most of the prisoners still huddled quietly on the stone floors, trying to ward off the cold creeping from the stone into their bones. The uniformed man stopped in front of Victor's cell.

"Hey, you there!" he called harshly, waking the sleeping captain. "Get up if you want to get out of here!" He clanged the bars loudly with the ring of keys he held, then unlocked the door as Victor sat up. "Let's go!"

Victor eyed the man with suspicion. "Where are we going?" he asked.

"Wherever you want to," the constable replied, "as long as it's not here." Victor stood, but still did not move forward, the confusion thick in his expression.

"Someone paid your fees, and you'd better take advantage of it. Now get outta here before that someone changes their mind!" The constable held the door open, waiting impatiently for the captain. Victor did as he was told and exited the cell. In the hallway, he turned to the cell next to his and looked disbelievingly at the woman in a fine dress with disheveled hair, who was watching him with a smile.

"Lady," he said, "I never met anyone like you before. I hope your God does help you."

"We will meet again, Victor," Josephine answered. "Please take care of yourself, and your cargo – and may God richly bless you."

Victor cocked his head to the side in confusion. "My cargo?"

"Come on, come on! I don't have all day!" the uniformed man urged. "Or I might just put you back in there!"

Victor quickly nodded to Josephine and followed the constable down the aisle to the iron door that marked his freedom. As he did so, he noticed that the two cells housing the prostitutes were mostly empty. There had been at least a dozen girls there when he came through four days ago.

There was no time to dwell on it, though. The constable opened the iron door and led Victor to the front exit of Leverett Street Jail. As Victor walked through to the frigid morning on the other side, the constable remarked to him, "It'd be best if you don't come back to Boston – ever." Then he shut the door tight and left Victor to his own devices.

The ship's captain didn't need to be told twice. That lady, Mrs. Dunham, had told him to take care of his cargo. That must mean she had somehow secured his ship! With hurried steps, Victor made his way from Leverett Street to the docks, looking for the familiar mast of the *Reina Dona Isabel* against the gray sky as he drew closer to the harbor.

Incredibly, it was there! Victor broke into a run when he saw the mast, almost not believing his turn of luck. As he approached the dock where his ship was tied, he heard an unfamiliar sound. Were those voices? Woman's voices? Coming from his ship?

Victor strode up the gangplank of the *Reina Dona Isabel* and stood on his deck, his mouth hanging open in disbelief. At least fifteen women were buzzing about the ship, going in and out of the captain's cabin, popping up onto the deck from below and excitedly remarking to the other girls about the upcoming voyage, or their incredible luck at being bailed out of the jailhouse, or their gratitude at being able to escape the Boston winter for the distant and exotic shores of Cuba.

It suddenly dawned on Victor what Mrs. Dunham had meant when she asked him to "take care of his cargo".

There were also busy deckhands on board, loading crates and barrels of food and water, winding around the excited girls to stash the cargo below deck. When one of the girls, very young and wearing suggestive tatters, saw Victor, she ran over to him and took his hand.

"Thank you, Captain!" she cried. "Thank you so much for this!" Victor looked down at her as if she were mad, but other girls had seen him come aboard, and now they were also crowding around him, showering him with their thanks and embraces.

"Of course, ladies," he responded, not knowing what else to say. He kept nodding and smiling until he could make his way through the women to his captain's cabin. When he was finally inside, he shut the door firmly behind him, happy to escape the delighted girls milling about his deck. He turned to the wheel, then almost jumped out of his skin as saw another woman sitting calmly in the corner, looking over one of the charts.

She was older than the other girls by a few years, dressed well but sensibly, and quite stunning, with blonde tendrils of hair escaping her bun. Victor stood aloof, not knowing how to react to the beautiful woman in his captain's cabin, or this situation, or to any of the events that had transpired this day.

The woman gracefully rose and extended her hand, a mischievous twinkle lighting up her brown eyes. "You are Captain Victor, then?" she asked.

"I am," he answered, taking the extended hand and having the presence of mind to kiss the back of it. The woman smiled.

"My name is Ophelia Adams. I am here at my mistress's bidding. She sent this for you." The woman reached into the pocket of her full dress, pulled out a new deck of cards, and handed then to the befuddled man. "She sends her thanks." Victor reached out and took the cards from Ophelia, shook his head, and smiled. He turned them over in his hands. Brand new. He wondered if there was an implied message in the gesture. He dropped the deck into his shirt pocket.

Victor finally found his voice. "I am to take all of these women to Cuba, then?"

"And me, if you are willing," Ophelia answered. "My mistress feels that I am in danger here, and she wishes for me to flee Boston for the time being."

Victor frowned. "What am I to do with all those women once I get to Cuba? And what about the trip? You can't have women on a sailing vessel. It's bad luck!"

Ophelia nodded in understanding, as if she had been expecting his resistance. "I will take care of everything when we arrive, as well as your fee for transporting us. In addition, Mrs. Dunham was hoping there could be a permanent business relationship between you and her that would be profitable for both. Perhaps that possibility would outweigh any 'bad luck' we might bring to you or your vessel."

Victor eyed the woman's face as he mulled the prospect over, then patted the deck of cards in his pocket. "I would be happy to take you to Cuba, Miss Adams. You and all of your ladies."

Ophelia smiled largely, her beauty once again stunning the captain. "Thank you, Captain," she said. "You have my thanks, and that of my mistress. How soon can we be off?"

"As soon as we have all the supplies we need." Victor gestured to the deckhands loading the hold. "It seems you have taken care of that, as well."

"Yes," replied Ophelia, "and the crew. If they meet with your approval, of course."

"Then we can cast off in the hour."

Ophelia nodded and said no more. She resumed her seat in the corner of the cabin as Captain Victor left for the deck to make ready for departure. She wondered, not for the first time, if Josephine had made a wise decision regarding this situation. In any case, she was happy to be leaving Boston for a while, though she would severely miss Darcy, Shannon, and Josephine. She might even miss Mr. Dunham.

With the recent turn of events, however, Byron Drake was certain to want her dead, and Ophelia Adams was very opposed to that idea. Yesterday, she could not have imagined any circumstance that would ferry her off to a foreign land, much less Cuba. Today, it was the only logical course of action. She grinned as she watched the girls, deckhands, and mildly stunned captain through the window of the cabin.

It seemed that God had a sense of humor.

38

Josephine's miserable stay in the Leverett Street Jail lasted for almost two weeks, during which time she was allowed no visitors and no messages. She had not made another friend, either. Unlike Victor, the other occupants of the jail seemed uncomfortable even looking at her, much less engaging in conversation. Her fine dress and apparent status made those around her uneasy, and her presence here indicated something so out of place that the others avoided her universally.

So she pursued her prayers with even more fervor, grateful for the peace and serenity she found when spending time with her Lord. Time was a lonely companion, however, and Josephine felt her spirit slip from sureness and confidence to a place shadowed with uncertainty and sadness. Her thoughts followed suit, and more and more she found herself wondering how long she would have to wait here, how long God would allow her to be in this place.

That first day, her thoughts had lingered with joy on the Apostle John and his imprisonment, and the opportunity it had afforded him, his opportunity to see Jesus. Now, she thought more on his loneliness and suffering, and the long years in captivity his Lord had required of him. What did God have prepared for her? Would she be able to go through the trials He had in store?

She thought again of Byron Drake standing in front of her cell, holding the indentured servitude papers for each of the twenty-three girls she had rescued. One hundred and fifteen years. If things went terribly wrong, if her plans fell to tatters, she would be sentenced to one hundred and fifteen years in this place.

Give me Your strength, Lord, the strength to endure Your will. Josephine slipped to the floor and knelt at the bench, more prayers falling from her parched lips and tired mind. So engrossed was she in her activity that she did not notice the sound of boots striding down the aisle to her cell.

"Josephine?" William's astonished voice caught her attention as a constable fitted an iron key into the lock of her cell. She looked up to his concerned face and saw worry etched in every inch of his handsome features.

He stared for only a moment, taking in her drawn face and disheveled hair, then burst inside the cell and pulled her up from the floor. She threw her arms around his neck, reassuring herself that her husband was truly there.

"I have come to take you home!" he exclaimed, pulling her close. "And it is long overdue! Judge Patterson released you to make ready for court."

"I am so very glad," she answered, her face still against his chest. "So very glad. When is the hearing?"

"Tomorrow," he answered, pulling away gently and holding her at arm's length to look her over properly. "They did not take care of you by any means!" he remarked, casting a hot glance to the constable. "You are thinner and wearier than I have ever seen you!"

She smiled happily. "We are truly to go home? This very minute?"

William took her hand and led her out of the cell. "Before another second goes by!" he answered, brushing past the constable as quickly as Josephine's stride would allow. He waited impatiently for the man to unlock to iron door at the end of the aisle, and when he did, William did not wait to be escorted to the main door of the jailhouse, but hurried through the office with his arm around his wife's shoulder.

After they exited the vile place, he helped his wife to the carriage, opened the door for her, and nimbly climbed in the seat beside her. The driver flicked the reins and eased the horse into a trot, each step taking them away from Leverett Street and closer to Hamilton Manor. Josephine leaned wearily against William, and he wrapped both of his arms and a thick blanket around her in the privacy of the cab.

She closed her eyes and sighed happily, the jarring contrast of her situation from only ten minutes earlier very welcome. "Have you any news from Ophelia?" she finally asked. Her eyes were still closed, and she made no move to unsettle herself from his embrace.

"No," William answered. "I am quite certain we will hear nothing for many weeks. She is probably still en-route, and a message will have to be sent back by steam, taking another two weeks, at least." He kissed her hair, though his nose crinkled a bit. "I am sure she is fine."

"Of course you are right," she answered. "Is there any other news from Mr. Blythe or Mr. Graves?"

"Ah," answered William, his tone causing Josephine to sit upright and give him her full attention.

"What did they find?" she asked, her eyes lighting up with sudden interest.

William smiled. "Mr. Graves has been sifting through all of the court records of property transfers that were filed in the past few months, and he found the identity of the young lady Byron Drake transferred his property to."

"And?"

"Erin Moore is the lady," William said.

"Of course!" Josephine exclaimed. "Mr. Drake still thinks she is dead. He thought he could transfer everything over to her and still retain control of his funds, with no one being the wiser!"

"I have already been in contact with Miss Moore and explained the situation," William continued. "She was quite happy to learn Byron Drake had made her a rich woman."

"I am sure she was," Josephine replied, but her tone was grave rather than merry. "When Mr. Drake learns of this, however, he will take steps to remedy the situation and reclaim his possessions. Miss Moore will be in more peril than Ophelia."

"Perhaps," said William thoughtfully. "But Mr. Graves has already met with Miss Moore several times. He has changed the documents to ensure that Murray is Miss Moore's heir instead of Drake. Should anything happen to Murray, then all of the property will be distributed to various charities throughout Boston. But it would have been better if she and Murray were also on their way to Cuba."

"True," she answered, "but I see you have things well in hand, William," Josephine commented, smiling. "You are becoming quite the shrewd businessman. Is there anything left for me to attend to before tomorrow?" she asked.

William raised an eyebrow as he sniffed her hair again. "Well," he answered, somewhat reluctantly, "perhaps a bath is in order?"

Her laugh was genuine. "Yes," she answered. "I could not agree more."

William smiled as well, then became abruptly solemn. "Josephine?" he asked, his voice burdened with concern, "what will happen if tomorrow does not go as planned?"

Josephine sighed and returned to her place of security against his chest. "Then I will go to prison, William," she answered, "for the rest of my life."

"I would not be able to bear it," he answered.

"Then pray, William," she said. "Pray."

William was silent, though he pulled her against his chest again despite the lingering odor of the jailhouse clinging to her hair. Pray? He had been reading the heavy, old Bible left by Mr. Hamilton, especially when the nights had been long and lonely. That Book was interesting, sometimes even fascinating, but did the God in that Book even exist? If He did, did He give regard to human prayers?

He knew Josephine believed so with all her heart, and that Mr. Hamilton had, as well. He thought back to the day when Josephine poured out her heart to God, and William had unintentionally heard her struggle with Him. Would Josephine truly yield her will to an imagined being?

Unlikely. However, William could not bring himself to talk to a force that might not be there. The idea felt too foolish and childish. For now, he would hope for the best instead of pray for it, and enjoy the warmth of his wife against his chest. Tomorrow, the chance might be gone forever.

39

Byron Drake sat comfortably in the courtroom next to his lawyer, his smile as cold and persistent as the January chill clinging to the brick building. Judge Patterson had just seated himself at his bench, a white collar and black tie visible beneath his austere robe.

Drake nodded to the man, who raised an annoyed eyebrow, then continued rifling through his papers. Josephine Dunham and her idiotic husband sat just across the aisle, their lawyer whispering directions and suggestions as they listened attentively.

Her time in the Leverett Street Jail had affected her physically. She was thinner, and her face was drawn, which did nothing to improve her already homely looks. No matter. It was her spirit Drake was interested in. Did her time in jail give her enough perspective to seriously consider his offer? Drake was almost giddy with anticipation as he noted Mrs. Dunham's grim expression.

The lady at least had the good taste nod in his direction, while the man glared hatefully at him. Drake smiled graciously at Mr. Dunham. He was certain Mr. Dunham would try to take his head off were they in any other venue. But they were not, and Drake was about to strip everything away from them. From the look on Mr. Dunham's face, Drake could tell the man knew what was coming. The day was shaping up to be a very fine one, indeed.

The resounding boom of Judge Patterson's gavel echoed through the courtroom, signaling the beginning of the hearing. All the whispers and comments grew silent as the judge's eyes fell heavily on Mrs. Dunham.

"Mr. Graves," he began, his voice carrying an air of wearisome routine, "your client has been charged with a number of thefts against the plaintiff, Mr. Drake. We are here today to determine..."

"Excuse me, Judge Patterson." The lawyer for Byron Drake stood and brazenly interrupted the judge. The judge turned his attention to the man, then looked at Drake and sighed.

"Yes, Mr. Thompson?" he acquiesced unceremoniously.

"My client, Mr. Drake, has graciously offered to drop all charges against Mrs. Dunham if she agrees to his terms of financial compensation. I already have the contract in order, and would like to extend the formal offer to Mrs. Dunham before this hearing begins."

"Proceed."

Mr. Thompson met Mr. Graves in the center of the aisle and handed a sole document to the aged lawyer. Mr. Graves looked at the paper through his glasses, then cast an incredulous look at the other lawyer. Mr. Thompson shrugged without concern, then returned to his place beside Mr. Drake.

With seeming difficulty, Mr. Graves placed the document in front of Josephine. Drake watched closely as she read it over without any hint of surprise. Mr. Dunham, on the other hand, read the brief document and turned to Drake with a look that would have withered many other men. Drake took it as a good sign.

He watched expectantly as Josephine grasp the pen Mr. Graves offered her, then sign the document with no expression on her face. When she finished, she handed the paper to Mr. Graves, then looked over at Byron Drake, her eyes flat and emotionless. With obvious objection, Mr. Graves passed the signed document to the bailiff, who then handed it up to Judge Patterson.

The judge read it over without any surprise. "It seems that this matter has been resolved without any intercession from the court," Judge Patterson announced. "Mrs. Dunham has transferred all of her properties and holdings to Mr. Drake, who will be the sole owner. In exchange, Mr. Drake has dropped all of the charges against Mrs. Dunham, and agrees not to seek any further civil or legal action regarding this matter."

As the gavel's heavy thud brought finality to the decision, Drake could barely contain his ecstasy. He had won! He had faced his enemy and stripped her of everything – absolutely everything! Rising from the seat, he joyously shook his lawyer's hand, then turned and bowed deeply in the direction of Mr. and Mrs. Dunham.

"It has been an absolute pleasure, my lady," he remarked gleefully. With a sardonic smile he added, "You never need be without a home, Mrs. Dunham. The full terms of my offer still stand." He winked gregariously, and Mr. Graves had to physically insert himself in front of Mr. Dunham to keep the man from inciting violence in the presence of the judge.

Drake only laughed, then sauntered merrily out of the courtroom. His very first stop would be the bank, where he would immediately transfer all of the Dunham's liquid funds to his own account. After that, he would be off to his new home, Hamilton Manor.

He was certain Shannon Tiernan would not be there, as she had probably fled Boston in anticipation of this moment. However, someone at Hamilton Manor knew where she was. He was going to find that someone, then wrench the information from him or her by any means necessary. He would have his child – and the woman who still haunted his dreams. They both belonged to him.

Drake would also find Darcy Adams. He would spare no expense in that search. When the wretched man was finally in his reach, he would kill Adams in the slowest, most painful manner possible while Shannon watched. He almost skipped to the carriage as the scene played out in his mind.

He called to his driver as he snapped the door shut, "To the bank, now!" The wheels seemed to turn more slowly than ever before, and Drake could barely stand the anticipation that was building in his chest.

"Faster, man, faster!" The driver urged the horse into a dangerously quick trot through the Boston streets. Finally, the prestigious exterior of the bank came into view, and the carriage pulled up to the front, depositing Drake at the foot of the steps. He wasted no time in climbing them and making his way to one of the bankers' desks sitting alongside the wall.

"I wish to withdraw all funds from the accounts of William and Josephine Dunham and have them transferred over to my own." The stunned man behind the desk did not respond at first, but looked at Drake as if he were insane. Drake leveled a severe stare at the banker, then added, "Immediately."

"If you will excuse me for one moment, sir," the banker replied, "I must verify this transaction before I proceed."

Drake reached into his pocket and handed him the single document signed by Mrs. Dunham. "This is all the verification you will require," he answered tersely. Taking the document, the man unfolded it and examined the signature, then motioned another, older man over to the desk.

"Mr. Blythe, sir," he began when the man arrived at his desk, "Mr. Drake is asking to withdraw all of the Dunham's funds and deposit them into his own account."

"Ah, yes, Mr. Drake. I was made aware you would be coming in today." Mr. Blythe then turned back to the confused banker. "Go ahead, Ames. This is a legitimate transaction between Mr. Drake and the Dunham's. Do everything that Mr. Drake asks." Mr. Blythe left the two men at the desk, returning to whatever task he was engaged in.

"As I said, Ames," Drake added, "immediately."

The banker's confusion did not abate, but he obeyed nevertheless, leaving his desk and disappearing into the back offices. For Drake, the wait seemed an eternity, but only a few minutes passed before Ames returned to the desk where Drake sat, a few notes in his hand. Drake looked at the contents of the banker's hand and frowned. Ames seemed nervous as he placed the notes on the desk. They totaled $115.

"What is this?" Drake asked, his voice harboring a dangerous edge.

"That is the sum of the funds in all of the Dunham's accounts, sir," the man replied anxiously while beads of sweat started to form on his balding forehead.

"Are you mad?" Drake began, his voice rising. "They are the wealthiest couple in Boston! Now do as I ask and transfer all of their funds into my account!"

Ames held up his hand defensively. "This is all there was, sir," he replied as other customers began to look curiously toward their corner.

"Then what happened to all the money, man? Blythe!" Drake roared. "Blythe! Get out here now! I want my money!"

Mr. Blythe hurriedly emerged from the back offices, though his face showed no alarm or surprise. "Gracious, Mr. Drake!" he exclaimed. "Would you kindly lower your voice and explain to me why you are causing such a disturbance in my bank?"

"Where is my money, Blythe?" Drake asked, his tone implying threats and murder. "That much money doesn't disappear overnight! Now where is it!?"

Mr. Blythe excused Ames and sat down behind the desk himself.

"Mr. and Mrs. Dunham bequeathed all of their belongings and possessions to their heir about two weeks ago," Mr. Blythe explained calmly. "But they were very clear about leaving the sum of $115 for you. Mrs. Dunham said you would know the significance of the amount."

Drake felt the rage start to build inside him, but he maintained a calm exterior. "Everything, Mr. Blythe?" he asked. "Did they bequeath everything to their heir?"

"I believe, so, Mr. Drake," Mr. Blythe replied.

"And who is that person?"

"I am not at liberty to say," Mr. Blythe replied calmly.

Drake stared at the man for a few more moments, his expression barely hinting at the violence boiling underneath. He would wait until Blythe left the bank this evening, then have one of his men slit the banker's throat – perhaps the same man that had dispatched Mrs. Dunham's driver. Yes, he would do nicely.

Drake smiled curtly. "As you wish, Mr. Blythe. There are consequences for this, however." Drake sat back in the chair and folded his hands, resting them on top of his legs. Then he looked directly at Mr. Blythe. "I wish to close my accounts in this bank immediately. I want all of my money now! Every last penny!"

Mr. Blythe nodded in understanding. "Certainly, Mr. Drake." Reaching toward the desk, Mr. Blythe picked up the $115 and handed it to Mr. Drake. "There you are, sir," he said. "Now would you kindly leave my bank?" Mr. Blythe signaled to two uniformed officers, who immediately placed themselves behind Mr. Blythe's chair.

Drake leaned forward, ignoring the men and glaring hotly at Mr. Blythe. "It is a dangerous game to part a man with his money, Mr. Blythe. Give me the sum of my accounts now, and I will not bring charges against you."

Mr. Blythe sat forward and placed his elbows on the desk, folding his hands as he did so, and looked at Drake through his spectacles. "Mr. Drake," he explained, "you have no accounts at this bank. Apparently, you transferred them to a certain young lady, an Erin Moore, I believe, some time ago. She visited the bank yesterday evening to take possession of her accounts."

Drake sat back, and his eyes grew large, his rage momentarily twisting into confusion. "Erin Moore?!" he exclaimed, shocked. "But that's not possible!"

"I am quite certain it was her," Mr. Blythe responded. "There are not that many ladies in Boston with those curly, red locks – and her younger brother, Murray, was with her. That lad has run many errands to this bank. I would know him anywhere. Now," Mr. Blythe rose from his chair, "kindly leave my establishment!"

As Drake stood, the full realization of his situation impacted him all at once. He had nothing, absolutely nothing in Boston, except for the $115 left for him by Josephine Dunham. He understood the significance. One dollar for every year she would have served in prison.

Drake's pistol beckoned to him from its holster. He could easily draw it and do away with this contemptuous banker, perhaps even one of the guards standing behind him. However, the other guard would most certainly have shot him by then, and Drake was not ready to enter a foolish gun battle with no way of escape.

He had other plans.

Slowly taking the money from the desk, Drake deposited the notes into his pocket while keeping his eyes locked on Mr. Blythe. "You and I will cross paths again, Mr. Blythe," Drake said, his voice masking the hatred and malice just underneath his exterior. Mr. Blythe did not flinch. Neither did he answer.

Drake turned on his heel and marched out of the bank, down the stairs, and into the waiting carriage. "To the tavern!" he snapped to his driver. Drake's brow furrowed in confusion and worry. How could Erin Moore be alive? He had seen her carriage go over the bridge, heard her screaming until the Charles River had swallowed her whole. It could not be. Josephine Dunham had somehow discovered his property transfer, and then hired someone to play her part. It was the only explanation.

He would have to find that woman and make her see his point of view. He also needed to deal with Blythe and Adams, as well as locate Shannon. It would take a small army to accomplish all of that, but his men at The Crimson Dagger had no idea about his financial destitution, and would be none the wiser until their paychecks were noticeably absent at the end of the month. He was certain they would all walk out on him then, but he still had almost three weeks to use their talents.

That was more than enough time to kill Blythe, hunt down Adams, locate Shannon, and do away with Mr. and Mrs. Dunham. He was certain Blythe would reveal the identity of their heir if enough pain were applied to him, then he could formulate a plan to deal with the heir and recover his money. The Dunham's may have kept their money from him for now, but Drake would take everything from them eventually, down to the last drop of blood in their veins.

As the carriage rounded the corner and turned onto Ann Street, The Crimson Dagger's hanging sign and large front door became visible. Most of his men would be awake by this hour, and he would lose no time in employing them to the tasks at hand. The carriage stopped at the front door and Drake exited briskly, determined not to waste any time in dispatching his enemies.

"Sam!" he yelled loudly as he threw open the door to the dark interior, "We have a lot of work to..." Drake stopped in his tracks, and his eyes locked onto the long, red curls of Erin Moore as she leaned casually against the bar. Sam, and the other dozen or so of his men were sitting around the tables. All heads turned to look at Drake as he stood still as death in the doorway, staring at the young woman who now owned everything he once had.

"Erin?" he said, softly, trying to think fast. "I thought you were dead. I am so glad to see you!" He started forward toward the young woman, but Sam stood and drew his pistol, pointing it directly at Drake. Several other of his men did the same.

"What do you think you're doing!" Drake growled menacingly, his eyes narrowing dangerously as he surveyed the hostile room.

Still leaning on the bar, Erin Moore answered, "They are protecting their new employer, Mr. Drake." She smiled shrewdly at him, then continued, "You did try to kill me once, and I would rather live to enjoy all of my newfound wealth." She raised a glass to him. "I must thank you for that, by the way."

"You wretched harlot!" Drake spat. "How dare you come into my tavern and try to take it away from me! I will make you pay for this!"

"I didn't take it, Mr. Drake," Erin answered calmly, picking up a stack of documents from the bar and holding them in front of her. "As I was just explaining to my new employees, you gave it all to me. Every – single – penny. Now, get out of my tavern!" Erin Moore was no longer smiling,

Drake stood unmoving, his breathe becoming heavier as he tried to contain his wrath. "Is this all the loyalty you men can muster?" Drake fumed, his fists clenching at his sides. "Is this how you're repaying me?"

Sam drew back the hammer on his pistol before answering. "To be quite honest, Mr. Drake, workin' for you was never all that nice. I'd rather work for Miss Moore here anytime – especially since she gave us all very generous raises. Now you'd better do as she asks and get outta here."

Drake's face twisted into a hateful grimace, and his voice betrayed the malevolence seething inside him. "I will kill you for this, Sam!" he breathed hotly. "I will find all of you and repay this betrayal! Especially you!" He pointed his finger at Erin and poured all of the evil he could muster into his voice. "Especially you!"

Drake turned abruptly and exited The Crimson Dagger, making sure to slam the door with a thunderous bang on his way out. The carriage had already pulled away, and Drake was left standing on the street with nothing, not even a means of vengeance. The only things he had left in his possession were the clothes on his back, the money in his pocket, and the pistol in his holster.

Josephine Dunham! He had underestimated her cleverness, and it had cost him. But not as much as it would cost her! Drake was not going to let the sun go down before unleashing his wrath on that woman!

Two horses were tied across the street, their owners somewhere inside the establishment. With a resolute expression set on his grim features, Byron Drake untied one of the horses, nimbly mounted it, and left Ann Street behind at a full gallop.

40

The eventful morning at the courthouse had been quite disconcerting, but at least the legal battle with Byron Drake was over. However, Josephine was sure there would be repercussions. Drake had likely been to the bank by now and learned that winning the legal victory had gained him nothing financially. By now, he might even know Erin Moore was alive and well, and the rightful owner of all of his possessions. He would not be happy. Not happy at all.

Josephine sighed as she looked out the carriage window, and William squeezed her hand. "What are you thinking, Josephine?" he asked. "Are you not pleased with the turn of events?"

She turned to him with a concerned smile. "I am," she answered, "but I know this is not the end of Byron Drake. I fear that stripping him of his financial means has not taken the teeth out of his bite."

"Aye," he responded, putting his arm around his wife and pulling her closer. "I was thinking the same thing. When we get home, I will find Darcy. Perhaps the two of us can contrive a plan to remove him from Boston altogether."

Josephine laughed softly. "I know of a ship's captain that will happily transport him to Cuba for us."

"That may be the way to go." William smiled, but his tone was serious. "Darcy and I must find a way to get Drake out of Boston. We will have to keep a careful eye on him until them. It will not be easy."

"No," she answered, "but it is necessary." They were silent for a few more minutes as the carriage made its way down the cobblestone lane that wound to Hamilton Manor. Josephine finally broke their silence.

"Are you more comfortable with our financial situation than before, now that our plans have succeeded?"

William laughed out loud. "You mean to ask if I am comfortable with Ophelia being the owner of everything we have? Of course not. But," he added, his tone turning tender, "I would rather give her every penny I own if it means keeping you by my side."

She placed a reassuring hand on his cheek. "Thank you, William. And I am certain she will return the bulk of our properties after she comes home."

"The bulk?" William questioned. "Not all?"

"Really, William," she said, "don't you think Ophelia deserves something after saving us like she has? I mean to make her a wealthy woman."

William shook his head. "I will never get used to Ophelia being our equal, she is too spirited and too vexing."

Josephine laughed. "Then she is good for you. You had better become accustomed to the idea. She will be back shortly after we send her word."

William was still looking unsettled as the carriage pulled up to the stone steps of their home. "You go in," he said. "I will accompany the driver to the carriage house and find Darcy. The sooner we can discuss a plan to deal with Drake, the better I will feel." He kissed her cheek before she exited the open door the driver held for her.

"Josephine," he called as she ascended the first step. Josephine turned to her husband, a quizzical look on her face.

"I love you," he said simply.

Her smile was radiant. "And I you," she responded, thinking of how good God had been to give her William. The driver climbed back into his seat and snapped the reins, taking her husband down the lane and out of her sight. When they had rounded the curve and Josephine could no longer see the carriage, she finished climbing the steps and made her way into the foyer of Hamilton Manor.

Shannon took her coat as she entered. "I have tea waiting for you and Mr. Dunham," she offered as she hung Josephine's coat in the foyer closet.

Ever since Ophelia had left, Shannon stepped in to take her place, even though Josephine initially objected. But Shannon had persisted, claiming that staying busy helped her to pass the time until her child was born. Josephine finally relented, but only with the promise that Shannon would refrain from any activities that could be considered strenuous.

"Mr. Dunham has gone to the carriage house to find Darcy. Will you share tea with me instead?" Josephine answered. She saw Shannon's reluctance, and quickly added, "I would love to hear about the baby. Please sit with me for a while." Shannon nodded happily, her reluctance fading with the mention of her baby, and the two retired to the sitting room where Jeffrey was adding another log to the fire.

Josephine sipped her tea and happily viewed Shannon's large tummy. "How have you been feeling? Has the baby been moving much?"

Shannon placed a delicate hand over her stomach and smiled. "I have been quite well, but this little one seems to have settled down a bit. He was very feisty until a few days ago, now he seems to sleep most of the time."

"He?" Josephine asked. "How do you know it's a boy?"

Shannon sipped her tea thoughtfully. "Well, I just know. I really can't explain it."

Josephine laughed. "I can," she surmised. "A woman's intuition has been widely dismissed, but I think..."

Her words were cut off by a sudden and thunderous commotion in the foyer. Both of the women froze as the voice of Byron Drake roared through the downstairs.

"Josephine Dunham! You and I have unfinished business! Where are you, woman?!"

Shannon's eyes grew wide with terror as Josephine quickly rose and helped her from her chair. "Go! Find a place to hide! Now!" She almost shoved Shannon through the door to the kitchen at the opposite end of the room. "Do not come out for anything!"

Shannon heard Jeffrey's elderly voice sound from the foyer as she ran to the kitchen. "What business is this, sir!?" the old man demanded. "Leave this house at once, or you will be removed by force!"

A loud pop cracked through the house, and Josephine screamed Jeffrey's name in horror. Shannon caught her breath, realizing that Drake had just murdered the old servant. She covered her mouth to keep in the cry threatening to escape her throat. Tears were coursing down her cheeks, but she dared not vent her sobs.

"Shut up, woman!" She heard Drake's harsh words cut through Josephine's cries, then heard the familiar sound of Drake's hand strike flesh. Josephine cried out in pain and shock, and Shannon almost bolted through the kitchen door to defend her mistress. But fear kept her glued to the wall – fear for her child, fear for her own life. She could only listen, weeping silently as she heard Drake strike Josephine again.

"You're coming with me!" Drake commanded, his voice hot with hatred. "You and I are taking a trip to London."

"Let go of me!" Shannon could hear Josephine struggling against Drake, and heard something crash to the floor in the foyer. "No!" Josephine's frantic struggles continued, but their voices grew fainter as Drake dragged her out of the house. Shannon heard the thunder of a horse's hooves through the open door as Drake galloped down the lane with Josephine in his possession.

Everything was eerily quiet for a moment, then Shannon flung herself through the kitchen door and to the foyer. Jeffrey, the old man, lay unmoving on the floor, a blood stain seeping through his white shirt from a hole in the center of his chest. Shannon tried to scream, but couldn't. Her head began to spin, and she felt as if her tea was going to be ejected from her stomach. She turned around as quickly as she could and fell to the floor.

She must find Darcy! Darcy and Mr. Dunham. They had to go after Drake and rescue Josephine!

This one thought echoed through Shannon's head again and again. She clung to it and used it to propel herself to her feet and out the back door of the kitchen. The open air helped to ease her nausea, and she began to run toward the carriage house. She had to find Darcy!

After a few yards, Shannon's legs gave way and betrayed her, and she went toppling to the ground, belly first. Something inside her stomach felt like fire, and she cried out in agony. Still, Shannon pulled herself to her feet, wrapped her arms under her belly, and started for the carriage house once again, every jolting step inflicting more suffering inside her.

"Darcy!" she screamed, hoping she was sufficiently close to be heard. "Darcy!" No longer able to stand the pain, she fell to her knees, barely noticing the trickle of blood running down her leg. "Darcy!" she screamed again, over and over, though panicked sobs broke her voice. Finally, the sound of sprinting feet caught her ear, and Darcy and Mr. Dunham were soon kneeling beside her.

"Shannon!" Darcy's distressed voice echoed the alarm on his face.

"Drake took her!" Shannon began, crying almost hysterically and grabbing Mr. Dunham's hand. "Drake came in the house and killed Jeffrey! Then he took Mrs. Dunham!" Mr. Dunham turned white as Shannon sobbed out the words.

"Where!?" he asked hurriedly, bending down to look Shannon in the eye. "Did he say where, child?"

She nodded through the sobs. "London. He said he was taking her to London!"

Darcy looked at Mr. Dunham as he pulled Shannon into his lap, his hands gently feeling over her stomach. "The wharf, William!" he shot the words out as quickly as he could. "He will go to Captain Munstead and his ship, the *Charlotte Jane*!"

Without answering, William bolted for the carriage house as fast as he could force his legs to go. Already, Hans and a few other servants were running toward Darcy and the pregnant girl, and William held out his arm to stop Hans.

"Ride to Dr. Stone!" he commanded. "Bring him back here at once! The girl is injured!" Hans turned and ran with William back to the carriage house.

"Where are you off to, sir?" he asked, seeing his master hastily lead Hero out of his stall and saddle him in record time.

Without pausing, William answered, "Drake took my wife!" Hans' look changed from mild alarm to outright apprehension, but William was already mounting the stallion and riding down the lane before Hans could say anything more.

God, William prayed under his breath as Hero flew down the road toward Boston, *if You are really there, then help me. Help me get my wife back, and I will give You whatever you want. Just keep her safe. Just keep her safe.*

His prayer repeated itself over and over again, a hundred times or more, though William didn't count. All he knew was that time was standing still, and though Hero was moving faster than any horse had a right to, it still wasn't fast enough.

Oh God, he pleaded, *please!*

41

Josephine cringed as Drake sharply yanked the reins, stopping the horse abruptly. She was still praying, just as she had been for the last twenty minutes. She could feel the anger seething from this man, spilling out onto everyone and everything around him.

Drake vaulted off the horse and violently wrenched Josephine from its back, his hand still latched tightly around her wrist, just as it had been since he had dragged her out of her home. Josephine's heart sank to her stomach. Anchored to the dock in front of them was a small sailing vessel called the *Charlotte Jane*, making ready to set sail. To her horror, she realized Drake was not planning on her ever leaving that ship alive.

William, she breathed silently. She would never see him again. Oh, God, she prayed, why is it Your will that it end this way? Drake pulled her up the gangplank and threw her to the deck, where she landed hard at the feet of a bewildered Captain Munstead.

"Ay now!" his old voice grated with displeasure as he saw this lady dressed in finery being thrown onto his ship. "What manner of business can this be?" The old captain was not concerned for the woman herself, but rather the trouble he could face if he was an accomplice to mistreating a woman of means.

From the captain's demeanor, Josephine sensed that salvation was in her grasp. "Sir," she began hastily, "my name is Josephine Dunham, and I can give you whatever money you desire for delivering me from this man!"

The captain's eyebrows raised with great interest, and he looked from Josephine to Drake. But instead of challenging Drake's gaze, he was looking down the barrel of a cocked revolver. Every crewman froze in place, watching the confrontation between their captain and the armed man.

"That money won't do you any good with a hole in your head, Captain," Drake said coldly. "Now throw off the lines and leave port at once. We make for London."

Captain Munstead took a cautious step back and raised his hands slowly. He valued his life above all else, but if he could finagle a way to calm Drake, release Mrs. Dunham, and line his pockets handsomely, he would be a truly happy man.

"Look here, Mr. Drake," the old man began, his voice slow and careful. A loud shot rang out, startling Josephine out of her skin. The old captain crumpled onto the deck next to her. She stared helplessly at the dead man, too shocked to even utter a cry of surprised grief.

Drake looked each of the deckhands in the eye, his gun still level in front of him. "I am your new captain. Are there any objections?" The wide-eyed men each shook their heads, standing otherwise motionless in front of the man with the gun. "Good," continued Drake, almost cheerily, "then throw off the lines and leave port at once. Make sail for London."

He strode to the terrified Josephine and grabbed her under the arm, yanking her up from the wooden planks. "And roll that filthy corpse off this ship!" he shouted over his shoulder, shoving her through the captain's cabin door. The men acted instantly, jumping from the ship to the wharf to disengage the docking lines and prepare the rigging for departure. Drake's satisfied smile as he pulled her into the stateroom and locked the door behind him frightened Josephine more than the murder of Jeffrey, and that poor, dead captain. But she stood tall, silently praying, as Drake strode to the opposite end of the room.

He turned to face her and unbuttoned the top button of his shirt. She looked him steadily in the eye without flinching. "Make no mistake, Mrs. Dunham," Drake began, "you are going to die." She could see the delight creeping into his eyes, but stood unmoved by his words. "However," he continued, "you have made my life a living hell these past few weeks." He moved on to the second button on his shirt. "So before I strangle you, I am going to make you suffer." He smiled at her and unbuttoned the third button.

Josephine could feel the evil pouring out of Byron Drake, filling up every space in the room where they stood. She could also sense the spirit of death lingering near, its tendrils dancing closer. Without any doubt, she knew these next few moments of life would be her last.

She was afraid, but deep in her spirit a soft whisper echoed, *Do not fear, I am with you.* She recognized the voice of her Lord, and it made her eager to see Him.

The ship lurched slightly as it was released from the dock, free to make its way into the churning Atlantic. With its freedom, Josephine's fate was made sure. Drake finally undid the last button and stripped his shirt from his torso, throwing it to the floor.

Josephine felt peace settle into her, and she looked Byron Drake directly in the eye. "I know what waits for me, Mr. Drake," she said, "and I am at peace. I have prayed."

Drake laughed. It was an evil, vile sound. "You pitiful woman!" he said, the laughter finally dying from his voice. "Do you know how many times I have heard a woman praying for God to save her?" He spat the holy name out of his mouth like poison. "He never saved one of them! Your God can't save anybody, Mrs. Dunham!" He started toward her.

"You misunderstand, Mr. Drake," Josephine answered, her voice sure and solid. "I have not prayed for myself, but for you," she said simply.

Drake froze in his tracks, his face contorting in rage. "How dare you!" he hissed. All of the hatred he had ever felt culminated in this one moment toward this one woman. He closed the distance between them like a freight train and pinned Josephine against the wall, his hand tightly gripping her throat. "Never mind the suffering, Mrs. Dunham," he whispered in her ear as she gasped for breath. "You meet your God now."

William drove Hero hard, not even mindful of the poor beast's labored breathing and the sweat pouring off of his great body. It had been at least twenty minutes since Drake had charged into his home and taken Josephine. He could be anywhere, could have done anything to his wife, but he trusted Darcy's instinct and made straight for the docks. William felt the panic trying to rise from his gut to his throat, but he pushed it down mercilessly, angrily, as he drove Hero even harder.

The road curved gently as the tall masts of sailing ships in the harbor just above a thick fog came into view. How would he ever find the *Charlotte Jane* in that dense cloud? What if the ship was already gone? How could he possibly rescue Josephine under those circumstances?

"I need you, God!" he shouted in the wind. "Show me!" Another minute passed as he and Hero thundered down the street, every second taking him closer to Boston Harbor. As the first wharf appeared, the cloud of fog enveloped him and reduced his visibility to no more than twenty feet. William reined Hero to a restless stop next to a pair of very startled sailors. He hastily pulled his money pouch from inside his coat and held it in front of him.

"The *Charlotte Jane*!" he cried breathlessly. "Where is she docked?"

The two men looked wide eyed at the pouch, then at William.

"Now man!" William bellowed, shaking the pouch impatiently and causing its heavy contents to rattle.

"Eighth wharf down, sir," answered the older man, catching the pouch as William hastily tossed it to him.

Without wasting a second, William turned Hero and roared down the street once again, recklessly jumping the wooden crates emerging from the foggy mist. Only one thought reverberated through his mind, finding his Josephine. As he blew passed the seventh wharf, William's eyes strained through the fog to see any activity on the eighth.

A cool breeze began blowing in from the sea, sweeping the fog from the docks and toward the city, allowing William to see the wharf and make out the stern of a small sailing vessel. The boat had just cast off and was moving slowly into the harbor. It was too late.

"NO!" William's voice blasted from his chest even as he drove his heels into Hero's side. The horse replied by surging forward, using every last ounce of his mighty strength as he sensed his rider's urgency. William steered Hero down the wharf, gaining speed as he closed the distance between him and the end of the wooden structure. Without any hesitation, Hero's strong legs propelled them into the air, horse and rider making a graceful arch toward the ship.

Several of the crewmen cried out in alarm when they saw Hero launch from the end of the wharf, realizing that the destination of the massive animal was their own deck. William drew his gun in midflight, preparing for the instant he would land.

With the booming clap of hoof on wood, Hero touched down squarely on the deck amidst yelling crewmen scrambling to get out of the way. Before the horse had completed his sliding stop, William leapt off his back onto the confused deck, gun held in front of him. The bloodied trail from the deck to the railing caught his immediate attention.

The next instant, the door to the cabin flew open and a shirtless Byron Drake emerged, anger and hatred seething from his face as he shouted, "What the...!" His voice caught as soon as his eyes fell upon William Dunham. He hesitated for only a moment, then bolted for the side as William pulled the hammer back on his pistol. A shot raced through the air and tore clean through Drake's arm.

Drake didn't stop, but jumped onto the rail and into the air above the dock. William cocked his revolver and fired again, this time catching Drake in his torso as he fell into the waters of the Atlantic. William bolted to the side of the boat and emptied his pistol into the dark ocean where Drake had fallen. He waited for a few seconds to see if the man surfaced, but the fog was once again becoming soupy.

He turned to the bewildered men standing in shock on the deck for the second time that day. His expression was deadly, and the men parted before him without a word, bunching close to the stomping horse.

Without giving any explanation, William replaced his gun and ran through the open door of the cabin where Drake had emerged. A quick glance around the room revealed a small, motionless form lying in the corner.

"No, no!" William whispered, rushing over to where his wife lay and falling on his knees next to her. He turned her over and pulled her in his arms, hastily assessing the ugly, bruised ring around her throat and listening for any breath from her nose. "Josephine!" He shook her hard and listened again. Nothing. "No, God!" He cried, his voice rising with panic and anger.

"I trusted You! You weren't supposed to let this happen!" He grabbed Josephine's shoulders and shook her body violently, desperately wanting his efforts to bring back his wife. He stopped and watched her chest for movement, then put his ear to her nose again. Still nothing.

"No!" he cried, pulling her body into his arms and against him. She was still warm. He had been so close. Tears streamed down his face as he pulled her to him tighter, knowing he had almost been soon enough. Almost.

"God," he echoed, grief consuming his whisper, "You weren't supposed to let this happen." Two of the crewmen were peering through the door, slowly piecing together what had just transpired on their ship.

"Josephine." William wept into her hair, and his body heaved with sorrow as he squeezed her tightly and rocked back and forth. Like an unexpected gust of wind, William felt Josephine's ribs expand as she gasped in a great quantity of air, then another. He pulled back in disbelief and saw Josephine's eyes open and look directly at him. She breathed in another great breath and grabbed onto William's coat with both fists.

"Josephine!" William exclaimed, shock radiating from his words. "Thank you!" He pulled her to him again, this time ecstatic. "Thank you, God. Thank you!"

One of the men called to the others on deck, "She's alive, mate! Pull back to the dock." There was a hurried bustle of bodies and voices as the men returned the vessel to the dock.

After a few moments, William held Josephine in front of him again, gently cradling her face in his hands. "Can you see me?" he asked, looking intently at her, his blue eyes somber and filled with tears. "Can you hear me?"

Josephine brought her hand to his face. "You're here," she answered, though her voice was strained. "I didn't think I would ever see you again." Tears began to fall from her eyes as well, and she leaned onto William's chest. "All I could think of was how much I would miss you."

"No, no," William responded, kissing her hair and wrapping his arms protectively around her. "I daresay you will not be rid of me for anything after this."

Josephine nodded, resting heavily against her husband's chest. "I am agreeable to that," she answered wearily.

A crewman popped his head in the door. "We are tied up at the dock, Mr...er..sir. Would you like me to fetch a doctor?"

"Yes," replied William, not taking his eyes from the woman who lay in his arms. As the man left the door, William called, "Young man! Have someone tend to the horse as you go."

The young man nodded. "Already done, sir." Then he was away.

William returned his attention to his wife, stroking her hair and gently rocking her back and forth on the floor of the stateroom. "I did not know how much I loved you until I thought you were gone," he said. "I am so sorry for that, Josephine. So sorry."

He felt her smile, and she breathed in a heavy, satisfying breath. "No, William," she said softly. "Don't ever be sorry." They sat contentedly for a few minutes more, then Josephine jerked upright suddenly.

"Drake?" she asked. "Where is he?"

"Dead," William replied, gently easing her back to his chest. "Dead and at the bottom of the harbor." Josephine nodded and relaxed again.

"I prayed," William said suddenly, softly to Josephine, who quietly listened. "After Drake took you from the estate, and I did not know how to save you, I prayed."

"Thank you," she whispered, tears once again filling her eyes. "You don't know what that means to me."

"I am beginning to understand," he answered. They spent the rest of the time in silence, while William continued to cradle Josephine on the dirty planks of the dead captain's cabin, waiting for the doctor to arrive and tend to his wife.

42

The day proved uneventful at the brick office on Hanover Street. Just one patient had come in all morning, and he was ailed only with a minor cough. Dr. Stone gave the older man a jar of sticky, bitter fluid, told him to keep a kettle of water on his stove, and sent him on his way. He watched as the man hobbled out the office through the front door, then he turned his gaze onto Elisabeth. She was seated at the opposite end of his desk with three books open before her and an exceptionally accurate sketch of the lungs and bronchioles taking shape in her notebook.

He had taken Miss Beech on as a favor to Josephine, really, as a way to ease the pain of separation from Mr. Dunham. After the events at the Spring Ball, he had expected to have an ill-mannered, heartsick child to deal with. For the most part, he had found Elisabeth to be the exact opposite of his expectations.

She had proved to be intelligent, even cheerful after the first two months, enjoying the studies that Dr. Stone had piled on her. And she was compassionate. She had a way with the patients who came through his door, a wonderful bedside manner that put them at ease and facilitated his work.

What had he done before she came into his life? He had gotten by well enough, not knowing what more life could offer. Now, he had, dare he say, a colleague of sorts? Dr. Stone turned his head to one side as he studied her. Her knowledge and skills already made her a competent nurse, but could she one day be a physician? Could she one day be his wife? Would she even want to? He was her senior by at least twelve years, perhaps more.

Elisabeth raised her head and caught him staring. She smiled quizzically as he stood there. "Dr. Stone," she finally said, "you seem to be contemplating something serious."

Dr. Stone shook himself from his thoughts as her voice broke his concentration. "As a matter of fact, I was thinking about your future, Miss Beech. "What I am trying to say, Elisabeth, is that..."

The bell rang furiously as young Hans burst turbulently through the office door. "Dr. Stone!" he exclaimed, his excited panic causing him to breathe heavily, "One of the girls on the Hamilton Estate has had an accident! Her baby is coming too soon!"

Dr. Stone pointed to his shelves in his office as he addressed Elisabeth. "Gather my bag and extra suture supplies!" Elisabeth was already up from her desk and heading toward the shelves. He addressed Hans, "What sort of accident?"

"It was Miss Tiernan. She fell while running to fetch Mr. Dunham and Mr. Adams."

"Why on Earth was she running?" Dr. Stone replied as he fetched his coat from the wall. Elisabeth hurried from the office to Dr. Stone's side, bag in hand and coat on her arm.

The worried Hans was thinking hard, obviously trying to convey information in the clearest, shortest way possible. "Mr. Drake burst in to the manor and took Mrs. Dunham right out of the house. He shot poor Jeffrey dead! Miss Tiernan ran to get Mr. Dunham, but fell on the way." Elisabeth gasped in disbelief and horror as the young man spoke.

Dr. Stone's expression was grave. "Have they recovered Mrs. Dunham?"

Hans was almost to the point of tears. "No, sir," he answered, choking on the words.

As they spoke, another very excited man pushed through the front door. He wore a sailor's raggedy garb, and had streaks of blood on his shirt from where he had wiped his hands. "I need a doctor down at the harbor right away," he began.

"For who, man!? Who sent you?" Dr. Stone demanded.

"Don't know his name, doc," the man replied. "Only know that he is a fancy fella who shot the man who shot our captain. Rescued his fine lady, he did. Though I'm not sure she'll make it." The sailor paused, as if sifting information. "You're needed for the lady, by the way. Pretty sure the other two are goners."

Dr. Stone threw up his hands in frustration. "It has to be Mrs. Dunham! Where do I go first?" He turned to Elisabeth, then pointed a bold finger at her. "You!" he exclaimed as she took a step back. "You will go save Miss Tiernan and her baby! I will go and save Mrs. Dunham!"

Incredulity seized Elisabeth's face. "I cannot possibly do this without you to instruct me!" she objected.

"There is no time, Elisabeth! You must!" he replied as he made his way to the office and grabbed another bag, hastily stuffing medical supplies into it. He returned to Elisabeth and placed both of his hands on her delicate shoulders. "You have helped me deliver a dozen babies. You will be magnificent! Now off you go!" Without pause, Dr. Stone hastily followed the sailor out the door.

Elisabeth gave only a moment to her surprise, then she turned to Hans. "You heard Dr. Stone," she said. "Off we go!"

They hurried out the door and Hans mounted a great beast of a horse that was waiting for them. He pulled Elisabeth up behind him and kicked the horse into a gallop. She buried her face in Hans' back and clung tightly around his waist, terrified of falling off. The handle of the black bag was still tightly clenched in her fist.

Fear stirred her chest – fear of the immediate situation of galloping madly through the streets of Boston, and fear of the very near future, when the life of a woman and her infant would be placed in her hands. A thrilling sense of adventure also rose in her gut, and she almost laughed out loud at the insanity of the whole situation.

Would this be the kind of life she would have with Dr. Stone? One moment full of quiet study and dull mediocrity, and the next moment madly racing off to rescue someone? It was a life she would have never had with William Dunham. Suddenly, Elisabeth was truly grateful for Duke Dunham's cruel twist of circumstance. It had brought her here, to this unexpected adventure and happy insanity with Dr. Stone.

They finally reached the cobblestone lane that wound into Hamilton Manor, and Elisabeth saw a large, stone home emerge from around the corner. Under the porte-cochere, just outside the stone steps leading to the entry, Elisabeth saw two young men struggling with an object bundled in a sheet. Red stains blotched portions of the sheet, and Elisabeth realized the men were tending to the old man that had just been murdered. Had the same thing happened to Josephine Dunham?

Her earlier sense of adventure vanished, and a feeling of dread fell in the pit of her stomach. This was life and death, and she suddenly felt terribly inadequate knowing that the consequences of her actions in the next few minutes could cost a woman and an infant their lives. Her stomach almost rejected its breakfast, but Elisabeth held herself together. People were depending on her.

As Hans approached the young men and the body, one of them pointed further down the lane. "They're in the carriage house!" he called over the thunder of the horse's hooves. Hans adjusted his course accordingly, and he and Elisabeth were once again galloping like mad. It only took a moment for the carriage house to come into sight, and Elisabeth saw streaks of blood on the pathway below her as they neared the smaller stone structure, as if someone had been pulling a red rag behind them as they walked.

Before Elisabeth had time to nurse any more fear, they were already dismounting the horse and running into the carriage house toward the agonized screams coming from the comfortably furnished bunk room in the back. Elisabeth passed Hans and ran into the room where a dark haired man held the hand of a delicate, blonde girl who was lying on her side on the bunk. Her belly was heaving as she breathed hard, and her legs were covered with streaks of fresh crimson.

The man was wiping her sweating forehead with an already drenched handkerchief while she squeezed his other hand tightly and cried again in torment. Her unearthly wail caused him to looked at Elisabeth with terror and helplessness in his eyes.

"Can you help her?" he cried, the desperation ringing in his voice. "Please! Help her!" Elisabeth hurried to the girl's side and ran her hands smoothly over her swollen, solid stomach. The baby was still high in the girl's abdomen, much too high to be properly born.

The dread and panic that had enveloped her moments earlier fled, replaced by a calm confidence as Elisabeth began mentally reviewing scenarios from one of Dr. Stone's dusty medical books.

"How far along is she?" Elisabeth asked the distraught man, who was breathing almost silent prayers over and over again.

He stopped praying for a moment to answer her. "I think she is almost the full nine months, though I am not certain."

"Are you the father?" she asked as she lifted the girl's dress to check the flow of blood and the positioning of the baby.

"No," he answered, his eyes never leaving the girl's face. "Not yet."

"Darcy!" the girl's pain found a tormented voice as a particularly difficult contraction gripped her stomach. "Help me! Darcy!"

Darcy grabbed Elisabeth's hand in desperation. "Can you help her?!"

"I can try," she answered. Opening the black bag, she retrieved a bottle and cloth from its depths and placed them on the table next to the bed, while Hans hurried in with steaming water and extra sheets. She looked Darcy squarely in the eye, "I need some of those prayers."

She nodded to Hans, who was still standing in the doorway. "I need a clean cup." He raced off to retrieve the needed item while Elisabeth pulled a small, sharp blade from the bag. She placed this on the table next to the bottle, then added a curved needle and sinewy looking threads next to it.

Darcy's eyes widened as he realized what was about to take place. "Is this the only way?" he asked, his voice lowered beneath the continuous cries of the girl.

"Neither of them will live if I don't," Elisabeth answered matter-of-factly, but her face was etched with concern.

"Will Shannon survive?" Darcy's voice broke on the last word, and Elisabeth could see this girl was his world. "Please tell me she will live."

She was silent for a moment. "I don't know." Hans returned with the cup. Elisabeth took it, placed the scalpel in the cup, and poured the boiling water over the instrument. Next, she opened the bottle and held the handkerchief over the opening while turning the bottle upside down. She held it there and nodded to Darcy.

Darcy understood. He might never be able to speak to his Shannon again. He knelt close to Shannon's ear and placed his hand on her cheek. "I love you, Shannon Tiernan," he whispered, "more than all the blue in the sky. May God be with you and give you peace." Tears spilled down his face, and Shannon grabbed his hand and began to cry.

"Take care of him, Darcy!" she pleaded, placing her other hand on her stomach. "Promise me you'll take care of him!"

"I promise, Shannon." Another contraction seized her, and Elisabeth mercifully placed the handkerchief over her nose before the pain could reach its full fury. Shannon's eyes drifted, then closed as her whole body slumped into unconsciousness. Elisabeth quickly turned the girl on her back and hastily covered her with the sheet, while simultaneously pulling her dress up and out of the way, leaving only her belly exposed.

Darcy hung his head, then looked away. "Should I leave?" he asked, uncertainty clouding every word.

"No," Elisabeth replied, "I will need you here." Then she reached for the scalpel while Darcy prayed.

43

Dr. Stone found Josephine resting wearily in her husband's embrace, both of them reclining against the cabin wall of the *Charlotte Jane*. The bruises circling her neck were severe, but a careful examination determined her airway was intact and her faculties were still her own. He sent for a carriage, and rode with them back to Hamilton Manor, keeping an observant eye on his friend for any subtle signs of damage.

After finding that Josephine had survived the encounter with Drake, Dr. Stone's thoughts drifted back to Elisabeth time and again. What if this birth had been difficult? What if one, or both, of the patients did not survive? Would Elisabeth be able to bear that kind of burden on her shoulders?

Circumstances would have worked out much better had Dr. Stone sent Elisabeth to Josephine and taken care of Miss Tiernan himself. But one does not know such things in advance, and this line of work had taught him to dismiss regret over which he had no control. It was incredibly destructive.

Only after Josephine was securely tucked into her own bed for an extended rest did Dr. Stone leave her in the care of her husband. He climbed down the stairs and left through the kitchen door, taking the stone path to the carriage house, his thoughts keeping him company. The grounds were oddly quiet, and the lack of activity only accentuated the sense of wrongness hanging in the air.

In the distance, he heard the clopping of hooves, and his eyes found a wagon moving further down the path. The driver did not seem to be in any hurry, and in the back of the wagon lay a white, shrouded figure.

Dr. Stone wondered if the figure were the remains of old Jeffrey or of Miss Tiernan.

The carriage house finally came into view, and Dr. Stone quickened his step. As he quietly entered through the rustic, wooden door, only silence met his attentive ear. The door latched loudly as he pulled it shut. A second later, the sound of a newborn's delicate cry filled the air as Darcy poked his head through the far doorway of the bunk room.

Darcy smiled widely as the rest of him emerged from the bunk room, a tiny, very unhappy child resting snugly in his arms. Relief flooded through Dr. Stone as took the child from Darcy and starting rocking it soothingly in his own arms. The child quieted slightly, then rooted around Dr. Stone's vest for some type of sustenance.

"How is Miss Tiernan?" Dr. Stone asked. He offered his pinky finger to the child, who started sucking on it enthusiastically.

"Your Miss Beech is just finishing with her," Darcy answered. "She is hopeful."

Dr. Stone smiled at the child. "Boy or girl?"

"A son," Darcy replied, taking back the little boy that Dr. Stone offered him, his eyes never leaving the child.

"Have you named him?" the doctor asked as Darcy also offered his little finger to the baby.

Darcy's expression took a serious, thoughtful turn, and he looked directly at the doctor. "That is for his mother to do, if she recovers."

Dr. Stone nodded in understanding, then walked past Darcy into the bunk room. Miss Tiernan lay on the bunk, resting uneasily. Elisabeth was sitting by her bedside, watching her patient carefully. She looked up at Dr. Stone as he entered.

"I think she will survive," Elisabeth offered as Dr. Stone knelt next to the girl, his eyes and hands examining her carefully. "The uterus was torn where the placenta was attached. I was not certain what to do."

The doctor nodded as he examined Miss Tiernan in more detail. Uncovering the remnants of the procedure, which Elisabeth had wrapped in the sheets Hans had brought, he carefully prodded through them with the scalpel and tweezers.

When he was finished, he sat back on his heels and looked at Elisabeth as if in a new light. "You absolutely made the correct choice, Miss Beech," he said, pride running through his tone. "I was worried I had pushed you into an impossible situation, but you handled it beautifully."

Elisabeth nodded, then admitted, "I was completely terrified at first, then I remembered the procedure described in the obstetrics text."

Dr. Stone nodded as well, then inched closer to Elisabeth, still kneeling. "Quick to think," he said, smiling in approval. "Miss Beech?" he continued.

"Yes?" she answered after a moment of silence, not sure what his mannerism or his smile implied.

"Well," he continued," I would like for you … to be my … my partner."

Elisabeth faltered for a moment, and she frowned in confusion. "Did you say … partner?"

Dr. Stone hurriedly continued, "I know it is no small matter, asking this of you. But we work so well together, and you are already more competent than I could have ever hoped for."

"More competent?" Elisabeth echoed, her voice full of bewilderment.

"I want you to work for me, formally, as my nurse." Elisabeth looked over Dr. Stone's face for a moment, taking in his solid features and piercing eyes. She was quite certain Dr. Stone was about to ask her something entirely different.

Was she ready to move up from her studies and become his nurse? Was this what she really wanted?

At that moment, Darcy entered the bunk room, the little boy finally sleeping in his arms. His eyes barely saw the two people at Shannon's bedside, instead they settled on the unconscious girl. "Will she be all right, Dr. Stone?"

Dr. Stone rose and smiled largely at Darcy. "Time will tell, Mr. Adams," he replied. "But I believe she will recover." Relief overflowed from Darcy's expression, and he finally pulled his gaze away from Shannon to make eye contact with Elisabeth.

"I cannot ever thank you enough, Miss Beech," he began. "She would have perished if not for you." An immense sense of satisfaction filled Elisabeth chest. It was so gratifying to see Miss Tiernan alive, and she was alive because of her. In that moment, she knew her place was with Dr. Stone.

"Knowing she will be all right is my thanks, Mr. Adams," Elisabeth replied.

"Darcy," Dr. Stone interjected, his tone becoming serious, "you need to know that Miss Tiernan will never be able to bear another child. The damage caused by the fall was too severe."

"It does not matter," Darcy replied without hesitation. "She is alive, and she has already given me this fine, young lad." He looked down at the sleeping child with adoration. "What more does any man need?"

Dr. Stone simply nodded. He rose from his place at Elisabeth's side and held out his hand to her. "Shall we away, my dear?" he asked. "I think we are finished here." She looked from his hand to his face. Dr. Stone's eyes were twinkling and happy, and fixed on hers. Elisabeth took his hand.

"Miss Beech," he asked after a few moments of silent walking, "Will you accept my offer?"

"Of course I will accept your offer," she replied, smiling. "How could I refuse you?" Dr. Stone's eyes widened slightly at her choice of words. This one was bold, but it would serve her well.

"In that case," he responded, "I have another request of you."

"Oh?" she said. "So soon after the first?"

He laughed. "It is nothing so serious. I would like to have the privilege of addressing you by your first name."

"Of course," Elisabeth answered. Then she frowned slightly. "And will you extend the same opportunity to me?" she asked.

"Absolutely," Dr. Stone replied.

"And what is your first name?" she asked. "You have never made mention of it."

"I have good reason," he said laughing. "But if you can determine my first name, then, by all means, you may call me by it."

Finally, they reached the carriage in front of the main house, and Dr. Stone opened the cab door for Elisabeth, where they continued their easy conversation as the carriage drove them toward the heart of Boston.

44

The lovely, spring afternoon could not have been more perfect. Golden rays of sunlight spilled onto the few guests that sat on the lawn, their warmth chasing away the slight hint of coolness lingering from winter. Josephine looked down at the little boy in her arms and pulled the delicate blanket that swaddled him over his fine, blonde hair. He nestled contentedly against her in his sleep. William looked down at the sleeping child and smiled happily at his wife, reaching his arm around her shoulder.

The baby's mother, Shannon Tiernan, stood just a few feet in front of Josephine, holding the hand of Darcy Adams. The couple was standing before the same minister that had married Josephine and William last spring, though this time the bride and groom were clearly enthralled with one another. The two exchanged vows and rings, and then kissed for the first time as Mr. and Mrs. Adams. Josephine could not help but think they were the most perfect match she had ever seen.

The evening ended late, and the newlyweds were the last to leave the Dunham's ballroom, calling their good nights to the master and mistress of the manor. William and Josephine remained, quite alone, swirling slowly to the music of the quintet, who was happy to stay for as long as there was a couple still swaying to their melodies.

"It has been a good day, my love," William said as he turned Josephine in his arms. Now that all the guests were gone, they danced with no distance between them. Josephine leaned her head on William's shoulder, her face resting close to his neck.

"An excellent day," she replied. "It would have been better if Ophelia were here to see her brother's wedding."

"Still no word?" William asked.

"Not yet," Josephine answered, "though we should hear something any day, now." There was a touch of concern in her voice.

"These things often take time, my dear," he answered soothingly. "Messages sent across the sea are notoriously slow."

"True, but I feel so unsettled without Ophelia here."

William nodded in understanding, then changed the subject. "I couldn't help but notice how lovely you look with a child in your arms," he offered, turning her gracefully so that she spun under his arm. He pulled her against him, her back was against his chest, his left arm supporting hers, and his right hand resting on her hip.

She laughed softly, and extended her neck to kiss his chin. "He is a beautiful child," she answered. "I am so happy Darcy adores him like he does."

"Aye," he answered. "Their story ended quite well. I hope there are no more trials for them in the future."

"As do I."

"So," he ventured, pulling her even closer, "when should we begin a family? Seeing you and the child... it made me long for one of my own."

Josephine smiled wider and brought her hand up to her husband's cheek. "Perhaps in seven months? Would that suit you?"

"Seven months?" he replied, slightly confused. "I thought a woman carried a child for..." He suddenly stopped dancing and turned to her. "Josephine?" he asked, delight sweeping his face.

"I thought this evening would be the perfect time to tell you," she answered, the happiness radiating from her eyes. William kissed her passionately while the quintet still played, though their surprised expressions indicated they seldom witnessed such intimate affection or happy news during a performance.

William placed both hands tenderly on Josephine's face. "I love you, Josephine Dunham."

"And I you, William," she answered.

They continued dancing for a long while, quite content in the other's embrace, before retiring upstairs. One of the new housekeepers, a young woman named Helen, had already turned down their bed, and was making ready their bedclothes.

Her clever eyes caught Mr. Dunham's hand cradling Mrs. Dunham's stomach, and she smiled. Her ears had already gleaned several events of importance from the guests that evening, and this unmistakable gesture on the part of Mr. Dunham could only mean one thing.

"Will there be anything more, Mrs. Dunham?" she asked with a smile, her voice soft and pleasant.

"No, Helen, you have done wonderfully. Thank you," Mrs. Dunham returned.

Helen curtsied and left the couple to themselves. She made her way to the foyer, retrieved her coat from the closet, and stepped out onto the stone stairs of Hamilton Manor. Hans was already waiting with a carriage. He opened the cab door as Helen made her way down the steps.

"You really don't have to make a fuss, Hans," she said as she climbed into the carriage. "I am perfectly able to walk home."

Hans shut the door securely and looked through the window at Helen. "Mrs. Dunham would be beside herself if any harm came to you. And," he added, "I rather enjoy the drive."

She smiled shyly and turned her eyes away. Hans vaulted himself to the driver's seat and snapped the reigns, taking his passenger just a few miles down the road beyond the manor. When they arrived at a tiny lane that could barely be seen from the road, Hans stopped the carriage and opened the door for Helen once again.

"May I walk you to your door this evening?" he asked, looking at the darkness around them.

"Oh no," she countered, "It is not far at all, and my mother is not overly fond of strangers. She would resent me bringing you to the door."

"Of course," Hans replied. "Then promise to be careful."

She smiled again. "I promise. Until tomorrow." She turned and strode confidently down the lane. After a hundred feet or so, it turned a sharp corner and revealed a tiny cottage. The windows were dimly lit, as if the fireplace inside needed tending.

As Helen entered through the rustic, wooden door, she saw this was indeed the case. The fire was almost out, even though there was a pile of oak logs sitting just to the side of the hearth. She removed her coat and stirred the dying embers, temporarily ignoring the figure sitting in the corner.

"Well," she finally said, "you'll be interested to know that Mrs. Dunham is expecting. And that couple you keep talking about, Miss Tiernan and Mr. Adams, they finally got hitched. It was a proper party and everything. And that little boy of hers, such a beauty!"

Byron Drake took a long drink from a bottle in his hand, then smiled. "You are the most wonderful woman, Helen. Come here." She obediently crossed the small distance from the fireplace to Drake, and he pulled her into his lap.

"Be careful, Byron!" she chided. "You're not fully healed yet!"

"Don't worry about me," he answered, pulling one finger down the side of her cheek. "You just worry about keeping those pretty eyes and ears open."

She smiled again and looked into his icy, blue eyes. "Anything you want, Byron."

Far to the south, the moon rose bright and full over the warm waters of the Atlantic, illuminating the shoreline in clearly defined whites and grays. Waves washed over the rocks and boulders that littered the beach, flooding the sand beyond with gentle foam. Before the waters retreated back into the ocean, they caressed the crushed remnants of a wooden hull.

Just visible in the moonlight, etched silver against the battered grain, was the ship's name.

Reina Dona Isabel.

About the Author

Elm Bryant has a heart for girls and women who are trapped in the horrific world of human trafficking. The best way to battle this malignant evil is to make people aware of what is happening, and the best way to do that is to tell a gripping story.

This book is her battle cry.

Thank you for reading *The Black Sea*. Though this story is fiction, so many women in our world live its cruelties every day.

You can make a difference for them.

Visit my website to find a list of organizations that fight against human trafficking and work to rescue these women from their captors.

Please consider supporting one of these organizations on a regular basis.

Be the hero! Save a life!

ElmBryant.com

Printed in the United States
By Bookmasters

Printed in the United States
By Bookmasters